Tilly shivered as she eyed her nocturnal visitor.

"If it's true that I saved your life, Mr. Flynn, don't you think you owe me an explanation?"

"No, Miss Templeton. Too much knowledge is a dangerous thing. You'd best get back to bed and forget this ever happened."

"Just like that?"

"Yes. You're a sensible woman."

A smile touched her mouth. "A sensible woman would not be standing in her nightshift, beside a man she had concealed in her bedchamber."

Flynn grinned, and the warmth of his expression eased her chill. "Your logic is undeniable. I retract my statement. You are quick-witted, beautiful and hopelessly insane. What a terrible shame."

Tilly shook her head. "I see now, Mr. Flynn, why you have such a colorful reputation."

Flynn looked suddenly rueful in the half-light. "I beg of you, Miss Templeton. Do not believe everything you hear. I am not the scoundrel you have every right to think me...."

Dear Reader,

Once again, let us take you on an unexpected journey into a past you might not have thought of exploring before. In *Tilly and the Tiger*, bestselling author Marianne Willman begins her tale in Jamaica, then follows her characters to the mysterious, ruin-filled jungles of the Yucatán. Adventure and danger go hand in hand with love as dashing Tiger Flynn courts the only woman fit to be his match. For Matilda ''Tilly'' Templeton, Tiger is a riddle, but one she can't help falling in love with, so she's more than happy to find out that her dangerous, enigmatic tiger *can* be tamed.

Jo Ann Algermissen has developed a strong following as a writer of contemporary romances. Now, in *Golden Bird*, she works her storytelling magic on the past, as well. This is a down-to-earth story of a Louisiana belle who finds love—and laughter—in the arms of a rugged Texas rancher. You won't want to miss a moment of their delightful tale.

Next month, the excitement continues with new books by Kristin James and Erin Yorke, and there's more to come after that. Pick up a Harlequin Historical—the past has never been so romantic.

Yours,
Leslie Wainger
Senior Editor and Editorial Coordinator

Tilly and the Tiger

Marianne Willman

Harlequin Books

TORONTO • NEW YORK • LONDON
AMSTERDAM • PARIS • SYDNEY • HAMBURG
STOCKHOLM • ATHENS • TOKYO • MILAN

Harlequin Historical first edition October 1990

ISBN 0-373-28655-4

MARIANNE WILLMAN

is an established author in both the historical and contemporary romance genres. She was born and raised in Detroit, and now lives close by with her family.

As a child, Marianne haunted the local libraries, and she still manages to read volumes of history as well as fiction of all kinds. When her hobby of collecting antique inkwells finally forced her to acknowledge that she wanted to be a writer, she gave up her critical-care nursing career and turned to writing. She's been busy ever since.

For my sisters,
Jane Clark and Betsy Clancy (Liz)—
wishing you love and luck
in all of life's adventures

Prologue

Jamaica 1858

The night scene was innocent enough—soft music wafted through the open French doors, and far below the lamps of Kingston glowed and the harbor waters glimmered like black satin. Then the moon peeked slyly from behind a drift of cloud, and the dark figure swinging over the second-story balcony froze. *Damn! Everything had gone so smoothly up to now.*

The moon winked and hid her face again, and the man went into action. With scarcely a sound he was over the rail and hanging from the upper story by his fingertips. He gauged the distance and jumped, landing on the soft earth in the garden below. The sound was covered by the strains of music.

Hidden in the shadows of the colonnade, he took out a handkerchief and carefully wiped the soil from his leather soles, then tucked the cloth away in an inside pocket. As he straightened his cravat he checked his surroundings. Not a soul in sight, thank God. On his own, he would have preferred a more open method, but there were others to consider. It was risky. Damned risky. But he'd work it out.

He had to.

Quickly he moved around the sprawling house and into the bedded gardens leading to the terrace. The wide French doors stood open to the night air, and it wasn't difficult to work his way into the crowded drawing room without attracting notice. For a moment he was poised on the threshold, wide shoulders and lean body in silhouette. The ladies and gentlemen assembled at the plantation were busy exchanging news and bits of gossip. Not a single questioning glance was sent his way as he stepped through the door. No one looking at his handsome countenance and impeccably tailored clothes would guess that he had just searched his host's bedroom and made his escape via the balcony.

"Tiger! Over here."

He heard Lord Edgecomb call out to him but pretended not to. A moment later he was lost in the shifting crowd. Candlelight fell softly on his sun-streaked hair and profiled his strong jaw. In a deeply tanned face his green eyes glittered with satisfaction. He'd just proved how easy it would be to move in and out of Coeur d'Émeraude while his host was occupied with his guests. It took less than a minute to work his way through the elegant throng and into the hallway.

He slipped along the corridor and went into a study, closing the door behind him. The room was dim with only the two candles in the sconces lit, but his eyes were as sharp as a cat's. Or a tiger's. "How did I do, Lara?"

A delicate blonde with anxious eyes moved out of the shadows and glanced at the mantel clock. "Four minutes exactly. Oh, Lucas! I was so afraid you'd be caught or that someone would come here looking for me."

"Well, we've proven it can be done. Now go out and mingle with your guests. I'll slip away and join you again shortly."

She reached out and touched his sleeve. "I don't think I can carry on much longer under the strain!"

Flynn took her hand in his. "Chin up, my dear. I'll find a way out of this coil as soon as possible."

Smiling tremulously, Lara straightened her shoulders and left the room. Flynn counted out several minutes and opened the door to the hallway with careful nonchalance. He'd almost reached the drawing room when a voice hailed him.

"Lucas!"

He turned on a lazy smile and looked up as a stately dowager came down the long staircase toward him.

"There you are!" Lady Steadmore called out as she bore down upon him, the plumes in her satin turban bobbing with every step. "I declare you have been avoiding me all evening, and I have been wanting to introduce you to my charming niece."

He bowed and gave her an engaging grin. Would she be as eager to make the introduction if she knew what he'd just been up to? Nothing of his thoughts showed in his face. "I'd be honored to meet your niece, Lady Steadmore. Introduce me to this paragon."

Lady Steadmore grimaced. "She's actually rather dreadful. A simpering, rabbit-faced girl with more hair than wit. Her parents sent her out here, dreaming I could make a match for her, but it is beyond any hope! I really can't blame you for keeping your distance."

Flynn laughed. "I assure you that I wasn't in hiding. I merely stepped out to the terrace for a breath of air."

"Sneaking out to foul the garden with one of those filthy cigars, no doubt!" The matron's voice was still stern, but Lady Steadmore couldn't hold back a smile. She had always had a soft heart for a handsome rogue.

Flynn read her face easily and his eyes twinkled. "You're merely envious, ma'am. Only last week you complained to me that women's bad habits are condemned by society, while men's are indulged."

"You are impertinent, sir! No woman in her right mind would so much as touch one of those filthy tobacco sticks." She gave him her hand to kiss. "What you need is a wife. A good woman to cure you of cigars and all your other bad habits."

As they continued to the drawing room Flynn's mouth turned up at the corners and his eyes blazed as green as the emeralds hidden inside his waistcoat.

His smile was light with just a hint of self-mockery. "A good woman," he said, "would have nothing to do with me."

Chapter One

The yellow beam of the lantern swung around the ancient chamber, illuminating the rough blocks that formed the walls. In the flickering light, the bizarre figures painted upon them leapt to sudden, menacing life—Chac-mool, god of rain, and An Puc, the skeleton-jawed representation of Death. Tilly swung the lamp toward the far corner, and her keen eye caught the telltale gleam of gold. Her heart pounding with excitement, she crossed the littered floor and stepped over the scattered bones.

Yes, it was gold. The massive gem-studded collar and pectoral gleamed on the suit of jade mosaic, which covered the remains of a once-proud Mayan priest. She moved in for a closer look, and the engraved glyphs confirmed what she already knew: after months of searching, she had at last found Queptil, the lost city of the Mayas.

Suddenly, there was a sharp sound behind her. Whirling about, Tilly prepared to face danger, eagerly seeking the face of her adversary, the secret enemy who had dared to follow her into the tomb. The leering skeleton of Death rose up before her in the dimness, bony arms reaching out to embrace her, and...

...Tilly jerked awake. The pagan splendors of the Mayan tomb faded into the dark-paneled confines of the familiar, shabby sitting room; outside the window, instead of emerald jungles and rainbow-hued birds, there was only rain. Rain and the endless Yorkshire moors. Her eyes focused on the kindly face of Mrs. Pimm, her elderly housekeeper, looming over her in the dimness.

"Dozed off, did you?" Mrs. Pimm shook her grizzled head. "Working too hard again, dearie, that's what it is. All them committees and ladies' auxiliaries and such."

Tilly confessed openly, "I'm sorry, Mrs. Pimm. I was woolgathering and didn't hear a word you said."

"What I was wondering," Mrs. Pimm repeated, "was would you be wanting a nice cutlet for your dinner? Or there's a bit of lamb shoulder I could put into a meat pie, if you'd rather."

It was difficult for Tilly to concentrate after the shock of finding herself yanked from her exotic daydream into mundane reality. The sitting room was dark, all gray and brown, like a bowl of congealing oatmeal. Her eyes ached for color and light the way her spirit ached for adventure and life; but instead of the daring woman of her dreams—Miss Matilda Templeton, archaeologist, explorer and world traveler— there was only Tilly Templeton, a spinster of almost twenty-six years, tucked away in an obscure Yorkshire village.

She sighed, a sound that surprised her housekeeper. Mrs. Pimm blinked anxiously and pushed her eyeglasses up her formidable nose. Miss Tilly was always so brisk and full of energy. It wasn't like her to sit around with idle hands. Not with the church bazaar coming up in three days and so much left to do.

Mrs. Pimm folded her hands across her stomach. "Now, about that cutlet, then?"

"Oh, yes. A cutlet would be very nice." Tilly glanced at the open book upon her lap. "I'm afraid my thoughts were quite far away."

"Aye." The housekeeper nodded. "You looked to be a million miles off."

"And so I was."

"'Tis no wonder, reading such drear stuff. No good can ever come of poking about nasty heathen ruins, is what I say!"

Tilly glanced down. The open volume on her lap was an abridged version of Stephens's and Catherwood's *Inci-*

dents of Travel in Central America, Chiapas and the Yuca-tan. The black-and-white engraving depicted the ruins of an ancient Mayan temple city, buried for centuries beneath mounds of encroaching jungle. Profiles of grinning, hawk-nosed gods peered out between curtains of living vines, conjuring images of strange rites and blood sacrifice. Mrs. Pimm might find the illustrations dreary, but Tilly did not—she found them fascinating. And, contrary to Mrs. Pimm's reasoning, it was boredom and the lack of any real work that had sent her mind wandering. She longed for the exhilaration of discovery, the thrill of not knowing what would—or could—happen next!

Instead she was entombed in her family home, where one day followed another and weeks grew into months, with only the change of season to distinguish them. Despite her craving for adventure, the greatest challenges she had faced in her twenty-five years were stretching her tiny household allowance from one quarter to the next and playing peace-maker between Mrs. Todd and Mrs. Wicken, who should have never, *never* been put on the same church committee.

The housekeeper paused in the doorway. "Oh, I almost forgot. I was to tell you that Master Durward has come in and is waiting for you in the library." She shook her head. "Like clockwork, he is."

Mrs. Pimm bustled away while Tilly checked the watch pinned to the pocket of her starched shirtwaist. She and her brother were as different as water and stone. They had both inherited the straight Templeton nose and their father's rich chestnut hair, but the resemblance ended there. Tilly's quicksilver traits were a direct contrast to her brother's leaden ways. Durward's days were marked out by the ticking of his pocket watch and the tall case clock that stood at the foot of the stairs. He had no yearning for adventure and loathed change of any kind.

Tilly set aside her book and rose. There were times—like now—when Durward's passion for punctuality and slow, methodical habits irritated her to distraction. Then she was filled with guilt. After all, it wasn't Durward's fault that she had inherited all the mental liveliness and physical vigor he lacked.

Passing one of the long windows that fronted on the overgrown garden, she eyed the draperies with misgiving. The silk brocade was faded and fragile with age. How she was going to keep them from rotting off their rods in another year was beyond any reach of her imagination. If only poor Papa had been more provident in his investments, how different life would have been!

In the dark hall she met Sturgis, the ancient retainer who served as butler and Durward's valet.

"These just arrived from Hollowdean Hall, Miss Matilda." His arthritic hands held a silver Charles II tray, which he had scrupulously polished, and which bore a large posy of wilting spring flowers. "Shall I put them in water for you?"

"Oh, dear! Yes, thank you."

Sturgis nodded in sympathy. There was no accounting for where Cupid's arrows struck, the villagers all agreed, holding their sides with laughter. How old Sir Harold, with his crotchets and gout and red-veined face, expected to woo so lively and forthright a young lady as Miss Matilda Templeton was a topic of general hilarity in the village. He was known to have proposed at least three times already. The fact that the entire countryside interested themselves in this non-romance was quite a trial for Tilly, but no matter how often and how firmly she refused, Sir Harold was determined to wear her down.

Durward was just finishing the last section of the paper when she entered the library, and Tilly knew he would not look up until he was through. A small fire burned in the grate. The only other light came through the tall windows overlooking the windswept moors. She took one of the brown upholstered chairs and leaned her head against the worn fabric, half irritated and half amused. For all Durward noticed, she might be invisible.

Any moment, she knew, he would fold the morning paper into precise quarters and lay it to the left of the desk. Then he would ring the bell, and Sturgis would enter with the afternoon post on a silver tray. When the butler withdrew Durward would examine each letter and sort them into two neat stacks, squaring the corners. Finally he would clear his throat and ask, as always, what her plans were for the rest of the day.

Dear Durward. So meticulous, so exact. So utterly predictable, yet touching, in a rather poignant way. Tilly had a fleeting vision of herself, twenty years hence, sitting in the library at two o'clock, waiting for her brother to sort the mail. A wild, rebellious impulse came over her. She wanted to startle him out of his rut.

"Durward," she said clearly and firmly, "I have decided to run away with Colonel Meecham's stable boy and live the life of a Gypsy."

"Um," her brother replied, turning to the last page. Tilly sighed. It was just as well he hadn't paid her any heed. He wouldn't have gotten the joke, and the smallest upset to his routine would roil his digestion and disrupt his sleep. *Of course,* she thought guiltily, *he needs a great deal of rest to keep up his strength.* Durward suffered terribly from insomnia and resorted to horrible diets in order to maintain his health. It really was unfair that she had inherited so much of Papa's energy, and he so little.

Tilly idly examined the yellowed wallpaper, wishing they could afford to replace it, and waited. On cue, Durward folded the newspaper into precise quarters and rang for Sturgis. The butler entered, soundless as a wraith, with a small pile of notes and letters upon his tray. Removing the assortment of correspondence from the silver tray, her brother dismissed the butler and began sorting the mail into two stacks. Tilly selected a lemon drop from the dish on the table beside her and waited expectantly, a twinkle in her fine gray eyes, as he squared the stacks with his hands.

Durward cleared his throat. "Matilda, my dear, have you given any real thought to accepting Sir Harold's offer of marriage?"

Tilly choked on the lemon drop. After a confusion of coughs, spilled ink, scattered letters and Durward's alarmed thumps between her shoulder blades, she was finally able to speak.

"Marry Sir Harold? He is sixty-two years of age and afflicted with gout and a dozen unpleasant relatives who expect to be his heirs! I'd rather die a withered spinster a hundred times than accept his offer. I suspect he only wants a wife so he can dismiss his nurse and save her wages! And," she added, "who would look after you?"

Flushing unbecomingly, Durward resumed his seat. "You have kept house for me since Papa died. It has been brought to my attention that I have been, perhaps, a little selfish in expecting you to continue on this way. I . . . I would not like to think that your concern for me has kept you from following the inclinations of your heart."

A peal of laughter burst from Tilly. "My heart is perfectly content with *not* marrying Sir Harold. I'd rather hire myself off as a kitchen maid at the Blue Swan! Let your conscience be easy, Durward. We'll live out our days at Oak Manor until we are both doddering octogenarians."

He gave her a doubtful look but didn't pursue it.

"Good Gad!" Durward exclaimed sharply, interrupting her train of thought. He was eyeing an envelope with the aggrieved air of a man who has found a spider in his teacup.

It couldn't be another tradesman's dun: Tilly was sure she'd paid the last with the remnants of her meager personal allowance—and given the man a piece of her mind for his impertinence.

Durward waved the offending missive in the air. "I cannot believe it. Jamaica! Who on earth could be writing to you from such an outlandish place?"

Tilly extended her hand eagerly. "I shall never know, Durward, unless you let me open it."

Still disapproving, he held the letter out to her, his jowly face ruddy with indignation. "Pirate's haunts. Nothing but black sheep and women of low character!"

Ignoring him, Tilly slit the envelope with an ivory-handled opener. The page of heavy-pressed paper was crossed and recrossed with lines of script, in letters so small and close together they resembled some exotic alphabet. Her eyes opened wide with pleasure.

"Oh! It's from my old school friend, Lara Burlinghome. Or rather, Lara Whitby. You remember, Durward, she married a wealthy merchant and went off to live in the islands."

As Tilly deciphered Lara's words the dull library vanished and her mind was filled with visions of crystal beaches glittering beneath a benevolent golden sun. Her ears filled with the siren song of the Caribbean Sea. Lara was inviting her for a long visit.

...a long and much overdue visit! I cannot promise you the elegancies of London, but you will find the company here both refined and stimulating. There is no lack of sparkling conversation—or, I might add, of handsome, eligible men. I can promise you sailing parties, balls, yachting excursions and alfresco dining beneath the palm trees. Do say you will come, dearest Tilly! I must see you. There is someone I want very much for you to meet, my dear friend, Tiger Flynn, and I hope...

The last words of Lara's writing blurred into an indecipherable scrawl. *Tiger Flynn.* What a ridiculous name! But possibly she'd misread it.

Tilly sat abstracted, while her head whirled with possibilities. For just a moment she let the Dreamer, the adventurous woman who lived hidden inside her, hold sway. She could envision it: towering palms, brilliant sunshine dazzling her eyes and, all around her, the warm, jewel-colored sea. Moonlight and the fragrance of night-blooming blossoms stirred by the tropical breeze. Glittering, candlelit parties and romantic walks beneath the stars with... with whom? Her imagination faltered.

During their days at Miss Martin's Select Seminary for Girls, Lara and Tilly had exchanged their ideals of the perfect romantic hero. He would be tall, but not too tall. A man of affairs, a prince among men. As at home in grand company as upon the hunting field. An Englishman, of course, golden-haired, with blue eyes and thin, patrician features—and bearing a distinct resemblance to the hero in a book of fairy tales, endowed with every virtue the world had ever known.

There was only one problem. Reviewing with the adult eyes this imaginary hero, this paragon, Tilly couldn't help but notice that he seemed . . . well, rather dull.

"Matilda!"

Suddenly the sunlight faded and she was back in the small library with its lovely faded curtains and drops of wind-driven rain splattering against the panes.

"What was that, Durward? I'm sorry but I wasn't attending."

Durward was apparently in the middle of a long list of waiting duties. Her duties. "And if you do go into the village, don't forget to stop by the vicarage and ask Reverend Toomey for that volume of sermons he promised to lend me."

"But Durward, only listen! Lara has invited me to Jamaica, for an extended visit."

"Impossible! You could not go abroad alone, and my health, as I must sadly remind you, would not allow me to accompany you on an arduous sea voyage. I must also point out that it would take an enormous amount of money to pay for your transportation. And I suppose you would want to purchase expensive fabrics to prepare a suitable wardrobe. No, it is not to be thought of."

Two spots of rosy color tinged her cheeks and Tilly's eyes shone. "But you wouldn't be put out at all! Lara writes that I could sail under the chaperonage of a Mrs. Langdan, a most proper widow of her acquaintance. Oh, Durward, I could remake my summer frocks. And I would sail upon one of her husband's ships, so the financing of such an expensive journey would not be a burden to you."

"But who would look after the household while you are gallivanting around the globe?" he answered in shock. "You know how prone I am to colds and fevers this time of year."

The glow died in her eyes. "Furthermore," he added, "You have promised to supervise the Annual Church Gala and the Ladies' League Tea. You know how they all—how *we* all depend upon you."

Tilly glanced at the letter, the delicate color ebbing from her face until it was as pale as she sheet of paper in her hand. Durward was right. The Templetons always lived up to their duties and obligations.

She put the letter into her pocket and rose. As she reached the door Durward put down his coffee cup and called after her. "The next time you are in the village I think you should pick up another bottle of Dr. Brough's restorative tonic for me. I am not quite certain, you understand, but I do think I feel an attack of pleurisy coming on."

It wasn't until the next day that the rain let up enough for Tilly to take her daily walk on the moors. After delivering some of her calves' foot jelly to old Mrs. Creasey she set out at a brisk pace. Beneath the dry brown grasses and gorse the first adventurous plants were pushing up their tender green shoots. The playful wind that rippled the hem of her tawny cape and tugged strands of chestnut hair from beneath her bonnet carried the promise of awakening life. Usually the early days of spring filled her soul with pleasure; today Tilly was filled with a restless yearning instead.

She sat on a great slab of stone known as the Norseman's Bench and looked down over Hollowdean, cupped in a fold between the enormous, windswept hills. This was all the world she'd ever known—and all the world she was ever likely to know. Once a bustling stage stop, it was now an isolated, dying place ringed by a few poor farms and inhabited by the elderly. At times she felt as if she'd been walled up alive. The exotic lands, the emerald jungles and golden islands basking beneath a molten sun, were places she could only visit in books.

In dreams.

If Durward's health was not so frail she might have escaped somehow. Even the life of a governess, scorned and relegated to the chimney corner, would have been more interesting, but Tilly knew she wouldn't have been a good governess: she had no talent for meekness.

If only she had been born a man, Tilly thought, she would have made an excellent tutor. Although denied the classical education her brother had tossed away so lightly, she had a passion for knowledge and had educated herself at home. She chafed at the great discrepancy in the education of English boys and girls. Young gentlemen were trained to go out and rule the world while young ladies were trained to take their places as "ornaments to society." Tilly couldn't imagine herself serving as a mere accessory to a hypothetical husband. The very idea stuck in her throat like a bone.

The sound of an approaching gig interrupted her reverie. Dr. Brough was driving down the rutted track from Willow Farm behind his brown mare. He pulled up when he spotted her. He was a spare, good-humored man of sixty years with a ready smile, warm hazel eyes and a comfortably rumpled air. Since she was always as healthy as the proverbial horse, Tilly's rare dealings with the doctor were social.

"Good afternoon, Miss Templeton. Lovely day! But if you're done admiring the view I could give you a lift to the village."

She rose and took the hand he held out to her, but when she was seated beside him she smiled ruefully. "I'm afraid the view holds no charms for me today. It was the island of Jamaica I was picturing in my mind's eye."

He snapped the reins, and the mare set off. "Ah, Jamaica! One of God's more beautiful creations! Paradise is not too strong a word to describe its scenery."

"You know it?"

"Spent fifteen of the best years of my life there. But the missus was lonesome for her own kith and kin, so we came back to Yorkshire. Can't say as I'm not content here, though." He gave her a conspiratorial grin. "Except on hard winter mornings when I wake up to find four feet of snow on my doorstep. Are you thinking of taking a journey to the Caribbean, Miss Templeton?"

Tilly shook her head. "I have been invited to spend some time there with a friend from my school days. But of course,

I could not leave my brother alone in his frail state of health.''

There was something in her voice the doctor hadn't expected to hear. He turned his face toward her and frowned. "Frail state of health? What nonsense is this? You go and have your visit, young lady. It will do you good. And it would do Durward a deal of good, also, to be on his own."

She was startled. "But who would look after him? He told me only yesterday that he felt a touch of pleurisy coming on, and you know how bad his chest is in damp weather."

Brough's reply was sharp. "I know nothing of the kind. And why, if he thinks he is falling ill, do I see him riding along the bridge road with Lady Helena Blandford in an open carriage?"

Tilly followed his pointing finger. The two figures in the vehicle approaching the old stone bridge were doll-like with distance, but in the clear air they were easily recognizable. Her mouth dropped open in surprise. "But I thought . . . he said . . . why, I believed Durward was at the vicarage visiting the Reverend Munson. Oh, dear, to be riding in this weather! He'll surely come down with an inflammation of the lungs!"

"He'll come to no more harm," the doctor replied mildly, "than either you or I."

Tilly blinked. "I think I cannot have understood you correctly. You know that Durward has been subject to various ailments since birth. Why, he was far too sickly to even attend school. And any strenuous activity puts him sadly out of frame for days."

Dr. Brough lifted a bushy eyebrow. "Name one."

"I beg your pardon?"

"Name one strenuous activity that he has ever indulged in, Miss Templeton, and I will gladly eat my hat." He eyed her bonnet thoughtfully. "And your's, too—if you can think of any occasion when poor health has kept your brother from doing anything he really wanted to do."

As they turned right at the main track Tilly cast her mind back in time for an example. Her earliest memories were of tiptoeing around the house because "Dear Durward has the headache." Or the earache. Or the stomachache. Why, dear Mama, who had been rather an invalid herself, had spent most of her days nursing him; and Tilly knew what great anxiety their father had over his heir's state of health. Indeed, she could not remember a time when the activities of Oak Manor had not revolved around Durward's many infirmities.

Yet Dr. Brough was right: try as she would, Tilly could not recall a single strenuous activity in which Durward had ever engaged—nor could she remember one time when illness had ruined his plans for pleasure. Her frown deepened, and she smoothed a wrinkle from her skirt.

Only a week ago Durward had been poorly for several days but improved miraculously in time to attend a party in honor of Lady Helena. And not two days after declaring his liver felt grossly inflamed, he had gone off with the Squire's son to attend a cockfight some sixteen miles from Hollowdean. In retrospect she saw a string of such occurrences stretching back as far as she could remember. She felt like an utter fool.

"I don't understand—" She broke off, shaking her head.

The physician cleared his throat. "Let me be perfectly frank with you, my dear Miss Templeton. Some people are said to enjoy bad health. In reference to your brother, that can be taken quite literally. I brought Durward into this world, you know—a sturdy, squalling infant with all his fingers and toes. There was nothing wrong with him then, and there is nothing wrong with him now."

Tilly digested this for several seconds. "Then," she said spiritedly, "if my brother is not ill, why do you dose him with your draughts and remedies?"

"They are nothing more than tonics and physics to maintain his health when he quacks himself with one of his ridiculous food cures."

The doctor turned the gig from the cart track onto the narrow lane that bordered the village. He glanced at Tilly.

"Don't blame yourself, Miss Templeton. You were just a child when Durward was born. After two stillborn sons, your parents cosseted and indulged him to extremes. I can't tell you the number of times I was roused from my bed after midnight, for nothing more than the cutting of a baby tooth or a touch of colic! But if a child is taught that the sky is red and not blue, the child will grow up thinking it is red indeed."

They'd reached the rusted gates of Oak Manor. "You may let me down here, if you please." Tilly started to climb down before the doctor could assist her. He touched her sleeve.

"All your life you have been brought up to think of Durward as just one step away from the reaper's scythe. It was ingrained in you to coddle and protect and mother him. In fact, I blame myself for the fact that we did not have this little talk several years ago."

Tilly's gray eyes looked into his steadily. "And why did we not?"

For the first time in their frank conversation, Dr. Brough looked embarrassed. "Plainly speaking, I thought you were one of those unmarried women who enjoy catering to the whims of a self-supposed invalid."

Tilly wondered how many of her acquaintances had shared the doctor's mistaken notion, and her face flamed with mortification. "Thank you for being so frank with me, Dr. Brough. I do appreciate it."

"No thanks required. Just get out to Jamaica and enjoy yourself. A long and leisurely visit is my prescription for you, young lady. You're long overdue for it."

He handed her down from the gig, smiling a bit. He could almost hear the wheels turning in her head. What he wouldn't give to be a fly on one of Oak Manor's walls this afternoon!

She waved and started up the weedy drive, her boots crunching on the thin gravel, unaware that there were more shocks in store for her. Tilly was so deep in reflection she didn't glimpse the back of the elegant vehicle pulled up in the neglected stable yard. She slipped in the big front door and stopped in surprise. Sturgis stood in the hall, a caped overcoat folded over his arm and a burnished top hat in his hand.

"Your uncle has arrived from London, Miss Tilly. I have put him in the library."

They had only one living relative, her father's brother, whom she had not seen in some nine or ten years. Uncle Hannaford had returned to London from Bombay two years ago, but had never bothered to visit his niece and nephew in Yorkshire. Tilly decided that only an affair of great urgency would force him to journey to the north country.

She paused to check her appearance in the damp-spotted console mirror. The wind had brought rosy color to her cheeks. She tucked a stray wisp behind her ear and went in search of her uncle. The library fire had been banked with a layer of ashes, and its feeble warmth did nothing to dispel the chill. Despite his aversion to Yorkshire springs, Uncle Hannaford was not warming himself at the fire, but prowling the room with a baffled and rather belligerent air, chomping fiercely on the ends of his bristling white moustache.

"Egad," he said with no other attempt at greeting, "I swear not one thing has been changed in this room in the past thirty years!"

"It is exactly as it was in my father's day," Tilly responded calmly.

"Ha! Thought so. And the rest of the place, I suppose?"

"Except for the draperies in the dining room. They were hopelessly beyond repair and had to be replaced."

Uncle Hannaford nodded so hard his jowls waggled. "I should certainly think so. Everything is as shabby as a seaside rooming house. I can't believe a dwelling as fine as Oak Manor has been reduced to this!"

Tilly was a lady, born and bred, but it took an effort to control her rising temper. It would be improper to reply as sharply as she wished, but the provocation was great. He pulled an old-fashioned quizzing glass from his pocket and examined her through it. "That gown of yours has seen better days, I'll be bound. Why, that style of bodice has been out of the mode these past five years and more. Don't tell me you've become as big a nip-cheese as your brother.''

To her annoyance, Tilly could feel a dull flush spreading over her face. She was very aware of the worn cuffs of her sleeves beneath the bit of velvet ribbon she'd salvaged from an old dress in the attic. The gown was her second-best day dress, and this was its third incarnation. Cuffs and collar had already been replaced twice, and although she was a notable needlewoman, her skills could not preserve the gown another season.

"I've been out walking on the moors," she answered stiffly.

Uncle Hannaford tisk-tisked loudly and shook his head. "I never thought I'd see the day when a Templeton would jaunter about the countryside dressed in rags a scarecrow would scorn. I hope you're not turning into one of those old spinster gels with a hundred cats and a pipe in your pocket!"

That was too much. Tilly bridled. "I don't dress this way to be eccentric, I assure you. But my vanity isn't so overwhelming that I would let Oak Manor fall around my ears in order to put new fashions on my back."

Now it was his turn to be taken aback. "No, why should you? But if you're trying to make me believe you've run through your fortune already, you're wasting your breath."

"Fortune!" she protested, wondering if her relative was becoming senile. A *fortune*? "I would call it a mere pittance."

Uncle Hannaford's eyes bulged and his ruddy face grew redder. "If you do not consider eighty thousand pounds a fortune, my dear, you must have quite extravagant habits."

"I don't know where you came by that figure, but you're in error. Durward leased the manor lands years ago, and we've been living modestly on the rentals ever since."

"I remember now. You were away at school when your parents died." A strange expression came over her uncle's florid features. "I forgot that you were underage and excluded from the reading of the will. Of course, so was Durward, but he was there as your father's heir. And there was indeed an estate of eighty thousand pounds, invested in the Funds. I was one of the executors, you know, and I am very sure of the facts.''

He folded his hands behind his back, in the way of retired navy officers. ''Except for your mother's jewels, your late father left his entire estate to Durward, with the understanding that his only son and heir would provide adequately for you until you either married or attained your majority, at which time he was enjoined to make a healthy settlement upon you from the estate's coffers.''

For the second time that day Tilly felt her world going topsy-turvy. She sat down abruptly on the sofa. ''No. I cannot believe it.''

''My dear Tilly, why else do you suppose the widowed Mrs. Blandford has been making up to Durward? Her brother is a junior partner at Dobbs, Cranford, where *your* brother has long had his accounts. And that is how his entanglement with her came to my ears. I came immediately when I heard of it. The woman is a harpy.''

Tilly scarcely heard. The mention of jewelry had chased a memory out of the long shadows of the past. ''My mother's jewels—was there a sapphire brooch, shaped like a butterfly, among them?''

''Why, yes, now that you mention it. Part of a set, in fact. Necklace, earrings, bracelet. Excellent stones.''

Yes. Tilly remembered now—and she had seen the butterfly pin not a week since, decorating the bodice of Lady Helena's blue cloak.

Until this very moment, she had always thought that ''seeing red'' was only a figure of speech. Now she knew it was not. The red mist was only a symptom of the righteous anger burning within her. It burned for the years of saving candle stubs and the ends of soap bars and doing without. For being early to bed and early to rise in order to take advantage of the daylight, with no fire in her bedchamber, except in the dead of winter. For all the gaiety, the witty conversation, the London Seasons and the friendships she had missed.

And most of all, for her mother's brooch, which should have been hers, and was instead adorning Lady Helena's proud bosom.

Her mouth trembled as she surveyed the library with its water-stained wallpaper and sturdy but worn furnishings. She supposed that was exactly how her brother saw her: homely, useful and convenient. Tilly squared her chin, not knowing if she was more angry with Durward or with herself, for being so taken in. *Eighty thousand pounds!*

Uncle Hannaford turned abruptly and began to pace the frayed carpet. "I see that I have neglected my duties to you, Tilly, without meaning to and I . . . damn!" The toe of one polished boot caught in the worn threads and set him stumbling against the heavy mahogany desk. He righted himself, chewing his moustache violently.

"I am going to drive into Huddersfield to confer with your late father's solicitor and have the matter looked into immediately."

At the sound of carriage wheels Tilly rose and went to the window. "There's no need. Durward has just returned. If you'll provide me with a copy of the will and a list of Mama's jewelry, I shall handle the rest myself."

The moment she heard the sound of the opening door Tilly stepped into the hall. Sturgis was still in the butler's closet as her brother helped Lady Helena out of her cloak. A gleam of gold and sapphire caught Tilly's eye. She bore down upon them, took the cloak before Durward knew what she was about and removed the brooch.

"Tilly, whatever are you doing?"

"Reclaiming my property. And I expect you to hand over the rest of the jewelry which you've kept from me all these years, without delay."

While Lady Helena stared with her boiled-gooseberry eyes, Durward clutched at his sister's arm. "Have you lost your mind? Give me that brooch at once. I gave it to Lady Helena as a betrothal gift."

"Then you will have to give her another. The brooch is mine."

Lady Helena looked down her long patrician nose at Tilly. "Perhaps you don't understand, Miss Templeton. Your brother and I are going to be married."

Tilly smiled as her anger dissolved in the face of their arrogant absurdity. "I wish you joy of each other," she announced, "and hope you'll give me your good wishes, also."

Durward's mouth dropped open. "Do you mean you have accepted Sir Harold's offer of marriage?"

She had started down the hall toward the staircase with a light step and lighter heart, but Tilly paused when she reached the first step. "Marry Sir Harold? Not for all the Queen's horses. I have a much better plan. You may be going down the aisle, Durward, but *I* . . . *I* am going to Jamaica!"

Chapter Two

The West Indies! Tilly leaned against the rail of the *Montego Bay*, filled with pure and exquisite happiness. She was intoxicated with the beauty of the islands. Emerald-green mountains rimmed with opalescent sands. Sapphire waters paling to incredibly clear, warm aquamarine in the distant shallows. Every breath brought the tang of salt-sea air mingled with spices, exotic flowers and the scents of endless summer. And most of all, somewhere ahead, waited Lara and adventure.

She could hardly believe she was the same sheltered young woman who'd set sail from London. She felt different. Expectant. More alive than she had ever been. It was as if at any moment something utterly delightful might happen, something so impossibly wonderful that she had no name for it, only an intense and unidentified yearning that grew with every nautical mile.

Tilly heard footsteps behind her and turned. George Keating, Jonas Whitby's junior partner, joined her at the rail. He was quietly assured and rather distinguished with his neat beard and gold-rimmed glasses. A typical colonial Englishman, his fair good looks were only slightly impaired by his peeling sunburn. He'd done much to make her voyage a success, and Tilly greeted him cordially.

His answering smile was warm. "Life at sea seems to agree with you, Miss Templeton."

"Oh, yes, Mr. Keating. I feel like a pampered princess. After such a wonderful voyage, I'm afraid I'll be reluctant to step ashore."

"No fear of that. I think you'll find the island very much to your liking. Some people fall in love with it at first sight and never leave."

She laughed. "Perhaps I'll be one of them."

"I certainly hope so."

Tilly blushed. She wasn't used to pretty compliments, but there was no doubt that Mr. Keating intended it as such. She looked into water so clear she could see fish and sand and coral formations, with the shadows of the hull and rigging flying across them.

She squeezed her eyes shut a moment, then, was afraid to open them, afraid that it would all melt away before her eyes, and she would find herself a prisoner of England's cold gray winter. But it *was* real! The steady vibration of the ship as it cut through the waves, the mingled aromas of varnish and tar and the sea and the warm caress of the afternoon sun proved it.

"When will we arrive?"

"We'll be in Kingston Harbor within the hour."

"Then, before we reach the harbor I'd like to thank you for everything you've done to make the voyage enjoyable."

Keating gazed at Tilly earnestly. "It has been my great pleasure to do so."

The sudden warmth in his blue eyes threw her off stride. "I know that Jonas Whitby commissioned you to see personally to my comfort, and you have done so unstintingly, in addition to your other duties," she replied a bit stiffly.

The man's sunburned face grew redder, as if he thought she'd snubbed him for impertinence. "Forgive me, Miss Templeton, if my marked preference for your company has caused you distress."

Now Tilly *was* distressed. He had been so kind, and she had hurt his feelings. There were, she knew, rules for engaging in polite flirtation: unfortunately, she had never learned any of them. "Not at all, Mr. Keating."

"I am relieved. We shall be thrown in each other's company a good deal during your visit, and I hope our acquaintanceship will continue to flourish—and perhaps ripen into deeper friendship."

As the mistress of Oak Manor Tilly had handled everything from a leaky roof to an epidemic in the village, but she found herself quite unable to handle Mr. Keating's words. His announcement was a declaration of his intention to court her and Tilly, who had never been at a loss for words before, was rendered speechless. She had become quite used to thinking of herself as a settled spinster. All her brisk confidence deserted her, and she looked toward the water rather abruptly.

George Keating didn't press his luck.

"It has been my pleasure to serve you, Miss Templeton. And now, I will wish you good day. We'll meet again at Coeur d'Émeraude this evening."

He still looked mortified—even angry—as he took his leave, and Tilly wished she'd been able to accept his compliments without blushing and turning prickly as a hedgehog. It wasn't that she didn't like receiving them as much as any other young lady would—it was only that she'd had so little practice at it.

The wind picked up and she tied her bonnet more tightly beneath her chin. The thin green ribbon of land ahead grew larger until she could make out the vague outlines of the Blue Mountains, which formed the island's spine. Jamaica!

She strained her eyes as details became clearer with every passing minute. Tilly felt a strange sense of homecoming. Somewhere in those foothills was the extensive Whitby plantation. Coeur d'Émeraude—Heart of Emerald. The very name conjured romantic images. And today, she would be there.

Excitement sent shivers of anticipation along her skin. A door had opened, paving the way to the adventure she had always craved. She stood at the rail until the thin green ribbon grew to lush hills dotted with pastel buildings and backed by the misty Blue Mountains. The island grew bigger with every passing moment, and at last the lower sails were furled as the *Montego Bay* slowed for the approach to Kingston. Tilly gazed up into the rigging. The trim clipper was the pride of the Whitby line, and her tall masts, with their wide spars and graceful grids of ropes, made an elegant design against the bright blue sky.

Just inside the harbor the *Montego Bay* dropped anchor. The ship would wait for permission to proceed to the docks and unload her wares. Nearby two other vessels rode out their turn at anchor. One, a black-hulled frigate, heeled closer as an errant wind caught its still unfurled topsail.

As Tilly watched in alarm sailors swarmed along the frigate's lines amid shouts and curses. The acres of canvas fluttered and sagged and were drawn inexorably upward as she watched. Now the ship was so close to the *Montego Bay* that only a distance of several yards separated the vessels. The loudest voice, the one giving the orders, acknowledged the sailors' quick response with congratulations that were as profane as they were sincere.

"Look lively there, Bailey, or I'll flay your wrinkled old hide from your bones! Good work, MacRae! Good lad!" The deep, booming baritone, for all its cant phrases, sounded educated, and there was a definite lilt to it. The lilt of Ireland, Tilly realized, and quickly located its source.

A man stood on the foredeck, stripped to the waist. With his booted feet planted wide apart and hands fisted at his waist, he alternated threats with encouragement. His skin was deeply bronzed, and the stiffening breeze ruffled his light brown, sun-streaked hair. He leaped up to catch a shroud line, lean and lithe as a cat. The disciplined muscles rippled across his back and arms with every quick, agile movement.

There was a magnetism to him that drew the eye and held it. At least it drew and held Tilly's. She couldn't take her eyes away from him. His chest was as muscular and well-developed as his back, and the wide shoulders tapered down to a trim waist. He radiated a coiled, animal power that hit her with sheer physical force. While she stared, totally fascinated, he turned toward the frigate's rail and spied her watching him. Still she couldn't look away.

The man was neither embarrassed nor abashed by her frank scrutiny, and eyed her with equal interest. He seemed to like what he saw: a cloud of chestnut hair coming loose beneath her wide-brimmed bonnet, a trim figure in a white skirt and shirtwaist piped with navy, and an oval face with clear gray eyes that watched him with startled curiosity. His wide, sensual mouth turned up at the corners and he flashed her a grin, a slash of white against his deeply tanned face.

Tilly was caught quite off guard. She could feel a deep blush rising up her throat until her cheeks flamed with it. She was unaware that the flush enhanced the sparkle in her eyes and emphasized the delicacy of her skin. The sailor, however, took in everything. Laughter and appreciation sparkled in his eyes.

"And a very good day to you, ma'am!" he sang out in his deep, musical voice. "I'm happy to have afforded you some entertainment." He put his hands on his hips and gazed at her boldly. "Have you seen enough—or would you like me to come aboard so you might have a closer look?"

Tilly could have died with humiliation. Every hand aboard the frigate—and several on the *Montego Bay*—had looked up at his voice. The man—he looked like a pirate with his handsome, laughing face and easy masculine arrogance—put her all out of countenance. She pried her hands off the rail, but before she could back away he removed a make-believe hat from his wind-blown curls and with careless grace made her a low and sweeping bow. His eyes were green, filled with mocking laughter and little dancing lights.

Recovering herself, Tilly turned and proceeded to her cabin, wrapped in the tattered remnants of her dignity. A roar of unrestrained male laughter followed in her wake.

Lucas Flynn, hands still braced upon his hips, watched her go with a smile on his firm mouth. So that was Lara's friend from school. From Lara's comments he'd pictured Miss Matilda Templeton as one of those crisp, no-nonsense English women who terrorized the world and its inhabitants by attempting to recreate a little bit of England wherever they went.

Not that Lara had ever said so. Although she had described her as clever, competent and knowing her own mind, she'd also stated that she'd never known anyone with a kinder heart. *"At school all the girls turned to her in times of trouble, with certainty that she would find a solution."*

Exactly the kind of woman Flynn least wanted on the scene now. Of course, Lara had no intention of telling her friend everything, she only wanted the comfort of her presence. Well, Flynn had already taken the first steps toward keeping Miss Templeton out of his hair. At their next meeting she was sure to avoid him like the plague.

It was too bad. Under other circumstances he would have enjoyed getting to know her. There was a good deal of intelligence in her dark-lashed gray eyes, and her lips were softly curved and sweetly kissable. He suspected she'd have a lively sense of humor, too, but that rosy mouth also revealed determination and a firm sense of purpose that could cause him real problems.

With a shrug of regret he turned his back on the *Montego Bay*. There was merchandise to unload, including a few things he would see to personally.

Meanwhile Tilly made her way to her cabin. It was hot and stuffy inside but she would have perished from the heat rather than go on deck again. She would not be the butt of that wild, half-naked pirate's vulgar jokes. There was no reason a lady should expose herself to such rudeness. And that was exactly how she had felt. Exposed. Vulnerable. Because something about that rude, insolent man had shaken her badly. She sat on the edge of the bunk, trying to explain it to herself. It was his clothing—or rather lack of it—that had upset her composure. Except for statues and illustrations she had never seen a man's body. It was rather overwhelming and so different from her own. His arms, she thought hurriedly, so dark and hard and corded, while hers were white and soft and round. She tried to convince herself that it was only intellectual curiosity that made her wonder how it would feel to touch his arm, his shoulder. His chest. To be held against it in a close embrace.

She stood up so abruptly she bumped her head on the low lantern. What on earth had made her think of something so...so.... There were no words available to her. Even thinking of it brought a rush of heat to her face and caused a most peculiar sensation in her stomach. In her heart Tilly had suspected herself of having a cool, dispassionate nature, because not one man of her acquaintance had ever evoked any romantic feelings in her. But then, she'd never met anyone like the man aboard the frigate—thank heavens!

Anger helped blot out the mental image of the tall, swaggering figure as she stripped off her hat and threw it on the bunk. The mirror above the washstand reflected her face, still red with embarrassment. What was the matter with her, that such a silly incident should make her react like a gauche schoolgirl?

She poured tepid water from the china pitcher and splashed it on her face as her mind circled to the man on the frigate. He was crude, obnoxious...and physically beautiful, like the engravings of Michelangelo's statue of David. And his smile, she had to admit, held a great deal of charm. She wondered who he was. Most likely one of the black sheep that Durward had mentioned, a handsome ne'er-do-well paid by his family to go away and stay away. A handsome devil.

Tilly refused to let him dominate her thoughts at a time when she should be looking forward to Kingston and her reunion with Lara! She fanned her warm face with her bonnet and resolved to put the entire episode out of her mind.

After all, it was highly unlikely she would ever see him again.

Tilly stayed in her cabin until she heard the clanking and felt the reverberations as the capstan was turned to lift anchor. Her heart gave an eager leap. The real adventure was about to begin!

She went on deck, unaware that the heat had loosened a few tendrils, leaving wispy curls at the nape of her neck. Suddenly she realized they were passing alongside the black-hulled frigate. She turned her head away and pretended not to have noticed.

"What?" a familiar deep voice called out. "Not waiting for me?"

She knew who it was, of course: that bold-eyed pirate from the frigate, ridiculing her again. Tilly wouldn't give him the satisfaction of acknowledging that the taunt was meant for her. By the time they reached the wharf her back ached. Head up, back straight, she ignored him. Flynn grinned. Against his better judgment, knowing she might prove dangerous to him, he found himself looking forward to their next meeting. He'd have to be very careful.

Tilly had no time to think of the man once she had set foot on the bustling wharf. There were naval officers and uniformed customs officials and sailors from every corner of the earth, all so dark from sun exposure she couldn't distinguish them from the true Jamaican islanders. Wagons and vendors and flower sellers crowded the harbor, and everywhere she saw graceful women carrying baskets upon their turban-wrapped heads.

"Tilly! Dear Tilly!"

A spanking open carriage had just pulled up, not twenty yards away. It had barely halted before a vision in white ruffles and matching parasol alighted and came tripping daintily toward her.

"Lara?" For a moment Tilly thought her eyes deceived her.

Her former schoolmate had been a soft girl, pleasantly rounded with dimpled arms and masses of bright, unruly curls. The woman coming toward her so eagerly was thin as a flower stem, and as fragile. The bones of her face stood out too distinctly beneath her delicate skin, her long neck was corded, and her elbows showed beneath the sheer sleeves of her driving dress, sharp as sticks.

Even the thick golden hair was altered, ruthlessly tamed and carefully restrained beneath the brim of a frilly lace hat.

Only the soft voice and the eloquent dark eyes were the same. "Oh, Tilly!" the woman cried out, "I have been counting the days till your arrival."

"Lara! It is really you!"

Years fell away. Tilly dropped her bandboxes and ran to greet her friend. It was only after the embraces and happy tears were exchanged that she got a second and much closer look. There were fine lines at the corners of Lara's shadowed eyes, and deeper ones bracketing her thin mouth. Creases marked her high white brow, and beneath the bubbly greetings and exclamations there was a thin, nervous quiver to her voice. Tilly knew it was more than the effects of the sunlight on a delicate complexion that had aged Lara. But there was no time for speculation.

"Well, what do you think of Jamaica?" Lara asked.

"It is beautiful! I have already fallen under the island's spell."

Lara smiled archly. "There are many handsome and eligible gentlemen among our friends and acquaintances, as I wrote you. Perhaps you shall take such a liking to one that you will extend your visit—or even decide to make your home here."

Tilly hoped that it wasn't Mr. Keating her friend had in mind. Although he was interesting and good-looking with an excellent future, he wasn't a kindred soul—that other half of her that Tilly knew was missing and hoped to find one day. But at least George Keating didn't fill her with confusion and make her blush like that rude green-eyed pirate she'd seen aboard the frigate.

While they drove up King Street Lara pointed out various landmarks. Steepled churches and tidy government buildings stood cheek by jowl with stuccoed remnants of the Spanish occupation, but the prim British buildings could not restrain the profusion of flowering trees and shrubs that rioted everywhere. Kingston was an explosion of color. Hot reds and golds and oranges dotted the soft pastel walls, and the emerald hues of the foliage were enhanced by the changing blues of the sea.

Tilly was eager to see the island and its people, but Lara was full of plans and chattered excitedly of the activities she had laid for her guest's entertainment.

"In honor of your first night we are holding a small, select dinner party. Nothing fancy, mind! I knew you would be more comfortable at a small gathering, so we shall dine informally, with only sixteen covers laid."

Sixteen for an informal dinner! Tilly felt a shiver that was half anticipation and half alarm. She had never dined with such a large party before. Indeed, there weren't that many of the gentry in all of Hollowdean. If a party of sixteen was Lara's idea of a small, informal arrangement Tilly could scarcely conceive of what a formal party might entail.

Lara saw her look of comical dismay. "Don't worry, Tilly, I've placed you between two congenial gentlemen."

"Will your brother Christopher be attending the dinner? I am looking forward to renewing my acquaintance with him. Even when I was at my most shy and awkward stage, he was always able to put me at ease."

A shadow passed over Lara's face, and she looked away. "I am afraid Christopher will not be able to join us. He has been dividing his time between Jamaica and archaeological research in Central America."

"Oh. Will he be back in Kingston before my return to England?"

"I—I can't say. Really, I don't think so. You see, for the past few weeks he has been . . . been away on one of his expeditions in the Yucatan."

Tilly had the uncanny sensation that Lara had been about to say something entirely different. And she was equally sure that her friend did not wish her to pry into the matter.

"I met an archaeologist on the way out. He is excavating near Chichen Itza. A Dr. Challfont."

Lara dropped her parasol, and the breeze almost carried it away. In the intervening commotion Tilly almost forgot her question. Lara had not. She gripped the ivory handle so tightly her knuckles blanched.

"Dr. Challfont! What a coincidence," she said hoarsely. "He is quite well-known in Kingston. Did he...did he speak of his expeditions?"

Out of courtesy, Tilly pretended not to notice Lara's agitation. "He was a bit of a recluse. I didn't see him after the first night at the captain's table, when there was no chance to discuss the Mayan ruins with him. It was quite a disappointment to me, for I'm very interested in the subject."

The carriage turned a corner while Lara stared blindly ahead, twisting her thin fingers in her lap. "I...I suppose I should warn you, in case the topic arises. Originally Christopher was attached to Dr. Challfont's party, but they...they had a falling out. At times it does make things awkward, since our circle of society is so limited here on the island. But let me tell you about the other guests tonight...."

Lara chattered on in a manner that was as bright as it was false. Barely pausing for breath, she launched into a list of the people Tilly would be meeting that evening. "...and Lady Steadmore will very likely send you a card of invitation to the ball she is giving next week in honor of her niece. If she approves of you, every door in society will be opened to you. She has a great deal of influence."

Tilly's temper flared. "I'm sure you'll think me quite provincial, Lara, if I don't go out of my way to court her influence. The Templetons have lived in Hollowdean for nine hundred years and are known and respected. Consequently I'm unused to being weighed and judged as if I were a prize pig entered in competition at a county fair."

"Oh, dear!" Lara laughed. "I've given you quite an erroneous impression. I think you'll take to Lady Steadmore quite easily. At first meeting she seems a most formidable dowager—a dragon, in fact—but I know that her prickly exterior hides a kindly heart."

Tilly felt a bit prickly herself. She bit her tongue, not wanting to distress her hostess.

"Her niece," Lara continued, "is Miss Eggleston. She has come out from London in hopes of meeting some eligible gentleman. She seems pleasant, if perhaps a bit affected."

Tilly groaned inwardly. So far she could look forward to meeting an overbearing tyrant and a simpering bore. Life in Jamaica was not as different from life in Yorkshire as she had imagined. She might as well have remained at Oak Manor, listening to Durward and Lady Helena rant on about her ingratitude!

Lara clasped her hand. "I am looking forward to introducing you to Tiger Flynn. I know you will like each other immediately."

Tilly wasn't so sure. "Tiger? Surely that isn't really his name."

"No, but I'm one of the few people who uses it. His given name is Lucas. He is, I may have mentioned, a particular friend of mine."

Tiger Flynn. A particular friend of mine. Was this man the cause of the change in Lara? There was a hollow feeling in the pit of Tilly's stomach as she envisioned a sleek carnivore stalking women through the social jungle. Someone dangerous and ruthless, but with devilish charm. Someone like that man aboard the frigate—but much more polished, of course.

"Tell me, how did he obtain his unusual name?"

"He refuses to say, but my brother told me Lucas killed a man-eating tiger when he was in India. With his bare hands."

Lara shivered but Tilly hid her skepticism. She had seen a tiger once on display in the cage of a traveling fair. Despite the creature's advanced age and scruffy coat, she'd seen the rippling strength beneath that striped fur, the huge fangs in that enormous mouth, and the ferocity in those wild eyes that had made a deep impression upon her. She'd felt pity for it, and fear. No man alive could throttle such a great-clawed, great-toothed beast with his bare hands! Furthermore, any man who would let such a story be spread about, unrefuted, must be full of conceit.

Unless, of course, he was the one who had made up the story in the first place. Tilly had already made up her mind to dislike Tiger Flynn.

The carriage wound higher into the green hills, past large
homes in the Spanish or English style, framed by majestic
palms. High walls surrounded many, but through their
gates, glimpses of colorful tiled roofs and shady colon-
nades were visible. Fantastic blooms splashed against the
walls and gates and filled the sides of the road with their
glory: pink and rose and salmon, white and yellow and
glowing gold, nestled among glossy dark green leaves. Despite the ordeal of the dinner party, Tilly was glad she'd
come.

Lara echoed her thoughts. "Tilly, I am so glad you are
here." The thin, nervous fingers clutched at hers. "You
cannot possibly know how much it means to me to have a
friend..."

She trailed off anxiously, as if afraid of how much she'd
revealed in that last cryptic sentence. Tilly was filled with
uneasiness. It was impossible to follow up such an intriguing lead in an open carriage with the groom able to over-
hear their every word. She gave Lara's hand a comforting
squeeze and fixed her interest on the passing scenery.

A line of Jamaican women in colorful clothing walked
along the edge of the road with baskets on their heads, a
little girl of three or four holding on to the skirts of the last
one. Lara didn't even notice them, and the carriage passed
by without any sign at all from the women. But the child
turned her head and stared after them until she realized Tilly
was smiling at her. The small, curious face went blank and
the girl turned away.

Tilly felt as if a door had been shut in her face. The British government might own the island but it didn't own its
people. It was only thirty years since slavery had been abolished on Jamaica, Tilly soberly reminded herself. The lush
scenery hid a dark and bloody history, one that would take
generations to wash away. She had thought the island was
nothing short of paradise. Now she remembered that even
Eden had had its snakes. Here the serpent had been—perhaps still was—the injustice of man against his brothers.
Cain and Abel surrounded by the warm, tropical sun.

She shook off her thoughts as the road ended at a pair of open iron gates. "Welcome," Lara said, "to Coeur d'Émeraude."

The carriage rolled up a long avenue lined with palms and rhododendrons. It was like driving through a cool, green tunnel. Tilly realized how the plantation had gotten its name: Heart of Emerald, indeed! The house was of stone and whitewashed stucco, with tall arched windows on all three floors. The rose-colored tiles of the roof framed a square, shuttered tower.

Her friend followed her line of vision. "That is the Master's Walk. You can see all the way up to the Blue Mountains, or out to Gallows Point beyond the harbor."

"So the master could watch for his ships in the harbor?"

"Yes." Lara lowered her voice out of consideration for the driver. "And, before slavery was abolished, to watch for signs of riots or insurrection."

Tilly felt a cool breeze upon the back of her neck. Even this beautiful plantation lived in the somber shadow of past cruelty. Or perhaps it was just that the sunlight did not penetrate this section of the drive. By the time they emerged again into sunshine they were at the front entrance, and the sensation had passed.

After refreshments and a brief tour, Lara escorted Tilly to the bedchamber that would be hers. As they came up the stairs a footman was bearing away one of her trunks, which the maids had unpacked. The room was large, high-ceilinged and airy, a combination of European opulence and tropical inspiration. At present it was difficult to tell much else. The chamber was awash in numerous bandboxes, portmanteaux and two upright wardrobe trunks. A smaller, humpbacked one was partially emptied.

In the center of it all, a woman of indistinguishable age stood directing the chambermaid. She was tall, impossibly thin and impeccably British—and she was in a very sour mood.

"This is Agnes, my dresser," Lara said, ignoring the woman's frigid manner. "She has been with me since my marriage. The maid assigned to you has injured her ankle, so we will have to share Agnes for awhile.''

"I can manage quite well without a maid." Tilly chuckled. She had managed without one all her life.

Lara gave Tilly's arm a tweak. "I won't hear of it! Agnes will manage for us both. I am sure it will prove quite satisfactory."

From the way she said it, Tilly could tell that Agnes had already protested the arrangement. The servant and Tilly sized one another up as Lara left them. Agnes pursed her thin lips and fired the first shot. "If Miss had only lingered over her afternoon tea, I should have had all of Miss's belongings disposed of properly."

Tilly smiled. "I am quite sure of that. If you would find me a needle and thread, I would like to repair my cuff. I seem to have torn the trimming."

Agnes was scandalized. "After Miss has removed her traveling garment, I will be happy to repair the damage—as is my duty."

Properly chastised, Tilly agreed to leave the task to the maid. Agnes sniffed and removed a handsome bed jacket and matching night robe from the wardrobe trunk. She mellowed somewhat when her fingers touched an enchanting bed jacket of blue silk, adorned with ribbons of rose-colored satin and insets of gossamer lace. She ran her bony hand over it lightly and reverently.

"Oh, my! What lovely embroidery!" she breathed, without realizing she had spoken aloud. "And the seam stitches—so tiny."

"Thank you," Tilly said in a gratified tone. "It is my own handiwork."

Agnes was scandalized. It was one thing to set a few dainty stitches in an embroidery frame, Agnes's face plainly said, and quite another to actually sew one's own garments like a common tailor. Tilly realized her social status had just plummeted.

Frostily, Agnes indicated the humpbacked trunk. "The chambermaid has placed your volumes on the bookshelves, as you see, but there is not room enough for them all. If

Miss would care to sort through them, I will have a foot-man carry the rest down to the Yellow Sitting Room.''

Tilly glanced in the open trunk. There was only a layer or two left, and several of the books were intended as gifts for her host and hostess. "Leave them for now. I shall see to them myself.''

"Miss may, of course, do as Miss likes with her own pos-sessions. However it would be most peculiar. I would be re-miss if I did not put them away for Miss. At once.''

So, Tilly thought grimly, *I am going to be Missed to death, unless I settle the matter here and now.* There was really no reason for Agnes to make such an adamant point of the matter, but Tilly was no fool. She recognized it as an opening gambit, her response to which would forever set the course for her future relationship with Agnes. A strong mistress was respected; one too soft would be thought weak.

It went against the grain but she had to do it. "Thank you, Agnes, that will do.''

The affronted dresser stared at her a moment, then ac-quiesced. She, Agnes Chuffey, who had once been lady's maid to the Dowager Countess of Denville herself, was not to be shoved off lightly to care for the needs of a mere Miss Templeton. And before many days went by, she would make her feelings known!

There was a sudden flash of golden-orange as a fur ball with four agile feet and a great sweeping tail streaked across the floor. With a leap and a pounce a big marmalade cat settled itself in the middle of the bed and began licking one graceful paw.

Agnes dropped the shawl she was holding and flapped her hands at the animal. "Shoo, you nasty creature! Shoo!''

The cat gave her a green, enigmatic stare, but as the maid advanced the offended feline bristled and arched its back. The loud hiss it gave sent Agnes back three feet in one leap. Tilly intervened.

"Let it stay. I am fond of cats.''

As if knowing it had found a champion, the cat fixed her with its wide eyes and squeezed them shut in delight. He rose and stretched before making himself at home in a patch of sunlight, purring contentedly.

As Tilly's remaining garments were unfolded and shaken out, Tilly inspected the bed. Clouds of gauzy mosquito netting hung from the arms of a gilt cherub suspended above it, and painted medallions decorated the head and foot. She reflected with a good deal of amusement that she would be lost at night in all its magnificence. The rest of the room tickled her fancy, too. An overhead fan moved lazily, its basketwork blades turned by the light breeze. On the opposite wall a sofa of formal French design stood beside a series of open shutters that formed the fourth wall and framed a view of the harbor. Tilly wondered if life on the island always produced such strange and interesting blends.

Like that man aboard the frigate. Yes, he must definitely be one of those black sheep, a social exile who roamed the far corners of the empire in humiliation and defeat. But his bold smile and jaunty bearing had looked neither humiliated nor defeated. In fact, if she remembered correctly, he had seemed to enjoy the episode immensely.

She noticed then that there were two sets of shutters, one inside the room and the second outside the house. "For the hurricane season," Agnes said smugly. "And now, if Miss would care to put on a wrapper for your nap, I will deliver your outfit to the laundress."

"A nap?" Tilly was startled. "I'm not the least bit tired, I assure you."

Agnes smiled with malicious satisfaction. "In the islands it is the custom for *ladies*—" she emphasized the word "—to have a little lie down in the heat of the day. I'll be back to dress you for dinner."

Regardless of the custom, Tilly was too energized to nap. She wrote a brief note to Durward, advising him of her safe arrival, and a longer, more chatty missive to Mrs. Pimm. When she'd finished the sky was filled with gold and orange light, turning the harbor to a lake of liquid fire. The elevation of the house gave her a marvelous view. Dusk stole in from the east, and soon there was nothing left on the far horizon but a thin bar of luminous green light. It was gone in a flash.

Night fell abruptly, and the room behind her was dark until Agnes entered and lit the candles. Tilly stood at her window until she noticed a movement below. Someone was coming along the garden walk in the velvet dusk. She snapped out of her reverie. It wouldn't do to be standing here in her thin silk wrapper, with the light shining behind it. She stepped inside and pulled the shutters closed, and the marmalade cat slipped out to the veranda just in time to make his escape.

An hour later she left her room with a rustle of silk and crinolines for her first real party. Tilly felt suddenly nervous. The neckline of her rose-petal gown was much lower than any she had ever worn before, displaying her rounded white shoulders and a good deal more of her bosom than she felt was necessary. However, Madame Fontaine had insisted it was both proper and in the highest style of fashion, and when Tilly had visited the opera in London she had seen immediately that the modiste had been correct.

Agnes might resent her, but she hadn't stinted on her services. Tilly's hair was pinned high atop her head, with a series of ringlets cascading down the back, and she wore her mother's necklet of garnets and pearls and graceful teardrop earrings to give her courage.

Tilly descended the long staircase with growing anticipation. She felt like a small green bud about to blossom without knowing if she was to be a colorful, exotic flower or a plain brown weed. Time would soon tell her, for as she reached the upper landing she heard the sound of carriage wheels upon the drive.

Voices filtered up from the long drawing room, and Tilly hurried down. The room, ablaze with warm candlelight, reflected Lara's infallible taste. Treasures of Europe, the Orient and the tropics were displayed against walls of blue silk. The mantelpiece held huge seashells carved with intricate cameo scenes and rare Chinese porcelains flanked by antique English silver. Against the elegant background

Lara, dressed in ivory satin and an abundance of diamonds, was a beautiful jewel in a perfect setting.

As Tilly entered, an imposing matron in heavy bronze
satin and a feathered turban lifted her lorgnette and scrutinized her intently. "A nice little filly. Good carriage, excellent countenance. Breeding in every line of her. If her
manners are as good as her appearance, she'll do you credit,
Lara."

Tilly, who had entered girded for battle, couldn't keep the
laughter from her eyes as they were introduced. The woman's engaging frankness took the sting from being examined like a horse on the auction block. In fact, Tilly was sure
Lady Steadmore must be very fond of horses—she would
have to be, since she resembled one so strongly herself.

She addressed the dowager with a warm smile. "Thank
you, ma'am. And let me assure you that I've never been
known to throw out a spavin, or get winded trotting up a
hill."

"Ha! A sense of humor, and intelligent, too." The matron nodded, and the plumes waved wildly. "You'll do very
well, Miss Templeton. I cannot abide an insipid girl," she
added with a needle-eyed glance at her niece.

The latter was a rather proud girl with prominent blue
eyes and yellow hair. Her gown was frilled and ruffled and
tucked in a hundred places, and the unflattering shade of
yellow-green reminded Tilly of her first two days aboard the
Montego Bay, before she had gotten her sea legs. Five minutes of Miss Eggleston's smug conversation, peppered with
constant reference to members of the British aristocracy, her
personal friends and endless discussions of who was related
to whom, had Tilly groaning inwardly with boredom. If the
girl had any thoughts in her head except for fashion, society and the latest gossip, they were well hidden.

While Miss Eggleston rattled on Tilly had an opportunity to study her hostess unobserved. Lara's too-thin face
was animated; but underneath there was incredible strain,
as if a fine wire was drawn out almost to the snapping point.
She clasped and unclasped her hands, and her eyes darted
to the doorway at the slightest sound.

Then Jonas Whitby came in by the glass doors that opened to the back terrace. He was tall and stocky, with the crisp, dark hair that Tilly remembered, but now there were threads of silver woven through it. Lara followed her gaze and gave a little start.

"Why Jonas, I didn't know you'd gone outside."

"You'll be amazed," Jonas announced, "to see the suspicious character I've found prowling about our gardens." He was laughing, and he was not alone. A large potted palm hid his companion from Tilly's view.

"Lucas, you scoundrel, what have you been up to now?" Lady Steadmore said severely, but her face was wreathed in smiles.

"I am planning to abscond with the silver plate," a deep baritone replied, "and was seeking out the best route of escape."

A ripple of laughter followed this sally. Tilly could not see the speaker clearly through the spiky fronds, but he was well above her height and seemed to wear his beautifully molded evening clothes with a decided air of fashion. As he moved forward Tilly heard one of the ladies sigh. She turned, but couldn't tell who had made the telltale little sound. Lady Steadmore's plumes dipped and quivered as she extended her hand to the newcomer.

"Well, Lucas?" she said as the newcomer bowed over her hand. "What were you doing skulking about the gardens?"

His reply was soft and meant for her ears only. "Why, looking for a good woman, as you advised. I'd heard there were to be one or two beautiful English roses on display tonight at Lara's dinner party."

Unfortunately Tilly had very acute hearing. She turned her head involuntarily—and found him looking straight into her eyes. His bronzed features were oddly familiar beneath his sun-streaked brown hair. His eyes locked with hers. They were the most unusual eyes she had ever seen. His irises were a clear dark green in the center, rimmed by rays of gold. Like emeralds surrounded by facets of clear topaz. Cats' eyes.

Tigers' eyes.

A shiver played along her spine. Beneath the elegant evening clothes, his lean muscles rippled, and behind his smile lurked the heart of a predator. But unlike the captive beast she had seen long ago, this one roamed unrestrained. The image was frightening.

Before she could recover, his smile widened to a startling slash of white against his deeply tanned face. Recognition hit her like a cold wave of seawater and sent color into her cheeks. He looked very different in his expensively tailored clothes, but there was no mistaking the easy elegance of his movements or that brilliant, mocking smile. She had seen it only briefly, but it was indelibly imprinted on her memory.

Lara's "particular friend," Tiger Flynn, was the very same man who had bowed to her from the deck of the frigate. She wished she hadn't recognized him and prayed he wouldn't recognize her.

The prayer went unanswered. The corners of his mouth quirked upward with ironic amusement, and one eyelid closed and lifted in a quick wink.

Tilly blinked. What utter gall!

Flynn sent her a subtle nod that managed to signify both acknowledgment and amusement before transferring his attentions to his hostess. Tilly noticed the intensity in Flynn's eyes and registered the quick, eager look Lara gave Flynn. Her vulnerability was nakedly exposed as he clasped her hand reassuringly in his. Tilly wanted to look away, but could not. Flynn's touch seemed to exert a magical force on Lara. The strain in her rigid shoulders drained away, and her pale cheeks took on a healthier glow.

Tilly glanced away and found Jonas watching his wife and Flynn through narrowed eyes. Of all the others in the room, only he seemed to be aware of something amiss. His jaw tightened. Although a cordial smile remained on his lips, it didn't quite reach his eyes. After a pause he turned to speak with another guest, but his eyes sought out a mirror reflecting the little tableau that included his wife and Tiger Flynn.

Suddenly Tilly almost wished she hadn't come to Jamaica. She had stepped into what she had thought was a tropical garden, only to discover she had stumbled into a swamp.

There was sure to be quicksand ahead.

Chapter Three

Lady Steadmore nodded indulgently. "A charming rapscallion!" She leaned toward Tilly and lowered her voice. "Anyone listening to gossip will hear a good deal of speculation about Lucas Flynn, but a wise woman will disregard it. And you, my dear, appear to be a young woman of much sense."

"Mr. Flynn," Tilly answered acerbically, "seems to be a prime favorite—but since I've had no experience with charming rapscallions I haven't any opinions one way or the other."

Lady Steadmore leaned even closer and rapped Tilly's knuckles gently with the end of her fan. "No hoity-toity airs with me, if you please. I have experience enough for both of us, Miss Templeton. And I have always said that a reformed rake makes the best husband."

The dowager turned to Lara, leaving Tilly to digest her comment. Tilly was no prude. She knew that polite flirtations were the rule rather than the exception; but she firmly believed that marriage vows should not be contravened by a third party. Friendships were allowed between men and women, but only on the most platonic level. The burning looks Lara fixed on Tiger Flynn, the way her whole attention was focused on his face, told Tilly that Lara's involvement went deeper than casual friendship.

As she watched them, his actions reinforced her opinion. Flynn's gaze was so personal that he seemed to speak to Lara in a silent code. Her brown eyes widened briefly, and he gave an infinitesimal nod, one that only someone as observant as Tilly could have seen. She wished she had not.

She wanted the floor to open up and swallow Flynn whole, before anyone else became aware of what was so apparent to her.

Lara placed a hand on hers, and Tilly realized with a start that she was being formally introduced to Flynn. "... and this, Lucas, is Miss Templeton, my bosom friend from school days."

He bowed over Tilly's hand, a conspiratorial gleam in his eye. "Ah, yes. Miss Templeton. But we've already met, have we not?"

She almost snatched her hand away. How dare he remind her! The warm imprint of his long fingers burned against her palm. "You are mistaken, Mr. Flynn."

His thick, dark lashes swept lazily over those strange green eyes and up again in a long, significant look. "Forgive my error, Miss Templeton. Perhaps it's because I have heard our hostess speak so often of her very dear Tilly that I have such a feeling of familiarity."

Your familiarity, she thought irately, *is part and parcel of your brass-plated gall!* Outwardly she remained calm and poised. Only her eyes gave her away.

Lucas Flynn's well-chiseled mouth curved up at the corners and Tilly felt her face redden. It was as if he knew what was going through her mind and was amused by it. He regarded her with a glint of laughter, as if to ask if she was as pleased with him as he was with her.

What an impossibly arrogant man! Tilly pointedly ignored him and asked a question of Miss Eggleston. The girl's simper had spread into a kind of leer. "I see, Miss Templeton, that you're in danger of falling under the sway of Mr. Flynn's fatal charm. Let me warn you, he is a known breaker of hearts."

"I am not such an easy victim," Tilly replied, with more force than she had intended. "And, as I told Lady Steadmore, I have never been partial to rakes."

Although Flynn had given his attention to the dowager, he grinned in appreciation, and she knew her shot had gone home. The other guests arrived almost immediately, and another round of introductions followed. George Keating came in behind Captain Giddings, who had a lovely redhead on his arm. She wore a gown with the unmistakable stamp of Paris on it, and a flashing diamond choker. Her eyes had the same hard glitter.

"Mrs. Thorne," Lara said with just a hint of restraint, "Let me present my dear friend, Miss Templeton."

Tilly offered her hand, and it was taken in a limp embrace. Mrs. Thorne cast a swift glance at her, decided she was no threat and tendered a smile as brief as it was insincere. Never before had Tilly been treated with such casual disdain. Not even Helena Blandford would have dared. An awkward silence ensued, but as her temper simmered, rescue came from an unexpected quarter.

Lucas Flynn pulled out his gold pocket watch. "I hope we dine soon, Lara, for as you see Mrs. Thorne is so faint with hunger she can hardly speak. I fear she might fade away at any moment."

His outrageous breach of etiquette made Tilly gasp and Mrs. Thorne glower coldly. The others pretended not to notice, but it was impossible not to hear Lady Steadmore's forthright bark of laughter and Miss Eggleston's nervous giggle. Flynn bowed to Mrs. Thorne, taking her hand in his. Instantly the ice goddess thawed.

"You're abominable, Lucas," she complained, smiling at him. "I really don't know why we tolerate your monstrous behavior."

Lucas Flynn, Tilly realized, was the kind of man that no one—no woman, in particular—could ignore. His presence dominated the room, making him the center of all eyes. It was that strange magnetism that he had in abundance that drew people to him. Some, like herself, against their will.

The other guests arrived in a blur of names and colored satin, until Tilly was sure she would never remember them all. Lara rang a silver bell and the butler, a dignified black man with snowy hair, entered to announce dinner. The party went into the small dining room. This chamber opened to a lovely garden, where white paper lanterns hung from the trees. The effect was charming.

Tilly hoped she wouldn't be seated next to Lucas Flynn; yet when she found her place card she was disappointed to discover herself at Jonas Whitby's right hand, across from Lady Steadmore and flanked by Mr. Keating. To her chagrin she found her gaze moving down the table to see where her nemesis was placed.

Flynn was on the opposite side of the table, to the left of his hostess, with Captain Giddings across from him. He caught Tilly's eye, winked so quickly she was hardly sure she really saw it, and addressed a comment to Lara. Tilly glanced anxiously around. She didn't want the other guests to think she shared secrets with a rogue like Tiger Flynn.

No one seemed to have noticed and she heaved a sigh of relief. Then she saw the table reflected in the long mirror above the carved mahogany sideboard. Mrs. Thorne was staring at her from the looking glass, such venom in her face that Tilly almost dropped her goblet. Lucas Flynn, she thought wrathfully, was a very busy man.

Jonas offered a toast in honor of Tilly's arrival and Lara, ever the excellent hostess, made an announcement: "We shall not be formal tonight. Conversation back and forth across the table is not only permitted, but expected."

Tilly relaxed. Having to divide her time between George Keating's fulsome compliments and Jonas Whitby's forced bonhomie would have been a strain. Despite Lara's attempts at informality, the dinner talk was less than scintillating. It lay, as Captain Giddings might have phrased it, dead in the water. Jonas became so absorbed in his own thoughts, and his junior partner so particular in his attentions to Tilly, that she found it embarrassing. She wished the dinner would end.

Not so Tiger Flynn. His deep voice, with its faint lilt of Ireland, caught her attention time after time. Although he kept up a lively flow of talk with Lara and Mrs. Thorne, he watched the byplay between Tilly and Keating with sparks of laughter in his green eyes. Every now and then he made a remark intended to get a rise out of her, and she sent him a glance to let him know she was not amused. It didn't seem to work. The man was impervious to snubs.

By the time the ladies retired to the drawing room Tilly felt a headache coming on. The effects of her weeks at sea, meeting so many new people at once, and the tropical heat made it worse. Dinner parties, if they all followed tonight's pattern, were not nearly as enjoyable as she had expected.

Lara turned back the lid of the pianoforte. "I thought we might entertain the gentlemen with some music. Mrs. Thorne, I know, sings beautifully—and perhaps Miss Eggleston will play for us, as well."

There were murmurs of agreement and Lara brought out a stack of sheet music. Mrs. Thorne and Miss Eggleston went through it, looking for a selection they both liked, while the other women drifted into small conversational groups. The men were still in the dining room with their cigars and brandy. This was Tilly's chance. No one would notice her brief absence.

She slipped out the open doors to the wide terrace for a breath of fresh air. A cool breeze brushed past her and she turned her face into it. There was a salt tang and the call of adventure on the wind. She had always felt it, always been tempted by its siren call. For years she had stifled that longing, but the past weeks had changed her. She was lured deeper into the garden. The moon was still low, barely visible over the garden wall, and just ahead was the entrance to a shrubbery, flanked by wrought-iron settees. She would just peek into it and . . .

"Running away, Miss Templeton?"

"Oh! You startled me!"

Lucas Flynn stood a few feet away, the red tip of a cigarillo glowing in his hand. He discarded it in a convenient flowerpot and ambled closer, smiling. "You won't escape, you know. They'll send out search parties and drag you back to hear more about tariffs and gowns, and the diseases affecting the tobacco crops."

A chuckle escaped her. "Did my boredom show so badly?"

"Not at all. You are much too well brought up." He held out his hand to her. "I, however, am not. Will you take a turn with me in the shrubbery, Miss Templeton?"

"Thank you," she said after a brief hesitation, wondering why his words reminded her forcibly of those of the proverbial spider to the proverbial fly.

They strolled arm in arm away from the house along a brick path that wound through the silver-black garden. The scent of flowering jasmine came on the breeze like a sweet, séductive perfume. Candlelight from the drawing room filtered through the leaves, and Tilly was so caught up in the shadowed beauty of her surroundings that she started when her companion spoke.

"Tell me, Miss Templeton," he said amiably. "How does the hunt go?"

"The hunt?"

Flynn gave her a quizzical look. "In my experience—which is considerable—a beautiful young heiress travels across the ocean unescorted for only one reason. To catch a suitable husband. One who is willing to accept her on face value, without inquiring too closely into her past."

"How dare you!"

Enraged, Tilly yanked her arm from his. She was too angry to separate whether the emotion sprang from the unjust implication concerning her past or the fact that she did indeed hope to find a husband. He made it sound cold and mercenary; but it wasn't just any willing husband she had in mind, but that one special man, who could win both her heart and her respect.

Flynn gave her a quizzical look. "What, did I cut too near the bone?"

She drew herself up with dignity. "You are insufferable, sir! My past is entirely respectable and unblemished. And I am *not* an heiress, and I am *not* hunting a husband, as you so rudely put it!"

"No? Well, you *are* beautiful." He began walking again, as if he had said nothing unusual. "I accept your word that you're not an heiress with a past, but it seems perfectly natural to me that an unmarried woman might contemplate any bachelor she meets as a possible mate.''

Tilly was so furious she could only sputter. After counting to three she tried to speak calmly, but the quaver in her voice gave her away. ''I assure you, Mr. Flynn, that I am not the designing kind of female who sees every eligible man as a potential partner.''

''Oh? Then what kind of designing female *are* you?''

He was only teasing her, yet, to her surprise, the words came pouring out. ''One who finds aristocratic lineage and the latest fashions great bores as the chief topic of conversation. One who craves adventure and is no more suited to knitting quietly by the hearthside than . . . than you!''

''Ah, an adventuress. I was right.''

His unflappable composure stung her. ''Why is a man who seeks adventure thought to be a fine, sporting fellow, while a woman with the same inclinations is branded an adventuress?''

He didn't interrupt. ''You cannot know,'' she said vehemently, ''what it is like to be denied the opportunity to put your brain to practical use, except in the domestic sphere. To feel the universe shrinking around you day by day, until the most urgent concern is to decide whether to have a bit of veal or a lamb cutlet for dinner. To realize there is a colorful, exciting world all around—one you can only view through panes of glass.''

Flynn was silent and she turned away, her voice low with suppressed yearning. ''You wouldn't understand. You're a man.''

He moved to face her and lifted her chin with his index finger. ''I think I do, Miss Templeton. And I apologize for doing you a great injustice.''

Again he had disarmed her. Tilly felt awkward and vulnerable. ''I wish you would not be kind, Mr. Flynn. I seem to deal with you much better when I'm angry.''

She saw that they had gone deeper into the garden. A fountain splashed nearby but the hedge of pale flowers cut off the moonlight ahead. Flynn took her arm and tucked it in his.

"The path is dark. I wouldn't like you to stumble."

"Thank you. You're most considerate."

"What, no missish airs or protests that the others wouldn't approve of us strolling out of sight? You astonish me."

Tilly chuckled ironically. "I am sure Lady Steadmore would approve of anything you did, short of an ax murder! You are a prime favorite with her."

"But you neither like nor approve of me, Miss Templeton. Why?"

"It's not my obligation to either approve or disapprove of you."

"Little prude! You believe the very worst of me, don't you?"

She was unprepared for such a frank verbal assault. "Why—why, whatever do you mean?"

He shook his head. "I'm quite disappointed. After such a promising start I didn't think you'd retreat like a coward."

Tilly glowered. "I am not a coward!"

Flynn grinned reluctantly. "No. I suppose not. No coward would come out into the shrubbery with a man of my reputation."

He advanced. Tilly backed up slowly, as if she was in the company of a madman. "I think I should return to the others."

"Nonsense. You said—quite correctly—that it's intolerably warm inside, with all those candles. Or do you think I mean to have my way with you?"

"Oh!"

Her hand swung out in a wide arc but Flynn caught it effortlessly. "You're not in any danger. I've never used force where charm will do."

He captured her other hand. "You really should get to know me better, Miss Templeton. We are more alike than you suspect. Come, let us cry friends!"

Tilly felt her breathing quicken at the change in his demeanor, from humor to menace to a magnetic intensity that

mesmerized her. She did not know what she would do if he
came one step closer.

There was no opportunity to find out. Suddenly he spun
around with the speed and agility of his namesake. A servant materialized on the path behind them. Tilly was caught
by surprise. She had not heard a sound.

Flynn relaxed. "Yes. What the devil do you want?"

Before the man could answer, an angry female voice cut
through the night. *"Flynn? Tiger Flynn, where are you?"*

The rest of her words were drowned out immediately by
an infant's enraged squall.

The servant shifted from one foot to the other uneasily.
"There is an . . . er . . . a young female person with . . . with a
baby. She is demanding to see you, Mr. Flynn."

Then, louder than before, the female voice called out in
shrill accents. *"Tiger! Tiger? I know you are out there!"*

A peculiar look came over Flynn's face. Past his stony
profile, Tilly could see the open doors of the dining and
drawing rooms. Although the Whitbys and their guests
looked to be deep in conversation, they had the strained,
intense mannerisms of people who are pretending—very
hard—not to notice some appalling faux pas.

The infant's wail grew louder, a banshee cry splitting the
night. Tilly glimpsed someone moving along a parallel path.
A handsome dark-skinned woman with high cheekbones
and night-black eyes. The light from the terrace windows
brought out the colorful pattern of her long skirt and ov-
erblouse. The woman called out from near at hand, *"Tiger?
Where are you? I need you!"*

Flynn made a sound of exasperation and turned to the
servant. "Damn it to hell, Leonie knows better than to come
for me here! Tell her I'm on my way."

The servant vanished discreetly and Flynn turned to Tilly.
Shock and disgust were etched in her every feature. In the
moonlight, twin green devils danced in his eyes.

"Don't look so horrified, Miss Templeton," he said with
a slight, mocking smile. "I am not a philanderer."

She was stunned at the way he read her mind. He chuckled and took her hand, bringing it slowly to his lips. They

brushed her skin with warmth. He lifted his head and met her gaze squarely. "Neither, you little termagant, am I an adulterer."

She gasped audibly and he laughed. "Some free advice, Miss Templeton. Learn to hide your thoughts a little better. Every emotion shows on your face as clearly as though it were written there."

He took her chin in his hand, and before she could protest dropped a quick, warm kiss on her lips. His mouth was hard and not particularly gentle. It robbed her of her very breath. Before Tilly could react he spun away on his heel. There was a ripple of foliage and he was gone, like a tiger in the night.

Slipping into the drawing room unnoticed didn't present Tilly with a problem: the other women, clustered here and there in the room, spoke with unusual brightness and volume, covering the sounds of her return. Her absence seemed to have gone unnoticed. She stepped inside and joined the nearest group.

A thin matron of forty, whose name Tilly had forgotten, was dispensing bile with artificial sweetness. "His mistress, most likely. After all, a man of Tiger Flynn's reputation would have at least one *chérie amie*, and quite possibly more than one."

"It is the climate," Miss Eggleston said knowingly. "I have read that the English climate toughens one, both physically and morally, while the warmth and languor of the islands induces a regrettable moral laxness."

Her voice died away as Tilly fixed her with a pointed glance. "Is this something you have been told," she inquired dulcetly, "or is this knowledge you have acquired of your own experience?"

Miss Eggleston's pasty complexion went white with anger, then a blotchy red. "I . . . of course . . . most definitely not!" she stammered. "It is a topic I have discussed extensively with Mr. Keating."

The matrons turned to Lady Steadmore's niece with startled disapproval. "Surely an indelicate subject for conversation between a man and an unmarried lady," one whispered rather loudly.

Another raised her lorgnette and inspected the embarrassed girl like a scientist examining a rather unpleasant specimen. "I neither understand nor condone the odd manners of young ladies in today's society," she remarked in resonant tones. "Such forwardness would never have been tolerated in *our* day. And to discuss it in our presence!"

Miss Eggleston's mortification was complete. The conversation now centered around the sad want of conduct in young ladies, the decline of modern manners and the deteriorating condition of the world in general. The look Lady Steadmore's niece gave her tormentor would have withered flowers on the vine, but Tilly was immune. Satisfied with her work, she moved on to the next group. After an uncertain pause, Miss Eggleston followed.

"Of course," the dowager was saying loudly to Mrs. Thorne, "the Fayne Rubies are in a class by themselves. But if only you could have seen the sapphires that my dear friend, the Countess Povisky, wore when she visited us from Warsaw! As big as hens' eggs, and the same deep blue as her eyes. An accredited Beauty. I am sure I must have mentioned her before."

"Many times," her niece said, and was rewarded with a piercing look.

Miss Eggleston, realizing her gaffe, blushed deeply. "I believe it is going to rain," she added desperately, but no one took up on her lead.

Tilly realized that Lady Steadmore was fighting a losing battle, and did her valiant best to keep the conversation afloat. It was no use. Mrs. Thorne sat rigidly on the edge of her gilt chair, a look of cold fury in her eyes. Lara's abstraction had returned in full measure. Although she replied and smiled appropriately, her hands gave her away. The delicate fingers were never still, twisting a bit of lace or knotting one of the ribbons that adorned the skirt of her exquisite gown.

While the others inwardly prayed for the evening to end, Tilly dreaded it. Earlier she had hoped Lara would unburden herself of whatever was troubling her. Now she was in no mood to hear Lara pour out her confidences. Not if they concerned Lucas Flynn.

The minutes passed like hours. Around the drawing room women clustered in small groups, looking shocked or interested or frankly titillated, and their prim faces, coupled with shrewd nods and glances at the garden door, proved that Tiger Flynn was still their main topic of conversation. From time to time scraps of it drifted into the range of Tilly's acute hearing.

"...positively scandalous..."

"...like you, I have heard the rumors, but he always has acted more gentlemanly to me..."

"...merely sowing his oats... They all have mistresses, you know..."

"...that is true, and it would not do to cut him, for he is such an amusing creature..."

Tilly was surprised by the censorious comments. It was not as if Lucas Flynn had been found in a compromising circumstance. The woman with the squalling baby wasn't necessarily his mistress, as the others seemed to think. She might be a servant or a friend. Not that there seemed to be any true socialization between the island's indigenous inhabitants and the British colonists. In her few hours ashore she had seen that the classes were rigidly defined by rank, position and the color of one's skin. That ruled out any open relationships.

Somehow Tilly had imagined society would be a bit more flexible here than in England. After all, this was Jamaica, where the dreaded pirate Henry Morgan retired and rose to the rank of lieutenant governor; where the wicked city of old Port Royal had sunk beneath the waves like something out of a folk tale; where even the fishermen's daily catch consisted of fish in unbelievable colors of bright red, iridescent purple and canary yellow. But from the reaction of the majority present, it was quite plainly the opposite.

While the gossipers stood apart in animated groups, Tilly found the quartet of ladies that included her hostess to be quite subdued. Mrs. Thorne sulked, Miss Eggleston simpered and Lara was locked away in some cold, private hell. Tilly was torn between wondering about her little scene in the garden with Lucas Flynn and trying to keep the floundering conversation afloat.

Between them, she and Lady Steadmore kept up a flow of small talk to gloss over the awkwardness until the men joined the ladies in the drawing room. They had not lingered long over their cigars and brandy. Jonas came over to his wife.

"Miss Templeton has had a tiring day. Perhaps you would like to ring for the tea tray a bit earlier than usual, my dear."

An audible sigh of relief ran through the guests, and Lara sent her husband a look of heartfelt gratitude. Lara rang the bell for tea immediately, and the butler and maid brought in the carts. The party had really ended with Lucas Flynn's abrupt departure, and there was no sense in drawing it out.

Lara poured and Tilly assisted with handing out the cups. As George Keating came up for his, he smiled at them. "I was hoping to see your brother tonight, Mrs. Whitby. I trust he is well?"

Tilly turned to Lara just in time to see her face go white. The teacup rattled in Lara's hand, spilling hot liquid into the saucer. Only Tilly's quick action prevented an accident.

"Oh! So clumsy of me," Lara exclaimed breathlessly, looking around with wide, blank eyes. "Christopher has been...detained. On business. He will be away several more weeks."

Tilly handed Mr. Keating another cup and he had no choice but to retire. "Thank you," Lara whispered. "I don't know what came over me. A...a moment of dizziness."

"You are merely tired." But Tilly knew it was something more than tiredness. Something was very wrong.

The next half hour was social agony. Those not embarrassed by the evening's prime event were anxious to depart for a comfortable session of gossip and character assassination. Whether they liked him or not, Tilly speculated that none of the guests could avoid talking about Lucas Flynn.

Lady Steadmore, as ranking guest, brought the evening to a close. "We shall not keep you from your beds much longer, Lara. I am sure you will wish for a cozy tête-à-tête with Miss Templeton before retiring."

Within minutes the carriages had been summoned. The guests departed well before midnight, with the speed and dispatch of people fleeing a plague. Mr. Keating was the last to leave. As his carriage rolled away, Jonas pulled a cigar from his inner pocket.

"I'm going to have a smoke before coming up. Good night, Lara. Good night, Miss Templeton. I hope you've had a pleasant evening."

Tilly gave him her best smile. "It was certainly very stimulating," she said with complete honesty.

Leaving Jonas alone on the portico, the two women ascended the curving stairway. As they reached her room Tilly put her hand gently on Lara's arm. "You look tired. Perhaps we should postpone our little talk?"

Lara lowered her eyes. "Oh, yes. I am sorry, but I think I have a headache coming on. Perhaps tomorrow, after we return from our visit to the warehouses . . ."

"Of course."

Before Tilly could say anything else, Lara smiled perfunctorily and almost fled down the hall to her own boudoir. Tilly was glad the inevitable had been postponed, even though it made her feel like a coward. Tomorrow, when Lara was more herself, they would be more comfortable with one another.

Tiger Flynn had vowed he was no adulterer, she remembered belatedly, and at the time she had believed him; but perhaps the ability to seem totally convincing was part of his charm. Tilly was uneasy. There was something about him that attracted her strongly, while at the same time his look, his smile, his very nearness set warning bells ringing in her head.

She went inside and set the candle on the stand, but as she shut the door something in the hallway caught her eye. Just beyond the circle of light from the candelabra, a crumpled bit of white cloth lay at the head of the stairs. Without picking up her candle, Tilly went to retrieve the object. As she stooped to pick it up she knew at once it was not her handkerchief. This one was much larger, and in the light she was able to make out a bold, masculine monogram.

It belonged to Lucas Flynn. The square of linen carried his scent, an elusive blend of amber and sandalwood. Even blindfolded she would have recognized it. Tilly turned the handkerchief until the glossy embroidery caught the light. It proved her deduction: a large central "F" flanked by an "L" and a "P." Lucas P. Flynn.

Tilly wondered idly what his middle name was. She also wondered how he had dropped the handkerchief in the bedroom hallway, where no evening guest had any right to be. The more she knew of Tiger Flynn, the more questions she had about him. Caught up in her own thoughts, she was scarcely aware of Jonas's deep voice drifting up from the portico. His tones were low. It was merely a trick of acoustics that brought them so clearly to her ear.

"I don't want any of this to reach Lara's ears."

Surprise immobilized Tilly for several seconds. She abhorred eavesdropping, yet concern for her friend held her rooted to the spot. A moth fluttered between the banisters and toward the light, and a door closed on the lower floor, obscuring part of the interchange.

"Very well. It's been difficult to find out anything with Flynn about the docks today."

The other man's voice was barely audible yet there was something familiar about the rhythm of his speech.

"Hasty action would be regrettable," Jonas responded. "I'll make my decision when I have all the facts."

"Flynn's been asking awkward questions."

"You would be well advised to keep a weather eye out for him," Jonas warned. "He's not a man to trifle with."

"Faugh! The man is nothing but a fop and a dandy," his companion said. "There's not an idea in his head that doesn't concern the current fashion or his latest flirtation."

A puff from Jonas's cigar wafted on the breeze. "You couldn't be more wrong. Flynn is nobody's fool."

"Really, Jonas..."

"Don't cross swords with Lucas Flynn," Jonas interjected flatly. "He's a dangerous man. A very dangerous man."

Tilly had heard enough. Ears burning, she tried to stand up and discovered she was kneeling on her hem. Her efforts to free herself put her off balance, and she grasped the balustrade. It creaked faintly, a sound that seemed loud as a rifle crack to her ears. She rose hastily, the square of linen in her hand, and found Jonas looking at her sharply from the bottom step.

"I thought you had retired for the night, Miss Templeton."

"I discovered I had lost my handkerchief; it was here at the head of the stairs."

He mounted the steps firmly, his eyes never leaving her face. Tilly crushed the square of embroidered fabric in her hand, hiding its masculine size, and placed it in her reticule.

Jonas ascended to her level. She met his penetrating look with an innocent smile. "I would have been distressed to lose it. It was embroidered especially for me, by a friend."

Jonas peered at her a moment and seemed to decide she was speaking the truth. His frown eased. "You needn't bother yourself in future, Miss Templeton. One of the servants will see that any misplaced property is returned."

"Of course. How foolish of me!"

"I'll bid you good night once again."

He waited until she darted gratefully into her room. For some unknown reason, Jonas Whitby was suspicious of her actions. Perhaps he had observed her in the garden earlier with Lucas Flynn, or perhaps because she was Lara's friend and presumed confidante. Although her host had seemed genial enough at dinner and when they'd met earlier, she had the distinct impression that he had not welcomed her visit, and would be glad to see it end. It made Tilly very uncomfortable.

There were strange undercurrents at Coeur d'Émeraude and secrets that were none of her business. Tilly wanted nothing to do with them—especially if they involved the adventurous and enigmatic Mr. Flynn. Yet, knowing Lara's inner strengths, she could not imagine her friend involved in a scandalous intrigue and she believed Flynn's denial. It might be that Jonas had leaped to false conclusions, as she had done earlier. There must be a simple explanation. Everything would surely sort itself out.

She pulled the bell cord and summoned Agnes to help her remove her evening clothes. "You need not brush out my hair, Agnes. I will leave the braids in till morning."

She climbed into bed and let the maid arrange the bedclothes, sure she would fall asleep instantly; but after Agnes left, Tilly found herself wide awake. She lit her candle and padded across the cool floor in her bare feet to retrieve her journal. At the elegant desk she scrawled a few lines in her flowing script, jotting down impressions of Kingston and Coeur d'Émeraude and the various people she'd met at dinner.

Her words brought the evening's cast to life, but when she came to Lucas Flynn, her pen sputtered and stopped. Absently, she sketched in the shape of his face, the curve of his lips and the tilt of his eyes, hardly aware of what she was doing.

She looked down and saw the simple line drawing, more a rough impression than an actual portrait. It certainly didn't reflect the easy man-about-town she knew as Lucas Flynn. Oh, she had gotten the set of his shoulders right, and accurately depicted the firm chin and determined jaw. Even the slant of brows and eyes was accurately rendered. The features were correct, but the man in her sketch was a complete stranger. Beneath the lazy amusement and elegant posture, there was coiled-spring tension and the wariness of a jungle creature—the dangerous man that Jonas had described to his unknown companion. Tilly smiled at her overworked imagination and put her drawing materials away, then blew out the candle and got into bed once more.

The shutters were half open, letting in the soft silver moonlight. The furnishings were vague blurred shapes. She was still too stimulated to sleep. It had been a mistake to leave her braids in. They made her head ache. She swung her legs over the side of the bed and removed the pins that held her plaits in their shining coronet. It was wonderful to release the braids, and she felt some of her tension ease. A good brushing would feel even better. Moving to the dressing table, she picked up her ivory-backed brush, still going over the details of the evening in her mind.

She sat on the bench and began to brush her hair, from the nape to its shimmering ends. A scratching sound came from the direction of the latched shutters. *The marmalade cat,* she thought, and went to let it in. She pulled the right shutter open, and the cat streaked by her ankles. The single candle flickered and went out. For an instant moonlight flooded the room, only to be blotted out by a looming shape.

Before she could cry out, an arm clamped about her waist, a hand pressed over her mouth, and a low voice whispered urgently in her ear. "Not a sound, Miss Templeton, if you value your life!"

Unable to move, scarcely able to breathe, Tilly recognized her captor: the mysterious, maddening Tiger Flynn.

Chapter Four

Both our lives depend upon your silence." Tilly ceased her futile struggles. She didn't doubt that they both stood in peril of their lives. She didn't know the why or how of the situation, but his intensity communicated itself to her. Whatever he was engaged upon, it was no mere bedroom intrigue: if he'd been visiting a woman at Coeur d'Émeraude, his life might be in danger, but hers would not.

This was something deeper and more deadly.

His arms were like steel bands around her, crushing her dainty gown and bruising the ribs beneath it. Through her thin nightshift she could feel the dampness of his shirt and the strong, steady beat of his heart. His unorthodox embrace relaxed a fraction, but she remained still while his warm breath tickled her ear. She should have been frightened out of her wits, yet a strange calm pervaded her as they waited together.

The ginger cat, curled up on a pillow at the foot of the bed, stirred and opened one glowing, mirrored eye, and listened intently. Satisfied, it winked it shut again. With a slight shift of its fluid body, it settled in for the night.

From the garden below faint sounds drifted up: quick, stealthy footsteps crossing the gravel walk, the sigh and swish of disturbed foliage. Then, soft but distinct, a grunt succeeded by a hoarse curse.

"Quiet, you fool!" a deep voice hissed. Tilly strained her ears but only an eerie silence followed. Suddenly the skin at her nape prickled and crawled. She knew, without the faintest tinge of doubt, that the furtive men—whoever they were—were staring up at her balcony. A bout of uncontrollable shivering wracked her body, and Flynn's arms tightened reassuringly.

There was another crunch of gravel and a whisper so low she could almost have imagined it: "Not that way! We'll have to play it by the rules."

For a moment Tilly and her nocturnal visitor stayed locked together, like a Renaissance statue of entwined lovers. There was no sound at all. Surreptitious footsteps moved away, heading in the direction of the front portico.

Tilly had held her breath so long she thought her lungs were going to burst. Flynn released her. His changeable green eyes were warm despite the cool silver moonlight. His social facade of smooth, rakish charm was gone. Now she saw him as he really was: keen, alert and filled with a tense excitement. Her sketch of him had been true to life after all, and her eye had caught the very essence of him.

"Good girl! But we're not home safe yet," he murmured. "One's gone round to the front, but the other's on lookout below."

Before she could demand an explanation, he darted to the door. The clock on the landing chimed once. He paused, listening. "Too late."

A gust of moving air told them the big entrance door had opened, and a voice called out a sharp challenge to the empty foyer. Tilly and Flynn glanced around simultaneously and hit on the same thing at once. Working together, it took less than a minute to hide him completely from sight.

Tilly hurried across the floor in her bare feet, rumpling her hair as she went, to make it look sleep-tumbled and disordered. Not ten seconds after she scrambled beneath the covers, there was a soft rap upon her door.

"Miss Templeton?"

She made her voice listless and sleepy. "Yes? Who is it?"

"Jonas Whitby. I am sorry to disturb you at this hour, but I must speak with you immediately."

"Very well. You may come in." The door opened and Jonas Whitby stood beyond the threshold, a branch of candles in his hand. Tilly clasped the bed linens over her breast and tried to look properly shocked at his intrusion. Her indignant expression took him aback.

"I beg your pardon, Miss Templeton. Bernard was bothered by a touch of insomnia. He thought he spied a prowler in the gardens, and I am checking the house."

She sat up a bit more stiffly. "As you can see, there is no prowler here!"

His gaze swept the room in the wavering candlelight, pausing only briefly as it passed the tall mahogany wardrobe. She wondered if he noticed that the wardrobe doors were open a scant half inch. She was sure she had closed them tightly. Her palms were sweaty and she wiped them surreptitiously on the coverlet. Jonas turned his hard, unswerving gaze upon her.

"You heard nothing, Miss Templeton? Nothing at all?"

"Oh, no! I was asleep quite soundly, until you roused me!"

Her remark backfired. "Then," Jonas announced, "your chamber must be checked thoroughly, to ensure your safety."

Tilly stifled her dismay. "Of course, if you think it necessary," she replied, in what she prayed was a convincing tone. It didn't sound particularly strong to her own ears. She hoped he would attribute the slight quaver in it to a mild case of nerves at the thought of a prowler on the loose, and not to its actual cause.

Jonas stepped inside, and she realized he was not alone. The shadow in the corner stepped into the circle of candlelight, and she saw he was accompanied by a muscular black man. While Tilly's heart beat in her throat so loudly she feared they might hear it, Jonas swept his hard gaze around the room. He fixed on the opposite corner and braced for action.

"Search the wardrobe first, Leander."

While Jonas blocked the doorway the other man strode across the floor. He noticed the open door and paused, nodding his head significantly. Jonas acknowledged the warning and moved closer. Huddled in the middle of the big bed, Tilly watched the unfolding drama. The man called Leander grasped the bottom of the door and flung open the wardrobe. A pastel rainbow of silk and satin shone in the flickering candle glow, moving slightly in the draft. Leander plunged his head and shoulders into the wardrobe and pushed the garments ruthlessly aside. He searched behind the gowns.

"Nothing here, Mr. Whitby."

"He's got to be here somewhere!"

While Tilly tried to calm her accelerating heartbeat, the servant opened the cupboards flanking the fireplace, rummaged behind the window draperies and peered behind the tall rosewood desk. She glanced quickly at Jonas and away again. In that split second she had noticed that he held the candelabra in his left hand, while the right one hovered near his coat pocket. Only a pistol within it would have that size, that shape.

Her heart hammered so forcibly that she feared he would see the telltale pulse at her throat. Luckily, he wasn't watching her. Leander shrugged his shoulders. "All clear."

"Damn!"

Tilly spoke up, her voice thin with tension. "You haven't looked under the bed."

Arms around her knees to keep them from knocking, Tilly waited while the servant knelt and checked beneath the heavy frame. His sharp exclamation brought Jonas to his side, and she could see that it was indeed a gun that had been hidden in his pocket. He pulled it out and the barrel collected the light. To Tilly's horrified eyes, it gleamed as big and bright as a brass cannon.

"Step away," Jonas ordered.

Instead Leander laughed, a low, rhythmic chuckle that shook his brawny shoulders. "No prowler under here, Mr. Whitby. Leastwise, not now."

He scrambled to his feet, something dangling from his hand. Something small and brown and furry. "Looks like that cat's been here before us."

Jonas gave the dead rodent a look of disgust, and Tilly seized her chance. "Oh!" she shrieked. "A mouse! Remove it at once! Help!"

"There's need to shout the house down. It's quite dead."

"Dead!" she screeched.

"Get rid of that damned thing!" Jonas commented, trying without success to hush Tilly's agitated cries.

The marmalade cat lay on a pillow atop the small humpbacked chest in the far corner of the room. As he lifted his head and regarded them all with royal contempt, Tilly scolded him roundly.

"Horrible creature! I thought you were my friend. How dare you leave me such a ghastly present!"

The cat shifted and its eyes shone like gold coins. It rose and stretched with complete disdain, then turned in a circle and settled comfortably once more.

Holding the limp rodent by the tail, Leander opened the shutters and flung the body out into the garden. "I'll pick it up when I get outside."

He turned and grinned at the sight before him. Tilly, sitting upright against the headboard, had pulled the bed linens up to cover her face.

"It's all right, Miss Templeton," Jonas assured her. "Leander has disposed of it."

Tilly lowered the bed sheet. "Prowlers! Mice. *Dead* mice!" Loathing and horror underscored every word. "This is terrible. I shall not sleep another wink tonight. I shall have to take a sleeping powder."

Doors opened and voices murmured in the hall. Jonas recovered his composure. "Perhaps that is the wisest course, Miss Templeton. The prowler was probably nothing but a figment of Bernard's imagination, and you may repose yourself in complete confidence."

He signaled Leander to follow him out, and the men left. Tilly waited a few minutes, then hurried to the door. There was no latch, so she put the desk chair under the handle, then crept to the shutters, closed the louvers and secured them. She could hear Jonas talking to someone in the hallway.

"Go back to bed, all of you. Miss Templeton was merely frightened by a mouse."

Tilly bit her lip at that. She hated to be branded a silly fool for raising such a ruckus over a mouse; but it was far better than the alternative. She climbed back in bed and lay there for a long time. She was so tired she could barely hold her eyes open. It took a sheer effort of will to keep from nodding off.

After another ten minutes elapsed, she slipped out of bed and made her way to the corner of the darkened room. Twin green lamps glowed like evil emeralds in the dimness. She put out her hand and stroked the marmalade cat between the ears.

"Good cat. *Very* good cat. I shall have to reward you with a nice fish, since you don't seem to care for mice."

The creature began to purr loudly, rubbing its head against her palm. Their mutual admiration was interrupted by a faint but persistent thumping from within the chest.

"Down you go," Tilly said, and set the cat on the floor. It stretched, yawned and moved away to explore interesting scents behind the wardrobe.

Removing the pillow, Tilly tossed it aside and unlatched the trunk. As she lifted the lid a low groan sounded. "Hush!" she admonished. "You'll rouse the household again."

"I'm suffocating in here."

"Nonsense."

Lucas Flynn unfolded his length from the pretzel shape he had forced it into. The process was slow and painful but he was grinning as he clambered out. "I was crammed in there like a jack-in-the-box," he grumbled softly. "I've been ready to spring out for the past hour! What did you do, fall asleep?"

Tilly was indignant. "Of course not. And it hasn't been hours. More like minutes."

"I fear your watch must have stopped."

It had been hot inside the trunk. His shirt was plastered to his chest. He stretched as gracefully, but far more interestingly, than the marmalade cat. Tilly had never realized there were quite so many muscles in the human body.

She looked away. "You owe a debt of gratitude to the remarkable feline. Without its superb cooperation, you would surely have been discovered. Indeed, I don't know how or why he stayed put during all the uproar."

Flynn's answering laugh was as low and soft as hers. "He did it because I wanted him to do so. He's highly intelligent, and very loyal."

Tilly's eyebrows rose. "Do you mean the cat is yours?"

"Nobody owns a cat, Miss Templeton."

"Yet you claim you can control his behavior?"

Flynn stepped toward the shutters and silently unlatched them. "I no more control his behavior than he controls mine. But there *is* such a thing as accommodating a friend."

"If you expect me to believe that, you're either mad, or you think that I am."

"Believe what you wish. I think you're quite sane, Miss Templeton. And very quick-witted." He was serious now, and she saw the lines of strain etched in his face. "If you had stopped to ask for explanations, I might be lying at the bottom of Kingston Harbor at this very moment."

"You mean Jonas—"

"I'd rather not tell you what I mean. It's not your affair, after all."

She shivered and crossed her arms over her breasts. "If it is true that I saved your life, don't you think you owe me an explanation?"

"No, Miss Templeton. Remember that too much knowledge is a dangerous thing. The less you know, the greater your safety. You'd best get back to bed and forget this ever happened."

"Just like that?"

"Yes. You're a sensible woman."

A tremulous smile touched her mouth. "I doubt that. A sensible woman would not be standing in her nightshift beside a man she had concealed in her bedchamber."

He grinned, and the warmth of his personality eased her chill. "Your logic is undeniable, Miss Templeton. I retract my statement. You are quick-witted, beautiful—and hopelessly insane. What a terrible shame.''

Tilly took a step back, shaking her head. "You are a very strange man, Mr. Flynn. I see now why you have such a colorful reputation.''

In the shadowed light he looked suddenly rueful. "Don't believe everything you hear about me, I beg you. I am not the scoundrel you have every right to think me.''

For the first time she noticed the dark, glistening patch on his arm. "You are bleeding.''

"It's nothing. A mere scratch.''

"Yes," she said, examining it in the dimness. "But you've been bleeding all over the inside of my trunk.''

He chuckled softly. "Most ungrateful of me, I'm afraid.''

"I'll bind it up for you." She opened a drawer of the dressing table and took out one of the linen neck cloths she wore with her riding habits.

He watched her with amusement. "You needn't bother. I'll survive without your tender, if rather reluctant, ministrations.''

Tilly shut the drawer. "Yes, but now you are bleeding all over my floor!''

Picking up her silver-handled scissors, she slit his shirt sleeve past the elbow. The laceration was jagged and deeper than she'd expected. She wished she hadn't been so abrupt with him. The truth was that she was badly shaken. Pistols, dripping blood and midnight callers were not part of her life in Yorkshire. Experience in handling a hundred village emergencies, including the choirboys' picnic, came to the rescue. She bandaged his arm neatly and quickly.

He examined her handiwork. "Expertly done. I'll have no qualms in calling upon you in future, should the occasion arise.''

Tilly was still rattled and made no reply. He took her hand in his and held it a moment, his face suddenly serious in the barred moonlight. "I am forever in your debt, my dear. If ever I can repay the favor, I am yours to command.''

He raised her hand to his lips and kissed her fingers. In the darkness it seemed a highly personal and intimate gesture. Each touch of his lips sent tiny jolts of lightning up her arm. Staring into his face, seeing his eyes glimmer gold and green like a tiger's, she almost felt she was dreaming. He had the power to render her motionless with a look, to make every thought vanish from her mind like summer smoke. He kissed her fingers again, one by one, and released her hand regretfully.

"Good night, Miss Templeton."

"And you're really going to go away, leaving me completely in the dark?" she asked, without really expecting him to do otherwise. Tiger Flynn was a man who would keep his own counsel.

"Yes, I am. Good night, Miss Templeton . . ."

Before she knew what he meant to do his hand caught her chin and tilted it up. His mouth came down on hers, gentle at first but warm. Burning. She was dizzy with sensation, her mind unable to concentrate on anything but the kiss. It sparked something deep inside her, and that spark ignited an unexpected fire in him. Flynn's arms went around her waist, drawing her close against his body. Heat radiated through his damp shirt and the thin fabric of her nightshirt. They might as well have been naked. With her breasts crushed against him, she could feel the crisp curls that covered his chest. Her nipples tingled and swelled in response.

A soft moan reached Tilly's ears, but whether his or hers, she didn't know. Or care. She was only aware of the hardness of his body, the strength of his powerful muscles, the masterful, arousing way his hands stroked her back—as if he was learning her every curve and contour through his fingertips. The universe had shrunk to the circle of his arms. She was scarcely aware of the incredible, instinctive way her body bent and curved to fit against his. She forgot everything but his touch and the pressure of his mouth on hers.

Flynn's kiss was hungry and possessive. His breath was warm against her skin, his mouth hot with need. The heat grew until it threatened to flare out of control. He felt her tremble against him as his lips trailed down the side of her throat, sliding lower over her skin toward the V of her neckline. Her gown was plastered to her breasts and their peaks stood out temptingly. He touched the top of her breast with his mouth, just above the fabric, and felt the deep pull in his loins. He fought the wild urgency.

From the first he'd been attracted to her, but he'd never intended the kiss to send them recklessly into this moment. She was sweet and innocent, and swept away by the passion his caresses had unleashed. She had no idea of what she was doing or where this was leading. The strangeness of a foreign land, their shared brush with danger, had shaken her from her foundations. Now she wanted him, but afterward, she would hate him. Deservedly so. But, God! how he wanted her!

He was tempted almost beyond endurance. To be the first to usher her into womanhood, to be the one to teach her the beauty of her soft, rounded body and the intimate pleasures of love. They were poised on the edge of the cliff. Another step and it would be too late to turn back.

When Flynn's lips skimmed over the tops of her breasts, Tilly finally realized her vulnerability. She was in danger of losing much more than her head, but she could not pull away. Wanting him to go on, her breasts aching to feel his hungry mouth, she clung to him. It was Flynn who ended the embrace. He knew that she was defenseless against the twin onslaught of his passion and her own need. Even though he felt her readiness, to take her like this would be the act of a complete villain. He wrenched himself away.

His sudden withdrawal caught her unprepared, and she almost cried out in protest. He held her away from him and searched her face. "I wish to God you had not come here, Miss Templeton. Especially not now, when I need to be awake on every suit."

She shook her head, not comprehending anything except that she needed him to hold her again. Flynn smiled ruefully into her dazed eyes. "You are a very dangerous woman. Do you know that you have the power to cloud a man's mind and make every rational thought fly away?"

She shook her head disbelieving; but when she tried to speak the words wouldn't come. He cupped her face between his hands. "Good night, Tilly. Until we meet again."

"Oh, wait...I mean..." She did not want him to go, and her breathless voice betrayed her feelings. She was babbling like an idiot, and unable to stop. "You...I have your handkerchief. You dropped it at the head of the stairs."

He frowned suddenly. "Did I? How indiscreet of me. Keep it for me until tomorrow."

He dropped a kiss on the tip of her nose, and while she was still recovering he exited, not furtively through the window, but boldly by the door.

"You can't go out that way!" she whispered urgently, tiptoeing to his side.

"It's the only way I can. There is someone watching below your balcony. But they won't expect me to march right out the front door."

Pulling the chair from beneath the handle, he set it aside. "Boldness usually pays off. And if I'm going to die, I'd rather do it like a man than slink away like a coward. But don't worry, my dear, I intend to live to a very ripe, old age."

Flynn opened the door a crack and surveyed the corridor, then slipped into it. Tilly was amazed at how silent he was. There was not a sound, not the faintest creak of a floorboard to betray him. He moved down the shadows of the stairwell as if he were one of them, and vanished from sight.

A moment later she felt a rush of fresh air sweep up the stairway as the front door opened and closed. She waited, rigid with fear, but there were no shouts. No shots.

Tilly closed her door softly and stood with her back against it, waiting for her tumultuous pulse to slow. Her knees felt weak, yet her blood sang: for the first time in her sheltered life she had known danger. And desire. She had not known that she could react so quickly to either one—or so deeply.

Flynn's touch, his kisses and his brazen sense of humor had stirred up emotions and longings within her that she had never known she possessed. She had thought, for many years, that she was a woman, fully grown. Now she knew she had been a mere girl, with no understanding of what womanhood was about. Beneath her cool, capable exterior, there was a fountain of passion she had never suspected. And it had taken Lucas Flynn only a few brief moments to show her that.

There was, she knew, a lot more a man like Flynn could teach her. He could have taken complete advantage of her. Only his control had kept her from disaster. She had always been sure she was the kind of woman who could not be seduced. Now she was only sure of one thing: he was a man, and he made her feel like a woman, in every sense of the word.

His lovemaking had flustered her so much, it had pushed everything else from her mind. What were Flynn's reasons for prowling the grounds of Coeur d'Émeraude by night? If he had been visiting a woman, his life might have been in peril—but not hers. No, his midnight business at the plantation was more than a romantic rendezvous. It was something deeper. Darker.

Why did he need to hide from Jonas. Would Jonas have shot Flynn if he'd been found in her room? There were too many questions, and they did not add up. She needed answers desperately.

There was trouble and mystery at Coeur d'Émeraude, and Tilly's sense of survival urged her to leave as soon as possible; but she could not callously abandon Lara, who was caught in the center of this web of intrigue. Not until she could find a way to help her. And then there was Flynn.

He was like no man she had known before: quick-witted, perceptive and resourceful. And, as Jonas Whitby suspected, highly dangerous. He was indeed a tiger, hiding his claws and playing some secret, deadly game of his own, in which they were all his pawns.

And now, she had become a part of it.

After a light breakfast in bed—oh, heavenly luxury!— Tilly rose and bathed, pondering the events of the previous night. It seemed like a bizarre, impossible dream in the clear golden sunshine. But she had not dreamed up Jonas's pistol. Or Lucas Flynn's kiss. It made her blush to think of it.

Almost to prove to herself that it had happened, she opened her reticule and found the linen handkerchief she'd discovered the night before. The monogram was there, but she had known it was his even before she'd seen the initials. She held it to her nose and inhaled. A subtle scent of sandalwood lingered, and beneath it, a certain something that was Tiger Flynn, and no other man in the world.

The scents brought back the warm intimacy of their embrace. For the briefest moment she remembered how it had felt to be in his arms, the touch of his lips upon hers, the deep, liquid heat that welled up inside her. Then the door handle rattled and Agnes entered with her vaguely superior air. Her keen eyes swept over her temporary mistress, and the thin mouth settled in sour lines.

"Miss has a cold this morning?"

Tilly whisked the handkerchief out of sight. "Not at all. Not even a sniffle."

The maid briskly took out a gown of ruffled organza, as fresh and yellow as an English daffodil, and a pair of matching slippers. They were not exactly what Tilly would have selected to wear down to the docks, or for the afternoon's picnic in the countryside, but she bowed to the maid's judgment. When Agnes finished, Tilly decided it was almost worth all the fuss and fidgeting. When every curl and ruffle had been tweaked into place, she hurried downstairs in search of Lara.

Bernard, the stately butler, was passing down the hall with a covered tray, and Tilly gave him a bright smile. "Good morning, Bernard. I hope you slept well last night?"

Unfailingly polite, the butler quelled his surprise. "Thank you, miss. I did indeed."

"And the prowler did not disturb you?"

"Prowler?" Bernard's brow furrowed in surprise. "I know nothing of a prowler, Miss Templeton."

"Perhaps I dreamed it, then."

With her suspicions confirmed, Tilly went down the long hall in search of her hostess. So Bernard, who supposedly had seen a prowler and then alerted Jonas, knew nothing of last night's events! How very interesting. Someone was lying, and as far as she was concerned, the burden of proof was on Jonas Whitby.

When she had first met him, Tilly had been inclined to like him well enough, and was as sure as Lara that he would make her an ideal husband. But in view of Lara's nervousness around her spouse, and Flynn's warning of danger, she had to make a major readjustment in her attitude. It seemed impossible that she had been so very wrong. There were invisible currents sweeping through the halls of Coeur d'Émeraude, and Tilly was determined to uncover their source, not just because she had become involved, but for Lara's sake.

As she neared the wide doors to the terrace, Tilly realized she was humming a gay little tune beneath her breath. Midnight prowlers, guns and threats, and she was humming! Far away from home and familiar things, thrust into a totally new environment, and faced with mysterious hazards, she felt more alive than ever before. All her life she had stood on the sidelines as events marched by. Now her role was no longer passive. She had joined the parade.

Lara, exquisitely dressed in Dresden blue silk, was sipping her second cup of tea as Tilly came onto the terrace.

"The island air must agree with you, Tilly. I have never seen such roses in your cheeks, or such a sparkle in your eye. It's no wonder that Mrs. Thorne had her nose put quite out of joint last evening."

"I hardly think she was aware of my existence. After your introduction, she did not address a single comment to me or even glance my way once."

"Oh, but she noticed that you had slipped out to the terrace alone," Lara answered casually. A little too brightly.

Tilly felt her cheeks redden. "Yes. It was quite warm and I needed a breath of fresh air, but what business that is of hers quite escapes me. I am surprised she would mention it to you."

Lara looked down at her plate, her eyes screened by her lashes. "Actually, I also noticed you had gone into the garden. I was near the open doors when you walked past with Lucas Flynn."

Silence fell as Tilly took a slice of toast and slathered it with marmalade. Lara concentrated on carefully lining up her fork with her plate. Her fingers trembled with the effort to control her strong emotion.

"Tilly, there is something I have to... Oh dear! I don't even know how to begin!"

Impulsively Tilly covered Lara's hand with her own. "Do not say anything you might later wish unsaid."

"But I must!"

Suddenly Lara tensed. Whatever she had been about to say was lost as Jonas came strolling across the lawn to join them. He seemed relaxed, and showed no ill effects from his late-night investigations.

"Still dawdling over breakfast, ladies? I have already been out for my morning ride."

"Tilly and I have much catching up to do," Lara replied quickly.

"Well, there will be plenty of time for that." He pulled a turnip watch from his pocket. "But not at the present. The carriage will be coming around any moment now."

"You will enjoy the warehouses," Lara said, as they put on their bonnets and gloves. "They are filled with wonders. Goods from every corner of the earth pass through them."

"Lucas is down there now," Jonas said, "buying up more trinkets for his place."

Tilly felt her cheeks redden. She hadn't planned on having to face Tiger Flynn so soon. Lara turned from the mirror and noticed her flushed complexion. "My dear, you look uncomfortably warm already. If you think the visit too much for you, we could postpone it until you have grown more accustomed to the weather."

"It is only anticipation that makes my face so rosy," Tilly replied quickly. "I assure you I am looking forward to the visit eagerly."

A half hour's pleasant journey brought them to the docks. The warehouses shone white against the sparkling sea, and beyond them the heights of the palisades rose in the sunlight. Tilly was awed to learn that all four buildings, which covered several acres, belonged solely to Jonas and his junior partners.

The warehouses were filled, as Lara had promised, with splendid treasures from exotic lands: silks and spices from the Orient and Africa, embroidered satin robes and chests inlaid with precious woods; vases and bowls and temple jars of Chinese porcelain, dreaming Buddhas in brass and jade and polished ivory; glowing rugs and carpets from the looms of India; mosaics and elaborate brasswork from the workshops of the Golden Horn.

"This is like Aladdin's cave," Tilly exclaimed. "How do you ever keep track of everything?"

"Believe me," Jonas answered, "there is nothing that passes in or out of these buildings that escapes my notice."

They strolled through shelves of New World artifacts, and Tilly stopped to admire some amusing pots and jars shaped like squat human figures. The others were some distance away. A shadow fell over the table.

"You look fresh as a rose this morning, Miss Templeton."

The cool voice from just behind her could only belong to Tiger Flynn. Tilly wished she'd had time to prepare herself for this first awkward meeting after what had passed between them the previous night. She felt as gauche as a schoolgirl.

"Oh, good morning, Mr. Flynn," she replied, much more coolly than she felt. From the corner of her eye, she saw that Jonas was looking their way.

Flynn gave her a blank, charming smile. There was nothing behind his eyes. "I trust you slept well after all the excitement of yesterday?"

Tilly stiffened with alarm. "Hush! We might be overheard."

"I was referring to your arrival in Kingston and the Whitbys' dinner party."

"How can you joke about it?" she asked beneath her breath. "Last night you said our lives were in danger, and today you act as if nothing unusual happened."

Flynn tilted his head and surveyed her. "Your face is quite flushed, Miss Templeton. You'd stand the heat more easily if you dressed for it properly. We are not upon the wild Yorkshire moors, after all. Just strip off a few dozen layers of petticoat, and you'll soon feel better."

Tilly moved briskly down the row. Had he gone mad, or had she? Whatever she had expected from him, it was not this.

Flynn followed leisurely. "Giving me the cold shoulder, are you? I really think you should reconsider, Miss Templeton. If Lara or Jonas notices, it might lead to awkward explanations—which I'm sure you would rather not make."

"I think you would have much more to explain than I," she replied shortly, "but I would rather not put it to the test." She favored him with a remote smile.

He shook his head. "No, no. That will never do, Miss Templeton. A man could die of chill from such a wintry look."

"A risk that I am willing to take, Mr. Flynn."

Before she could think he moved closer. So close his breath whispered past her ear. "I much prefer the way you were last night when I kissed you, warm and willing."

Tilly's face flamed with mortification. She prayed the rest of her party was fully occupied elsewhere. "You, sir, are no gentleman to remind of it."

His dazzling smile flashed, white as lightning. "I thought we'd already agreed upon that, during our stroll through the garden."

"Oh, do go away!" she said angrily. "I have no wish to cross swords with you now or ever."

He did. Tilly looked up a moment later and found herself alone and completely bewildered. It dawned on her then that his odd behavior was not normal. It had been carefully calculated to get a certain response from her—for the benefit of a third party. Flynn had not wanted anyone watching closely to think that they were on familiar terms.

It would have been much simpler to explain it to her first, she thought crossly. And the longer she thought about it, the more irritated she became. Her temper began to simmer. *Warm and willing!* Really, there been no need to insult her!

She ground her small white teeth and vowed that she would not get involved with Tiger Flynn and his escapades again. In retrospect, she could not understand why she had done it in the first place. At the time she'd been operating on impulse.

A mistake she would *not* repeat.

At the far end of the aisle, Lara and Jonas were laughing over a remark George Keating had made. Flynn joined them, and Tilly escaped a bit farther along the row, examining the mysterious wares spread before her. Some were still in the process of being unpacked. Grinning stone figures with long, rectangular faces and large ears marched in single file toward her. Unlike the pottery bowls, which were new, these had an air of great age about them.

She continued down the table, safely away from Lucas Flynn. At the end of the table were six small, wooden crates. One had its lid removed, along with a quantity of packing material. Unlike the others, which were stamped with the name of Jonas Whitby's company, this one was marked Private Property of J. Whitby, Esq., Coeur d'Émeraude. She peeked in.

Cradled in the remaining packing material was a life-size mask worked in dark green stone. The mouth was thick-lipped and wide, the nose jutting and sharply curved like an eagle's beak—but it was the eyes that held her. White shell mosaic inlaid around obsidian disks, blind and yet all-seeing. Impartially cruel.

A ghost danced up and down her spine. There was something repulsive about the mask. Something evil. She felt compelled to touch it. Her hand reached out and her fingertips rested on the high stone cheekbones for a fraction of a second. She drew them back instantly, then unconsciously wiped them on her skirt. They left a faint, light smudge.

Lara came up beside her. "You seem to have found something interesting." She peered into the crate. "Oh! What is it?"

"A burial mask, I think. There is something uncanny about it."

Lara's face mirrored her unease. "It is quite horrible, though I suppose Jonas would disagree with me. He is quite a collector of primitive art."

At the mention of his name her husband looked across the aisle. His questioning glance changed to a scowl when he saw the crate. He hurried over. "This should not be here! I instructed McDonald to have that taken directly to the house the minute it was unloaded."

"Oh, Jonas!" Lara exclaimed. "I do not want that horrid thing in the house. It gives me the oddest feeling!"

"Nonsense, my dear. I shall mount it in my study, where you won't have to look at it every day. It is really a fine example of Mayan work."

Flynn, who had been deep in conversation with Mr. Keating, now made his way in their direction. Jonas put the lid on the crate. "Keating, have this put in the safe until we are ready to depart. And if you see McDonald, tell him I wish to speak to him."

"Yes, Jonas. Of course."

Keating signaled a workman, who hefted the crate in his brawny arms, and the two hurried toward the office. Tilly forgot all about the mask when Jonas unlocked a cupboard. Inside were rolls of fabulous fabrics from around the world.

"These were just unloaded. It would please me if you would each select a bolt of cloth, to be made up into gowns for the ball we are to give next month."

They thanked him excitedly, and Jonas excused himself. Lara knew instantly which bolt she wanted, a figured satin of midnight blue shot through with gold. "I have been looking for just such a color. While you make your selection, Tilly, I will find a clerk."

When she glided off, Tilly looked around for Flynn. He was nowhere in sight. Perhaps he had left the warehouse. Her disappointment was keen. She had told him to go away, and he had. What an abominable man! Heaven knew when she would have a chance to talk sensibly with him and discover what was going on.

She touched the fabrics spilling from their wrappers. They ranged from the sheerest imaginable silks to fine jacquards and heavy-weight damask. A length of peach taffeta flowed through her fingers, but it was the white spiderweb gauze, spangled with crystals and silver thread, that caught her eye. She had never seen anything so beautiful.

"What do you think?"

Tilly looked up. She thought Jonas had addressed her, but when she turned she was alone. Lara was at the far end of the building with a clerk, who was busily scribbling down her instructions. Jonas spoke again, his voice low and impatient. Tilly realized belatedly that the warehouse offices were on the other side of the partition. She didn't mean to eavesdrop. She started to leave but the words, although muffled, were distinct enough.

"Missing?" she heard Jonas snap. "Impossible, I tell you."

Mr. Keating answered. "I warned you. I don't trust him. I think we should remove him, at once."

"No! Let's not be too hasty. I don't want to do anything drastic until I've given it some thought."

"Then what? Something must be done as soon as possible."

Tilly sped up her pace, embarrassed at overhearing Jonas's private business. She was almost out of range when his reply brought her up short.

"I'll look into it myself, Keating. Take Lara and that damned girl off my hands for the afternoon, and keep them occupied. I'll join you later at the house."

Tilly's ears burned. After hearing her host refer to her as "that damned girl," it might be difficult to greet him civilly. Well, she would try to do it—for Lara's sake.

Lara closed the cover of the gold timepiece pinned to her bodice. "Oh dear! It is much later than I thought. Lady Steadmore and Miss Eggleston are coming at two o'clock."

She showed the clerk the bolts they wanted, and he promised they would be delivered that afternoon. They walked into the sunlight. The loading area was inordinately hot and bright after the coolness of the warehouse, and not even their deep-brimmed summer hats provided protection. As they stepped into it, Tilly's eyes closed against the glare. Before she could blink them open, she blundered into someone.

"Oh! Pardon me!" she exclaimed.

She had bumped into a Jamaican flower woman. Sheaves of fuscia and gold blossoms scattered everywhere, and while Tilly bent to retrieve them, the woman righted the wide straw bonnet that covered her brown-patterned turban.

"No need to bother, mistress," she said in a soft musical voice. "There be plenty more o' them."

Tilly already held a bundle of blossoms. They were bruised and covered with dirt. "I am so sorry," she said. "I will, of course, pay for them. In fact, I shall take them all."

"That be kind o' you, mistress."

While Tilly fumbled to untie her reticule, Flynn appeared at her side unexpectedly, like a genie from a bottle. "Allow me, Miss Templeton."

He slipped some coins into the woman's hand and took the blooms from her. Lara's face lit with one of her warm smiles. She seemed much more at ease with Tiger Flynn than with her own husband. "How gallant of you, Lucas."

Flynn bowed to her, then to Tilly. "Any man would have done the same," he said charmingly. "Who could resist buying flowers for the fairest flowers in all of Jamaica?"

Lara laughed, the first truly gay and carefree sound Tilly had heard from her since she'd arrived. "Why, Lucas, if I did not know you so well, I would take you for some silver-tongued trifler."

He shot Tilly a sideways look. "Silver-plated over pure brass, is what Miss Templeton is thinking. You have only to look at her countenance to see I am right."

Tilly's cheeks grew crimson. He had read her face—or her mind—quite accurately. She was really going to have to learn to quell her tendency to blush. Flynn cocked his head and grinned.

"You blush charmingly, Miss Templeton. It seems to be a lost art these days."

That put her back up. "It is not an art, but an affliction!" The man was much too sure of himself! "And please, do not put words into my mouth, Mr. Flynn. There is not the slightest need for you to do so."

He sketched her a slight bow. "Exactly my point, Miss Templeton. Your face is like an open book."

Tilly stepped past him quickly without glancing his way again. Lara held him back a moment. "Really, Lucas, must you provoke her so? I saw you earlier, putting her to the blush. I've never known you to act so, and hope you will refrain. I had hoped you would learn to like Miss Templeton, for her sake as much as mine."

Aware that Tilly was still within earshot, Flynn raised his voice even more. "I find Miss Templeton quite to my liking, but from the cool look in those icy gray eyes, she is less kindly disposed toward me."

"That is to be expected, when you keep teasing her so. But that will change, I'm sure, when you've spent a bit more time in one another's company."

The devilish green lights danced in Flynn's eyes. "If you'd like to know the truth, I spent a good deal of time with Miss Templeton last night, attempting to, ah . . . overcome her reserve."

How dared he! Her ears burning, Tilly didn't hear Lara's reply; but the memories his words invoked made her face flame fiercely. She opened the Italian fan that dangled from her wrist and waved it briskly, more to hide her face than for its fragile breeze.

Jonas came out of his inner office. "Why, Miss Templeton, you are suffering from the unaccustomed heat."

Not again! If one more person tells me that, Tilly vowed, *I shall scream.*

She controlled herself with effort. "It is nothing. Only a touch of sun. I am quite well, I assure you."

"I am afraid," Jonas informed Lara, "that I won't be able to accompany you to Crystal Falls this afternoon. A trifling matter of business, but one that demands my personal and immediate attention."

A strange expression, almost of relief, flickered over Lara's delicate features. It came and went so quickly Tilly thought it might have been a trick of the light.

"It is vexing, but of course we understand," Lara said.

Flynn offered his escort for the picnic, in case Jonas should be detained later than expected, and arrangements were made for him to set out with them from the plantation. He assisted Lara into the carriage and turned to aid Tilly. "I do hope you are enjoying Jamaica, Miss Templeton."

She inclined her head with what she hoped was chilling formality. "It is certainly the most amazing place. One feels that anything might happen."

Her response amused him. "We shall, no doubt, discuss it more fully later. Tonight, perhaps."

Tilly fumed. With a grin and a wave, he left them. Lara signaled the groom, and the carriage rolled away. Upon arrival they learned that Lady Steadmore would be delayed.

"If you don't mind," Lara told Tilly, "I think I will lie down for a while and refresh myself before the picnic. I have a bit of a headache today."

Two headaches in two days. Tilly didn't remark on it as she escorted her hostess to her bedroom door. "Shall I fix you a headache powder?"

"Thank you, but lying down in a darkened room is the best remedy."

Tilly went to her chamber, glad for the opportunity to be alone. Without ringing for Agnes, she took off her dress and put on a silk wrapper. A rest didn't tempt her. She wanted to think, not nap. She realized that she had left her reticule in Lara's sitting room and went to get it. If she slipped in quietly, she wouldn't disturb Lara in the next room.

The door was ajar, and the reticule on the table where she had left it. Tilly entered and picked it up. As she was leaving, she noticed the door to Lara's bedchamber was half open. Perhaps she should shut it. She poked her head in to ask.

The bed was made and the room untenanted. From the tall sitting room window, Tilly saw a flash of blue on the terrace below as, with a furtive glance over her shoulder, Lara vanished into the rose arbor.

Tilly returned quickly to her room. Everyone at Coeur d'Émeraude had secrets, it seemed. Even herself. But Lucas Flynn seemed to have the most secrets of all.

She sat in the armchair with the reticule on her lap and reached inside for her nail file. Her fingers curled around something that should not have been there. She pulled the object out. It was a small, chamois bag, secured with a drawstring and filled with what felt like pebbles. She opened it and spilled the contents into her palm, then stared in disbelief.

Not a handful of pebbles, but a fortune in emeralds. Some were natural crystals, perfectly clear or clouded with feathery inclusions. Others were cut en cabochon or simply faceted.

She held them up. The gemstones gathered the sunlight into their hearts until they glowed deeply green. As green and mysterious as tigers' eyes.

Chapter Five

Footsteps came down the hall to the drawing room, and Lara almost dropped her glass of lemonade. "Jonas! I was not expecting you."

He paused in the doorway. "I noticed you seemed a bit upset at the warehouse, and I didn't want to disappoint you, my dear. I'll ride along beside your carriage. That way, if I am needed, I can return without breaking up your party."

Lara was flustered. "I wouldn't wish to take you away from your business affairs at such a time."

"I left Keating in charge. He'll join us at Crystal Falls later." The look Jonas gave his spouse was a searching one. "I hope the change doesn't throw off your plans."

"I am so glad you're able to join us." Despite her assurance, Lara did not look glad at all—in fact, quite the opposite.

From her place in the window seat, Tilly had watched the interchange between husband and wife. It deepened her feelings of uneasiness. At the first sight of her husband, Lara's face had lit up; now that light was gone, and her face was a pale, plaster mask.

If Jonas noticed—and Tilly was sure he had—he didn't comment on it. "Well now, if you ladies are ready, I'll ring for the carriage to be brought round. Unless I am mistaken, Lady Steadmore and her party are arriving now."

Lara twisted her wedding ring around her finger and glanced in the direction of the fireplace screen. "Lucas is to go with us, also. He should have been here some time ago."

"He came up the drive as I stepped onto the portico. I believe he has stopped by the stables to speak with Leander."

Jonas looked bland, but his eyes were hooded by his lids. Lara picked up her bonnet from the sofa and tied the ribbons beneath her chin with hands that were not quite steady. Her color had returned, though, and her voice was almost gay.

"Then we are all set! Come, Tilly, and we shall show you Crystal Falls."

Tilly put on her bonnet and followed her host and hostess to the portico. A light breeze had sprung up, blowing the heat and humidity away. Overhead, the sky was a clear, piercing blue, and the scent of flowers wafted on the air. One of the stable boys held the heads of the perfectly matched bays harnessed to an elegant vehicle.

The dashing carriage, with its exquisite upholstery and shining red wheels, she was certain, could only belong to one man. As if in response to the thought, Flynn appeared around the corner of the drive that led to the stable yard and greeted the others. "What a beautiful afternoon for our expedition," he said.

To Tilly, he added: "The kind of afternoon when anything might happen!"

Her mouth primmed into a thin line. "I believe quite enough has occurred already, at least from my point of view!"

"Indeed?" He took her arm. "Then you must tell me all about it. Later, of course."

She looked daggers at him. "You may be sure I will!"

The trip to the picnic spot was made in two carriages, with the butler and one of the maids following in the buggy. Tilly rode with Flynn, but as they were accompanied by Lady Steadmore and Miss Eggleston, there was no opportunity for private conversation. She had to settle for offering him a cold shoulder when the others were occupied.

Flynn leaned forward. "You are not your usual self. Do you have the headache, Miss Templeton?" he asked solicitously.

"No! Although I am bothered considerably by a rather persistent pain in the neck."

He smiled blandly. "How beautiful the sea is today! As green as emeralds."

Tilly gritted her teeth. What effrontery! He knew that *she* knew that he had hidden the emeralds in her reticule. No one else would have had the opportunity, except for Lara, and that was too ridiculous to even consider. Flynn's impertinence was exceeded only by his audacity!

Flynn was not nearly as composed as he seemed. Just being near her quickened his pulse. With their first kiss last night, he had sensed the untapped passion that lay dormant within her. It had surprised him, then it had aroused him, until he had almost lost sight of where he was, and why. A mistake like that could have proved fatal.

Fatal beauty. The phrase had always made him think of experienced women of the world, those seductive creatures with lush, voluptuous bodies and cold, calculating hearts. Miss Matilda Templeton could not be more opposite. Her unfeigned innocence awakened his protective instincts, but her artless sensuality provoked such wanton needs that it shook him to his foundation. She was a dangerous woman by his way of reckoning. Dangerous to his goals and to his peace of mind.

"What are those peculiar magenta flowers?" Miss Eggleston asked, snapping him out of his distraction. He replied absently at first, until he realized Lady Steadmore was watching him with a great deal of amusement. From then on he applied himself to making pleasant, if very general, conversation.

Further opportunity for private conversation was lost—for which Tilly was extremely grateful. The vehicles turned into the road, but instead of heading toward town, they took a less traveled way. While Lady Steadmore held forth on the latest government squabble, Tilly found herself free to watch the scenery. At first it seemed they were headed inland, but after a bit the cavalcade turned toward the sea. They passed cultivated fields and went along a lane that skirted the banana plantation. Soon the lane diminished to a simple track and entered a wooded area.

Miss Eggleston, who had been trying to attract Flynn's attention, pointed out a tree that was much taller than the others. "What kind of tree is that, Mr. Flynn?"

"It's a duppie tree," he said, with a significant glance at the groom's back.

"A duppie tree?" she echoed doubtfully. "I am not familiar with it. What species of tree is that?"

"It is actually a ceiba, commonly called a silk-cotton tree." He lowered his voice. "The duppies—spirits of the dead—live down among their roots. We must be careful we do not conjure one up."

Miss Eggleston was indignant. "I believe you are making that up to tease me."

Lady Steadmore shivered. "He is telling the truth, at least according to local belief. My own servants will not go past such a tree at night without special protective amulets. They even avoid them by day, whenever possible."

Tilly, who had listened silently, was glad when they broke into more open ground. There *was* something about the silk-cotton. She had felt it. Miss Eggleston had no more questions, and Tilly wondered if she had felt it, too; and when Lady Steadmore changed the conversation, everyone but Flynn seemed to breathe a bit easier. He, it seemed, was not subject to superstitious fancies.

"Lucas," the dowager commanded, "you must tell my niece and Miss Templeton about our annual Isle of Shells race."

"Ah, yes. The race," Flynn explained, "begins with an early morning voyage to the Isle of Shells. We picnic there, and the men exchange veiled taunts while the ladies compete in finding unusual shells. After luncheon we embark again for the second leg of the race, back to Kingston Harbor."

Tilly was captivated. "The Isle of Shells! How enchanting."

"It's quite small with few trees or enticing views, but the sands are paved with the most beautiful shells in the world," the dowager said. "It is quite worth the effort. And for first-time visitors, quite worth the aggravation."

Tilly looked a question at her but it was Flynn who answered. "It is the custom that all newcomers to the isle are put through an initiation of sorts. But of course, we mustn't spoil the fun by giving the secret away. You will have to find out for yourselves."

"Oh," Miss Eggleston said knowledgeably. "Like the practice of putting a dead fish in one's bed on the last night at sea."

Tilly almost burst out in laughter, and Flynn's face was a picture to see. Lady Steadmore gazed at her niece in resignation. "You're a fool, girl. Lucas, tell me about your new yacht."

"*Sea Urchin* is a thirty-foot, copper-hulled beauty, yet two crew can run her if need be. She's the fastest yacht afloat."

Miss Eggleston's mouth opened and there was no doubt she was about to invite herself aboard his yacht for the races. Flynn bestowed a mocking smile on Tilly. "Miss Templeton," he added quickly, "has promised to be my partner and sail with me."

The man had no scruples! Tilly wanted very much to deny his audacious statement; but she wanted even more to sail with him aboard the *Sea Urchin*.

Flynn grinned wickedly, knowing her predicament. She bit her lip. He couldn't help noticing how small and white her teeth were, and the rosy softness of her mouth. Remembering the taste of her lips and the way they had yielded to his kiss, he determined to repeat the process before the day was out.

Tilly felt herself blushing. She knew exactly what he was thinking, as if he'd said it aloud. Try as she might to deny it, there was a sympathetic connection between them, a silent vibration that tuned their thoughts to the same note. She was both fascinated and alarmed. Being alone with him was dangerous yet she had to speak with him privately. In fact, she meant to find out why he'd put the emeralds in her reticule, and just what she was supposed to do about it. And then she'd give him a good piece of her mind. His charm wouldn't save him from that!

The carriage had turned into a pleasant copse. Picnic cloths were already spread beneath the trees. While the china and silver were set out Tilly tried to signal Flynn that she wanted to speak with him alone. He leaned forward solicitously.

"Is there something in your eye, Miss Templeton? You are blinking most ferociously."

"No, there is nothing in my eye, Mr. Flynn." She lowered her voice. "But there is something very much on my mind."

He offered her his arm. "A little stroll before luncheon does much to soothe a ruffled mind."

"I am more than ruffled, I am incensed!"

"Come along, then." He led her away from the others, along the banks of a wide stream.

Beneath the feathered canopies of overhanging trees the banks were clothed in ferns and flowers. Droplets of mist adorned the nodding ferns, like strings of transparent pearls. A short distance away the stream bubbled and splashed into a deep, mossy-rimmed pool, as clear as rock crystal. There was an air of magic about it, as if Titania and Oberon might peek out from beneath a leaf at any moment. Tilly reluctantly shook off its enchantment and went to the heart of the matter.

"Mr. Flynn, I demand to know why you—"

"Not here, Miss Templeton, if you value your lovely little neck." He took her arm and guided her farther along the track. To the casual onlooker it would appear he was escorting her in a gentlemanly way; only Tilly knew she was caught like a hare in a steel trap. She had no choice but to go with him. The alternative was to dig in her heels and scream at the top of her lungs, an action that would attract all the attention she wished to avoid.

The soft trickling of water changed to a splashing fountain as they followed the streambed. Flynn parted the low-hanging branches and they stepped through into a miniature paradise. The falls rose above the stream in seven magnificent tiers that plunged from the heart of the dark cliffs. Shimmering veils of water flowed through sun-dappled pools and over mossy ledges, then rushed past them, down to the distant sea. It was exquisite, and it took Tilly's breath away. Then she remembered her purpose.

"When you dragged me away from the others so roughly," she said, rubbing her arm, "I didn't realize it was to view the scenery."

"Ah, but this is the perfect place for a little tête-à-tête. We can't be heard over the thunder of the falls. I didn't mean to frighten you."

"I was not at all frightened," she snapped defiantly.

With her gray eyes alight and her cheeks flushed, she looked magnificent. Flynn's long fingers closed over her hand. "Do you know what I most admire about you, Miss Templeton?"

"No! And I don't care to know!"

"Your spirit," he went on, as if she had not interrupted. "Your hasty temper, of course, leaves something to be desired."

"I am generally thought to have a calm and mild disposition," she protested sharply. "There was no need to bruise me. I would have walked along with you if you had asked me."

"Forgive my brash behavior, my dear, but I thought it best to remove you from the others as soon as possible. I was quite sure you were about to say something, uh, shall we say *unwise*?"

"If you are referring to the emeralds, which I have no doubt *you* foisted upon me—"

"What?" He grabbed her by the shoulders and held her. "What are you saying?"

"I am referring to the bag of emeralds you slipped into my reticule while we were at the warehouse this morning! Or did you think me so stupid that I wouldn't realize you were the culprit?"

There was a strange, speculative look in his eyes. "I see," he said at last. "Very well, Miss Templeton. You have them, and I—" He broke off abruptly.

"Follow my lead. We are being watched." Without warning he pulled her into his arms and kissed her. She was caught off guard. He held her close, her arms pinned against her sides, and whispered in her ear. "Don't stand there like a stone, show a little interest! We are under surveillance."

Tilly was suspicious until she looked at him. Whatever he was about, it wasn't mere dalliance. His face was deadly serious. He moved his mouth near her ear again, and his warm breath tickled.

"I know you don't believe me, Miss Templeton, but it's imperative."

"That seems to be a favorite refrain of yours!"

She had no time to argue further. A twig snapped somewhere behind them, and she found herself locked in a crushing embrace. Thoughts of unknown lives in jeopardy fragmented and dissolved with his nearness. His lips brushed along her temple and her cheek before claiming hers, and she was no longer able to think of a single argument against it: the touch of his mouth rendered her incapable of thinking.

Impressions mingled. The hard strength and warmth of his body, the slight roughness of his cheek against hers, the light tingle of his breath against her skin, all clouded her senses. His hand pressed against the small of her back, drawing her closer into his embrace. Her mouth clung to his and her fingers curled around the edges of his collar as she lifted her face to him. His kisses grew more demanding, and she responded in kind. The world narrowed to the enclosing circle of his arms, and the sound of the waterfall merged and blended with the rhythm of her own heart.

The blood drummed in Flynn's ears, and his desire rose. She was so open, so giving—so completely unaware of what she was doing to him. To herself. For years he had thought himself immune, but she had pierced through his defenses in a way no other woman had before. He broke the contact, dragging his mouth reluctantly from hers.

Tilly was dazed and shaken. It had happened again. The habits of a lifetime, and all her fine resolutions, vanished like smoke when he touched her. She realized her arms were wound around his neck, though she had no recollection of putting them there. Her lips felt bruised from his kisses, yet they yearned for more. Her hands fluttered to her throat, as she stepped back a pace in confusion.

Flynn watched the emotions flit across her candid features. The light in his eyes changed as the heat left them. He cupped her face between his hands. The gravity of his face underscored the serious tone of his voice.

"You deserve explanations, Tilly, but I can't give them. Not yet. I'm a scoundrel for drawing you into this, but it's too late now. I'm asking you to trust me for a few more days."

She tried to read his face, and could not. "Without giving me a single reason as to why I should do so?"

"Not the slightest." His green eyes warmed. "But I promise I'll tell you everything soon. Meanwhile, I'm going to need those emeralds if I'm to extricate us from this mire. Will you trust me with them?"

The look in his eyes made her legs grow wobbly, and the note in his voice unnerved her. She tried to clear her brain. Hadn't Jonas said it last night? Flynn was a dangerous man. He had the charm and address of a practiced rake, and a reputation to match. He had come to her room like a thief in the night, hidden gemstones on her person and kissed her without a by-your-leave on two separate occasions. He had embroiled her, without her permission, in a hazardous game without telling her the goal—or the rules.

And yet, at least for the moment, she felt as if she would trust him to the ends of the earth. "If you won't go into details, at least confirm my own deductions. The emeralds were smuggled into Jamaica, which is why this whole thing has been hushed up. And I was used as an unwitting courier, to get them away from the warehouse unnoticed."

He scrutinized her face long and seriously, as if trying to anticipate her reaction before answering. Then the twinkle came into his eyes. "That's a fair way of putting it."

His frankness was unexpected. She thought his admission over for a bit. "I'm beginning to see. Their disappearance was the real reason that Jonas stayed behind this morning."

"Yes."

"And they . . . are they stolen?"

"In a manner of speaking."

"What do you mean to do with them?"

He regarded her with mock dismay. "What a lot of questions you have! And what an insult that last one was, to my integrity. Once I have them in my possession, I intend to return them to their rightful owner, as soon as possible. Until then, you will have to trust me."

She moved away from him, frowning in concentration.

Tilly struggled with herself. She had blundered blindly into the middle of this mystery and was operating in the dark. She was convinced that Flynn was no more a thief than she was. But then what *was* he? And *who* was he? And what in the world had she gotten herself into?

She might be a gullible fool—but if she had to trust one of them, she would chose Flynn over Jonas every time. "Very well."

Flynn clasped her hands. "Good girl! I knew you wouldn't let me down."

She shook her head ruefully. "I am sure I will have cause to regret it."

"Not if I have any say in the matter." He put his hand beneath her elbow and began escorting her back toward their party. "We'd better get back to the others before our absence causes comment."

"And the emeralds?"

"Sh!" He put a finger over her lips, then traced their outline with his fingertip. "I'll meet you tonight, when the others are asleep."

"Where?"

He leaned down and whispered in her ear, his voice low and laughter-filled. "Where, my dear? Why, the usual place!"

"You cannot come to my room again. It would be foolhardy to take such risk."

His smile warmed her to the core. "I'm gratified to know you're concerned about me."

Tilly frowned. "Are you never serious? Frankly, I'm more concerned for my own reputation and safety."

"Are you?"

Those curious green eyes dazzled her and she looked away. Flynn chuckled. "You are a lovely little liar, but not a very convincing one."

They made their way along the stream. She was right, of course. There was really no reason for him to risk coming to her bedchamber—at least, not a valid one. "Bring your little package with you to the governor's ball tonight. I'll arrange for us to be alone a few minutes, after the dancing is over but before the late supper begins."

Her relief was palpable. "In the meantime, what am I to do with the . . . er . . . ?"

"Nothing. Don't worry about the gems. They may be temporarily in your possession, but they are my responsibility. As long as they're concealed in your room, they're safe for a few more hours."

"Oh, but . . ."

Mr. Keating's voice, faint with distance, broke the silence. "Miss Templeton? I say, are you lost?"

A flash of white shirt showed through the ferns ahead, but Keating turned off in another direction. A sprig of orchids swayed, although there was no breeze. Flynn glanced around but saw nothing. "I'll take you as far as the clearing but it will look better if we return separately."

"Are you concerned with your reputation, Mr. Flynn, or mine?"

His face was enigmatic. "At the moment, neither."

They retraced their steps toward the pool and along the shadowed path. Suddenly Flynn stopped dead and spun her back the way they had come.

"Don't move," he ordered, "and don't look!"

"I already have." Tilly glanced over her shoulder and struggled for composure. "It's nothing but a dead chicken. I *have* seen dead chickens before."

"But not like this."

"No..." She had often seen barnyard hens with their necks wrung for the cooking pot; but never a white cockerel, with colored ribbons on its stiffened claws, its throat a horrible ruby slit.

Flynn's eyes narrowed. This was no fresh kill. Someone was trying to frighten his companion, either to make her cut short her visit or to keep her from exploring on her own. *Therefore*, he thought, *someone who knows Miss Templeton well enough to be aware of her curiosity and spirit*. He kicked the remains behind the ferns.

"Despite their Christian baptisms, many Jamaicans cling to the old religions and practice a mixture of both. Forget this happened, Miss Templeton. Mention it to no one."

"It is not," she said witheringly, "the kind of thing I would be likely to mention in ordinary society. Particularly at lunch."

He grinned at that and released her. "You are yourself again. A remarkably quick recovery."

Tilly heard a rustle of ferns and turned, startled. There was just a glimpse of movement, the flash of lemon that might have been a brightly feathered bird—or a piece of yellow patterned fabric—vanishing among the fronds.

"Look!" she said. "Over there! That bright yellow."

"The encounter has upset you. It was only a bird," Flynn said, and took her arm once more. "One of the hummingbirds that are everywhere. It has flown away."

Mr. Keating called out again, this time from much nearer. Biting back a retort, Tilly instead pondered Flynn's response. From his height and vantage point, he would have had a much clearer view than she had; and whatever had fled, it was no more a bird than she was. She kept her own counsel, silently adding to her list of questions to be answered when the day of explanation finally arrived. It couldn't be too soon for her.

They were back at the clearing. Flynn indicated she should go first, and Tilly slipped between two trees, pretending to admire the purple and white wildflowers blooming at their feet. As she stooped to pick a handful, she realized she hadn't corrected Flynn's erroneous assumption: the emeralds were hidden safely away, but not in her chamber. Presently they were nestled, in their little silken bag, between her breasts. Although she desperately wanted to be rid of them, she certainly couldn't undo her bodice and hand them over now.

Flynn had circled to the side of the picnic area, and was already engaged in handing out glasses of lemonade to the ladies. How did he move so quickly, and so silently?

Tilly moved into the periphery, gradually insinuating herself into the group. She sat on one of the cushions provided and helped herself to a bit of thinly shaved ham.

Her mouth felt tingly and full, and she knew her cheeks were still flushed with excitement. Did she look like a young woman who had just been thoroughly kissed? Or one who was carrying a fortune in emeralds on her person?

Tilly was glad to see that the other guests were all occupied. They didn't appear to have noticed either her defection or return. Miss Eggleston, blue eyes wide with admiration, was listening raptly to one of Mr. Keating's stories, while Lady Steadmore was more interested in wiping a bit of meringue crumb from her navy bombazine skirt. Lara was on the opposite side of the meadow, calling to her husband. When he didn't appear, she shrugged her shoulders daintily and joined the others.

Just as Tilly was congratulating herself on carrying it off well, she felt Lady Steadmore's gimlet eye upon her. She smiled disarmingly at the dowager and picked up a plate. "May I recommend these macaroons, ma'am? They are light as clouds."

Lady Steadmore ignored the delicately browned confections. "Why, Miss Templeton, your gown is quite damp with spray. I hope you didn't wander too close to the falls and those terrible rocks. For all its romantic aspects, such places can prove perilous."

She met the older woman's gaze steadily. "Thank you for your consideration, ma'am, but do not be concerned for me. I am always careful to watch my step."

The dowager nodded. "An excellent habit. Caution can prevent accidents, both away and at home as well. I've taken a liking to you, girl, and I would not wish you to come to any harm.''

Tilly merely smiled and took another bite of ham. What had prompted that veiled but definite warning? The aristocratic dowager was shrewd and knowledgeable about the world. Perhaps those sharp eyes had noticed that all was not as it seemed on the surface at Coeur d'Émeraude. More likely, Tilly thought, her own imagination had invested the words with their ominous note. But the riddle woven around Coeur d'Émeraude was a human one, and not a product of her imagination.

A little chill of premonition ran up the backs of her arms and she shifted uneasily. Tilly jumped as something tickled her cheek, thinking it was an insect. It was only a tendril of hair, which had come loose from her side comb. She pushed it behind her ear, but it refused to stay. Reaching into her reticule for a spare hairpin, her hand encountered a long, thin piece of metal. Surprised, Tilly pulled the object out. It was her fork.

She thrust her hand in again and raised the reticule. In place of the handkerchief, pins and other feminine necessities, there was nothing inside—except her hand. The reticule had been neatly slit down the side and the contents extracted. It must have happened about the time they'd found the slain cockerel. There had been that flash of yellow fabric, which Flynn had denied seeing. An unwelcome idea intruded. Flynn could have done it earlier, when he'd kissed her. She tried to remember if he'd moved his hands away from her waist or back, but couldn't. The only thing she recalled was the sweet, giddy excitement he stirred within her.

Mr. Keating had been watching. ''Why, Miss Templeton, you have torn your reticule on a sharp twig.''

''More likely a bit of rock,'' Lady Steadmore said. ''The edges are neat as a knife cut. We shall have to retrace your steps, Miss Templeton.''

Tilly didn't dare look at Flynn. ''There's no need to bother,'' she said. ''There was nothing of value in it.''

She took another macaroon from the plate before her. The chamois bag shifted between her breasts as she moved. The concealed emeralds suddenly felt as heavy as millstones.

Jonas checked his watch. "It is four of the clock, my dear."

"We had best be getting back," Lara announced, "or there will be no time for a rest before the ball."

Lady Steadmore nodded vigorously. "Yes, child, I'm an old woman now, and look to my naps with more anticipation than I do to a mere dance." She gave Tilly a friendly nod. "But I'm sure it is quite otherwise with you, Miss Templeton."

Tilly laughed. "With more eagerness, ma'am, than you can possibly imagine!"

The picnic party split up, and this time Flynn rode in the other carriage. Tilly was rather relieved. Under the circumstances, it would have been difficult to carry on a normal conversation with him in the presence of others.

The dowager and her niece were both too sleepy for talking, and Tilly could hardly wait to escape to the privacy of her room. She had always been up at dawn and in Yorkshire the entire household had retired by ten o'clock—even earlier on dark winter days, thanks to Durward's miserliness, to save candles and firewood. Here, no society lady rose until the sun was up for several hours and the Governor's Ball didn't even begin until ten. If she meant to dance all night a nap was indicated.

It was not to be.

Lady Steadmore dropped Tilly off at Coeur d'Émeraude. "We will not come in, child. At my age it takes too much energy to descend the carriage, only to have to make the effort to climb in once more within such a short time!"

"I suspect, ma'am, that you have more energy than a woman half your years, and that you use your age as a convenient excuse when it suits you."

Lady Steadmore laughed aloud. "Saw through my excuse, did you? You're a sharp-eyed gel, Miss Templeton. I told Lara that you were a noticing one!'' She waved languidly and was off.

The carriage bearing Lara and Flynn, which had detoured to drop Mr. Keating near the overseer's house, was just visible past the curve in the drive and Jonas had ridden round to the stables. It was too hot outside in the bright sunlight to wait for them. Tilly entered, to find the house in an uproar.

A gilt chair, from an alcove at the head of the stairs, lay on its side in the middle of the foyer. Shards of broken glass and porcelain littered the floor. Bernard, the unflappable butler, was shouting to one of the footmen, and a frightened parlormaid had just whisked out of sight around a corner.

At first Tilly thought one of the servants had accidentally broken something, and she hurried toward the staircase, in order to spare them embarrassment. She soon realized her error. Loud, angry voices penetrated through a closed door from the upper landing. As Tilly paused halfway up, a door banged open on the floor above and a gaunt, shabbily dressed man came hurtling down the steps.

"You won't get away with this," he shouted shrilly. "You can't keep me here!"

He rushed past Tilly without even seeing her, almost knocking her off her feet. A reflexive grasp at the railing saved her from a bad fall. She turned to watch the unfolding drama. The man reached the front door before coming to an unsteady halt. Whirling about, he staggered across the foyer.

Bernard flung the door open and Jonas entered, his stocky form outlined in the doorway. "Stop him!"

The order was unnecessary. The wild eyes rolled up in the thin face, and the man suddenly crumpled. Bernard and the footman were there to catch him as he fell. He was thin as a knife blade, but heavy-boned, and they were unable to maintain his weight.

"Lower him to the floor and send for Leander!" Jonas commanded. "He must be back by now!"

In the midst of this commotion the second carriage, bearing Lara and Flynn, arrived. With a cry of alarm, Lara jumped from the carriage, not waiting for assistance.

"Oh, Jonas! What has happened?"

Her husband answered curtly without looking up. "As you can see, my dear, your brother has come home."

Tilly was horrified. The emaciated giant bore little resemblance to the Christopher Burlinghome she had known so many years before. What tragedy had befallen him in the intervening years? He looked desperately ill. Then she noticed the strong odor of brandy he exuded with every unconscious breath.

The situation was extremely awkward. Tilly had no wish to intrude on their private family grief, but her way was blocked by two menservants bent on descending the staircase to help. She retreated to the foyer to let them pass and found herself trapped in a corner. There was no way to withdraw without stepping over Christopher.

A shadow fell across the prone man as Flynn entered and strode into the breach. "Is his room prepared?"

The butler gave a dignified nod. "It is always prepared."

"Excellent. Lead the way."

Flynn scooped Lara's brother up in his arms and, with a deft twist, threw him over his shoulder. The butler stood goggling at him, and Flynn raised his eyebrows. "Well?"

Bernard crossed in front of him and started up the stairs. Lara followed agitatedly, while Jonas did his best to calm her. Tilly waited until they reached the upper landing and began her own ascent.

The bizarre parade had reached a room at the far end of the corridor when Tilly opened the door to her chamber and stopped in astonishment. Despite the blazing sunlight from the open windows, it seemed to be snowing inside. Huge white flakes floated mothlike through the air, slowly settling to the floor, until a vagrant breeze started them up again. Tilly stepped inside. Not snow, but the entire contents of her pillows and the soft down coverlet. Feathers and bits of down sifted everywhere.

For a moment she was paralyzed. The room smelled strongly of perfume, and everything was in disarray. Garments of every description littered the floor. Her nightgowns and lingerie were crumpled together with scarves and gloves and evening shawls. Someone had ransacked the wardrobe and dressers and emptied every drawer upon the floor. Not content with ransacking the room, someone had wantonly ripped out hems and cuffs and wrenched off the heels of her boots and shoes.

Like a sleepwalker, Tilly went slowly to the center of the room, not bothering to close the door. The chaos was brutal and vicious. Books were open, face down upon the floor, some with their covers torn off or their spines slit. Her cutglass scent bottles lay on their sides, their contents evaporating quickly in the warm air. The inkstand on the desk was tipped over, and tendrils of dark fluid had dripped off the edge and splattered on her French silk dressing gown.

Nothing had escaped. A mound of pearly face powder streaked her ruined riding habit, and the floor glittered where minute flecks drifted in wispy patterns, like a discarded veil. She stooped to pick up the bed jacket it had taken her so long to embroider, and when she saw how it had been slashed, her hands shook so violently she dropped it.

All her life she had dreamed of owning beautiful things, and now they had been brutally destroyed. Tilly was torn between tears and outrage. She felt violated and vulnerable, and incredibly furious. What had she ever done to deserve such viciousness? Who could hate her so much? For the havoc had been deliberately, maliciously...

A sound made her whirl around. Flynn stood in the doorway, his face dark with anger. As he crossed the room to her side she faced him with brimming eyes, barely able to speak for the knot in her throat. She tried to say something. All that came out was a sob and a single word: *"Why?"*

Flynn drew her in his arms and she burst into tears. His embrace tightened while she fought for control, clinging to him desperately. An aura of protection and solid strength enfolded her, but she sensed his anger was as great as hers. After a minute she tried to pull away, embarrassed by her reaction.

Flynn would not let her get too far. He held her by the shoulders as she mastered her tears, and handed her his linen handkerchief to wipe them away. "Are you all right?"

"I suppose so. But I can't understand who would do this, or why!"

"I can," he said quietly. "This has distressed you greatly, but can you tell me if anything significant is missing?"

She was so upset she didn't grasp his meaning. "Nothing irreplaceable. Except for my composure and peace of mind!"

Comprehension dawned. "Oh." Tilly wiped her eyes and blew her nose angrily. "If you will turn your head, I will retrieve the emeralds and give them to you." A moment later she turned back and pressed a pouch into his hand. "I don't care what you do with these, as long as I never have to set eyes on them again!"

His fingers closed over hers. "Miss Templeton, you are a remarkable women." He picked her up and swung her around. "A pearl beyond price. When this is over, I shall buy you a new wardrobe that will be the talk of the town."

Tilly drew herself to her full height. He knew as well as she did that no self-respecting woman could accept clothing from a man who was not related to her.

"If I did anything so improper, my reputation would be the main subject of conversation. I will have to decline your generous offer, Mr. Flynn."

Her upbraiding didn't have the desired effect. A smile flickered at the corners of his mouth and set his eyes alight. She could not have been more indignant if he'd asked her to take her clothes off. Flynn leaned against the mantelpiece and studied Tilly. One moment she was fragile and feminine as a china doll, the next an ice queen no higher than his shoulder.

"Little prude! It's your finances I was considering, not your morals. My only intention was to replace the loss you've incurred because of me."

She flushed to the roots of her hair. "If I jumped to any unseemly conclusions, it is only to be expected under the stress of the circumstances. Circumstances, I might point out, that are more your doing than mine!"

Flynn's laughter spilled over into his voice. "Apology accepted."

He strolled over to her and clasped her hand in between his. "Ring for your maid. You'll be more comfortable when your room is set to rights again. And you can rest assured there won't be any repetition of this type of disaster."

She tried to withdraw her hand. "The room can wait, while you inform me exactly what *other* type of disasters I should expect in the near future."

"None at all." His grip tightened. "Whoever searched this room and caused this destruction must have known that the stones were slipped into your reticule without your knowledge. Since the emeralds were not found in your chamber or in your reticule, they will assume that I have already retrieved them—without your knowledge. They will come after me next."

"You have a ready answer for everything, it seems. But your glibness didn't save me from this! Had I been here, I might have been murdered!"

He looked at her intently, and his strange green-gold eyes burned like flames. Tilly had never seen him so stern, so dangerous. She turned away abruptly and tugged the bell-pull, then paced agitatedly among the wreckage.

He wished he could erase the frown between her brows and ease her mind. "Don't fret so, my dear. No harm will come to you while I'm around."

Running the back of his hand down Tilly's cheek, Flynn bestowed one of his blinding smiles on her.

"That's better," he encouraged. "I think you've earned the right to be told just what has been going on. If you'll meet me tonight at the ball—there is a small, little-used salon on the second floor, with the engraving of Wellington and the Meet at Melton. I'll meet you there at midnight. Don't fail me."

"I would not miss it for all the tea in China! Or," she amended in a lower tone, "all the emeralds in Jamaica."

He raised her hand to his lips and kissed her fingers. His mouth was soft and warm against her skin. This gentle tenderness was far removed from his more passionate caresses, but equally potent.

Flynn seemed to be under the same spell. His eyes held hers. Slowly, deliberately, he turned her hand over and dropped a kiss into her palm. The jolt that shot up her arm seemed to explode in her brain and midsection simultaneously. She was melting, like a candle in the sun.

Suddenly he dropped her hand and stood back. Agnes came hurrying in, then stopped short. "Oh, miss! What has happened? Who has done such a wicked thing? And look at your poor gowns! And your slippers!"

She swooped down and began gathering up armfuls of silks and linen, making distressed clucking sounds. Tilly, struggling to recover her composure, was relieved that no answer was expected. "I'll set some of the chambermaids to righting this," Agnes promised, picking up a nightgown of sheer muslin.

There was nothing more that Flynn could do here. He made a formal bow, but Tilly saw he was still flushed beneath his tan.

"Now that your maid has come, Miss Templeton, I will leave you in her capable hands. I'm very sorry you had to endure such a distressing episode. I do trust you'll be able to rest this afternoon, before the ball."

She clutched his sleeve with her fingertips. "You will be there?"

"You may count on it, Miss Templeton. Just as you may always count on me."

There was a swish of skirts and a gasp from the doorway. Lara stood there, one hand pressed to her mouth. "What has happened here?"

"Someone," Flynn said, "has torn Miss Templeton's room apart."

Lara's dark eyes widened in distress. "This is my fault, Lucas!"

With a glance at Agnes's energetic form, he stepped toward her quickly and grasped her wrist. "Naturally you are distressed, in your position as mistress of the house. But how you can blame yourself for the depredations of an intruder—one whom none of the servants heard or saw climbing through the balcony—is beyond me."

A look passed between them that Tilly could not decipher, but Flynn's meaning was clear, at least to her. He was telling Lara to hold her tongue. It worked. With a visible effort, Lara forced herself to become the proper hostess once again. She smiled weakly, and Flynn nodded encouragement.

"I will leave you ladies to your domestic arrangements, and look forward to seeing you at the ball tonight."

After he left Lara seemed nervous again. The reason was obvious: not knowing about the emeralds Tilly had been carrying, Lara had jumped to the wrong conclusion and thought her brother had caused the destruction in her bedchamber.

"Flynn was correct," Tilly said briskly. "It is most unfortunate, but you could not have foreseen such an incident. Fortunately, I had no real valuables to tempt the thief, and he took his frustration out upon my belongings."

Lara seemed about to speak, and Tilly took her arm, leading her toward the door. "There is no need for you to linger. You have your hands full with other matters, but perhaps you might send up one of the undermaids to assist Agnes."

"Of course. Thank you." Lara hurried away, but not before Tilly saw the tears that glittered in her eyes. Marriage and Jamaica had transformed a merry, bubbly girl into a haunted, jittery young woman. The change was alarming.

Tilly felt a headache coming on. So many peculiar things had happened to her since the first moment she'd met Flynn. Her mind was whirling with jaguar masks and emeralds, fairy falls and mutilated cockerels and ransacked rooms. Chaos seemed to follow in his wake, catching up everyone and everything he touched.

His touch. Her skin still tingled with it, and her palm still burned from the imprint of his lips. She curled her fingers against her palm and let the tips rest where his mouth had touched. Thinking of him, remembering the way he had looked at her, made Tilly's heart accelerate. She stood in the center of the room for several minutes before noticing that Agnes was watching her with great curiosity.

Tilly shook off the mood and began salvaging what she could from the ruins. Her second-best ball gown had escaped the carnage with only a few powder stains. That was some comfort. She wanted to look her best for her first real ball. Tonight she would be formally introduced to the inner circle of British society and whirl around the vast ballroom—she hoped—in the arms of several charming and handsome men. All of whom, when she tried to envision them, looked exactly like Tiger Flynn.

She sighed without being aware she'd done so, and retrieved a pair of pearl earrings from the floor. Flynn had said that no harm would come to her as long as he was near.

But—a nagging little voice asked in her head—who would keep her safe when he wasn't?

Chapter Six

Tilly fastened a pair of dazzling diamond earrings to her lobes and tilted her head to see the effect. The stones glittered like ice crystals in the candlelight, and darted rainbow fire with the slightest movement. The earrings had been her mother's, and though their style was old-fashioned, the antique settings suited Tilly.

At the moment, on the brink of her first ball, she had no thoughts of Durward's miserliness. She was wishing her mother could have lived to see this night. The first gong sounded. Lara and Jonas would be waiting for her in the drawing room but Agnes was still rummaging through one of the cupboards.

"What is it, Agnes?"

"Your shawl of Norwich silk is gone, miss! One of those heathen servants has stolen it!"

Tilly whirled, astonished at the bitter accusation. "You are mistaken. One of the undermaids took it away to try her hand at removing a spot."

The news did not mollify Agnes. Her thin face turned an angry mottled red. Once she had been a provincial upstairs maid, but years of watching and learning and pushing her way forward had paid off when she became first a ladies' maid then a very superior dresser. She was very conscious of her station and jealous of her duties.

Being forced to wait upon Tilly instead of her mistress had, she was sure, already lowered her status; and now her responsibilities were being given over to the servants she considered her inferiors. It was, in Agnes's narrow mind, a direct slap in the face. Her petty antagonism toward Tilly hardened into frank and implacable hostility. Mouth hard and eyes glittering, the dresser put a spangled shawl over Tilly's arms.

Agnes knew all the tricks and aggravations: the unnecessarily sharp tugs while dressing a lady's hair, the unexplained snags in expensive silk stockings, the French perfume that seemed to evaporate so quickly, even the spider in the flower-sprigged water pitcher. And Agnes would see that Miss Templeton would soon know all, too, she decided sourly. Of course, nothing that could be blamed directly on herself.

Unaware of the plans swirling in the dresser's mind, Tilly went down to join her hosts for dinner. George Keating stood before the tall windows with them, a drink in his hand. He set it down when he saw her and came forward to take her hand. Formal evening clothes showed off his fair good looks to advantage, but his wide smile and warm greeting didn't affect her the same way as one of Flynn's sardonic grins.

But then, nothing did.

No one else had Flynn's way of lighting up a room or filling the air with crackling excitement. Tilly knew she'd enjoy the coming meal much more if he was to be her dinner partner. She greeted her hosts. There were fresh lines of strain at the corners of Jonas's mouth. He looked grim. Lara, though ethereally beautiful in cascades of lace and ropes of incredible pink pearls, seemed distracted. Tilly wondered if they had been quarreling.

Lara seemed to recall herself with an effort. She came up to Tilly, her hands extended. "You look radiant," she said in low tones. "I am so glad that the upsetting events of the day haven't affected your spirits."

"What is this?" Keating asked, overhearing. "Has there been trouble?"

"A minor domestic disturbance," Lara said, turning away.

Jonas put his hand on her shoulder. "No need to dissemble with George, my dear. He is more or less one of the family."

Lara lapsed into embarrassed silence, and her husband filled his partner in. "The afternoon was a disaster. We returned to discover that Miss Templeton's chamber had been disarranged and some damage done to her wardrobe."

"Servant trouble at Coeur d'Émeraude? I wouldn't have expected it here, of all places."

Jonas frowned. "Nor I. It was not a servant who ransacked Miss Templeton's room. We searched the grounds but could find no trace of the intruder. I've set Leander and some others to watch the house tonight."

Tilly's heart pounded. Jonas thought it was an ordinary thief who'd turned her room upside down, but she was sure the intruder had come with one purpose in mind: to find the emeralds. Thank God she'd given them to Flynn. Now they were his worry. But when she thought of the grief they'd caused her, she could hardly forgive him for foisting them upon her in the first place. She couldn't wait to corner him at the governor's ball and get some answers from him.

Keating was asking about Lara's brother when she rejoined the conversation. Jonas set his glass on a walnut side table with a sharp thump. "Christopher returned home today unexpectedly and in poor health. He collapsed in the foyer at Miss Templeton's feet."

Keating was instantly all concern. "I hope it is not serious."

Lara flushed. "He contracted malaria several years ago, and suffers recurrent bouts of it."

Tilly lowered her lashes. It was the first time she'd heard that the strong odor of brandy upon a man's breath was a symptom of malaria.

The conversation had put a damper on the group. Dinner was announced and they dined in oppressive splendor in the Gold Dining Room. Many-branched candle holders of Venetian glass gleamed at each end of the long table, and the porcelain and gold plate shone in their soft light, but shadows swallowed up the high ceiling and the corners of the room.

Now and then Tilly caught the flash of her own diamonds in the curve of a stemmed goblet or the silver serving dishes. Their places were so widely separated that easy conversation was impossible. Eventually nothing shattered the silence but the ring of fork and knife upon bone china.

It was the longest meal of Tilly's life. Perhaps the Whitbys were always so formal on special occasions, but she found it terribly awkward. If only it was Flynn sitting across from her, his mouth curving up and green eyes glinting with amusement! He'd share her feelings of absurdity at being isolated in the center of the enormous table. Why, with Flynn an entire conversation could take place without a single word being uttered!

When the servants withdrew, Keating broke the silence. "I've been thinking of the unpleasantness in your room, Miss Templeton. Have you discovered any particular valuables missing?"

Tilly shook her head. "No. My jewel case was intact."

"How fortunate—especially with earrings as lovely and valuable as those you're wearing tonight."

Panic flushed her cheeks. "Perhaps I returned too soon, and almost surprised him in the act."

Jonas finished off his wine, looking at her steadily over the rim. "Perhaps."

He rang for the butler and ordered the carriage brought around.

The sky was black velvet, strewn with stars. It was a perfect night for the ball, and as they neared their destination, Tilly was filled with the expectation of dancing with Lucas Flynn. Her feelings toward him were confused. She could not deny her strong attraction to him, yet when they were apart she was embarrassed at how readily she had responded to him. She had no experience to guide her, and wondered if she would have reacted the same way to Mr. Keating's embrace. Somehow, she doubted it.

She looked at him from beneath her lashes as he spoke with Lara. He was handsome, well-formed and very much a gentleman. She could no more imagine him climbing over balconies than . . . Nothing came to her. Tilly couldn't imagine him doing anything out of the ordinary. George Keating was everything that was respectable and proper. She was beginning to believe that she was not.

The carriage slowed to a crawl. Light spilled from the open doorway ahead as the vehicle inched its way forward, behind a long line of others.

"Oh," Lara exclaimed. "There is Mrs. Thorne approaching the entrance. How smart she looks in that red crepe!"

The lady in question was escorted by a dashing young officer in full dress. Her shimmering gown had a daring décolletage and the unmistakable stamp of Paris in every elegant line. Tilly was surprised that a widow with only a modest jointure could afford such splendor.

Their carriage inched forward until they were second from the lamplit entrance. The vehicle ahead disgorged a trio of laughing redheads in clouds of white gauze sashed with pastel ribbons. A tall woman with coils of dark auburn hair accompanied them. They seemed to float effortlessly along the runner that stretched to the door like nymphs gliding through a forest. Tilly was enchanted.

"What a charming picture they make. Who are they?"

"The McDonnel sisters and their aunt," Lara said. "Americans, and quite delightful. Not a feather to fly with, yet she always turns them out in style. Despite their lack of fortune, they never lack for suitors. Mrs. McDonnel is an old friend of Lucas Flynn's."

Tilly made a wry face. There didn't seem to be a woman in Jamaica who wasn't. There was no further opportunity to talk. The carriage stopped before the runner, the steps were let down, and Jonas alighted to assist the ladies. Soon they joined the colorful throng in the vestibule waiting their turn for the reception line. The governor could not have been more charming, and welcomed Tilly warmly.

"Your uncle, Oliver Hannaford, and I have been friends since we were sent up to Oxford together," he told her, and extended an invitation to a coming garden party.

They moved along the reception line and eventually reached the ballroom. Masses of flowers trailed from marble columns flanking the doors, and the long chamber was filled with the brilliant pageantry of Kingston's high society. As they passed among the crowd, one elderly woman raised her lorgnette and stared at Tilly as if she were a rare specimen of insect.

"That is surely the new heiress," she said in a voice that carried. "Not a classic beauty, but quite presentable."

"But my dear Mrs. Cliffton," a sultry voice answered, "it is widely said that *all* heiresses are beautiful."

There were titters of laughter but Tilly kept her head high as Lara and Jonas guided her through the crowd. She would not deign to let show that she recognized the speaker—but that voice had belonged to Mrs. Thorne. Tilly's palm itched to slap the woman. Other people glanced at her, but their eyes held only curiosity.

"You mustn't mind," Lara said. "Within our constricted circle, any new face causes comment. Especially," she added with a meaningful smile, "when that face belongs to a beautiful and eligible woman. Oh, look! Lady Steadmore is waving to us."

Knots of people gave way to let them through, naval officers in full dress, ambassadors beribboned and bemedaled, debutantes in sweet pastels and older women in exquisite, and expensive, gowns. Jewels sparkled and gleamed as brightly as the massive chandeliers, and the entire ballroom was a kaleidoscope of swirling color.

Tilly's excitement was hard to contain. Under the aegis of Lara and the aristocratic dowager, she was introduced to so many would-be partners that she couldn't remember all their names. Before the ball officially opened her dance card was almost filled. Her first partner was Mr. Keating, but she needn't have worried about him hovering over her.

"I wish I could solicit you for the next set, but it would set the old tabbies gossiping in outrage," he said, guiding her to the sidelines. "If you'll put me down for the Quadrille later, I will relinquish you to another of your conquests."

Her next partner claimed her hand, to be followed by a succession of eager swains. They were mostly young and their conversation was less than scintillating. It skipped from solicitations of Tilly's reactions to Jamaica to comments on the remarkably fine weather, then inevitably on to the annual Isle of Shells race, which was scheduled to take place in four days' time.

"Small craft only," Lord Lithermore told her, as they waited for the waltz to strike up. "The fastest is rumored to be *Sea Urchin*, Lucas Flynn's new entry. A real beauty. She was built to his specifications, and cost him a pretty penny, I dare say."

Tilly imagined she'd dare say the same—having an uncomfortable idea of just where he got those pretty pennies from. No, that was unjust. Although Lucas had admitted the emeralds were stolen, he had said there was an explanation for his actions, and had promised to return them to their rightful owner. She wanted to believe him. Desperately. It was only when they were apart that the doubts crept in, fogging her mind.

Aware that she had just stepped on Lord Lithermore's toes, Tilly tried to devote herself to the music. It was heady to be a success at her first formal ball, but her pleasure dimmed as one dance succeeded the next, with no sign of Tiger Flynn. The dancing, at first so delightful, had lost its charm. The air was hot and stuffy, the ballroom too crowded, her partners seemed dull and indistinguishable from one another—until Tilly realized the fault was in herself. No amount of flattering attention or fulsome compliments could make up for Flynn's failure to attend.

She began to envision all sorts of morbid things: that he had fallen ill or his carriage had overturned; or that he had been attacked and injured—or worse—by the same person who'd ransacked her room in search of the emeralds. It was nearing midnight, and the closer the hands of the case clock in the hallway drew together, the more worried she became.

Tilly knew she was working herself into a state, but was unable to rein in her wild imagination. She had, at first hand, a minor taste of the ruthless greed that drove Flynn's unknown adversary. The person who had destroyed her room in broad daylight, with servants in the house, was desperate enough to do anything. Tilly noticed that her hands were damp and unsteady, and the butterflies in her stomach felt as big as bats. When Mr. Culpepper came to claim her hand for a set of country dances, she asked him to procure a glass of punch for her, and retreated to a seat in the alcove beside Lady Steadmore.

The dowager looked down her long, equine nose and raised her eyebrows. "You're pale, gel. Too much gallivanting?"

Lady Steadmore, Tilly thought, is far too noticing. "I'm enjoying myself tremendously. It is just that I am used to keeping country hours."

As the polite fabrication rolled off her tongue, she realized that Mrs. McDonnel and one of her lovely nieces were on the dowager's other side. "I cannot think what is keeping Lucas Flynn," the girl was saying. "He made me promise to save one waltz for him, and now I find myself on the sidelines, when I could be dancing with John Clark. It is really too bad of him!"

"Ah, you know what a will-o'-the-wisp that man is! He will turn up in a few days or weeks, full of charming apologies and his arms full of gifts, explaining that he had to sail to St. Kitts or the Straits of Florida at the last minute."

Lady Steadmore nodded. "Yes, and Lucas was to have danced with my niece, also." She tapped her fan on Mrs. McDonnel's arm for emphasis. "I wouldn't be surprised to learn he'd left Kingston as suddenly as he arrived two years ago, without a word to anyone! I wonder what that rapscallion is up to this time?"

Tilly couldn't help wondering the same thing. Climbing balconies by moonlight? Depositing emeralds in the pocket of some other unsuspecting woman? The set was forming for the country dance, and she saw her prospective partner trying to make his way toward her through the colorful throng. While the others were conversing, Tilly escaped to the terrace and took refuge in the shadow of a potted plant. Spying a wrought-iron bench farther along, she moved out of the lantern light and into the anonymity of the shadows.

Low voices came from the direction of one of the sheltered walkways while she sat in restless contemplation. They grew more audible, but she was too preoccupied to pay attention. A series of horrible suspicions was flitting through her mind, and growing stronger by the moment. What if he had never intended to attend the ball tonight? What if he was neither detained nor injured, but had instead absconded with the emeralds—and was even now sailing away to a new life, with his ill-gotten treasure?

Had she been a complete and utter fool, the naive pawn of a captivating and unscrupulous rogue?

No. Tilly refused to consider it. Her experience was limited, but her judgment of human nature was sound. There was some other reason for Flynn's absence. There *had* to be. Something commonplace but unavoidable.

She held on to that belief like a talisman.

The voices broke off, and a figure came up the steps from the garden, then stopped abruptly. "Hiding, Miss Templeton?"

Tilly turned quickly toward the open windows, dismayed that her hiding place had been found. George Keating stood in front of her, smiling. Her polite social mask dropped in place, but he noted the change in her expression and smiled with gentle regret.

"Your look of disappointment, Miss Templeton, has dealt my pride a severe blow. I see that you were expecting someone else."

"I? Oh, no," she answered quickly. "In fact, I was taking a moment away from all the gaiety. It is quite warm inside, isn't it?"

Keating bowed. "Will you take a little turn in the garden with me? There is a pleasant breeze."

There was no polite way of refusing him. Tilly put on her best smile and let him take her arm. Once away from the colored lanterns that hung along the terrace, the night was brilliant. Handfuls of stars were scattered across the cloudless sky. He led her toward an arbor. Brief glimmers of yellow-white light shone through the open lattices. Tilly was surprised to see fireflies out so late in the evening.

Beneath the arbor was a semicircle of benches, and one of these was occupied by Mrs. Thorne and her handsome young escort. The fireflies Tilly saw to her dismay, were not flying free: they were imprisoned in a bit of gathered net, held with a jeweled pin at the woman's bodice and hem. It was a cruel vanity.

"Look who I have found, sitting all alone in the dark on the terrace," Keating said. "Miss Templeton is such a success tonight, she was forced to hide away for a few moments of peace."

Lieutenant Metcalf, whom Tilly had met earlier, rose and bowed. Mrs. Thorne was not as cordial. She greeted Tilly with faint warmth and immediately began a conversation with Mr. Keating that excluded the others. The lieutenant engaged Tilly in small talk.

"You really must take part in the great race, Miss Templeton. It's jolly fun, and there are trophies for the winners, and prizes for all the ladies. Are you a good sailor?"

She chuckled. "I don't suffer from mal de mer, if that's what you mean, but I'm certainly not experienced. You see, I've never sailed on anything smaller than the *Montego Bay*."

"Excellent! That is the whole point of it—every crew must consist of an equal number of experienced sailors and novices. Ever so much more sporting, don't you think?"

Mr. Keating overheard them and joined in. "I'm planning on giving Tiger Flynn a run for the Gold Cup this year, if I can clear the time. If not, Lieutenant Metcalf is going to command the *Whisper* in my place. Perhaps, Miss Templeton, you would be my guest along with Mrs. Thorne."

Metcalf added his entreaties. "All you and Mrs. Thorne will have to do is look charming and unpack the picnic hampers. Do say you'll join our party!"

Mrs. Thorne had been watching Tilly closely. Now she favored the two men with a coquettish glance. "Before you get too deep in your schemes, I must tell you that I have already agreed to sail with Tiger Flynn. In fact, I accepted his offer just this afternoon. He stopped by on his way home from some outing or another.''

Tilly was grateful the arbor was in shadow. Disappointment and chagrin chased each other while she fought to keep them from showing in her face. He had left her at Coeur d'Émeraude, surrounded by chaos, and made the time to stop by and ask another woman to be his guest aboard his yacht. And after all she had endured on his behalf.

She was so furious she almost missed Lieutenant Metcalf's response. ''I only hope,'' he said laughing, ''that you make better time on the return leg than you did last year.''

The widow shrugged her shapely shoulder and appealed to Tilly. ''Surely no reasonable person would have expected Lucas to set sail in such high seas, with me so ill? If he had not lain over until the wind died, I assure you the gossips would have had my demise, rather than my tardiness, to discuss. Don't you agree, Miss Templeton?''

Tilly seethed inside but managed a civil smile. Mrs. Thorne was telling her, in the oblique language of feminine rivals, that she and Flynn were linked romantically and that Tilly was wasting her time. Well, if Mrs. Thorne expected to wound her with such a revelation, she was in for a surprise.

''I quite agree,'' Tilly replied smoothly. ''How could he have done otherwise? It would have been most ungentlemanly to put such a strain on a woman of mature years.''

Her shaft sank deep and drew blood. The widow's lips drew back from her teeth in a grimace, and Keating hastened to intervene. ''Then you must promise you won't fail me, Miss Templeton.''

Tilly made up her mind in a flash. Let Mrs. Thorne and Flynn sail off together into the sunset. It made no difference to her! ''Why, Mr. Keating,'' she said dulcetly, ''I would be delighted.''

The governor's ball was a great social success, but for Tilly it was a personal failure. She'd eagerly anticipated making her first appearance at such an elegant affair. Initially it had met her every expectation. George Keating and the others were flatteringly attentive, and she'd never once lacked for partners. She had planned to enjoy herself, to laugh and flirt—at least a little—and dance till dawn. Until she realized that Flynn wasn't going to show up.

It seemed very strange that the absence of one man should make a glittering ball seem dull and insipid. She'd been ready to depart long before Jonas ordered their carriage brought around.

"Did you enjoy the ball?" Lara asked sleepily as she left Tilly at her chamber door.

"Immensely!" she lied guiltily.

Tilly couldn't wait to tell Flynn she had changed her mind about sailing with him in the Isle of Shells race. However she had no opportunity to do so in the days that followed. He seemed to have vanished off the face of the earth. Although the English social circle was small and tightly knit, no one expressed concern when he dropped from sight.

"My dear, there is no keeping up with Tiger Flynn," Mrs. Thorne said airily at Lady Steadmore's garden party, as she daintily sipped her lemonade. "He goes sauntering off on one adventure after another, without warning."

Miss Eggleston leaned forward eagerly. "I have often wondered how Mr. Flynn came by his unusual nickname."

The dowager was happy to talk about her favorite. "It came about because of his daring act of heroism."

Miss Eggleston was goggle-eyed. "Really?"

"Oh, yes! In the Bengal a remote village was terrorized by a stalking tiger, which had killed several men. The villagers were near starvation because they feared to venture out to tend their crops, but Lucas, whose family was old but no longer wealthy, came through and heard of it. He was so incensed he went out, quite alone, and killed the tiger. And he was only a youth of sixteen or seventeen at the time. The maharaja heard of his bravery and rewarded him with a coffer of gold and priceless jewels, which he parlayed into his present fortune."

It was a tale similar to the one she had heard from Lara, but although this more elaborate version sounded vaguely familiar, Tilly was quite certain that the name Lucas Flynn had never entered the story before.

The fluttery wife of one of the under secretaries set down her teacup. "How strange, for I have heard it a bit differently. While in India ten years ago, seeking to restore his family's fortune, Mr. Flynn rescued the Maharani of Ajipur from the attack of a man-eating tiger, throttling the beast with his bare hands. The maharaja, thankful that his favorite wife was spared, presented Lucas with a flawless ruby the size of a hen's egg. In fact, that jewel was the foundation of his present prosperity."

Miss Eggleston was in raptures. "What a wonderful story! Quite like a fairy tale."

"Exactly so," Tilly murmured, before lapsing into brooding silence. The second version was as familiar to her as the first, and now she recognized their sources: Lowell Montgomery's *Tales of the Orient*, which her father had given her for Christmas one year. The volume, lovingly worn, still resided on the bookshelf in the old nursery of Oak Manor. Tilly wished she had the book in hand at the present moment. Tiger Flynn was no more the hero of either tale than she was—and Tilly would have wagered everything she had that he was the source of the misinformation. The man had no scruples!

Dismay filled her. She had willingly handed over the packet of emeralds to him, to restore to their rightful owner. Her belief in him was based on nothing more than his assurances—and, she feared, his magnetic charm. That belief, which had been eroding day by day with his nonappearance, crumbled completely. No doubt he had gone off somewhere to sell his ill-gotten gains, and was laughing up his sleeve at her naïveté.

She had been a fool to trust him. He had the ability of his Irish forebears to fascinate and delight all within the circle of his enchantment. The Good Fairy at his birth had gifted him with a silver tongue to match his golden presence. Only later, in his absence, did the doubts creep in. She would

dearly love to open her mouth and tell all, exposing him to
the censure he so rightly deserved.

Unfortunately, there was no way of doing it without embarrassing Lara and Lady Steadmore and implicating herself. If her fears proved true, Tilly fervently vowed to find
out who the gems had been stolen from and try to make
reparation. And do so she would if it took the rest of her life
and every shilling she had.

After the tea party her spirits went steadily downward.
The days flew by quickly, leaving her thoughtful and out of
sorts. With their many social engagements, the days and
nights were highly structured, and there had been no time
for that little tête-à-tête with Lara. Tilly was just as glad.
Any exchange of confidences might lead her to blurt out the
truth of her involvement with Flynn and the mysterious
emeralds—mysterious, because there were no rumors
abroad involving any missing gems, and her few attempts to
steer conversations to lost or stolen jewels were unsuccess-
ful.

By the morning before the race she was not looking forward to the event with the slightest anticipation. The day
was incredibly brilliant, but as the sun moved higher it grew
humid and hazy. Jonas had been up to the lookout several
times to check the weather.

"You may rest easy," he announced when the ladies returned from an evening's drive. "Not the slightest sign of a
tropical storm brewing."

Tilly looked disappointed. "I had rather hoped to see one
of the storms that are so famous here."

Lara's astonishment was great. "You would not enjoy it
at all. They are nature's fury, terrible and frightening!"

"But surely not from the safety of the house, so far from
the water as we are at Coeur d'Émeraude."

"These are not mere thunder- and windstorms," Jonas
replied. "Hurricanes may be a hundred miles or more in
diameter."

Now it was Tilly's turn to be astonished. She knew the
island of Jamaica was one hundred and fifty miles long by
some fifty miles across, at its widest. She had not realized

the size the massive storms could reach. And Jonas had not finished his warning.

"Hurricanes do not stay out at sea, and frequently veer inland. The wind is phenomenal. It tosses the trees like jackstraws and rips roofs away like paper sheets. When a storm of such magnitude merely passes near Jamaica, torrential rains and winds lash the island, and the coasts flood from the high seas. A major storm is devastating."

"Goodness, I can see why! I think I would much rather *not* witness a hurricane, after all," Tilly amended.

Lara gave her a reassuring smile. "Don't be concerned, it is much too early in the season. The natives have a saying:

"June—Too Soon
July—Stand By
August—Come They Must
September—Remember."

"Then it is just as well," Tilly replied, "that my return sailing is set for mid-July."

"Ah," Lara said brightly, "but we hope to convince you to extend your visit."

Tilly glanced up and caught a flicker of expression on Jonas Whitby's face. He was a generous host, unfailingly polite. And without a doubt, he was counting the days till she left.

After the tea tray was brought in at ten o'clock, Jonas retired to his study, leaving the two ladies to discuss their plans for the coming week in desultory fashion until bedtime. The air was oppressive, and neither of them could concentrate. "You have been fidgety all day, Tilly. I hope it is not because you find Jamaica dull, after the wider society of England."

"There is very little social life in Hollowdean," Tilly said, laughing. "I have found more gaiety in one week here, than I would in a year at home."

"Then what is it?"

"You will think me terribly ungrateful, and indeed I'm greatly enjoying my visit—it's just that I have nothing to do but indulge myself shamelessly! I think perhaps my conscience must be pricking me."

Tilly tried to explain to Lara. In Hollowdean she had been busy overseeing the household and the Ladies' Book Circle, the Orphans' Aid Society and the Home For Unfortunate Girls. Visiting the sick and elderly of St. Anselm's parish had been another duty she'd willingly shouldered. It had been demanding at times, tedious at others, and it did not provide the intellectual stimulation she yearned for. Still it had kept her busy from dawn to dusk, and it was satisfying in other ways, because she knew that what she did mattered—that her existence had purpose.

But it was difficult to see what function she served in the greater scheme of things by driving around Kingston day after day, or filling a place at some grand dinner table night after night.

Lara was amused. "I am sure we can put you to work in the scullery, or if you'd rather, in the stable yard. After a day or so, I'm sure you'd find it no penance to put on a beautiful gown and dine by candlelight."

"You are quite right," Tilly replied. "Tomorrow, during the yacht races, I will remind myself I could be mucking out stalls, and congratulate myself on my good fortune."

She touched Lara's hand. "There are more important matters on your mind, I know. Something is worrying you. If it would help to discuss it, you know you will find a willing ear with me."

Lara bent her head. "Thank you. You are most kind. It is only the moist air and the continued worry about Christopher's health. Indeed, I think I have one of my sick headaches coming on. I will take one of Dr. Jenkins's patented powders when I retire tonight."

Tilly noted how shadowed Lara's eyes were, how tense her posture. "You need not stay up for my benefit. Why don't you go up now and take the powder? I shall help myself to one of your novels and read in bed awhile before blowing out the lamp."

"Yes. I think you are right. No doubt I will feel better in the morning. The newest ones are on the table in Jonas's study," Lara added. She stood abruptly and hurried from the room.

Tilly made her way to the study and selected an interesting-looking volume from among the stack on the table. *Confessions of a Sinner* turned out to be a series of sermons, and quite failed to capture her attention. She picked up another. *Stories of Parisian Life.* That looked more promising. Flipping it open, she read the introduction, but the words blurred and danced before her eyes.

With a sigh she replaced it. It was not the fault of the late hours of the previous night, nor the several glasses of wine she had imbibed with dinner. Part of it was, astonishingly, nothing less than boredom.

The British colony was an artificial society, a bit of England imperfectly transplanted to the Caribbean. It was highly structured and formal, in direct contrast to the vibrant life of Jamaica's own population. And that was another thing that bothered her—the way the island's other inhabitants were deemed socially invisible. In the twenty years since slavery had been abolished on the island, there had not been any great strides toward equality. The transplanted society flourished in a vacuum, and Tilly felt she might as well have been in York or Bath or Dover.

She wandered around the room, examining the various artifacts in her host's collection. His interests ranged from Egyptian busts and amulets to Venetian glass and Chinese jade. Again she had trouble focusing her attentions. Jonas had his work to occupy him, but she was having difficulty adjusting to a way of life as indolent as it was elegant.

And of course, there was nothing to keep her from dwelling on the problem of Flynn's disappearance. It ran through her mind in an endless loop. If Lucas was the scoundrel he seemed to be and had absconded with the emeralds, she was in a good deal of trouble.

Tilly leaned down for a better look at a Mayan sculpture on the desk. It hadn't been there on her last visit. It set her thoughts circling to Lucas Flynn. On the other hand, Lady

Steadmore had told her that Flynn always kept his word, but he hadn't shown up for the dowager's dinner party last night, or sent his excuses. It was an unparalleled breach of etiquette, and Lady Steadmore had been quite put out by it. So, either he had indeed absconded with the emeralds, or....

A man's shadow fell across her and Tilly jumped. From past experience, she expected it to be the man of her thoughts. *Speak of the devil.* Her eagerness vanished when strong fingers closed around her throat and began to squeeze. The shock paralyzed her for a crucial second. The fingers dug into her windpipe as she desperately tried to pry them loose and escape. It was too late. Her scream was cut off by the bruising pressure, and she clawed futilely at the hands that were throttling her.

Dizzy with air starvation, she felt herself weakening. Her pulse was throbbing in her throat, at her temples, in her eyes. The blood drummed in her ears, beating a deadly tattoo. It was impossible to draw a breath, and her chest felt as if it were bursting. Holes burned in her vision, dark spots that spread until they blotted out the light. Tilly fought desperately until the blackness closed in. It surrounded her like a heavy cloak, muffling all sound, pulling her down from awareness into a dark netherworld.

Hearing was the first sense to return. The urgent sound of running feet upon the staircase. Impassioned voices, shrill and distant, over the roaring in her ears.

Dimly she recognized Lara's frantic pleas: *"No! Oh, no!"* Tilly tried to open her eyes. Her lids barely lifted, but she was able to see that a man leaned over her, his hands upon her shoulders. Jonas, she realized, as consciousness seeped back like a sluggish river. Her throat ached abominably, and her breath whistled in and out while she coughed and choked. She gasped, trying to gulp the life-sustaining air.

Lara ran into the room and threw herself down beside Tilly. "Oh, Jonas! Have you . . . Is she . . . ?"

"Get hold of yourself," Jonas ordered. "She's coming around."

"But why . . . ?"

"She had the mask in her hands."

They looked up sharply as a figure lurched through the door to the library, weaving from side to side. Tilly's eyes opened wide. Lara's brother was clean shaven now, his hair cut and brushed, but he looked as strange as when he had collapsed the previous week in the foyer. His clothes draped so loosely over his bony frame they gave the impression that they still hung from the peg. The mouth that she had once thought sensitive and expressive was slack and weak. And his eyes! Purple shadows ringed his pale blue eyes, making them seem almost colorless.

He shambled toward them, knocking over a small side table in a clatter of brass and wood. He didn't even seem to notice what he'd done.

"Fiend! You won't get away with it," he raved, waving one fist in the air. His voice rose to a banshee wail. "You think you can shut me up, but you can't. I know what happened.... I'll tell everything..."

Leander and two servants burst into the room and hurried to subdue him. He threw them off like jackstraws, and Jonas launched himself at his brother-in-law, bringing him down. They fell in a tangled heap, wrestling for mastery. Christopher fought with a madman's energy, an astonishingly equal match with Jonas's superior strength and cooler head. They fought in tense silence, with only the thuds of their effort and Lara's soft weeping to fill the room. Just as Leander was about to join the fray, Jonas sent a sharp uppercut to his opponent's chin.

Christopher slumped suddenly, all the fight and rage escaping from him like hot air from a balloon. He lay on his side, drooling. Jonas got to his feet heavily. His mouth was bleeding at one corner. Lara rose, hands clasped to her breast, and looked away.

"Take him to his room, please," Jonas directed, wiping his mouth with his handkerchief.

The two servants hefted Christopher's limp body as if it were an empty sack. Leander picked Tilly up, and she closed her eyes against a wave of giddiness. He placed her on the sofa.

Tilly opened her eyes in time to see Leander assist his master from the room. As they passed by her, Jonas placed a hand upon his wife's shoulder. "Don't hate me, Lara..."

Tilly was surprised by the gentleness in Jonas's voice. He hadn't been very gentle in subduing Christopher. Lara didn't move, but a single tear worked its way down her cheek, to splash silently upon her hand.

Jonas's hand fell and he strode angrily from the room. Lara put her head against the door frame, and her shoulders shook with a bout of uncontrollable weeping. Tilly struggled to sit upright, still trying to understand what had happened to her, and why. Lara rushed to her side, tear streaks visible on her face.

"He...he has been under a great strain. Forgive me, Tilly, for subjecting you to this!"

Tilly tried to talk, but couldn't. Only a painful squeak came out. Her mind was still clouded and her throat was bruised and swollen, but at least she was alive. Agnes arrived on the scene. Lara twisted her fingers nervously.

"Miss Templeton was taken faint."

Together they assisted Tilly to her own chamber, dosed her with medicine and put her to bed. She was groggy but wanted answers. What was the reason for the unprovoked attack upon her? And why had Lara lied to Agnes? Once again she tried to talk, but a hoarse croak was all she could manage.

Lara leaned over the bed. The turmoil of her emotions was evident in her soft, dark eyes. "Don't try to speak, Tilly dear. Rest. In the morning I'll try to explain as much as I am able. Meanwhile, you are safe."

The laudanum was making her warm and drowsy. Tilly could feel herself sinking into drugged sleep. She fought against it, forcing her eyes open.

The room was dim and Lara paced the carpet, wringing her hands and talking to herself in agitation. "I have known about him for some time, and been too cowardly to face up to the fact, and now poor Tilly has suffered for it."

She stopped suddenly and buried her face in her hands. "What should I do? What *can* I do?" Lara cried softly.

"The situation is desperate now. Oh, if only Lucas Flynn was here!"

As Tilly slipped into pain-free sleep, her last waking thought was that she couldn't have agreed more. She'd get the truth out of him if she had to shake it out! Only let her get her hands on Flynn and she'd....

But Tilly's dreams were not so martial. In them, she walked hand in hand with Flynn through a paradise of flowers. They paused by sparkling diamond waterfalls and he pulled her into his arms. Her body shaped itself against his hard contours as his mouth came down on hers, warm and possessive, and his eyes were green as the emeralds scattered at their feet.

Chapter Seven

The rocking of the ship woke Flynn. He was instantly awake, instantly sorry. Cymbals crashed and banged inside his head, and his tongue felt like a piece of wet leather. When he tried to move, it was worse. There didn't seem to be an inch of him that didn't ache or throb in protest. He sat up. The pain in his head was viciously sharp as though a spike had been driven into his skull.

With every roll of the hull his brain seemed to expand and shrink like a concertina, but his thoughts were starting to clear. Thirst was a worse torture than the physical pain. *Dehydrated as a prune,* he thought. Water would have to be the first priority. The rest he could sort out later. He didn't quite know who he was, but he knew damn well *where* he was. In the hold of a ship under sail.

It was dark as a mine shaft, but the vessel's mighty timbers creaked and groaned their song of the open sea. But how did he know that? He realized the sounds and vibrations of the hull were as familiar to him as the rhythm of his own heart. He must be a sailor, then. But he felt his garments. Linen shirt, gentleman's coat, leather boots. Not a sailor, after all. And the only reason they'd left him the boots, he surmised, was because they were too long and wide to fit any of them. The coat pockets were empty.

Slowly a name swam into recognition. Lucas Flynn. *Tiger* Flynn. He turned it around in his mind, examined it from every direction. Then something clicked. It was his name.

He was Flynn. He tried to concentrate, but that only made it worse.

"Damn it to hell and back!" His throat was parched, and he scarcely recognized his own voice.

A rusty exclamation from across the way answered his oath. "Awake now, be ye? Praise God. Ye stopped thrashing and mumbling in the early watches of the night. I was like to fearing they'd done fer ye, lad."

Although low, the voice lanced through his brain. Wincing, Flynn peered through the gloom to the bulky shape lying across from him. There was something familiar about the other man, yet no name popped into his mind. "Who are you?"

"Why, 'tis old Red Skelly! Aye, who sailed with ye around The Horn these five years and more, all the way to the China Sea. Never say ye've forgot me, lad!"

Memory was seeping back. A picture formed in Flynn's mind, unmoving but sharp and clear, like a bright-painted canvas: a three-masted ship just off Tierra del Fuego, and a huge man with dark russet skin and a hawk-nosed face that mingled the heritage of the Arawak Indians with those of England, Spain and Africa. A good man, quick to laugh and quick to act. It seemed long ago, in the far distant past.

"I remember you, Skelly, and damn glad I am to know you're close at hand. Together we'll find a way out of this fix. How did I get here?"

"Same ways I did. T'was a powerful knock on the head they give ye. At the Crown and Garter, it was. We met up and had a tankard or two together and I gave ye the information ye'd asked me to git. Then the landlord joined us and I shut me bone-box. Ye'd been asking after an old acquaintance o' ours—Christopher Burlinghome, God save him. The next thing I knew, one o' the men nearby coshed ye with a pistol butt. Ye went down like an old horse in the knacker's yard. Then a chair broke over me head and 'twas the end o' me. Didn't come 'round till we was trussed up like Easter hams."

It was all coming back now, tumbling into place with dizzying speed. The night of Lady Steadmore's ball. A seaman's hangout near the harbor. Dull gold light leaking around the edges of the shutters into the street. Inside, the smell of greasy food, the sweat of unwashed bodies and the growing sense of danger. A toothless man leading him to a sooty, low-beamed back room of the Crown and Garter, lit by a single dirty lantern.

Rough company, crowding the two small tables, and a sudden shadow falling over him. He'd tried to rise and...that was all. The rest was a blank, until he'd awakened in the hold of this ship. Flynn probed his head gently. There was a knot the size of a puffin's egg at the back, the strands of hair over it stiff with dried blood.

The last of the pieces clicked into place. Christopher Burlinghome's expedition. The emeralds. Jonas Whitby's warehouses. And that gray-eyed armful, Miss Matilda Templeton. Lord, he'd give a pony to know what she was thinking right now!

Propping himself up on one elbow, he gritted his teeth as whirling red lights filled the darkness. It took several seconds before he realized they weren't really there, but only the product of his aching head. He felt along the back of one boot. So, they hadn't found his hiding place. That was a small advantage. His companion might be another. Flynn spoke to him.

"What are you willing to risk to escape?"

The other man chuckled dryly. "If ye've got a plan, mate, I be ready to give it all. But I wouldn't give ye good odds of our chances."

"A slim chance is better than none, and that's all we've got to look forward to. This is no ordinary conscription, as I'm sure you well know."

"Aye. 'Tis plain ye've got powerful enemies." The wheezy chuckle came again. "And now they be mine as well. Whatever ye've a mind to, I'm game."

"Good man! It will have to be a spur-of-the-moment affair, so keep yourself at the ready."

"That I will."

Flynn thought rapidly. "How long since they took us?"

"Three days, near as I could keep track."

"Three days!" Flynn was astonished so much time had been lost, but the throbbing of his head and his fragmented thinking convinced him it was true. "We must be halfway to Brazil by now."

"Nay. Set course for Hispaniola first, they did, but hit a storm. The seas was uncommon rough. Yestidy they turned back toward Kingston, 'cording to the one that brings the food and water."

Lucas was thinking fast. "Did he say why?"

"Mum as a spar."

Distant calls came to Flynn's ears, indistinct yet familiar enough to decipher their meaning. A short time after he heard the rumble of the capstan and the clanking of the great anchor chain as it rattled its way down. They'd reached their destination—wherever it might be. If he meant to make a move, now was the time.

A scraping sound came from overhead and a shaft of lamplight blinded them as the hatch cover was removed. Flynn recognized Skelly instantly, and had a vague recollection of seeing him in the back room at the Crown and Garter. Except for a few grizzled hairs at his temples, that dark, seamed face was unchanged. Flynn whispered, and his companion nodded.

Above, the sinewy, towheaded seaman set the lamp on a hook and swung down the ladder, agile as a monkey. A canteen of water and a net bag of hardtack dangled from a loop in his waistband. When he jumped free of the bottom rung, Flynn was flat on his back, eyes closed and unmoving. His stocky ally sprawled on his side, moaning terribly.

The sailor prodded the man's arm.

"Here now, what's the matter with you?"

A garbled word and another moan were the only response. The sailor stepped closer, then hesitated. Fever and pirates were the only things he feared—and of the two, sickness had sent more seamen to the grave than any crew that flew the Jolly Roger. He hunkered down to examine the man without touching him. Skelly rolled on his side, and as the sailor ducked to dodge a flailing arm, he was momentarily off balance.

Instantly Flynn sprang into action. He had the mariner immobilized with his arms pinned back and a sharp and exceedingly wicked knife at his throat.

"Not a word, or by God! it will be your last."

Skelly jumped up and pulled out the long steel blade that had been sheathed at the sailor's side. He brandished it menacingly. "Aye. Any tricks and you'll be shark rations."

The sailor rolled his eyes from one to the other and swallowed. The blade that Flynn held was against his neck below his Adam's apple. As it bobbed he felt the blade scrape. He nodded only enough to let them know he understood. For the first time Flynn let out his breath. It was only a small chance. But it might work.

Ten minutes later they were marching along the upper deck in the indistinct predawn light. Patches of fog covered the water like a blanket of dirty snow, making a ghostly landscape of sea and ship. The vessel sighed and creaked as it drifted at anchor, and the wind whistled through the rigging. The shrouds were furled and a portion of the mainmast and its spars hung like a gallows tree above them.

The ship was old, of Dutch make, and featured a raised cabin across the stern where an admiral had once planned the movements of his fleet. There was only one such vessel in Caribbean waters: the old *Black Tulip*, renamed *Venture* by her present owners. Flynn knew the captain by reputation, a hard man who would skin his own grandmother for the price of her hide.

Flynn proceeded toward the captain's quarters, prodded along by a gleaming knife, in the hand of the sailor who walked immediately behind. The watch wouldn't change for another half hour, and they passed unnoticed in the fog.

Inside the cabin Captain Folling studied a chart in a pool of light from the gimballed lamp. He was a big, impatient man, as dark of heart as he was of visage. The weather ahead had foiled his plans, and he was out of patience, and itching to be off at first light.

Two hours back to Kingston, if the wind held fair. But if it changed to another quarter there'd be the devil to pay, and no pitch hot! He rubbed his hand over his beard. *Now, if we could catch that current off the eastern end . . .*

A soft rap at the door interrupted his train of thought, and he stifled an oath. The first mate had gone up the crow's nest to see if the fog was lifting and was due to report at any moment. Without looking up from the charts before him, Folling measured a distance of nautical miles and barked permission to enter.

The door opened while he plotted his best route. "Well? Be quick about your business."

Outside his circle of light the room was in shadows. A vague sensation that something was not right brought his head up with a jerk. The man he'd been paid to kidnap was being propelled across the room by the dark-skinned sailor behind him.

"By Blackbeard's ghost, what the hell do you mean bringing him here!"

"Says e's got a deal to strike with ye, Cap'n. Happen ye'll be interested in hearing wot e's got to say."

Before Folling could reply, Flynn held out his hand. A great, faceted emerald lay in his bronzed palm, and as the lamplight struck it, the gem came alive with green fire. It burned with an inner glow that seemed to dim the lamplight with its splendor.

The captain stared at it. He'd never seen one so large, so vibrant a green, or so perfectly colored. The kind of gem men killed or died for. Worth an empire. Flynn watched as awe and avarice altered and sharpened the man's wily face. He turned his palm so the light danced and blazed from within the jewel's bewitching heart.

Captain Folling was blinded by it, and by his own greed. He didn't notice that the prisoner's eyes burned with the same curious green flame.

"Well, Captain? An exceptional gem, you might think. Incomparable. Unique. But you would be entirely wrong."

Flynn leaned forward, his voice low, almost hypnotic. "There are more emeralds where this one came from, Captain. Equally as splendid. And I am willing to share them with you. My ransom, you might say. If you take me ashore and release me, I'll make you rich beyond any reckoning."

Folling stroked his bristly chin. "And where might these jewels be?"

Lucas smiled. "Hidden on the island, where no one but I can ever find them. I'm not a greedy man. Take me there, and I swear I'll split them with you."

Captain Folling's face grew crafty. Now he understood why he had been paid to capture this lynx-eyed gentleman, and to deliver him up for questioning in Hispaniola. The man who'd employed him had obviously planned to extract the location of the emeralds, either by force or by torture.

Greed was a habit with Captain Folling. So there were more of the emeralds ashore, were there? Well, why not help himself to all of them? And no need for anyone to know about it. But first, he'd have to persuade this fellow to tell him where to find the emeralds. There'd be no need to split the goods, either. There would just be another nameless body, washed ashore with the tide.

While his mental wheels were turning, he didn't notice that the husky seaman had changed position. Not until he felt the arm around his throat and the knife at his back. He went completely still. The evil plans in his mind were obliterated, and frustrated resignation took their place.

"A wise decision, Captain." Flynn came forward and took the man's pistol from his belt. He nodded to Skelly. "Good work."

"Treachery," Folling muttered, and received a jab just over his right kidney in response. The only sound in the cabin was his hoarse breathing.

Flynn checked the pistol. It was loaded, as he'd anticipated. Aiming it squarely at the captain, he cocked the trigger. "And now, Captain Folling, if you will be seated, you and I have business to transact."

Not long after a small dinghy was lowered over the side of the *Venture*. It was still gray out, and mist rose from the water, but the sun was just below the horizon. As the fog began to lift the first streaks of light painted the eastern sky with bold magenta streamers. The water was choppy, but calmer near the shore.

As they approached the cove the sun rose, burning off the fog rapidly. The ruddy light struck the water, staining its millions of broken reflections a savage hue. In the incandescent light the dinghy carved its path through shallows as blue as a morning glory. Below, red and yellow fish darted over the coral and sand, casting long, rippled shadows.

It was too beautiful a setting for bloody deeds, a morning from the dawn of time. With Captain Folling in the middle, Flynn at the stern and Skelly rowing, they reached shore quickly. There was no sign of human habitation among the trees in the secluded cove, one of a series that scalloped this side of the coast.

As they entered the frothing surf the shallows slanted up sharply and the bottom of the dinghy banged against a coral shelf. "Steady with that pistol, now!" Folling cautioned, sweat breaking out on his face.

Flynn held the long-barreled weapon easily, under cover of the long drab cloak he wore. "Just do as I say and you'll escape with a whole skin."

They beached the dinghy in the cove and climbed out, ripples of foam beneath their soles. Folling walked between them into the wooded point, and the mate aboard the *Venture*, trying to watch with his spyglass, detected nothing wrong. But once under cover of the foliage, Flynn brought the pistol out into the open.

"Before we let you go, there's one thing I need to know: the name of the man who paid you to have me knocked out and carried aboard the *Venture*."

"I don't know his name...."

"Enough!"

Once again the pistol was aimed at the captain's heart. Skelly looked from one to the other, wondering what would happen next. Fine tremors shook Folling's body. "I swear on my father's grave that I don't know!"

"Swear on anything you like, Captain. Just come up with that name." Flynn's eyes sparked green and gold in the dappled shade. He suspected the man was telling the truth; but it wouldn't hurt to push him further.

"I'm sure it has occurred to you that I might shoot you like the dog you are and leave your body under some convenient bush."

Fright dragged a buried memory from the depths of Folling's mind. "Fritz.... As they were leaving I heard the other man call him Fritz."

The look that came over Flynn's face made the captain think his end was near. He shook like a man with ague. Slowly, Flynn lowered the gun. "Go on. Back to the dinghy. And don't look back."

Folling took to his heels like a man possessed. They could hear him crashing through the brush toward the beach long after he disappeared from sight. "He'll have a pretty story to tell them when he returns to his ship," Flynn said with satisfaction.

Skelly chuckled, a deep rumbling sound that began in his chest and worked its way up. "'E won't be doing it anytime soon. I 'oled' the dinghy whilst ye two went on ahead. Won't get out fifty yards afore she sinks, 'e won't."

Flynn clapped him on the back. "You're an enterprising man, Skelly, and the information you brought me is invaluable. I can use a man like you on my payroll, permanently. What do you say?"

The dark face creased into a wide smile. "Well, I had me a pretty woman in the Canaries, but she run off with a Portugee. There be nothing to hold me back. I'd say ye got yerself a new man, Cap'n."

"Call me Flynn."

"Aye. An' now what's yer plan."

"Now we go back to Kingston."

"Then ye'd best start walking, or 'twill be tomorry afore we git there."

"We'll make better time than that. Follow me." He led the way across the point, and in a quarter hour they reached another small cove. The sun had ascended and the bay sparkled in golden light. Riding at anchor was a small yacht, sleek as an otter and built for speed. Fresh white paint gleamed along her thirty-foot hull, and her brass and varnish gleamed with polish.

Skelly was visibly impressed. "A beauty. Be she yers?"

"Yes. Brand new, and ready for a good shakedown cruise. I moved her here, out of harm's way, for just such a situation as this."

"Where be yer crew?"

"Right now, we're it, but two can handle her easily. I left my men aboard another vessel. Meanwhile, I think you should lay low for a few days. I'll send for you if I need you. I have to make a few stops along the way, but if you're in no hurry I'll drop you off anywhere you like."

"Kingston town is what ye mentioned afore, and Kingston town is just where I'm wanting to be. I'll go to earth at Whiskey Nan's. Do ye know the place?"

Flynn grinned. "Better than you do, I'll wager." He boarded the yacht and threw the sailor a salute. "Welcome aboard the *Sea Urchin*, First Mate Skelly."

After a quick check for seaworthiness, Flynn grabbed the shroud line and ran the canvas up the mainmast, while Skelly took the other lines. The sails filled, dazzling white against the turquoise sea and sapphire sky. Flynn signaled Skelly to weigh anchor. A quiver of anticipation ran through the hull, as if the *Sea Urchin* were a living creature. It was a moment Flynn always loved. He set a tack to take them out of the cove, and the yacht moved smoothly through the water.

He had a score to settle with Fritz. He'd only heard the name once, but it had stuck in his mind like a burr. Yes, Fritz was in for a surprise. And, Flynn thought, so was Miss Matilda Templeton. That cool exterior of hers was wrapped around a fiery core; no doubt she'd been stewing and simmering over his defection. But when she'd learned he'd been kidnapped her anger would change to contrition—to be followed, if he judged rightly, by a great deal of sympathy and unholy curiosity about the experience. He could use it, if necessary, to parley himself into her good graces.

As soon as the matter of Fritz was disposed of, he would pay her a visit. He didn't like to leave loose ends. Meanwhile, it was good to know that she was safely at Coeur d'Émeraude, under Lara's watchful eye.

Not long after dawn, while the *Sea Urchin* rode the breeze toward Kingston, a swarthy sailor delivered a sealed message to an office along the waterfront. The man it was addressed to broke the seal impatiently and scanned the lines. Crumpling the paper in his fist, he swore viciously. "I should have known better than to trust something of such importance to a bumbling fool!"

He twisted the sheet of paper and touched the end of it to his oil lamp. A thin blue flame flickered at the corner, turning orange as it fed itself. The paper blackened and flaked away in pieces until he dropped it and ground the remains beneath his heel. Only then did he realize that the seaman was still watching nervously, shifting his weight from foot to foot.

"What are you standing around here for? Off with you!"

"Cap'n Folling told me to ask if there's any message."

"Only this— I'll do what is necessary myself. As for Captain Folling, he may go to the devil for all I care! Get back to the ship. No, wait!"

An idea was forming in his head. No need to be too hasty. His first trap had failed. The next one wouldn't. But he'd have to bait it differently. And he was fairly sure he knew the one lure that would prove irresistible.

He scribbled a few lines on a sheet of notepaper and sprinkled sand over them. When the ink was dry he folded and sealed the paper. There was no need for a signature: she'd know who it was from. He rose.

"Take this at once to Mrs. Thorne in Prince's Court. Deliver it into her hands personally. Not another soul is to touch it, or I'll have your head."

"What if the lady is out?"

"Then order them to send someone to fetch her, and wait."

"Aye, sir."

With the sailor gone, the man leaned back and went over his plan in greater detail. The more he examined it, the more plausible it seemed. If there had been more time he could have used more subtle means, but Flynn had forced his hand. Still, it was a pity. He'd had such fine plans for the two of them.

For just a moment he acknowledged stirrings of real regret. The plan required a personal sacrifice of sorts. Despite his original misgivings, he had grown fond of Lara's plucky little friend. It was a shame it had come to this. In fact, it really went very much against the grain. Of course there was always the chance his plan wouldn't work, but after Christopher's handiwork last night the opportunity was certainly there.

He turned away from the window and poured himself a snifter of imported brandy, and the early light struck fire from the glass. Yes, it would all work out. He was a gambler, and a gambler had to back his odds. And he hadn't acquired his wealth by hesitating to do what was necessary, when it was necessary.

No, there was no use repining. He really had no other choice.

A faint sound awakened Tilly. It seemed only a few minutes since she had closed her eyes in her candlelit bedchamber; but the bright sun, shining between the slats of the shutters, told her she had slept the night away. She dimly remembered Lara escorting her upstairs and making her drink a medicinal powder dissolved in a glass of water. Although Tilly would have sworn the shock of the attack would keep her awake all night, the compound had worked wonderfully. The last thing she remembered was settling back against her pillow.

The medicine's effects lingered a bit, as evidenced by her sluggishness, and her throat still felt bruised. A soft footfall explained what had awakened her. A young maid with pale hair and nondescript features stood by the washstand with a pitcher of water. She had knocked over a bottle on the dressing table and was frantically trying to right it without dropping the pitcher.

Tilly yawned and rubbed her eyes. "Good morning," she said in a slightly husky voice. "What time is it?"

The girl jumped. "Just after seven, miss."

"You may open the shutters, if you please."

The girl nervously hurried to do her bidding, casting an anxious eye over her shoulder. Tilly blinked at the sudden spill of light. "You needn't look so petrified," she said, stifling another yawn. "I won't bite you."

"Oh, miss! I didn't really mean to wake you. Mrs. Whitby will be so angry with me. She left instructions that I was not to disturb you, only to check on you every hour while she's away."

Tilly was confused and groggy. "While she's away?"

Where on earth had Lara gone so early in the day? She turned toward the window. The new day was fresh and golden, the sky a shimmering arc of blue. The very air held a waiting, expectant quality. A perfect day for sailing. She remembered all at once. "The race. Today is the Isle of Shells Race."

"Yes, miss. The mistress went off not a quarter hour ago with Lady Steadmore's party, with orders that I was to let you rest the day in bed."

Belatedly she reached into her pocket and pulled out a folded note. Tilly brushed a tumble of curls from her face and took the paper.

Please don't be angry. Everything is under control now and C. is in his quarters. I'll be back as soon as possible. All my love,

Lara

Tilly was dismayed. How could Lara have gone blithely off to participate in the yacht race after she'd been attacked? Comprehension dawned. She'd come to and found Jonas bending over her, and her first thought had been that he'd attacked her. The dizziness and pain in her head had made it impossible to think rationally at the time. Lara had been alert and unhurt, and it was plain that she'd concluded Christopher had been the culprit. That was a much more logical conclusion. Still . . .

Lying against the pillows, Tilly tried to reconstruct the events. She realized she wasn't at all sure of what had actually happened. She'd been turning the mask over in her hands when a shadow had fallen upon her, but before she could glance up she'd been struck from behind.

She had never seen her attacker before losing consciousness. Had it been Lara's brother—or Lara's husband? The bits of conversation she'd heard could be construed either way. Tilly shook her head to clear the fog that dulled her thoughts. It was a terrible mistake. Her head clanged like a broken brass bell.

"Where is Mr. Whitby? Is he sailing with your mistress and Lady Steadmore?"

"Oh, no, miss. The master went out for his morning ride. He'll be back shortly."

Lara gone, Flynn missing and Jonas on his way to Coeur d'Émeraude! Tilly threw off the covers, squinching her eyes against the throbbing between her temples. She had to talk to Lara, and she wasn't about to stay at the house alone under the circumstances. A quarter hour was not so great a lead, after all. And Mr. Keating's party was to meet at seven-thirty. If she hurried she could make it. She brushed aside the maid's urgings to remain in bed.

"I'm feeling much better and I wouldn't want to miss the race. Can you arrange for someone to drive me down to Deadman's Cove? I shall be ready to leave in ten minutes."

The maid looked alarmed. "But you really must rest, miss. The mistress will be so angry with me!"

"Nonsense. You make Lara Whitby sound like Lucretia Borgia!" Tilly threw open her wardrobe and took out the white shirtwaist and skirt she'd planned to wear, then located the corresponding slippers. "If you could fetch me a cup of coffee I'd be exceedingly grateful."

"Yes, miss." The girl bobbed a curtsy and, after looking up and down the hall quickly, slipped out. Tilly didn't notice. She pulled her hair back and pinned it with a clip, wincing only slightly. By the time girl returned she'd washed and dressed and was reaching into the wardrobe for a wide bonnet of white straw.

Tilly took the hot drink with thanks and gulped it down. The maid looked anxious. "If you take the servant's staircase, miss, and turn left at the bottom it will put you right at the side door. Just follow the brick path toward the bake house. Emmanuel will be there with the wagon."

Tilly followed her directions and found the brick path without difficulty. Long shadows from the early-morning sun striped the gravel paths and the beds of the kitchen gardens. She was glad there was no one to stop her. The only sound was the music of the birds and the crunching of her soles over the smooth stones. As she wound her way around the last bend, Tilly saw the small wagon behind a storage shed, with a plantation hand in the driver's seat.

He got down to assist her. "Good morning, mistress. It be a fine day for sailing."

"Yes, indeed." Tilly put one foot on the iron brace as he handed her up, but was so busy thanking him she snagged her sandal on a bit of splintered wood. Rushed, excited and still battling the persistent aftereffects of the sleeping powder, she didn't realize the bow had torn off and dropped to the ground.

The driver, a swarthy man with a rolling sailor's gait, climbed up beside her and snapped the reins. As they drove away, she glanced over her shoulder at the house. Something didn't look quite right, but Tilly didn't realize it was the fact that the shutters were still tightly closed against the light.

Instead of the main drive, the man guided the wagon in the opposite direction along the edges of the fallow fields, past extensive banana and mango groves. The strong coffee had helped to clear her head. Tilly was certain that Lucas Flynn would show up to take part in the race. He'd look incredibly handsome in sailing garb, his skin golden-bronze against the blue of the sea, and he'd be full of all sorts of plausible excuses for his absence. Tilly didn't intend to flatter his vanity.

Oh, really Mr. Flynn? I've been so busy I'm afraid I wasn't aware that you were out of town. She smiled to herself. That would show him how little she cared!

The track grew wilder, and they drove through a paradise of trees and ferns and bright-winged birds that seemed untouched by man. As they passed beneath the spreading limbs of a great silk-cotton tree, the driver made a hasty sign to ward off evil. She shivered. *A goose has walked over my grave,* she thought, recalling the old saying.

On the day of their picnic, Flynn had said that the Jamaicans believed duppies—the spirits of the dead—lived in the roots of the silk-cottons. The silence was so eerie and profound she could almost be convinced of it herself. She was glad when they left the track and the duppie tree behind.

The journey was short, and they arrived at a sheltered cove without seeing a living soul. The spot was secluded but charming, with clusters of bread-fruit trees and waving palms. The stiffening breeze whipped the sea into foaming lace ruffles.

At the end of a short dock a small sailboat rode easily at anchor, bobbing with the motion of the sea. There was no name visible from this angle, and the craft was in need of paint—not at all the sleek wave rider she'd anticipated—but it was the only one in sight.

"Are you sure this is Deadman's Cove?"

"Yes, mistress. I have been here many times before."

As she eyed the craft doubtfully, Lieutenant Metcalf and his crony, Franklin Thoms, came out of the whitewashed boat house, trim and athletic in white yachting clothes. "Miss Templeton! This is delightful. We had been told that you were indisposed."

Tilly realized her thinking wasn't totally clear yet, or she would have anticipated questions. "I'm afraid I was a slugabed this morning, after a restless night. But I really couldn't miss the race! I do hope Mr. Keating has room aboard for me."

"Room to spare. I'll be captaining our vessel today since Mr. Keating was required to stay in Kingston this morning.

The penalty for being a man of affairs." Metcalf laughed and preened his mustache.

"That's really too bad," Tilly responded as Mrs. Thorne came out of the boat's cabin, decked out in yellow frills with a parasol to match. It was a costume more suited to a morning's carriage ride than to the deck of a yacht. The lieutenant hailed her. "Mrs. Thorne, our luck is in. Miss Templeton is here."

Mrs. Thorne spun around abruptly. At first the widow seemed vexed to see her, but then smiled. Tilly could share the widow's chagrin. Sharing the voyage with Mrs. Thorne took a good deal of pleasure out of her day.

"Why, Mrs. Thorne," she said, "this is quite a surprise. I understood you were sailing with Lucas Flynn."

A frown marred the widow's white forehead. "I was not more than half an hour late in reaching his yacht, but he had already set sail!" Her indignation was amusing to see.

Lieutenant Metcalf laughed. "As he told you he would do, if you were tardy. You can't say you weren't warned."

Mrs. Thorne saw that Tilly was very pale. "I hope you are a good sailor, Miss Templeton. Yachting is not at all like the comforts of a clipper ship. You see, they pitch and yaw much more," she said maliciously. "Up and down, up and down. Side to side. Some people become quite ill from the motion. But I am sure *you* will not succumb."

Not if it kills me, Tilly told herself determinedly. The fresh air had cleared some more of the cobwebs from her head but she still felt woozy. Mr. Thoms helped her aboard. The yacht was ready, white sails unfurled in the breeze. They cast off.

"I am afraid," Metcalf said, scanning the horizon with his glass, "that we shall have our work cut out for us. The others are almost out of sight."

The horizon was lined with odd puffball clouds stretched out like a series of dots. Their bottoms looked perfectly flat. Tilly squinted against the bright light. "I can't see a single sail."

Metcalf handed her the glass. "Try this."

Tilly scanned the sea, blinking when the sun's rays were refracted from the water's surface. She examined the horizon patiently, but try as she might, she couldn't make out a single sail. The other racers had certainly taken advantage of their early start.

"Is there any chance we might catch up with them?"

"A very good one. The only yacht in the same class as the *Whisper* is Tiger Flynn's *Sea Urchin*. He set off from around the bay, which means we have the more favorable current. With a fair wind, we shall still reach the island first."

With the sun in her eyes and the wind in her hair, Tilly was unable to subdue a tingle of anticipation. She felt as weightless and insubstantial as one of those funny puffball clouds advancing toward the island. The very air crackled with excitement.

It was just eight when Flynn left his horse with one of the young grooms and entered the shade of the portico at Coeur d'Émeraude. As he reached for the knocker, the door was wrenched open and Lara came hurtling through like a loose cannonball. He managed to avoid a collision by grasping her shoulders; by the look on her drawn face he knew something was terribly wrong.

"Christopher?"

Unable to speak past the panic that filled her throat and threatened to cut off her breath, Lara could only clutch at his coat sleeve and shake her head. Flynn tried to get some sense out of her.

"Then what has set you all on end? Surely it cannot be so bad as you think."

Lara collapsed in tears and struggled to explain. Flynn found it was impossible to make out a single intelligible word due to her hysteria. He guided her slowly into the wide hall and toward the study, where he knew a decanter of brandy always stood on the side table. He shut the door and ushered her to an armchair, then poured a generous amount into a cut-glass snifter and handed it to her.

"Sit down, catch your breath and drink this."

Lara took a hasty gulp and neither choked nor sputtered. He eyed her thoughtfully. A fondness for drink was not a trait he associated with Lara Whitby; but evidently she was not a complete stranger to it. Whatever the truth, he had no leisure to study her now. The first matter at hand was to quiet her agitation, the next to uncover its source.

Under his soothing manner and air of authority she managed to blurt out the crux of it. "Oh, Lucas, it's ... it's *Tilly*! She's gone, and no one knows where ... or even when."

His air of patience evaporated. Every line of his body was taut, tense. "Start from the beginning. Slowly."

"I didn't think anything of it when Tilly didn't come down to breakfast. I was sure she would sleep late. Afterward I went up to her room. Agnes was there, putting something in the wardrobe. She said Tilly was already gone when she came in with fresh water this morning. She thought she had dressed herself and come down early. It was some time before we realized that she had vanished, without a word to anyone."

"Have the grounds been searched?"

"Thoroughly. There is no sign of her anywhere. No note. Oh, Lucas, I blame myself. There was trouble at Coeur d'Émeraude when I invited her, but I wanted so desperately to see her again. And I thought having her here would help ease the strain. I was selfish, I should never have—"

"When was she last seen?"

"Last night. I left her sleeping in her own bed, with Agnes keeping watch over her." Haltingly she told him about the attack. "Do you think ... ? Could the sleeping powder have affected her mind? Made her walk away in her sleep?"

"This is none of your doing, Lara." Flynn bit back an oath. His mind was working furiously. "Where is Christopher now?"

"Locked in his room, sleeping off a heavy sedative Jonas gave him. Leander checked on him five minutes ago."

"And Jonas?"

"He left early this morning. Some problem at the warehouse. As soon as I was certain Tilly had vanished, I sent a groom down to the warehouse with a note for him. If he is not there, it may take some time to reach him. In the meantime, if there is anything you might do to help..."

"I would like to speak with her maid."

"Very well." Lara tugged the bell pull, and when Bernard answered, requested him to send the maid to the study.

"And ask Leander to check with the stable hands," Flynn interjected. He took a turn around the room, pounding one hand impatiently into the palm of the other. The maid arrived shortly. "I do not know why you wish to question *me*," she said smugly. "Miss did not take me in her confidence."

"You are in no trouble, Agnes—" Lara began.

Flynn interrupted. "It is urgent that Miss Templeton's whereabouts be ascertained with all due speed. She may be in danger."

The slightly superior air deserted Agnes, but she tried to stare Flynn down. It was unwise. Flynn's eyes narrowed. "When did you last see Miss Templeton?"

"Last evening. I sat with her until she went to sleep. Then I retired to my own bed. When she did not ring this morning, I went to see if my services were required. She was already gone."

He wasn't satisfied. The words tumbled out too quickly and sounded rehearsed. The woman knew more than she was saying.

Her gaze faltered and fell. "I do not know where she is," she repeated woodenly.

He knew that she was concealing something, but was frightened into stubbornness. She would not tell him anything directly—at least, not yet. He took another tack.

"You are familiar with Miss Templeton's wardrobe, of course?"

"Yes, sir, that I am."

"Very good. I want you to go through her garments as quickly as possible, and return to tell me what is missing."

The maid dropped a nervous bow and hurried from the room. His suspicion hardened to a certainty. The woman was definitely apprehensive about something. But what?

Once he had taken possession of the emeralds, any doubts of Tilly's involvement should have been deflected. *Must* have been deflected.

Then why in God's name had she disappeared? The fear that she might be up to some sleuthing on her own he dismissed after a moment's consideration. Since she didn't have any real clue to what he was involved in, she wouldn't have either a reason or a clue to make her investigate—unless she had stumbled upon something. A growing suspicion crawled along his spine, and a muscle jerked at his jaw.

The strained silence was broken by the maid's return. Flynn spoke sharply. "What have you discovered?"

Agnes did not meet his eyes. She was seeing the ruin of all her dreams and schemes. Her pride had been offended at having to wait upon anyone other than her mistress, and to be supplanted in Mrs. Whitby's service by an upstart undermaid had been a blow to her self-importance. Agnes's proud ways had not endeared her to the other servants, and they had let her know it, in subtle ways. Goaded by her dissatisfaction, she had been ripe for mischief, and had been more than willing to cause embarrassment to the guest she been assigned to wait upon. Too late, she regretted her part in the morning's little charade.

A little trick on Miss Templeton, the girl had said. *A harmless jest. And no one need ever know your part in it.* From the expressions on the faces around her, it seemed that the jest had gone sour. Agnes was now frightened. The money had been an added bonus, but now it weighed upon her like a leaden yoke. She twisted the corner of her apron between her fingers.

"Miss's large straw hat and her white sandals are gone, and there is only one dress missing, sir. It is the white yachting ensemble that Miss had been planning to wear today, for the Isle of Shells race."

Lara looked at Flynn blankly. "But the race has been postponed. And why would she leave alone, before the household was awake, and wearing her sailing costume? And today, of all days!"

As if on cue they heard a gust of wind sighing through the trees, whipping the wide palmetto leaves. It was an ominous sound in the sudden silence, one familiar to anyone who lived on the island year round. Flynn turned on the maid.

"I think Agnes can supply the answer to that. The truth, if you please," he thundered.

"I swear that I know nothing." She held out her hands in protest, but her voice shook and her skin took on a waxy pallor. Agnes teetered on the brink of hysteria. Flynn pushed her closer.

"We're wasting time." He put one hand on the maid's shoulder and ushered her firmly toward the door. "Come along with me."

"Where are you taking me?"

"To the magistrate. He will want to detain you for questioning until you decide to tell us what you know."

His eyes were green and dark, mesmerizing her so that she was unable to look away. Flynn saw the panic she was trying to govern and pressed his advantage. The thought of Tilly in the hands of his enemies made his blood run cold. They would be ruthless.

On the heels of his words Leander strode into the study, accompanied by a sweating young groom. Agnes was trembling so violently her guilt was obvious to all. "Roberto was bribed to let a sailor use the wagon early this morning. Later, he saw him driving with a young Englishwoman, but he returned the wagon alone, within an hour. And I found this."

He held out a leather bow. Lara clutched a hand to her breast. "That is from one of Tilly's sandals."

They turned to Agnes, who saw there was no escape. Weeping and wringing her hands, she threw herself on their mercy, and everything she knew about Tilly's disappearance came out between gasps and sobs.

"It was merely a harmless prank, they told me. I was to provide a girl with a maid's uniform, and not to answer Miss's bell if it rang before eight this morning."

She fell into a sobbing heap at Lara's feet. Her mistress was too stricken to pay her heed. "Oh, Lucas, I am conscience-stricken. I should never have asked Tilly to come. Not when things were so unsettled here."

Flynn answered grimly: "No, by God, this is all Jonas's doing. I warned him he was playing with fire, and not to cross swords with me. Damn him to hell for it!"

He turned to Leander. "I will instruct Bernard to admit no one to the house. Meanwhile, do not leave Mrs. Whitby's side."

With a blur of movement Flynn was out the door and, seconds later, mounted on his sleek gray gelding. The animal responded to the urgency in his master's touch and broke into a gallop, streaking past the palms and poinciana trees that lined the drive. As they wound down the road toward the distant harbor at breakneck speed, Flynn cursed himself as furiously as he had cursed Jonas.

He had expected his attentions to Tilly would lay a false trail for his adversaries, throwing them off the track; instead he had drawn her into a deep and deadly game, one she was ill-equipped to play. He guessed where they had taken her, and why.

He only hoped he wouldn't be too late.

Chapter Eight

Beneath the bright sky, the sea was as blue as ink. They had left Devil's Cove an hour earlier, and though the yacht moved swiftly through the water, not one other sail was visible on the vast expanse. Mrs. Thorne leaned back against the cushions and sulked. "They've outdistanced us greatly. We shall be the last to arrive."

Lieutenant Metcalf shrugged from his place at the tiller. "We've got a late start, but the current and wind favor our position. Clap on more sail and we'll soon catch up."

Mr. Thoms nodded. "Yes, I believe we've got a fair wind with us, this time."

The two men seemed in very high spirits, in contrast to Mrs. Thorne, who was a bad sailor and had spent the first hour below deck in the small cabin. Tilly loved the feel of the wind on her face, but despite her hat and parasol, the reflection off the water was already turning her nose pink. The lieutenant had advised her to retire to the cabin until the sun was high enough for the canvas deck cover to shield her, but Tilly remained topside. She had no wish to spend any time cooped up with the whining widow.

"When do you anticipate we will reach the Isle?"

The lieutenant looked due west. "Not much longer. If you watch closely, you'll see a bit of land upon the horizon shortly—the Isle of Shells."

Tilly shaded her eyes but could see nothing but the bright, endless waves. For the first time it struck her that they were completely isolated in the middle of the sea. To be in such a small vessel surrounded by so much water was intimidating. Aboard the *Montego Bay* with its high decks, huge masts and acres of canvas, she had felt much safer. Compared to its greater mass, Mr. Keating's boat was a flimsy little cockleshell. Thank heaven that the sea was calm!

Mr. Thoms took the tiller while Metcalf went aft to adjust the halyards, and Tilly perched upon a storage locker for a better view. After several minutes of intermittent scanning, she finally made out a smudge in the distance. It seemed to stay the same size for the next quarter hour, but after that it grew and stretched with their approach, until it filled the skyline.

Wind-sculpted sand rose, blindingly bright, forming a dunelike mass, dotted here and there with clumps of grass, scrubby shrubs and scattered, stunted trees. The only evidence of the hand of man was a homely structure of weathered wood, like one of those known in her quiet village as a "necessary house." Her disappointment was keen. This was certainly not the tropical Eden she had pictured.

Returning, the lieutenant saw her dismay and laughed. "Don't be disheartened, Miss Templeton. To take advantage of the wind, we are approaching from the far side of the island. The tents will be set up beyond the dune's crest, in the shelter of the bay."

They strolled to the stern where Mrs. Thorne joined them. She looked a bit flushed. When Tilly neared she smelled spirits on the woman's breath and tried to be charitable. Brandy was said to be an excellent remedy for seasickness.

Metcalf glanced at the sails. "I've been thinking, ladies. The wind has changed quarter and it will take us quite a while to tack around the island. If it holds steady, heaving to on this side would be an advantage on the return voyage. We might make up enough time to place in the final leg of the race."

"Yes," Mr. Thoms agreed. "But that complicates matters. It would mean a long climb over the dune for the ladies, in order to reach the picnic site. I'm sure they would rather not go to such exertion."

Tilly wasn't paying any attention. Her eyes were straining for sight of Flynn's *Sea Urchin*. Wouldn't he be surprised to see her! He might think that just because he'd kissed her, just because he turned her knees to jelly and her mind to jam, that she was still susceptible to his masculine appeal. The best course would be to snub him completely and . . .

"What do you think, Miss Templeton?"

With a jolt, Tilly realized the lieutenant was addressing her. She tried to gather her wits.

"The dune doesn't appear to be so very high. If it will give us an advantage on the way back to Kingston, I'm certainly game, but perhaps Mrs. Thorne is not well enough for the climb."

To her surprise, the widow didn't object. "I will agree to anything that will get us to solid ground, quickly!"

The men set course for a small, sandy beach where a point of coral rock projected into the water like a natural dock. They were excellent sailors, spilling the sails and taking in canvas with easy competence. The yacht settled with the drift as the lieutenant brought her smoothly in. The ladies were able to step ashore without wetting their shoes.

Tilly realized the vast openness of the sea had tricked her into misjudging distance. The island's crest had seemed like a low hill from out a sea; from the shore, the smooth curve of sand loomed high above them, the sides terribly steep. At least she had reached her destination. Now, she only needed to speak privately with Lara and with Flynn and uncover the truth—and she would have climbed The Matterhorn in order to do so.

The men set down the large wicker hamper and glanced at the wall of sand. "I don't know exactly where, in relation to this spot, they have set up the tents," the lieutenant said. "If you ladies will make yourselves comfortable, Franklin and I will climb up and scout along the crest."

"And make sure," Mrs. Thorne added sharply, "that you find the easiest way across the top for us. Our sandals and dresses were not intended for mountain climbing!"

The lieutenant set out the two large cushions he had brought from the boat. Tilly was anxious to join the others, but she couldn't abandon Mrs. Thorne just yet. The widow plumped up her pillow in the only available shade and made herself comfortable.

After the men set out, Tilly disposed herself on the other cushion. She hadn't eaten a bite, and her hunger was keen. "Do you think we might have just a nibble of something before we climb the dune? I am sure I smell cinnamon bread."

Mrs. Thorne agreed. "After all, we have to keep our strength up. But first, now that they are gone, I shall leave you briefly." She rose, with a nod toward the necessary house.

The widow trekked off determinedly, sheltered from the sun by her yellow parasol and Tilly politely turned to gaze out over the waves. The sky was sunny and blue overhead, but to the southeast it took on a milky tinge. The odd little puffball clouds were larger now, and still advancing in a straight line, like a row of marshmallow soldiers.

Thinking of marshmallows reminded her that she hadn't eaten any breakfast. Sheer torture, to a starving stomach. If the men didn't return soon, she would be tempted to pilfer at least a roll from the hamper.

Pilfering. Stealing. Emeralds. Flynn. Unless she was occupied in conversation, her brain always circled back to him. The minute she saw him she would demand to know just what was going on at Coeur d'Émeraude, and how deeply he was involved in it. Memories intruded on her thoughts: that precise, masculine angle of his jaw; the shape of his strong hands. The touch of his mouth on hers. Possessive. Persuasive.

Seductive.

Tilly banished such disturbing remembrances. They were too dangerous to her peace of mind. Minutes passed and no one came to disturb her solitude. She watched the clouds move in. They didn't look like rain clouds. They didn't look like anything she'd seen before. After a while she was bored with sitting alone. Rising, she strolled along the beach.

From her vantage point, there was nothing but sky and sea in every direction. She could almost imagine herself alone on the edge of the world, or upon a forgotten isle, like Robinson Crusoe. Strange to realize there were dozens of her acquaintances on the far side of the dune.

She stooped to pick up a shell, mottled brown and ivory, with a hole neatly drilled through one side by a marine creature. There was nothing spectacular about the shell, and she dropped it on the sand. It was not until she'd gone farther that Tilly registered something that didn't add up. The Isle of Shells was supposed to be a treasure trove of exotic shells, but that was the first one she'd seen. A trick of the tide, she decided.

She started back and realized she'd gone farther than she'd intended. The curve of the land had taken her beyond the point, and she spotted the *Whisper* in the distance. Something about it looked odd. The mast looked short and squat. At first she thought it was a mirage, caused by the bright reflection. Then she understood: the craft was listing heavily, giving the mast a foreshortened appearance. She ran toward it, the soles of her sandals crunching over the gritty coral sand. "Lieutenant Metcalf! Mr. Thoms! Come quickly!"

No voice answered her cries. By the time she reached the point, the vessel had taken so much water it was half-immersed. Tilly called out again, without any response. There was no sign of Mrs. Thorne. She ran to the small wooden structure and rapped sharply on the wall.

"Mrs. Thorne, do come out! The boat is sinking. I shall have to climb the dune and try to find our escorts."

She started away and tripped on a piece of driftwood, falling heavily against the side of the tiny building. Tilly saved herself by catching at the latch, and the wooden door swung slowly open. It wasn't a necessary house at all, only an abandoned fisherman's hut. Except for a mildewed hammock, a broken lobster trap, an earthen pot and a very large black and yellow spider, the interior was empty.

She must have made a mistake. But no, there was the yacht they'd sailed in, slowly sinking into the clear green shallows, and there was no other wooden structure in sight. While she watched, horrified, the vessel rolled on her beam ends and settled. Only a third of the hull cleared the waves. Tilly turned, searching the landscape as far as she could see. Nothing moved. She called again.

No one answered.

A seabird's cry, lonely and haunting, was the only sound to override the restless splashing of the waves upon the shore. Racing up the dune, breathless and perspiring, Tilly tried to push away the fear that had her in its grip. After the first three yards she made little headway. The higher she went, the harder the going was. Her sides heaved with the effort. Her sandals were the wrong footgear for clambering up loose sand and for every two feet she rose, she slid back one.

Her legs were wood, then lead, and she grabbed at the stunted growth to pull herself upward. Her hair came loose from its simple chignon to lie damply against the back of her neck, and her lungs burned with effort. The silk stockings she'd been so proud of were shredded at toe and heel, and her palms were scraped from the hot sand. It took forever to reach the crest.

Tilly hauled herself over and struggled to her feet. She stared in disbelief. No yachts were moored in the wide bay at the foot of the dune. The bay was empty, and the land, for all its width, was a fragile, sandy crescent that formed the raw beginnings of a broken atoll. Someday it might become an island; for now, it was a curving rim of coral rock and sand. There was nothing else. No tables, no tents.

No people.

By straining her eyes Tilly made out the only sign of life: a small craft far out to sea, shrunken with distance. As it sped away, sails filled with wind, she thought she could just make out moving figures aboard the vessel—one of them holding a bright yellow parasol.

A stone rattled down the steep slope, then another. Skelly heard the sounds of someone approaching through the underbrush and hid in the shelter of a bread-fruit tree Captain Cook had planted generations before. Whoever it was had no fear of being heard. The sailor tightened the grip on his knife. Then a figure jumped from the rocky ledge above.

"Put away your weapon, Skelly."

The seaman recognized Tiger Flynn and relaxed. "Thought ye was one o' them piratical fellows a-coming back fer us." He tucked the knife into the waistband of his pants. "I was fixin' fer a fight."

"Good." Flynn led the way to the small, sandy beach. "Because we're liable to start one. That is, if you're willing to sail out with me."

The sailor's mouth fell open. "Be ye daft, man? In the face of that storm that's a-brewing?"

"Well then, I'll go alone, and no hard feelings. Only a fool would go out today, and I can't expect you to risk your life for a woman you don't even know."

"A woman?"

Flynn didn't answer. He looked seaward. The milky haze that obscured the sky was denser now, almost opaque. The surf was higher, assaulting the narrow strip of beach with increasing aggressiveness. The *Sea Urchin* dipped and bobbed with the rising swell. The storm was closing in rapidly. It was going to be risky as hell.

Only God knew what the weather would be in another few hours, and handling the vessel alone in a storm might be beyond him. But he didn't have any choice. Before leaving Kingston he had questioned the lookout on a Scottish merchantman seeking permission to ride out the storm in the sheltered harbor. Yes, the mate had seen a small craft, although it had been at the very limits of his long-distance vision. Small but trim, and heading almost due west, he said, scratching his jaw.

Fools, I called 'em. Nothing but ocean between them and the coast o' Costa Rica, 'cepting the sickle-shaped sandbar.

By the time Flynn reached the waterline there was another shadow moving in step with his. He turned his head and raised his eyebrows questioningly. Skelly's weathered face split in a wide grin. "Aye. Happen I be as daft as ye.

But I've nothing better to do, to pass the time o' day. And if there's a mermaid a-waiting fer me, I'd rather meet her in Davy Jones's locker than in Fiddler's Green."

Flynn grinned and clapped him on the shoulder. "What makes you think you'll go to such a fine place as either of those, Skelly?"

"I met the devil once, when the *Joseph Vaugh* went down in '52. 'E looked me right in the eye and said, 'Skelly, ye old rascal, Satan's hell is too small t' old us both, and I ain't about to give up me own home for the likes of a black old sea dog like yourself.'"

"Good. At least one of us will get ashore safely. But I have to warn you, we might run into a couple of ugly customers. Well-armed, no doubt."

"Ho! I'm as afeared as ye. Can ye hear me knees knockin'?" He guffawed. "Lead on."

Aboard the *Sea Urchin* they weighed anchor and hauled up the shrouds. The sails snapped and filled with wind. The yacht pulled swiftly away from the secluded cove and headed out to sea. Once clear of land, they trimmed the sheets and the yacht shot forward like a greyhound eager for the race. Skelly watched the foaming bow wave with approval.

"This be a sweet and sprightly goer, Cap'n. She's got the bone between her teeth now!"

"She'll have to go full out to get us into the bay and safely out again before it hits." By the time they reached it, the crescent of land might be underwater. It was directly in the path of the oncoming storm.

As he tacked around the headland, Flynn kept one weather eye to the east. That peculiar milky quality in the air was showing ominous signs of change—signs that meant the tropical storm was moving in with unusual speed. The distant sky was tinged a dirty gray, and the dark ocean streaked with frothing whitecaps. A hurricane was on a collision course with the Greater Antilles, and Jamaica lay directly in its path.

* * *

Tilly was hot, tired and irritable, but she was not prone to hysterics. There was no way she could leave this sandy spit of land under her own power, so she would just have to cool her heels until the others returned. She had no doubt that they would do so shortly, laughing at her discomfiture.

What puzzled her was the reason behind such a seemingly spiteful trick. Perhaps it was not meant to be malicious. On the island of Ruranta, she had once read, newcomers to the colony were told to dress in their best finery and were then doused with buckets of water to signify their acceptance into local society—but Jamaica was not the Pacific island of Ruranta, and she had never heard of such a strange custom here. Then she remembered Flynn saying something about an initiation required of novices in The Isle of Shells race— But where were the other victims?

Meanwhile, she refused to gratify Mrs. Thorne with the least show of anxiety. They were probably watching her with a spyglass, waiting for her to panic. Well, she would show them! Tilly lifted the lid and examined the basket's contents. Most of its space was taken up with cutlery, goblets packed in individual compartments, an assortment of dishes and three bottles of wine. There was also cold chicken, cheese, crusty bread and two pieces of fruit.

It was more than enough to hold her until the others tired of their little game and came back, but it was scarcely enough for a party of four. The servants must have misunderstood, thinking the basket was only to serve one person. Tilly smiled. When the trio dropped anchor once more, the tables would be turned, for she intended to eat as much as she wanted. And since she hadn't had any breakfast, that was considerable.

Piling sliced chicken and cheese on a plate, she set to work. Everything was delicious. Her only regret was that there was nothing but the wine to wash it all down. She removed the cork and poured herself a glass. During the next half hour she made severe depredations on the food, then wiped her fingers delicately on the embroidered damask linen. There was nothing left to do but wait—and sip a second glass of wine. She settled against the warm sand and closed her eyes, letting her mind wander. As usual it wandered for only a moment or two before arrowing straight toward a familiar target: Tiger Flynn.

He was an enigma. One that intrigued her greatly. A dandy by day. And by night? Several descriptions came to mind. Adventurer. Renegade. Hero. Thief? It was difficult to assess him accurately. Her brain tried to view him dispassionately but her feminine instincts were definitely biased. The wine made her warm, but she was incredibly thirsty. She poured one more glass and drank it, then returned to her obsession.

A good fairy had been present at Flynn's birth, endowing him with a handsome face and a lithe, powerful frame. But there was something beyond the appeal of his physical form. It had to do with the tilt of his head, the way the corners of his mouth quirked up when he was amused, the quick intelligence and warmth that sparkled from the depths of his eyes.

A gull screeched overhead, diverting her attention. The sky was still bright and blue all the way to the western horizon. She helped herself to another piece of bread and threw the crust to the bird. It swooped down, caught the bit of bread in its bill and flew off with a loud flapping of wings.

Tilly realized the other gulls had disappeared. Perhaps, she thought, they spent the afternoons riding over the waves or following the fishing boats. That made her aware of the passing time. She opened the case of the watch she'd pinned to her bodice. The hands pointed toward the six, and she realized she had forgotten to wind it that morning in her haste.

Tilly wound the stem and satisfied herself that it was ticking off the seconds again. At least she could keep track of how much time passed from now until they returned for her. The glare from the sand was adding to her sunburn. Although she meant to stay outwardly unruffled, inwardly she was fuming and anxious for her companions to return. This had gone far beyond the bounds of a joke!

Rising and brushing off crumbs, she climbed the dune to scan for a boat. Once she was out of the scrap of shade, the sun hit her like a blast from hell. It poured down from the sky and blazed up from below. The rough coral sand glittered in the fierce light, and she had to half close her eyes against its brilliance.

There was no sign of any craft on the shifting, swelling surface. Endless white-tipped waves tumbled over, spraying diamonds in the air and collapsing against the shore. The effect was hypnotic. After a while she realized they were much higher than they had been earlier. A gust of wind caught her, whipping her skirts around her ankles and trying to tear her hat away. Fixing her long hat pin more securely, she pivoted halfway around and gasped in dismay.

To the southeast a sooty blur was rapidly blotting up the blue sky, spreading outward and upward moment by moment; the sea, still a breathtaking sapphire here, was dark as slate in the distance. It had an ugly, menacing quality as it announced that a storm of tremendous magnitude was headed directly toward the puny little sandbar where she stood. Already the waves were taller and coming farther up the shore. The soft murmur of the surf was growing loud. Soon it would be a thunderous roar.

How high would the water come? Tilly had noticed no high-tide lines along the beach. A shiver of fear shot through her. That could only mean that the island was completely inundated by it. It wouldn't do much good to retreat to the crest of the dune. Unless they returned for her soon, it would be too late.

The truth hit her with stunning power. This was more than a trick gone awry. They were not coming back for her. They had never intended to do so.

No, it was the wine, befuddling her brain. Why should they wish to harm her? Any moment they would come sailing along, filled with laughter at her gullibility. It was only a senseless, harmless joke.

Wasn't it?

* * *

Beneath a lowering sky the sleek yacht plowed its way through the increasingly high seas. A few birds skimmed along the jagged waves, but none arced overhead. Flynn set his jaw grimly. Two hours offshore and there was no other sign of life. The yacht and its two-member crew existed in a cruel, watery world that tested their resolution as greatly as it tested their strength.

A wave broke over them, then another. Skelly glanced worriedly over his shoulder. "We be taking on water, Cap'n."

Flynn cursed beneath his breath. They were shipping water faster than the scuppers could handle it. With Skelly manning the pump they had managed to keep afloat, but they were sailing close to the wind. A change of direction would help prevent them from taking on more water, but a change of a few degrees might sweep them right past the Crescent.

The light was failing, although it was midday, as an eerie twilight turned the sky and sea to pewter. Flynn strained his eyes for the first sight of the curving reef. If his reckoning was true, the bulge of it should soon be showing above the waves. The *Sea Urchin* ran on and still there was nothing. A sense of foreboding hovered around him. Had he misjudged his bearings? Now, when every second was precious, a miscalculation could prove fatal—to Tilly, and to Skelly and himself.

After several nerve-racking minutes he saw something ahead. Not the great hump of coral and sand that he'd expected, but a ragged wall of rock no more than fifteen feet above the top of the highest waves. The action of the water had so thoroughly undermined the sandy dune it had collapsed into the sea. Flynn felt as if he'd been struck in the midsection. He threw off the reaction and fought to get the yacht in closer.

Spume spattered them as the waves crashed into the remaining shelf of coral rock. It took another thirty minutes of skillful tacking, and all his and Skelly's skills combined, to bring the craft around one horn of the crescent-shaped reef and through the opening into the little bay. They were drenched with salt water and sweat, and Flynn's hands were raw, but at last they had made it in. If the crescent had curved the other way it would have been impossible.

He saw her then, huddled into one of the crevices that marked the ancient coral growth. She was so still, her position so awkward that he thought the worst. He called out her name, but the wind snatched the words away. They maneuvered the *Urchin* in as far as was safe. Flynn wound a rope around his middle and plunged overboard, swimming toward what remained of the western beach. The waves were small inside the sheltering arms of the reef, but the surge and drag of the water threatened to pull him under time and again.

When he dragged himself out of the lagoon his limbs felt like lead weights and his lungs were starved for air. He staggered over the sharp surface, laid bare by wind and wave, dreading what he might find.

"Tilly!"

The huddled figure didn't move. He called out again, and this time was rewarded. She stirred and lifted her head. Her eyes were tired and glazed. Flynn dashed across the water-logged sand toward her. She was pale, and a lurid scratch crossed the angle of her jaw; but the sparkle in her gray eyes encouraged him to think she was in better shape than she looked.

Flynn lifted her to her feet and felt the tremors that shook her entire body. She was ice cold. "Thank God! I was afraid we wouldn't get to you in time."

"'Nother hour," she responded tartly, "and there would've been nothing left to salvage. I think you an' your friends are disgusting, and your stupid joke is not funny!" Tilly's voice slowed to a halt and she dissolved in tears.

Flynn leaned down and sniffed. "My God, you're drunk!"

"Am not. Just had a few glasses . . . to keep me warm."

"Good Lord! How much did you drink?"

"I'm still sober enough to figure out your schemes. You 'n Lieutenan' Me'calf 'n Jonas are all in this together."

Flynn groaned. He hadn't counted on this when he'd set out to rescue her. "Can you swim, Tilly? Because we can't bring the *Urchin* in any closer without risking its breaking up."

"Swim? 'Course I can swim. But I absolutely refuse to go into the water. It's cold 'n wet, an' I'm already cold 'n wet."

Flynn sighed. There was no way he could get a drunken, belligerent woman to the yacht without risking both their lives. It was a pity, the act of a real knave, but he had no choice.

He brought his right fist up so fast she didn't even see it and clipped her on the point of her chin. Her head snapped back, and she crumpled like a rag doll in his arms.

Flynn kept a watchful eye on the storm clouds as the *Urchin* ran close-hauled before the storm. She was a gallant craft, delivering all the speed and ease of maneuverability she was designed for. They continued to gather way under the freshening gale-force winds, but if the winds increased they'd have to reef the sails and hove to. That would be disastrous. With the strong currents, the yacht would be taken far off course with no hope of making the landfall Flynn sought.

"Here." Flynn held out a slim silver flask to Tilly. "Hair of the dog..."

Tilly rubbed the knot on her jaw tenderly and went back to bailing, although her head felt like a beating drum. "No, thank you. It is probably poisoned."

"Still holding a grudge? Why the devil do you think I'd risk my neck to save you, only to poison you later?"

"I have no idea, *Mr.* Flynn. But then, I've never understood any of your actions. Especially such ungentlemanly behavior as striking me with your fist!"

"We were in acute danger and you refused to go into the water with me," he answered sharply above the moan of the wind. "And there wasn't enough time to sober you up first. Now drink. It's perfectly harmless under the circumstances."

"So you say. But the word of a man who is vile enough to strike an unprotected woman is not something I value greatly."

"It must be one devil of a hangover that you've got." He eyed her grimly, then tipped the flask and took a swallow. "There. I haven't fallen dead at your feet. It's not poison, only rum, and it will keep you from catching a chill and make you feel warmer."

She hesitated.

"It will also," he added, "ease your aching head."

Since she was shivering with cold, the prospect was enticing. Reluctantly she unclenched her blue fingers and held out her hand. Flynn put the flask into it and sketched a mocking bow. "I only wish it were champagne, Miss Templeton."

Tilly took a healthy swig of its contents and choked. To her unfamiliar palate it was like drinking liquid fire. "Oh," she gasped, "I wish it were tea!"

Flynn laughed and capped the flask, then went toward the stern to assist Skelly. Tilly had heard that sailors were partial to spirits. Now she knew why. The illusion of warmth had trickled down her throat and into her stomach, spreading outward through her veins. Her wet clothes seemed less chill and clammy, and her icy fingers lost their stiffness. Even the bite of the wind was less keen.

Much as she disliked it, the rum would help keep her alive—as long as she didn't get so tipsy that she fell overboard. But with the cold and exertion, the spirits didn't seem to affect her that way. Taking up the bucket once more, she went back to her self-appointed task.

Her eyebrows and eyelashes were crusted with salt spray, and her clothing felt like sheets of ice. If her toes didn't fall off, it would be quite amazing, she thought with odd detachment. She had reached the point of weariness where the mind steps back from the body for survival. Her back ached as if it were breaking, and her arms and shoulders burned with unaccustomed effort, but still she bailed and bailed. It was hopeless. Inexperienced as she was, she saw they were losing the battle.

Chapter Nine

The yacht scudded along before the storm's wrath. Flynn conferred with Skelly and shook his head. "We're sailing as close to the wind as we dare. We might gain a bit of speed, but we're more likely to broach." If the *Urchin* fell into a wave trough, she could be dismasted or even capsize.

As he made his way toward her, Tilly knew the news was not good. She raised her voice to carry over the wind.

"What are our chances of making it safely to Jamaica?"

"The winds and tides are against us, and the sea is running too high. This craft wasn't made to withstand such conditions. We'd break up attempting it."

"I see." She kept bailing.

Flynn felt a surge of admiration. "No recriminations, no tears? You are indeed a remarkable woman."

"I believe 'maddening' was the descriptive term you used earlier. Well, I won't go down without a fight."

"Good girl!" He took the bucket out of her stiff fingers and covered one of her hands with his. At first they seemed as cold as her own, but gradually the warmth seeped from them into hers.

"There is still a chance that we might escape with whole skins, Tilly. It's a long shot. I can't promise anything but that I'll do my damnedest to see us safely through this."

Lightning flared, and his eyes were greener than the mountainous sea around them. "If we can continue running before the storm, we might reach land before the hurricane strikes."

Tilly tried to concentrate despite her aching head. Perhaps she had misunderstood him. "I think my geography has failed me," she replied. "To my knowledge, there is nothing but hundreds of miles of empty ocean between us and the Americas."

Flynn hesitated only a split second. "You're right as usual, my dear. There isn't."

Tilly swallowed hard, clutched at his hand with icicle fingers and kept her chin up. It took a moment for the implications of his words to sink in. It was terrible and frightening. The *Sea Urchin* was a needle in a watery haystack. They were somewhere in the Caribbean Ocean, and the gale-force winds were building behind them. Somewhere beyond that was a hurricane, a storm so massive and powerful she could not conceive of its scope. And landfall, even at the speed they were traveling, must be days ahead. It was impossible and ridiculous and overwhelming.

But it was their only chance. Hope rose inside her. Flynn didn't seem to think their situation was insurmountable. His main concern was to keep the yacht from swamping or heeling over in the winds. If they could keep afloat, they had a good chance.

She waited, superstitiously afraid to show her eagerness and tempt fate. It was ironic that she had traveled halfway around the world to die in a tropical storm. She didn't want to die. Not now, when she had just begun to taste life. She blamed herself for the fix they were in. Common sense should have told her that Lara would not have gone off to the race leaving her alone and unprotected after Christopher's attack.

Unfortunately, her common sense hadn't been operating at the time. The effects of the sleeping powder had clouded her judgment. Because of that, both Flynn and Skelly—who was a complete stranger to her—had risked their lives. At the moment Flynn had his hands full without having to worry over her reaction. She would not let her panic burden him.

Flynn watched her, interpreting the fleeting thoughts as they crossed her mobile features. Fear. Awe. Stalwart determination. The hysteria or despair that would have doomed them were absent. Despite the spray of water that spattered them with the next wave, he smiled. Her courage had considerably improved the odds for their success.

"If we get out of this alive, Tilly, I swear to God that I'll make it up to you."

She gave him one of her level glances. "If we do, I shall certainly hold you to that promise."

He threw back his head and laughed. "Keep bailing," he said, and went back to his own tasks.

Time passed in an agony of exhaustion, a monotonous pattern of effort and pain, interrupted only by the movement of the boat and the ceaseless writhings of the sea. There were periods when Tilly's muscles refused to obey her commands; when they twitched and quivered and lost all sense of feeling. But the moment strength came back she began bailing again.

Later, when they changed their tack, the yacht took on less water and the level dropped rapidly. Her actions were so automatic by then that she fell asleep for fleeting seconds, waking with a painful jerk to right her balance. Flynn let Skelly take the tiller and gestured for her to go below into the tiny cabin. She sat there, blinking her eyes dazedly. He had to pry the bucket from her cramped fingers.

"We're shipping less water now. Go below and strap yourself in a bunk. Try and sleep."

"I can't leave everything up to you two."

"I'll alert you if there's need. For now the best thing you can do is rest awhile and keep up your reserves."

He helped her up and guided her to the tiny cabin. Her legs were jellied, and she stumbled awkwardly. Flynn muttered something that was snatched away by the wind. Tilly's back and neck and arms felt as stiff and heavy as logs.

She ducked inside the cabin, curled up gratefully on the narrow bunk and strapped herself in. The blanket was damp, but the wool wicked the wetness away from her skin. She thought the danger and the pitching of the yacht would keep her awake, but neither was a match for her extreme fatigue. Just before falling asleep she realized, disinterestedly, that not even a call to abandon ship could have roused her from the bunk. She was utterly drained.

Tilly woke from a slumber disturbed by nightmares, unable to judge if minutes or hours had passed. It was dark, and the rolling had decreased. She went topside. The sails were reefed and the yacht was drifting to leeward.

Flynn saw her. "Stay below," he ordered. She did. There was nothing she could do to help above deck, and her presence was an obvious hindrance. At least she had gotten her sea legs, and could keep herself upright. Most of the time.

Horrible as the incessant bailing had been, the inactivity was worse. Being helpless with the yacht didn't mean she had to be useless. It was dim in the cabin, but Tilly rummaged around in the tidy lockers and found the food stores. The two men would need sustenance to battle the elements; as for herself, food was the last thing she required at the moment. The yacht pitched and she had to grab the unlit lamp to stay upright.

When she seemed to be right side up again, Tilly examined the stores. There were tins of bully beef and sardines wrapped in oilskins, but she had no means to open them. Just as well—she was more likely to accidentally open an artery than the tin. The canisters of English biscuits would have to do until Flynn or his companion could spare the time to open something more nourishing.

A sudden flash of lightning illuminated the small space in stark glare and shadow. The resounding crash of thunder came immediately on its heels. Tilly's ears rang with the furious sound. An eerie blue glow lit the cabin, and the air seemed to crackle and buzz. She felt the hairs on her head and the backs of her arms rise away from her skin. Another rocket of light burst overhead, blindingly bright. She dropped the canister and clapped her hands over her ears. They were no protection. The boom came instantly, with a roar like the last judgment's call. It was followed by a horrible crack that almost burst her eardrums. The mysterious blue light faded.

"The mast is sprung!" Skelly shouted.

Tilly pulled herself up to the deck and paused, framed by the opening. Flynn and Skelly hacked at the backstays that held the upper part of the mast, and it came crashing down into the water, just missing the deck. It was tossed like a straw on the looming waves. It sank while she watched, terrified.

Skelly took the tiller again while Flynn struggled with a tangle of rope and canvas. Tilly made her way across the slick deck, holding on to whatever was at hand to stay upright on the sharply slanting deck. A wave broke across it, almost knocking her off her feet.

Flynn spotted her. "Get below, god damn it!"

Shaking with fear and effort, Tilly worked her way up the slanting deck and braced herself in the doorway of the cabin. She was afraid to go inside, afraid she would be trapped if the yacht went down. She wedged herself on the top step while her teeth chattered with cold and fright. It was appalling to be so useless in the present crisis, but there was nothing she could do except stay out of their way and pray. She did both.

It was an eternity before she saw Flynn again. Although the rocking of the yacht had decreased he looked worn and haggard. His hair was plastered to his head and neck, and his shirt was ripped to tatters, baring the muscles of his chest and arms. But it was his eyes that astonished her. They were heavy-lidded and shadowed with exhaustion but incredibly alive. Her spirits lifted.

"Is the storm slackening?"

He shook his head. "It's going to get worse before it gets better, Miss Templeton." *If it ever does get better.*

The unspoken words hung in the air between them. "I just wanted to tell you..." Flynn stopped, then started again. "I'm sorry," he said shortly. "For this—and for everything."

Thunder rumbled overhead. Tilly tried to smile but her mouth trembled too much. "There's no use in our crying over spilled milk," she said. "What's done is done."

A reluctant smile spread over Flynn's features. "Spilled milk. By gad, you're worth ten of any other woman!"

She was too cold and wet and tired to discover what he found so humorous. "How desperate is our situation? The truth, if you please."

The slight tremor in Tilly's voice gave her away. He cupped her cheek in his palm and rubbed his thumb along her skin. "We've lost the top of the mast, but we can compensate for that if the wind drops. The real problem is the tiller. It's splintered to a stub. Until we can repair it, we're at the mercy of the storm and the sea."

She stared at him wordlessly for what seemed like a very long time. His face was barely visible in the darkness that had closed in around them. He started to speak, hesitated, then seemed to change his mind about what he had intended to say.

"It would ease my mind if you would rest. There's nothing you can do to help. It will be light in a few hours. If the seas drop, we'll try to rig something up for a sail and to replace the tiller."

He leaned down and kissed her on the mouth. His lips were cool and salty, and despite the circumstances, stirring. He caught her up in his arms, holding her so tightly her ribs protested. Tilly didn't care. She felt she could face anything as long as she stood within the circle of his arms. He kissed her again, a light, quick touch, and released her.

For a few seconds his eyes held hers. "Tilly…" was all he said, before turning away. That single word held volumes.

He went back to work, and she huddled on the top step just inside the entry. Although the electrical storm had moved away, the distant flashes of lightning gave the men something to work by. They rigged a piece of the broken mast to the stub of the tiller and bound it with rope. Anything more sophisticated would have to wait till morning. The heaving of the waves lessened, and the men took turns at rest or manning the tiller. Tilly dozed fitfully in her cramped little space, and came to with a start when she heard Skelly call out.

Gradually she perceived that the sky behind him was growing luminous. She stepped out and stretched her aching muscles. Ahead it was black as soot, but to the east a lurid bar of orange stretched across the horizon, staining the water like bleeding dye. Morning was dawning, bringing with it a promise of more rough weather to come. With the light, the yacht appeared to be cutting through the waves. She was puzzled. Tilly approached Flynn.

"We have no sail, yet we seem to be moving quite swiftly. Is it the tide?"

"No. We are in the grip of the strong current that flows toward the coast of South America, then up along the Yucatan Peninsula."

"Then we shall reach land eventually."

He couldn't burst her bubble of hope. "If the seas drop I can attempt to repair the rudder. Enough, at least, to bring us in close to shore." He left the rest unsaid—that otherwise they would be helpless, unable to keep from being swept past the peninsula and back out to sea.

"Then there is no need for total despair," Tilly remarked. "If one of you gentlemen will open a tin, we can eat. I, for one, am starving."

Skelly's deep laugh rumbled like an echo of thunder. "Ye be a brave lass, mistress. T'would be a shame to let ye starve, it would."

She brought him a tin of meat to open, glad that she had won his confidence. Skelly beamed at her. "Ye've come right about, ain't ye? Half seas over, ye were, when Cap'n Flynn hauled ye aboard."

A blush crept over her cheeks. It would be some time, evidently, before they stopped twitting her about the wine and dehydration that had made her so tipsy. Behind her brave facade she hid a great deal of fear. The ocean was so big, their disabled vessel ship so very small in comparison. Tilly had never dreamed there was so much water in all the world.

By the next morning she was sadly aware that all the water around them would not slake her growing thirst. They had sufficient food to last another week, but scarcely enough water to make it through another morning. Tilly found some pooled in the fouled canvas, but it was half rain and half salt water. Flynn snared a floating coconut in his net, but it turned out to be only a hollow shell.

"Aye, we've got to catch us some fish," Skelly announced darkly, as the scorching sun came out.

Tilly didn't understand. "Fish? But we have plenty of food. It's something to drink that we lack."

Flynn gave her an odd look. "He wasn't thinking of cooking them."

Her stomach turned over. "My thirst will have to get much worse before I could even remotely contemplate eating raw fish!"

"Another day of this and I can guarantee you'll be leaning overboard, searching for minnows with lust in your eye!"

The men went to their task of putting up a makeshift sail, and Tilly retreated to the cabin. By unspoken consent this was her preserve. By noon the sea was calmer, and it was hot. Too hot. She went on deck where there was a steady breeze to cool her skin. Flynn was sleeping on the bare boards in the minuscule shade of the cabin wall while Skelly took charge. The small but efficient sail they had rigged was filled with wind.

By afternoon the watch had changed again. Skelly was stretched out in the bow, snoring softly. Despite the clouds building up again, the glare off the water was blinding. She turned her eyes to the only thing worth looking at: Lucas Flynn.

Stripped to the waist, his body was as bronzed as his face, and as lean. She was endlessly fascinated by the play of muscle and tendon beneath his skin. Not just the splendid symmetry of his form, but the efficient and disciplined strength of it. The beauty and economy of movement as he knotted a loop or pegged a wedge into a rope stirred her imagination. The French had a way of describing someone like Flynn. *C'est un homme!* Yes, he was a man. Very much so.

That was what had made his languorous-dandy pose in society so out of character. This man, hardheaded and competent, was the same one she had first met in the shadows of her boudoir the night of Lara's dinner party. He was related to the man who had kissed her then and later at the waterfall, but in direct contrast to the flirtatious and fashionable upper-class favorite. The man who had risked his neck to save her was the same man who had knocked her senseless. Unconsciously she rubbed the tender lump again. There were layers upon layers of Tiger Flynn, it seemed, each so different from the others that she could only wonder at what really lay at his core.

Flynn completed his task and glanced up in time to read her expression. All that curiosity and not one question. His blinding white smile flashed against his tanned skin and dark growth of beard. "Did I ever tell you, Miss Matilda Templeton, that you are a woman in a hundred?"

She smiled back in response. "No, only one in ten. I didn't believe you then, and I am quite sure I don't believe you now."

"You are very right. You're not even a woman in a million. You, my sunburned little ragamuffin, are unique."

A flush rose beneath her already red skin. Was that a compliment? It had sounded like one. But a sunburned ragamuffin was not exactly the image a woman wanted to conjure up in the eye of the man she...felt very attracted to. Tilly looked away, afraid he would decipher her feelings as easily as he seemed to interpret her thoughts. She didn't dare examine them more closely herself.

Flynn lashed the repaired tiller in place, then eased the kinks from his back and rose. "We've been thrown together in rather singular circumstances. Even more extraordinary, although you've censured my actions, you haven't once beleaguered me for explanations."

"It would be rather stupid of me to badger you for answers when you are busy trying to assure our very survival. And I am not a stupid woman."

"Not in the least." He came toward her and stood so close she almost backed up. The light in his eyes as he stared down at her was so brilliant it dazzled her.

Tilly swallowed. "However, now that we've a bit more time on our hands, I would like a few answers."

"Such as?"

"Such as why you vanished from sight after I gave you the emeralds. And why Jonas—or Christopher Burlinghome— tried to throttle me. Or, more to the point at the present moment, why I was abandoned on the sand reef with a hurricane approaching by supposed friends. Even," she said firmly, "how you knew I was out on that tiny island, and why you risked your life to find me."

"There are some things that I can't explain to you yet. For one thing, it would take too much time. For another, I don't have all the facts assembled. You'll have to trust me a bit farther."

"Yes," she said stringently. "All the way to the coast of Central America!"

He threw back his head and laughed. "As to the why of rescuing you, I am deeply in your debt. And I always pay my debts." He frowned suddenly, and his eyes took on a distant look. "One way or another."

Tilly's disappointment at his impersonal reply was overwhelmed by the cold currents in his voice. She shivered. Lucas Flynn could be a good friend or a deadly enemy, of that she was sure.

He noticed how pale she'd gone beneath her sunburn. "You need to get some rest. If it is too hot below, I'll rig up a lean-to for you, but you must rest."

Her lips felt dry and cracked but she managed a brisk tone. "Very well. I'll sit in the shade of the cabin. But I will not go below except to forage for food. It's like a furnace down there."

He let her go. She was aware of him watching her, of the tension in his stance. He suspected her of losing her nerve. Well, she would show him she was made of sterner stuff. As the day wore on, Tilly knew he watched her from time to time with a frown between his brows. She stiffened her spine and ignored him.

The day was interminable. Skelly opened a tin of unidentified meat. It was tasteless and rather salty. Another, of oiled herrings, was even worse. "Axle grease," Flynn said, spitting a morsel over the rail. He used it for bait, without results. Even the fish spurned it. Later, they rejoiced when an unmarked tin was opened to reveal pulpy fruit, and savored every last drop of the precious liquid.

"We might save some for tomorrow," Tilly had suggested when they started. Flynn disagreed.

"What little there is will not help us tomorrow. We need it now."

The timbre of his voice told her there was more to it than that, but she didn't argue. By late afternoon an alteration in the current and a change in Flynn's improvised sail had them moving in a more westerly direction. They were on a collision course with the edge of the advancing storm.

"If we can keep just to the outside of it," he said, "we might draw some stray showers."

Skelly agreed. Death in the sea was preferable to the slow, agonizing alternative. Tilly was torn between her terror of being caught up in the storm and the appreciation that it was their only hope of fresh water. She gathered every possible container she could find, including the rum jar and Flynn's discarded boots.

The rain came after sundown. The first drops awakened Tilly, who had just fallen into a fitful doze. She lifted her face to the dark sky, unbelieving. One droplet touched her parched lips, and she felt scattered beads of water on her skin. The sprinkle turned to a fine, misty drizzle, and she flung her arms wide in welcome. It came harder and faster, each drip stinging like a tiny steel pellet. For a few more seconds she stood with her face upturned. Then she came to her senses, shook off her delight and began checking the receptacles she had set out earlier with more dogged determination than hope.

Rain rattled in the bucket and empty tins. It made wonderful pinging, sloshing noises as it filled the enameled tin basin and heavy pewter mugs from below deck. Soon her clothes were soaking wet and molded to her body, her hair loose from its serviceable braid and plastered to her head and back. She took a cup to Flynn, who stood at the tiller, and offered it up like a goblet of the finest wine.

"Ladies first," he said, and watched with satisfaction as she downed half of it at one swallow. "Not too much, though, or you'll be sick."

He finished the water and grinned at her, his hair sleek and dark and curling at the back of his neck. Tilly realized that she was grinning, too. Skelly threw back his head and laughed his booming laugh, and the others joined in for the pure joy of being alive.

Despite everything, Tilly was sure Flynn would manage to bring them to safe harbor. Relief made her giddy, and her confidence in his abilities was complete. "Now that we have the water we so desperately need, I am sure we shall reach land in safety."

Flynn's smile faded. They had dodged misfortune by a hair more than once, and it had given Tilly a false sense of optimism. Tilly knew that they had to reach land before the storm hit.

But she didn't know about the reefs.

Just after dawn Tilly woke to rough seas. She heard Flynn give a shout and came up on deck, wondering what was wrong. He was pointing west, and she followed his gesture. One moment there was nothing but gray waves and sky, the next, great frothing scallops rising above the silver-surfaced sea, the portents of treacherous shallows, sharp-toothed coral formations, lying in wait to rip out the hulls of trespassing vessels. But—miracle of miracles—beyond their threat was a thin, wavery black streak, like a line of India ink floating on the water. Land. *"Land!"*

Flynn scanned the roiling sea. There appeared to be no break in the reefs. They had to find a way in, and soon. The storm had veered in their direction, and when it reached them their little vessel would be dashed upon the coral and shaken into splinters. Climbing the fifteen-foot remnant of mast, he scouted the area, then slid down for a hurried consultation with Skelly. He would man the shroud lines, and the burly sailor would steer the craft.

As he was coming to speak to Tilly, a capricious gust of wind caught the sail and sent the yacht into the eye of the wind. Flynn shouted orders, but there was no time for Skelly to act. The ship rolled, and Tilly hung on for dear life. It was impossible to tell up from down or sideways. Another blast hit them, and the *Sea Urchin* bobbed like a cork in a whirlpool.

They rode it out for several minutes, and Tilly saw the land growing larger as they dodged past the first line of reefs. She held her breath. They were nearer every moment. They were going to make it. The sky opened without warning and dropped a wall of water upon them.

An enormous wave rose from the sea, a mountain of dark, foaming water. It slammed the hull with terrible force, like a blow from a giant's hand. A vibration shuddered through the keel, followed by the screech of ripping wood. "Her back be broken!" Skelly bellowed. "She be breakin' up!"

"Abandon ship!" Flynn struggled to catch the makeshift yard. Another wave hit, pushing them off the concealed reef. The vessel tipped so far over that the top of the broken mast dipped beneath the waves. A shroud line tore loose and whipped around Flynn's legs, bringing him down. Skelly saw the boom come around toward Tilly and lunged at it with all his weight before it could sweep her from the deck.

A wave broke in her face, and Tilly choked on the brackish water. Then Flynn came rushing at her, and they hurtled through space together. Water closed over her, and the sea clutched greedily at her body. As Tilly struggled an arm caught her around the waist and she was hauled to the surface, gasping and sputtering. Flynn held on to a piece of splintered wood.

"Hang on! Your skirts are pulling you down."

She could not see the yacht or the shore. Clinging to the wood with all her strength, she coughed as a wave crashed over them. Flynn disappeared beneath it, and she cried out in alarm. A moment later something entangled with her legs and she was out of her mind with terror. *Sharks!*

But sharks would have gone for her dangling legs, not her petticoats. A sharp tug almost pulled her underwater, and she struggled to hold on to the timber. Then her petticoats tore free, and Flynn bobbed up in the trough of a wave. She was slipping off the floating plank, and he pushed her higher until she was half on top of it.

"We're through the reef," he shouted exultantly. "I can see the shore—"

A wave caught him full in the face, and the rest of his words were lost. Except for sputtering and coughing, he seemed no worse for it, and Tilly clung to the timber, knowing it was her lifeline. Her only hope. If not for Flynn she would have been lost more than once. The hellish nightmare continued until she was so numb it would have been a blessing to give up the struggle. To let go. To rest.

She went under and Flynn caught her by the hair, pulling her to the surface. The pain shocked her out of her deadly lethargy. A wall of water shoved them forward. Tilly's bones were jolted and her knees smarted as she was pushed hard against the bottom, in the shallows. Another wall of water smacked them forward and she went sprawling head first. She flung her arms out just in time to save her neck. Her fingers grated against a rocky ledge.

Land! They had reached land.

A heavy thrust of water hit her in the small of the back, sending her up and forward, then dragging her back. Flynn got her around the waist and kept her from being sucked under again. Another wave slammed into them and Tilly bit her tongue painfully as the water flung them at the narrow beach. Hands and knees abraded, back aching, she crawled like a tortoise from the water. Her weight seemed to have increased a hundred times. She couldn't move another inch.

Flynn was next to her, his arm touching hers. At first they lay side by side, gulping in air, thankful for the solid ground beneath them. Her feet were still in the surf. Tilly's body felt awkward and heavy out of the buoyant salt water.

Each succeeding wave sent a cascade of water several inches higher. Past her knees. Past her waist. Up to her collarbone. The last one rolled beneath her cheek, and its recoil spilled gritty seawater into her mouth. It was too much effort to crawl to safety. Her sides heaved and her lungs were on fire, and every breath was flaming agony.

"Get up," Flynn said, rising to his knees and tugging at her arm.

"I can't."

"The tide is coming in."

Just breathing took all her strength. "Let it come. I don't care."

"Get up, god damn it! Don't quit on me now!"

Her sluggish brain responded to the command in his voice. She got clumsily on her hands and knees. The next wave knocked her flat again. Flynn swore. Half dragging, half carrying, he got Tilly up on the beach beyond the waves. She was almost delirious with shock, and her limbs, so leaden before, felt like willow stems, unable to bear her weight.

"This way," he ordered. She went mindlessly in whatever direction he guided her. Abruptly they came to a narrow canal that cut across the ground in either direction. She expected Flynn to curse and turn back; instead he got down on the bank and lowered himself into the water. Once sure of his footing, he held out his arms to her.

"Jump!"

Bewildered and exhausted, she stubbornly refused. "No. I cannot go another step, and I am wet enough already!"

"Then come closer so I can explain," he shouted over the wind, and she did. When Tilly stooped down to hear him more clearly, he grabbed her by the ankles and pulled her into the canal.

"Damn you!" she cried out, spluttering and splashing. "Let me go!"

"Not yet. We're going inland." He pushed her to the opposite side and to the bank. She was too tired to climb up, and he hauled her bodily out of the water.

"Leave me alone!" she howled, finding recourse in a refrain as old as Eve: "Oh, if only I were a man..."

"You would have been left on the Crescent to fend for yourself until it disintegrated under your feet."

"You are...are insufferable!"

"Only determined. We've a long way to go yet—but I think I know where we are. The only place with irrigation canals so near the sea is Quexiptil."

The name sounded familiar, and Flynn sounded hopeful. That cheered Tilly out of all proportion. With rekindled energy, drawn from some primal core, she followed him through the storm-lashed jungle. Years of striding up and down the moors and of riding in all weather had toughened her constitution and increased her vigor. A new surge of strength powered her muscles and gave her breath, although her respirations were rapid with exertion.

Flynn took heart from it. The indomitable Miss Templeton was as fit as she was brave, and not some fashionable hothouse flower, wilting fast in the face of adversity. When they got through this, *if* they got through this, he would have to show his admiration in more practical terms. For the time being he could only chivy her along as best he could.

Wind and rain savaged the palm trees and the shoulder-high foliage that surrounded them, and tore at her wet skirts. The texture of fallen twigs beneath her arch and heel brought the unwelcome remembrance that she had lost her shoes. A root tripped her up, and she stumbled and went sprawling.

Her chin grazed something cold and solid. Flynn lifted her to her feet and prodded her relentlessly on. Unbelievably, unmistakably, her bare feet touched cold pavement. She scraped the side of her foot on the edges of a block of stone and stubbed her toes on another. The pain seemed disembodied, real but unconnected to her in any meaningful way.

They came to second canal, then a third. Both times she jumped in willingly to get across, but each episode of cold water and knifing winds brought her body temperature lower. She was hallucinating now. For a moment she stood in Lady Steadmore's drawing room, held a teacup in her hand and felt the warmth transmitted through the fragile porcelain, smelled the wonderful aroma of Jasmine tea. Then the dowager's turban changed into a cap of leaves upon a squatty palm, and she was in the jungle again.

Flynn's arm was around her waist, helping her over the roughest ground.

"Keep going," he shouted encouragingly, but the words were almost inaudible in the hammering storm.

Tilly plodded on. Mist-enshrouded vegetation loomed menacingly. Gnarled limbs looked like ghastly, twisted arms. Twigs clutched at her torn and sodden clothes with bony fingers, and their jagged nails scratched her arms and cheeks. Flynn forced her onward when she would have gladly fallen where she stood. Tilly knew she danced on the edge of insanity when ghost images floated at the edges of her vision, huge snarling jaguars and hawk-nosed men with cruel eyes, like the jade mask Jonas had in his study.

Dimly, she was aware they were going up. At first she felt as if she'd shrunk to the size of a doll, then realized it was because the steps they ascended were so high and steep. Her breath came raggedly, and her feet moved to Flynn's command, for she had surrendered any control over them long ago. Even so, it was his pushing and pulling that was responsible for most of her progress.

Up they went, feeling for a sturdy toehold, struggling to maintain balance. Time and again Tilly wanted to rest, but he kept her scrabbling up the massive steps. Suddenly she fell forward, grazing her temple on something sharp and solid. Sparks flew up and danced before her eyes in dizzying patterns.

Flynn caught her just in time to save her from a nasty fall. "Are you all right?"

"I... I think so. I bumped my head."

Putting his arm around her shoulders for guidance, he led her along a level surface. It was darker here, but there was neither wind nor rain. The blow to her head had a delayed, numbing effect. She couldn't seem to feel her limbs. Perhaps she was dead. No, if one were dead, one did not hurt so abominably in so many places. Now the way sloped down at such a steep angle that Flynn had to put his arm around Tilly's waist to keep her from gathering dangerous momentum. Their progress was slow and halting and seemingly endless. Just when she was ready to sink in a boneless heap, they stopped.

"This is far enough." Flynn helped her down to the floor and propped her in the corner of two walls. More stone, she noted dully. Her head began to throb and the scraped skin prickled and burned. There seemed to be acres of it, especially on her knees and elbows. The pain was seductive, pulling her down until she drifted like a feather on the thin edge of delirium.

She was scarcely aware of it when Flynn came and sat beside her.

"We're safe here, Tilly. We've made it."

Safe. That was the magic word that released her senses from her bruised body. She heard Flynn's voice, becoming as distant and muted as the hum of bees in the meadow on a summer day. But she was not in a meadow, she was in an unknown place, waiting out a storm in total darkness.

She felt his arms around her, and her head was nestled in the crook of his shoulder. She was drawn to the warmth of his strong body, deriving strength from it. They were safe and Flynn was with her. She could let go now.

As she slid into the warm comfort of unconsciousness, one isolated part of her mind was briefly lucid. At Oak House, she had longed for adventure, the chance to live to the hilt. In her innocence, she had equated it with glamorous events, moonlight sails, exotic ports of call. Well, she'd gotten her wish.

And very uncomfortable it was, indeed!

Chapter Ten

The yellow beam of the lantern swung around the ancient chamber, illuminating the rough blocks that formed the walls. In the flickering light, the bizarre figures painted upon them leapt to sudden, menacing life—Chac-mool, god of rain, and An Puc, the skeleton-jawed representation of Death. Tilly swung the lamp toward the far corner, and her keen eye caught the telltale gleam of gold. Her heart pounding with excitement, she crossed the littered floor and stepped over the scattered bones.

Yes, it was gold. The massive gem-studded collar and pectoral gleamed on the suit of jade mosaic, which covered the remains of a once-proud Mayan priest. She moved in for a closer look, and the engraved glyphs confirmed what she already knew: after months of searching, she had at last found Queptil, the lost city of the Mayas.

Suddenly, there was a sharp sound behind her. Whirling about, Tilly prepared to face danger, eagerly seeking the face of her adversary, the secret enemy who had dared to follow her into the tomb. The leering skeleton of Death rose up before her in the dimness, bony arms reaching out to embrace her, and...

Tilly awoke to blackness, heart turning over like a mill wheel, and realized she was in bed. The mattress was incredibly hard and uncomfortable but the dream had seemed so real it was much more prominent in her awareness. Why, she could still smell the dust and the musty essence of the ancient tomb.

The nightmare still held her captive, and she was totally disoriented. *It is still the middle of the night,* she thought, *the darkest night she had known since arriving at Coeur d'Émeraude.* She could not even distinguish the faint outlines of the shutters. She rolled over and became aware of three things: every bone and muscle in her body ached; the mattress was not only as hard as stone, it *was* stone; and most frightening of all, she was not alone.

The warmth and human softness of another body beside hers would have alerted her, even without the sounds of soft, deep breathing. *I am dreaming. I have only gone from one strange dream to another.* Tentatively she reached out her hand—and touched a chest, solid and muscular. A man's chest. As she pulled her hand back, her fingertips brushed a face with a wiry growth of beard.

Tilly was unable to stifle a gasp as memories of Christopher's unprovoked attack came flooding into her mind. It was enough to awaken the man beside her. As she tried to scramble away a hand shot out and captured her wrist.

"Oh!" She tried to see something, anything, in the darkness. Dear God, was she blind? Panic almost overwhelmed her. "My eyes! Why can't I see?"

"There's nothing wrong with your eyes. It's black as the inside of Jonah's whale in here."

"Flynn! Oh, thank God it is you! I thought . . . I thought it might be Christopher."

He rubbed his hand up and down her arm soothingly and chuckled. "I didn't realize you were in the habit of waking up beside Christopher Burlinghome, Miss Templeton. If I had, I should certainly have left you stranded."

She laughed in relief. "Are you *never* serious?"

"You've asked me that before, you know. You should appreciate by now that I'm often most serious when I seem just the opposite."

Unsure of his meaning, Tilly didn't reply. She wished she could see his face. Words and tones could say so many things that were denied by a fleeting expression or the look in a person's eyes.

He spoke again. "How's your head? You took a nasty knock when we first arrived."

"A bit of a headache. Not bad. But I don't..." Then she fell silent, remembering. Pictures flashed inside her head, nightmare remembrances that were not a part of her recurrent dream. Abandonment on that isolated sandbar amid rising seas, the rescue by Flynn and his companion. The unending storm, and the wreck of the gallant *Sea Urchin*.

The rest was a blur. She had vague recollections of stumbling through the darkness, and of climbing up and over slippery stone blocks. None of it made any sense.

"Where on earth are we?"

Flynn moved closer. "Amid the ruins of an ancient Mayan temple complex. We're deep inside one of the buildings. I should imagine this section was once intended for use as a burial chamber."

"A tomb! Are we really? How fantastic it seems. Just like in my dream."

"I must say you're taking it very well. I dreaded telling you, in case it might result in hysterics."

"Nonsense! I'm not such a poor creature as that."

"Evidently not." He laughed, a deep, rich sound that warmed the darkness. "My abject apologies, Miss Templeton."

A thought struck her. "Where is Skelly?"

For a moment Flynn didn't answer, but his hand found hers and covered it. "He was thrown overboard after we hit the reef. I never saw him again."

Beneath the curt words she sensed Flynn's grief and anger. It might just as easily have been Flynn who'd gone over the side. Or herself. Fate was not evenhanded in granting favors: some lived and others died, standing side by side. It was a sobering thought. She wiped away tears for the brave sailor who had given his life to save hers, but couldn't banish the guilt.

"How terrible," she said into the stillness when she was able to speak again. "I am very sorry." She clenched her fists against her chest. "If I hadn't been so gullible, if I hadn't fallen into Jonas's trap, Skelly would still be alive."

Flynn knew she was struggling to maintain her composure. There was no sense trying to explain now. Better to distract her. "Tell me about this dream of yours."

"It's very vivid, and I have had it several times before. There is such a wealth of detail in it that it all seems very real."

She described it all: the rough stone blocks that formed the chamber; the desiccated remains of an ancient noble clothed in jade mosaic wired with bits of gold, and the golden pectoral that covered its chest; and the horrible, capering figures painted on the walls.

As she spoke, the feeling of dread returned and crept into her bones. "It seems significant, as if the dream is meant as a sort of warning. If, just once, I could see who is stalking me before I awakened, I would understand what it means."

"Don't you think you're reading too much into it? Perhaps your visit to the warehouses and that mask Jonas took home have set off unpleasant thoughts in your head."

"No." She frowned, trying to hold the image in her mind. "The first time I dreamed it I was still in Yorkshire. The Chac-mool is not three-dimensional like the mask but incised upon a flat surface or cut into stone walls. Not black and white, like Catherwood's drawings, but gaily colored."

"Gaudy as a parrot, you mean."

"Exactly! Silly, isn't it?"

There was just the slightest hesitation before he answered. "Not at all. The original buildings and stelae were once plastered and painted—rather garishly by our standards. I'm certain you must have seen tinted drawings somewhere."

Tilly was equally sure she had not. In fact, she hadn't even known that the Mayans had painted their intricate reliefs. But at the moment the renderings of ancient artists were not her prime concern; her rumbling stomach was. They needed food and water if they were to survive—and they must survive so Skelly's sacrifice would not be in vain!

"It's not very romantic of me, but historical research isn't high on my list of priorities right now. Do you think the storm has passed—so we could go foraging for food, or whatever one does in such circumstances? I'm famished!''

"Food is certainly a priority, but you, my dear, will have to bide here a bit longer. It would be most unwise for you to go out until I've scouted the area.''

"Surely you're being overcautious.''

"This is not Kingston, this is the jungle. There are many dangers, not the least of them being jaguars and bandits.''

"Oh!'' Tilly mulled that over. "Very well, but if I'm to kick my heels while you explore, I refuse to do so in this dark hole!''

"Very well.'' Flynn's hand closed over hers. "Follow me.''

They traced their steps from the previous night, Flynn feeling his way along the wall and guiding her with a few words and a firm but gentle hand at her back. There was no sound but the scuffle of their bare feet on the smoothly dressed stone.

As they reached the ascending slope the darkness grew less absolute. They went steadily upward, and every yard brought an increase in light. A dull gray rectangle beckoned. It was a section of wall that moved on a pivot and opened to another passage.

In the brighter light Tilly could see Flynn's dark growth of beard clearly. He looked like a pirate captain, or one of Francis Drake's bold companions. Despite the travails of the past days, he was incredibly fit, lean and limber.

Not a spare ounce of fat upon him anywhere, she thought, and felt her own ribs. They felt only slightly more prominent than before, but then she hadn't undergone as much physical exertion as Flynn had over the past few days.

It was growing warmer and more humid as they neared the entrance. When they reached the upper chamber Flynn slowed his pace and gestured for her to stay put. With the lithe grace of his namesake, he crossed the room and disappeared. She froze in place and waited. Time seemed to creep by until she discovered it was only because she had been holding her breath. Flynn reappeared and took her by the hand. Tilly didn't utter a peep until they reached the uppermost chamber.

They were both streaked with fine white dust from head to toe, but as Flynn drew her up the incline and around a corner, she forgot their ragged state and her gnawing hunger. No matter where she looked, every direction was down. They were atop a massive step pyramid, its green-furzed sides already in half-shadow, and impossibly steep. Other shapes rose from the level ground, still covered by mounds of rampant growth. But it wasn't their position or even the great ruins around them that had stopped Tilly in her tracks. It was the sky.

It was on fire. There was no other way to describe it. The very air seemed to burn and glow like a solid, shifting flame. Like the heart of a volcano, scorching reds and yellows shimmered and blended into one another, alive and deeply incandescent. Floating some distance above the far treetops, the molten sun poured out rivers of light along the horizon.

It was stunning. Unearthly.

Tilly could not tear her gaze from the view. She stared until her heart swelled and her eyes grew dazzled. Tears formed in them and she dashed them away. "So bright," she murmured, scarcely able to speak past the lump in her throat. Beauty always affected her that way. Flynn was not fooled.

"I've never seen its equal," he replied softly. "Not in all my travels."

"Surely it cannot be near sunset."

"No, we've at least three hours before night falls. That spectacular sky is a product of the same storm that blew us here." He touched her arm lightly. "As soon as the sun drops below the treetops I'll search the area. If it's safe, I'll be back to fetch you."

Flynn made his way around to the other side and began his descent. The ground seemed very far away. Even the leaves of the largest trees did not reach anywhere near Tilly's stony perch. The green canopy stretched like a restless ocean as far as the eye could see, pierced only by the vine-strangled top of another pyramid some distance away.

When she gazed straight down the stairway, the angle of descent was so sharp Tilly marveled to think they had climbed the stairs at all. She realized that she had been a grave hindrance. That they had made it to the top in the rain and wind was due to Flynn's dogged persistence and sheer brawn—and, she was certain, Divine Providence.

When the sun dipped entirely below the wide green umbrella of trees, a false dusk fell over the level space below, and over all but the tips of the pyramids. In the strange play of light and shade, the overgrowth of vegetation was concealed by the long shadows. The crumbling stones seemed new and deeply etched, and the comb roofs of the uppermost temples shone red as blood. As the jungle receded, the shapes of the mounds sharpened into the outlines of red stuccoed buildings, and the cleared areas were filled with ghostly life in the fading light.

The smell of incense wafted on the humid air and the rustling leaves changed to the murmur of prayers in an ancient tongue. Patterned shadows cast by leaves and branches made the massive steps swarm with movement, as if hordes of worshipers were ascending to her hiding place. Tilly felt as if she'd been transported back in time, to when the massive structures had formed an important center of commerce and worship.

A howler monkey cried out. She blinked and the illusion vanished. The jungle returned and there was nothing but leaves and vines and buried ruins—and Flynn, moving through it all. She stepped back until she was just inside the shelter of the temple and prayed for Flynn's safety and her own. It was daunting to find herself alone among the houses of the dead.

"Oh!" Another sudden blood-freezing scream from below made her jump in fright. A sleek form burst out of the trees into the light like a feathered projectile. The high screech of the soaring bird floated out over the stillness, like the dying shriek of a sacrificial victim. She wiped her sweaty palms against her salt-stiffened skirt and fought to control her nerves.

The monkeys chattered excitedly in the towering trees, and a set of unearthly howls echoed across the clearing. The sound alarmed her. Was this their regular nighttime ritual, or was Flynn returning? Or—heart-stopping thought—was it another form creeping toward her hiding place? *Jaguars and bandits.* She doubted one of the fierce panthers would climb the towering staircase—but bandits might be an entirely different matter.

Tilly held her breath and waited. No one came. She began to wonder what to do if Flynn failed to return. Should she go down and search for him or stay put? With him at her side she could face anything. His magical ways of diverting disaster had lulled her into false security until she had begun to believe he was indestructible. But there were dangerous beasts and poisonous snakes in the jungle, and great potential for other misfortunes—falls, broken limbs, concussion, internal injuries. All it took was a single misstep, a chunk of falling stone, a concealed pit.

Even now he might be lying alone and injured. Or dead. The thought was too terrible to contemplate. Panic rushed in, as the blinders fell from her eyes. If Flynn was dead it didn't much matter what happened to her. She loved him—had loved him almost from the beginning.

The revelation hit her with breathtaking force. Only her absurd doubts and uncertainties, the fear of making a fool of herself, had kept her from recognizing it sooner. She had tried to pretend that he was nothing but a charming rake, that her relationship with him was nothing more than a mild flirtation. She had pretended so well she had almost fooled herself. All the icy remarks she had directed his way, all her attempts at aloofness were nothing but a farce.

She'd been attracted to him from the first instant she'd seen him aboard the frigate, much as she had tried to convince herself otherwise. Now, after they'd been through so much together, she was even more vulnerable. The bond she felt with him ran deep; the need she felt for him ran deeper. The knowledge shook her. She was in love with a man who didn't return her sentiments. She'd been a complete and utter fool, flinging away the only heart she had to a man who flirted as easily as he smiled. Flynn must never know. It would be mortifying!

The sound of movement from just below the platform startled her. A moment later Flynn's head and hands came into view, followed shortly by the rest of him. He looked weary and worn, and incredibly handsome. Her relief at his safety was so profound that she threw caution away and ran to him.

"Thank God you're back at last!"

Flynn grinned. It had a devastating effect on her heart. "Well," he said, "I'd go away more often for a welcome like that." He took a bandanna-wrapped packet out of his shirt. "It's not what you're used to, but it will have to do for now."

Tilly hid her confusion. She had almost made a fool of herself. Acknowledging in her own heart that she loved Flynn was one thing. Confessing it to him was another. She took the bandanna from him without meeting his eyes.

"I've discovered my tastes aren't as nice as they used to be," she said lightly. "At the moment, eye of newt would taste like ambrosia."

She sat on the platform and untied the bandanna. Inside it, wrapped in several broad leaves, were two flat pieces of bread filled with a pasty substance redolent of garlic, cumin and oregano. It was still warm. It seemed like an eternity since she had eaten warm food.

"Where on earth did you get this?"

He gestured toward another step-sided pyramid, buried by an encroaching mantle of greenery. "Some of the natives still worship the old gods. It was an offering."

Although she had no idea what the paste was made of, she wasn't about to let such a minor detail affect her appetite. "Whatever is it, the aroma is mouth-watering! Please don't ruin it by telling me what the ingredients are."

Flynn laughed and took the portion she handed him. "Nothing horrible. Only maize and tomato and beans, with a few spices."

He tore off a piece of bread and showed her how to scoop up the mixture with it. She imitated his action and took a tentative bite. The taste was even better than the aroma. When she was finished she sighed in satisfaction.

"A feast for the gods. I never thought any food could be so delicious," she confessed. "Outside of a hot bath, a cup of tea and a change of clothes, there is not a single thing that could improve this moment!"

"Not one?" Flynn gave her an appraising glance from beneath his dark brows. "I can think of several."

When he spoke in that peculiar low tone she was never quite sure of his meaning, and when he looked at her that way it made her insides flutter. The smile that touched his lips lit his eyes. It held her as surely as a snare. A sudden bond of intimacy linked them, and it seemed perfectly natural to be sitting together in the dying light atop a thousand-year-old Mayan pyramid. Tilly fought to remember that he was a lusty and vigorous man, with many forgotten conquests in his past. She resolved not to become one more of them.

Deciding it intellectually and putting it into practice were two very different propositions. She resisted the urge to rest her head against his strong shoulder and let him decide the outcome, but couldn't vanquish the desire to feel the warmth of his mouth upon hers. Her fingers wanted to smooth the sharp line of his cheekbones and touch the crisp golden hairs of his beard. It was utterly ridiculous, but she had to clasp her hands tightly together in her lap to keep them still.

She looked away. "I do wish we had something to drink," she said, more out of need to redirect the conversation than out of thirst. Flynn reached into his pocket and took out a miniature pottery jug. Her nose wrinkled and she eyed the jug dubiously.

"Another medicinal potion, I'm sure. Is it as potent as the rum?"

"That is like comparing a firefly to the sun. This decoction would warm an Eskimo at the North Pole. For your sake, my dear, I wish it was tea."

"So do I!"

His eyes twinkled as he popped out the soft clay stopper and offered it to her. "Try it. Pulque, fermented from the juice of the cactus. Primitive and potent. However, milady will most likely need a nip of it before milady bathes in the canal."

"Milady will do well enough without it, thank you. She is most anxious for her bath."

"Then milady," Flynn said, recapping the jug, "had better bestir herself. Now is the best time to climb down. We'll be hard to spot as we make our way, and it will be safer on the ground as well. The day animals are heading for their lairs and the night creatures not yet stirring."

Animals? Swallowing her misgivings, Tilly took the hand he held out to her. It swallowed up her own in its callused grasp, and she felt the mantle of his protection drop over her. There was something about his nearness, his touch, that gave her courage for the trip down.

She went to the edge of the platform and was overcome by a wave of vertigo. "I don't know if I can do it. I feel as though I'm going to fall forward."

"That's because you're looking down. Turn toward the steps and kneel down, look straight ahead, and trust me to see you safely to the ground."

Tilly obeyed without a second's hesitation. Flynn jumped down to the step below and reached up to clasp her around the waist, lifting her as easily as if she were a child. From step to step, each almost three feet high, he lowered her to the next level. The humidity was punishing, each breath an effort, but as they reached the bottom third of the ceremonial stairway, her confidence was established.

"I believe I can manage the rest of the way myself."

"Why tempt fate?"

Flynn continued his assistance long after she needed it. Long after the imprint of his hands had burned through her tattered dress to kindle the flesh below. Long after his nearness had created an aura of tension that enveloped them both. By the time they reached the artificial twilight of the jungle canopy she was breathless, but not from exertion.

Her feet touched the paving stones of the central courtyard. Solid ground at last, but why did she feel she was
standing in quicksand?

She turned to find herself mere inches from him. To push
past him would be rude, to back up impossible. Her eyes
were on a direct line with his chin. She couldn't look into his
face. He would read her thoughts, as he had done so many
times before.

Flynn's hands captured her waist once more and held her
firmly. So small, so fragile, so full of life and passion. If he
put his hand over her breast he knew he would feel her heart
beating in time with his. But if he touched her, he might not
be able to stop.

"Tilly," he said softly. His breath stirred her hair; his
voice stirred her blood. She was afraid to look at him, afraid
that it would ignite a spark that could turn to a conflagra-
tion. It was her own need and vulnerability she feared, not
Flynn.

Never Flynn.

He didn't press her. She'd been through enough in the
past few days, but the urge to pull her into his arms and
make love to her was so strong! He waited for that one little sigh, that one soft yielding of her body that would tell
him she was caught in the same spell. It didn't come. When
the seconds flew by without any response from her, he let
her go.

"About that bath, Miss Templeton. We'd better hurry; it
will be dark in less than an hour."

In silence they crossed the central pavement, which the
jungle was trying to reclaim. Every crack and crevice between the paving stones was furred with green vegetation.
Vines snaked across their path, wound over the tumbled
blocks and garlanded the limbs and exposed roots of the
trees. Straight overhead the sky still flamed with reflected
light, but all around the perimeter of the cleared area, the
giant trees blotted out the view: mahogany, *cedro*, ceiba and
saspodilla and rubber trees. Flynn knew all their names.

"Watch out for the lianas," he warned, indicating twisted vines strung from branch to branch overhead. "Some, like the *lancetilla*, have needle-sharp spines."

It was too late. Already the sharp barbs had hooked a lock of her hair. "Oh!" She looked up, expecting to find some terrible-clawed creature caught in her tresses. Tilly tried to free herself.

"Hold still. Wriggling about will only make it worse."

Flynn ducked his head and stood to one side. They were both conscious of the other's nearness, of the magnetism drawing them together. Tilly's heart was beating so fast she was sure he could hear it. There was nothing she wanted more than to be held again in Flynn's strong embrace; and nothing she feared more.

She was not the same untried young woman who'd left England wide-eyed and innocent as a child. Tilly knew she had gone through life like a sleepwalker until she'd met Flynn. One kiss, one embrace and he had awakened all her womanly instincts, changing her forever. He confused her. He excited her. He broke all the rules, and made her want to break them too.

If he kissed her again she didn't know how she should react, but there was no question in her mind of how she *would* react. If the moment came when their needs merged, she would not be able to turn away. She would fling away everything she had ever held dear and take him on his own terms. She found herself trembling at the thought.

Flynn was unaware of the silent battle that raged within her; he had demons of his own to fight. He wanted to put his lips against the tender nape of her neck, to breathe in the scent of her hair and skin. She would taste of sea salt at first, then he would savor the taste and fragrance that was uniquely hers: flowers and sunshine and soft, tempting woman. He would leave a trail of kisses around her throat to the notch between her delicate collarbone, then follow a line down, into the cleft between her breasts. His fingers shook at the thought of brushing across her skin, pulling away the torn fabric of her bodice to reveal her breasts. He would fill his hands with their satin texture as his mouth roved lower...

Flynn yanked his thoughts away from temptation. With a last dexterous twist he freed her hair and started walking again. They'd been through fearsome times together, and there were likely to be more ahead. Instead of dampening his ardor, the danger heightened it. He wanted to hold her, to touch her, watch her catch fire from the flame that burned within him.

But this was neither the time nor the place.

There were low ruins all around them, beneath the tangled jungle. "Why on earth did we have to climb the highest pyramid?"

He chuckled. "Because it was the first one we came to in the dark. And I wanted us above the flood if the hurricane came inland. Fortunately, my precautions weren't necessary."

Tilly paused. "I thought that *was* a hurricane."

"No. We were just ticked by its outer edge."

"Poor Skelly..." Tilly's voice broke.

Flynn didn't answer. She was close to tears, he could see it in the trembling of her mouth, and he didn't want to push her over the edge. It was all he could do to keep from pulling her into his arms and covering her scratched, sunburned, beautiful little face with a hundred kisses. His eyes blazed with the thought and the need. Instead he reached out protectively and took her hand in his.

They were beside a pair of odd-looking hills, draped with the ever-present vines. Stunted trees had rooted on the summit, some thirty feet up, and others grew haphazardly along the sides. Flynn stopped and surveyed them. "One of the temples atop these platforms might be habitable."

"Unless they're crawling with vipers and poisonous insects, I'd much prefer it to climbing the pyramid again tonight. You must think I'm a terrible baby."

Flynn caught her chin with the tip of one bronzed finger. His eyes were warm and deeply green. "If we were safely out of this adventure, I would tell you exactly what I think of you."

Tilly pulled away, and he let her go. She could still feel his touch upon her skin, as if drops of melted gold burned into her flesh. She realized he'd said "if," and not "when."

She twined and untwined her fingers. "You will think me very näive. Once we survived the wreck and the storm, I imagined our troubles were over. Wishful thinking, I suppose."

Flynn hesitated, wondering how much of the truth she could take. While he weighed his response, Tilly lifted her chin and gave him a level look. "I am not a child."

He almost laughed aloud. She certainly wasn't. If she could see herself as he did, the rounded breasts and small waist, the soft flare of hip that tapered sweetly into the curving line of thigh and—he let his breath out. If she could see herself as he did, she'd slap his face.

Tilly thought he was trying to spare her. "Pray be honest with me. What are the chances that we will ever see Kingston again?"

"I can't give you any absolutes. The outcome depends on many factors, including the weather, the friendship or hostility of the natives and how far it is to Dr. Challfont's excavation site."

"And those jaguars and bandits you mentioned before!"

"You certainly seem to take everything in stride."

"I can't imagine that hysterics would be of any use."

Flynn's ready grin flashed out. "Not the least. And it would earn you a sharp slap for your efforts."

She didn't know whether to laugh or be indignant. Laughter won. "You are odious. However, since I'm relying upon you to get us out of our scrape, I will save my lecture for another day."

"Very wise. But the odds aren't all stacked against us. I still have a few tricks up my torn and tattered sleeves."

He broke off a spray of pink orchids for her and led the way toward the canal. Lianas coiled across the ground and slithered between the sharp fernlike plants and knotted roots. Tilly stepped on one and wobbled as part of it broke loose and scuttled away.

Flynn caught her around the waist and steadied her. Her body seemed to fit into the curve of his arm as if it had been planned. "Only a lizard. The place, if you'll excuse the pun, is crawling with them."

Tilly recovered herself. "I suppose they have more right here than we. And it lost a tail, while I only lost my composure."

"Don't worry, it will grow another."

"I hope none of their larger relatives are native to this place."

Again just the slightest pause told her he'd sifted his words before saying them. "There are tales of a type of crocodile in the general area, but none have ever been found near this site."

"How comforting! If one should seize me by the leg, I'll be sure to inform the creature that it has wandered out of its territory and gotten quite lost."

"That," Flynn said wryly, "is a novel approach. I'll have to remember to use it myself, if the need ever arises."

They had reached the canal. The air was brighter, since the sun was still above the horizon, and the branches of the forest giants had not completely closed over the ancient irrigation channel. There were others in the distance, crossing at right angles, like streams of polished silver. The closer they came, the more the logistics of bathing in Flynn's company filled her thoughts.

Flynn set her mind at ease with one of those disconcerting comments that made her certain he could read her mind. "This spot is sheltered and I'll leave it to you; I'll be around the corner—out of view, but still within earshot—should you need me."

He parted the reeds and disappeared among them. Tilly looked into the canal. The water was almost still, the surface dimpling around the reed shafts and the wide water-lily pads. She was tempted to tear off her clothes and dive right in, but she couldn't forget that Flynn was only a few feet away,

She hesitated, and the clear depths of the canal beckoned. Quickly, Tilly discarded her salt-stiffened clothing and slipped in. The water was deliciously cool and came to just below her breasts. It flowed like silk over her skin, caressing every curve. She caught up handfuls of it and bathed her face and throat, washing away the sweat and salt and dust.

Tilly arched backward and scrubbed her scalp until it tingled. Her hair floated out behind her like ribbons in the wind. She was refreshed and free and reveling in it. She stretched out her arms and floated like one of the water lilies, impervious to the now familiar background sounds of the jungle. Nothing disturbed her tranquility. Not even the long, dark shape that cut through the water behind her.

In the adjoining section of canal, Flynn scrubbed the salt from his corded arms and shoulders. His body was sore in a hundred places, and the abraded skin stung sharply as he dunked himself beneath the surface. When he rose, shaking his hair, he felt revitalized. The salt and sweat and grime had washed away, and with it went some of the strain.

At least they had made it this far. Far enough that his most pressing dilemma was not how to provide them with food and shelter, but how to keep himself from dwelling on the fact that a lovely and desirable woman was splashing about in the all-together a few short yards away. He tried not to think of the water sliding over her alabaster body, or the way her hair would stream out behind her like a satin shawl. That way lay madness.

She was totally in his power, more vulnerable than she knew, but trusting in him totally. She evoked his protective instincts even while she roused his deepest masculine urges. Flynn felt the heat rising inside him and ducked beneath the surface again, hoping the coolness would quench the fire. He came up an instant later, gasping for air, as the sound of her scream rang out.

With powerful strokes he shot through the water toward the spot where he'd left Tilly. She was nowhere in sight. He called out to her, but there was no sign that she had left the canal. Flynn was about to dive when she emerged, brushing a lock of dripping hair from her face with a rounded, glistening arm.

Flynn drew in a sharp breath. He had been about to call out her name, but the words were lost, forgotten in the vision before him. She was an enchanting water nymph, rising from her reedy home, one white breast seductively cupped in the curving petals of a water lily.

Her beauty struck him like a blow. Her shoulders seemed carved from ivory and her breasts were luminous and inviting. Droplets beaded on their tips like dewdrops on rose petals. He was spellbound, ensnared by her beauty and his growing hunger.

"Tilly..." His voice was deep and hoarse.

She opened her eyes. The pupils were wide and dark. "It was just a lizard," she began breathlessly, and stopped as he came toward her.

The stern beauty of his face held her mesmerized, and the desire carved in every line of it evoked an answering thrill. It frightened her with its intensity. Flynn stopped a foot away, outlined with golden light, his bronzed skin glazed with water. It rippled over his wide, sculpted chest, spangling him with light. He was magnificent, a primordial god rising from the waters. His bold masculinity was overwhelming, reminding her of her own nakedness. Her arms came up to shield her breasts, but the gesture was never completed.

He held his hand out to her. It was then, as the lowering sun gilded the irrigation canals, that she saw his hands. Now that the dust and salt were gone, she realized they were bruised and raw, scored with cuts, and abrasions. He was not an untouchable god, he was a very human man, and she loved him so deeply she ached with it.

"Flynn! Your poor hands!"

She remembered guiltily how he had clung to the piece of timber and brought them safely to shore despite her struggles; how once on land she had balked and fought him; how he had pushed and pulled and carried her over obstacles and through canals and around obstructions when her own strength had failed. He had suffered pain for her sake without once complaining. Gliding through the water, pushing small ripples before her, she reached out and caught his battered hands in hers.

She raised them to her lips, kissing first one then the other. Without conscious thought he closed the small gap between them. Freeing his hands, he pulled her into his arms, crushing her in his embrace. Her nipples brushed against him, swollen and ripe as berries. Her breasts were soft and yielding against the hardness of his wide chest.

His mouth found hers, gentle at first, tasting and savoring. The mood changed. His lips became demanding, claiming and conquering. His fingertips moved over the small of her back, feeling the delicate curves, the slender column of her backbone, the perfect texture of her skin. The fire in his loins spread outward until it engulfed him, and he was lost.

She clung to him as the first waves of tenderness and longing turned to alarm at the touch of his naked flesh against hers; but his urgency communicated itself to her and her response changed. She was filled with a strange, primitive power. As his mouth moved hungrily over hers she gave herself up to it. There was nowhere she belonged more than right here, in his arms.

Flynn took the kiss deeper. His tongue touched her lips and they opened to him. He took this first surrender gently, anticipating the next. He touched and taught and tasted, evoking sensation upon sensation and need upon need. She was falling into him, spinning dizzily like a planet around the sun. His warmth seeped into her until she was melting with it. His need became hers. She shifted her breasts against him and exulted in his sharp gasp.

Flynn was a man possessed. He lifted her off her feet, massaging the sweet curve of her buttocks, cupping them in his hands and bringing her hips forward to press against his throbbing loins. The need to possess her completely was growing stronger with every touch and caress.

Her back arched and her nails dug into his shoulders as the mounting urgency coursed through her. His teeth nibbled at the corner of her mouth and their lips moved in quick, hot kisses that robbed them both of breath. When

Flynn's hand closed over her breast she threw her head back in pleasure; and when his mouth claimed it she moaned with elation.

The soft, frantic sound inflamed him. He rained kisses on her face and throat as his other hand moved over her hips then around the front of her thighs in slow, seductive circles. She shuddered and pressed more tightly against him, her mouth hungry to know him. Her lips skimmed across his chest, leaving a trail of fire.

Lightly, gently, his fingers brushed across her abdomen, sending ripples of reaction through her. He sought her mouth again and again until they were both intoxicated with the wine of desire.

Fine tremors moved through her body as his hands dipped lower with each circling movement, until he felt her mounting tension and heard the swift acceleration of her heart.

Caught in the embrace of the man she loved, Tilly was willing to follow wherever he led. She wanted to get closer to him, so close that they were one body, one soul. The pressure of his mouth upon hers, the way her nipples tightened and tingled, the skilled touch of his fingers, all were driving her mad. She clung to his neck for support and lost herself in him. She wanted to show her love without reserve, to return in full measure the pleasure he gave to her.

Flynn seemed to read her mind, knowing when to advance and when to retreat, until they were both half-mad with the ecstasy. He had never meant it to happen this way, but there was no turning back for either of them. The piercing was quick, a fleeting second of discomfort that was nothing compared to the burst of sensation that flooded through her at their joining.

The sweet, hot pleasure wracked their bodies. His mouth never left hers and he felt her gasp as he thrust upward once, twice. Tilly was lost in a world of wild sensation. Somehow they were up on the bank in the gathering twilight, without her noticing how they'd gotten there. There was mossy ground beneath her, soft as velvet, and his magnificent profile was outlined above her in gold and black. The bright flame of passion burned and blazed like the heart of the sun until they were both consumed with it. She met him thrust for thrust and when Flynn shuddered and cried aloud, she thought the sound was hers.

Afterward they lay locked together in a close embrace. Dusk fell, accompanied only by the sounds of their breathing and the sigh of the breeze through the leaves. Tilly welcomed the silence between them. There was no need for words. Words were for everyday, ordinary things. There were none that could express what they had just shared, or the feelings welling inside her until she thought her heart would burst.

Flynn misunderstood her quietness. Words were wrenched from deep within him. "I never meant it to happen, Tilly. Not like this."

His voice was so troubled, his eyes so tender, that her own misted over. "No," she murmured. "No apologies. No regrets...*I* haven't any." She traced the outline of his jaw with her fingertip. His beard was soft and tickled her hand. "It's all right. I . . . I wanted you to make love to me."

He kissed the corner of her mouth. "Tilly, when I thought of making love to you—and I did!—it was always so different. I imagined moonlight and the scent of flowers. Champagne in crystal goblets. Silken sheets and flickering candlelight . . . all the romantic touches a woman like you should have."

She chuckled low in her throat. "Instead we had barbed vines and cactus juice and lizards among the ancient ruins. *I* think it was very romantic."

His breath stirred the hair at her temple. "You'll feel differently later. You'll hate me, then."

"I could never hate you. Never. Not when I have loved you for so long."

She heard his sharp intake of breath and reached out to him blindly, offering the reassurance of her touch. He pressed her head against his shoulder, burying his face in her hair. She clung to him again, as if the sheer strength of his body could protect her from all the dangers that threatened them. "All my life I've been so alone, so locked away from everything that is real. It took you to set me free."

Flynn pulled her tightly against him. His kiss was long and deep and satisfying. He pulled away and started to speak, but she stopped him. Her hands moved instinctively, affirming the truth of her words. Pledging and promising. Proving that she had given herself willingly. Joyfully.

The mist caressed their naked bodies but did not cool their heated blood. Soft rain fell from the sky like a benediction, pattering on the water and tapping gently on the massed leaves. Passion held sway among the curving reeds, with no other witness than the thin crescent moon. It hung in the sky, as luminous and new as the emotions revealed beneath it. The two lovers flew up together, higher than the topmost branches of the jungle forest, higher than the soaring temples and the gauzy veils of cloud that streaked the rapidly darkening sky.

Tilly had never dreamed such felicity existed, never imagined the joyous delirium of losing her separateness, of joining in the bond of love. Afterward, filled with peace and contentment, she lay in his arms. So much had happened, and so quickly, that she had no time to analyze it.

The last of the light was gone. A spray of stars was flung across the sky, their images reflected in the canal. She picked out the brightest one and made a wish: that the happiness and fulfillment she felt now was only the beginning, that her love for Flynn—and his for her—would burn as bright and eternal as that star.

Chapter Eleven

It was Flynn's kiss that awakened Tilly. She opened her eyes to find him looking down at her. They were inside the smaller temple in the predawn dimness, and memories of the previous night came rushing back. She felt shy until he leaned closer and kissed the tip of her nose. From there it was a natural progression to her lips. They softened and parted under the warmth of his mouth and her arms twined around his neck, pulling him close against her.

When he lifted his head, Flynn cupped her face in the curve of his palm. "The sun will be up soon. I hate to leave you, but I have to explore a bit. We'll be going east tomorrow, along the coast, and I want to scout the area."

Tilly ran her fingers through his soft growth of beard. "Surely you don't mean to leave me here alone?"

"You'll be safer here, and a lot more comfortable."

She tugged on his beard. "Give me a little more credit, if you please! It was not my own skin I was considering, but yours. If you expect to convince me that you aren't in great need of rest, the heat must have addled your brain."

"My profound apologies, you little termagant! But remember, I am used to this sort of life and it has hardened me. You, my love, are the one with shadows beneath the eyes. If you don't rest today, I'm afraid you'll never be able to keep up with me later."

She had been about to protest again, but his argument was too logical to dispute. In her present state, she would only be a burden to him.

"Very well. I won't dispute you. This time."

He took her hand and lifted it to his warm lips, kissing her fingertips. "The price of a wise woman is beyond rubies."

Tilly knew the Book of Proverbs. He'd gotten the quotation quite wrong. *Who can find a virtuous woman? for her price is far above rubies.* She wondered if he'd done it deliberately, not to taunt her, but to spare her feelings.

Flynn read her expression accurately, as usual. "Little doubter! I was merely tailoring the quote to fit the situation."

"I do not care for the cut of your tailoring, sir!"

"Would you have preferred 'lean, rent and beggared'?"

Tilly shook her head ruefully. "The Biblical quotation has greater elegance, but I must admit the phrase from Shakespeare is more apt."

He thought a moment, surveying her ruined dress. "I think you'll find this more fitting: 'Strength and honor are her only clothing.'"

A ripple of laughter came from Tilly. "You are shameless, sir! And well read, I must admit."

"I knew if we were acquainted long enough, you'd discover I have a few good qualities."

Flynn smiled down at her, a warm, intimate smile that turned her bones to taffy. She put her hand out to touch his cheek. "I already know that you have many. Be careful. Come back safely to me."

"'If I can not move Heaven, I shall bend Hell.'"

He gave her a light kiss that sent her heart pounding with its promise of more and put her reluctantly away from him. "I wish I didn't have to go." There was regret in his voice. "But we can't stay here forever, you know."

Why not, she thought. They were safe and warm and dry, wrapped in the cocoon of love. There was no need to think of a future that might not be nearly as pleasant. Tilly was well aware that her return to Jamaica, in Flynn's company, would ruin her in the eyes of society. She would be an outcast, a scarlet woman.

Yet that was not the true reason she wanted to keep him with her. The sharing, the joining had been so beautiful and fulfilling, and she didn't want to lose that closeness with him. Her lips remembered the touch of his mouth on hers and her fingers recalled every line of his lean, sculpted body.

Desire grew and blossomed. Her eyes were dark with passion in the half-light. "Why can't we stay here forever? Just the two of us."

"Temptress!"

He kissed her again, lingeringly, and she responded to the hunger in him. When he lifted his head he saw her eyes were closed, shadowed by her thick lashes, and her lips were parted in anticipation. Did she have any idea how seductive she was? How she made a man forget everything except that he was a man? No, he thought, she is too unaware of her own power, too innocent; yet she had responded to his lovemaking with a deep, welling passion that had startled them both. He had never meant for it to happen even once, and now it was happening again.

He was drugged with desire, wanting her with an urgency he had never known. Flynn fought to control it. Before, when they made love, their driving, mutual need had dominated. This time he vowed he would go more slowly, teaching her the sensual delights of her body, awakening her to the fullness of her womanhood. He held back the dark tide that threatened to overwhelm him. This time he would savor every taste and touch to its fullest, and teach her how to do the same.

His teeth caught her lower lip, nibbling at it lightly. She hesitated only a moment, then opened her mouth to his, seeking. She tasted like honeysuckle, sweet and fresh and flowery. Her gentle yielding inflamed his senses. He plunged deeper into her mouth and exalted when her tongue brushed against his. There was no shyness in her giving, no holding back in her eager surrender.

Her musky scent perfumed the air, mingling with her soft breath as his lips touched hers. His hand warmed the curve of her breast, and she drew a sharp intake of breath. His lips skimmed the side of her mouth and across her cheek, coming to rest in the tender spot below her ear.

Tilly was caught up in his fever, shaken with the intensity of her longing. She moved beneath him, scarcely aware of the hard floor as she wrapped her arms around Flynn to draw him close. Closer. When he murmured her name his breath whispered across her skin sending chills of pleasure racing over her skin. The touch of his tongue against the lobe heightened the intensity. She arched her back, curving against him with innocent abandon.

Flynn was caught up in a storm of desire. His thumb pushed aside the fabric of her tattered bodice, seeking the ripe tip. Her skin was satin against his palm, centered with a velvet rose. The combination of textures tantalized him. He circled the taut nipple lightly with his thumbnail. It swelled in response and he took it between his fingers, kneading it to exquisite tenderness. Tilly moaned and arched her back again, and he knew her blood was as hot as his. He could feel the wild thrumming of her heart.

His mouth, warm and damp, roved down the column of her throat, pausing to press a kiss in the delicate hollows before moving lower. More kisses trailed across the swell of her breast and down to its crest. He took the hard bud into his mouth, memorizing its shape and feel, delighting in its perfection. He wanted to give her every shading of sensation, from subtle to sharp. She moaned softly and reached out to pull him closer.

"Not yet, darling," he whispered. "There is so much more..."

Tilly's mind was reeling. Her excitement was so intense she didn't think she could stand much more, but Flynn would not let up. His mouth moved lightly to the valley between her breasts then up to capture the other peak. His breath was hot as flame, his lips hotter. That heat burned into her and she felt it concentrate in her loins.

Somehow they were both naked. She didn't remember him undressing her or stripping off his own clothes. When Flynn began to press his kisses lower, toward her waist, she was suddenly frightened—not of him, but of what was happening to her. She was spinning away again.

She clutched his hair, weaving her fingers into it, but when he tried to go past her waist, she resisted. "I'm afraid," she whispered.

"Don't be. I won't hurt you, love."

Gently, he untangled her hands from his hair and took her wrists. He placed her arms at her sides, holding them lightly. She permitted him to do so, but trembled uncontrollably. Ever so slowly, his lips traveled to her navel. Again, his tongue touched her skin and increased the heat of her blood. It flicked around the sensitive dimple, then across it rapidly until she writhed beneath him. Her bones melted away and her body turned liquid with pleasure; but he wasn't finished.

Flynn's head dipped lower. He released her wrists from their easy clasp and this time, although she was still afraid, she didn't resist. The backs of his fingers caressed the inside of her thigh. Her hands twined in his hair again, not to stop but to encourage him. She waited expectantly. Eagerly. Even her breathing ceased.

His touch was so tenuous she thought she'd imagined it; but no, he did it again, each time with more pressure. All the throbbing of her blood concentrated in that one spot until she thought she would burst. He waited, knowing how close she was to the ultimate sensation, wanting to prolong the moment for them both, wanting the tension to build inside her. She moaned low in her throat. Another light touch sent her plunging into the heart of the hurricane.

The strength of her reaction amazed him. The fury of it racked her delicate body again and again, and Flynn rode out the tempest with her. Tilly was flung helplessly through the storm. Only Flynn's strong arms kept her from being swept away.

When it was over she lay gasping, fulfilled yet wanting more. Breathless, shaken, she reached for Flynn and pulled him over her. Her arms wound around his neck passionately as her hips ground against his loins. She felt his readiness and shifted to cradle him. There was no need for words. They communicated silently, as they had done so many times before.

Flynn plunged the hardness of his body into the softness of hers, losing himself for a few savage seconds. He wanted to unleash his fever into her. Instead he went slowly, until the mellow glow that filled her kindled another blaze. A part of him needed to know that she wanted him, that it was her desire as much as his that drove them. Her hunger was as deep as his, her need as overpowering. Caught in the rhythms of love, they joined in mutual delirium, meeting and parting, then rocketing through a galaxy of molten stars together.

They lay for some time, still locked in that final embrace. Tilly would have been content to stay like that forever, feeling triumphant and complete in his arms. After a while he stirred, lifted his head and gave her one more kiss that was full of secret promises.

The sun was up, filling the open doorway with clear, golden light. A long rectangle of gold stretched from the threshold halfway across the room, and tiny motes danced in its aura. Reluctantly Flynn tore himself away. His eyes were so bright and green Tilly thought he looked almost angry. What an odd fancy, she told herself.

Flynn rolled over, one arm flung across his brow. He was angry, but not with her. All his wrath was for himself. His good intentions had fled once again. He could not more keep from touching her than a thirsty man could turn away from a cool, refreshing spring. And one day soon, she would hate him for it.

Without looking at her he got up and dressed. "I have to go now. There's water in that stoppered jug."

Tilly was startled by the change in him. She leaned on one elbow, unaware of the voluptuous curves and hollows of her body. He looked away.

"What is it, Flynn? You *are* angry. Is it something I did? Or something I didn't do...that's displeased you so?"

Instantly he was contrite. Kneeling beside her, he cupped her face between his hands. "It was wonderful." He kissed her mouth. "Amazing and perfect in every way, like you."

She was reassured, but something was still not quite right. He reached into the corner and picked up several odd-looking fruits covered with downy, pale-russet skin. "I got these earlier while you were asleep. I'm afraid they'll have to keep you until my return. I'll be back around sundown."

"So late!"

"I know it's difficult to sit and wait, but if fortune favors me, I might locate a village where I can obtain some more suitable clothing for us as well as food."

Rising, she brushed the fine limestone dust from the ragged ruin of her dress. "Of the two, I'd much prefer the clothing."

She'd washed her garments as best she could in the canal the night before and they had dried fairly well, despite the damp air. The worst of the dirt was gone, but there was nothing she could do about the stains and frays and outright gaps. The right sleeve hung by two loose threads, and the hem was gone in great jagged tears. As for the delicate lace that had formed the wide sailor collar and cuffs, it was only a fond memory.

A day earlier Tilly would have been dismayed by the amount of white thigh and bosom so wantonly displayed. Strange how one's attitude could change overnight. "I feel like Cinderella before the ball," she said, laughing, "although not nearly so respectable."

Flynn smiled. "But infinitely more alluring! I can't promise elegant gowns and glass slippers, but I'll do my best to come up with practical substitutes. Meanwhile, I want you to stay safely hidden here until I return."

"I was thinking of bathing in the canal again."

"It wouldn't be safe." His eyes held hers. "I don't like leaving you here alone. If there were any other way..." He raised her hand to his lips. "Promise me this, Tilly, that you won't go outside for any reason."

She didn't like it, but Flynn was right. Until he knew what they had to face, she would be a definite liability. "Very well. I promise."

"That's my girl." A last kiss, and he was gone.

It had been a long time since anyone had called Tilly a girl. Under other circumstances she would have resented it; coming from Flynn, it made her feel cozy and protected.

The only problem she had now was how to pass the long hours alone. Listing Flynn's virtues was one way; recalling every kiss and caress of their night of love was another. In reality she knew so little about him—and nothing of his background. He'd been raised as a gentleman, with a gentleman's education, yet the idle society life didn't seem to suit him, no matter how charmingly he played his part. On the way to Chichen Itza, she would have plenty of time to get to know him better: Flynn had warned her it might take them several days.

She ate one of the fruits whose name she didn't know. Its juice was rather sweet, the pulp smooth with the taste and texture of pears. Although it was delicious and filling, she would have traded it in an instant for a single cup of fresh, hot tea. Or, better yet, a brush and comb. She wanted to look her best for Flynn, but at this crucial juncture of her life, she was afraid she looked about as appealing as a beggar woman in an eastern bazaar—not exactly the image a woman wanted to present to her beloved.

Wriggling her dusty toes, she reflected wistfully that a pair of shoes would be a gift from heaven. How little she had appreciated the everyday possessions that made life so much easier! Well, she would never take them for granted again.

Attempts to braid her hair were futile, tousled and twisted as it was. She raked her fingers through it with scant results. A bit of branch with a few twigs might be of use in untangling it. Tilly decided to go out and find one, but before she could act she heard voices nearby.

Flynn must be back, bringing assistance. Eagerly she ran toward the threshold—and stopped just short of it. There were several voices, loud with anger or alarm—and none of them sounded the least like Flynn's. She listened. The voices were louder, and seemed to be coming in her direction. Her heart thumping, Tilly moved deep into the shadows.

Something white flashed through the jungle beyond the cleared area, visible at intervals behind the massive tree trunks. A man, running. Tilly strained her eyes for a better look. Others were in hot pursuit. She crept back to a hidden vantage point and watched. The runners came into clearer view, shouting to one another. She realized it was a trick of acoustics and not volume that made the words so clear. Unfortunately they were in a foreign tongue. Not Spanish or any language familiar to her.

Their quarry was screened by the vegetation but she had partial glimpses of his dark, terrified visage. The hunters broke into the open. There were two of them, with brutal, determined faces. Her blood chilled! These were surely the men Flynn had warned her of—*bandits!*

The fugitive broke into the open, heading across the clearing to Tilly's left. Suddenly he stumbled and went down. The others fell upon him and a furious struggle began. The still air carried the solid thud of knuckles on bone, the grunts of effort and pain. They were so faint she couldn't tell if they were real or supplied by her imagination. The smothering green vines trembled and shook, hiding everything but flailing arms and legs and one man's back. Light flashed, bright and metallic. The brief reflection blinded her.

She blinked against the glare. The fugitive made a sudden lunge and broke away from his captors. The trees and hanging vines obscured her view, and she lost him for a few seconds. Then he appeared at the edge of the clearing below. The shoulder of his white tunic was red with blood, and his left arm dangled awkwardly. With great consternation, Tilly realized he was heading straight toward her.

His pursuers were closing on him rapidly as he started to clamber up the great steps. In his haste he tripped and slid toward the ground. Once more he rose to flee, and this time something shone and glittered in the air. It struck him between the shoulder blades and went deep. Tilly felt horribly sick to her stomach.

The man spread his arms, then fell forward. He was hidden from view by the bulk of the stepped-sides, and she could not tell if he crawled away or not. While she held her breath, trembling, the other two ran across the court. Tilly discovered there was an emotion that went beyond fear, a numb acceptance that progressed to a profound calm. Her mind was blank as a slate, empty of all thought. She was not aware of her beating heart or her nearness to discovery and death: she simply *was*.

They were in a direct line with her vantage point. The mumble of their voices drifted up to her but she couldn't distinguish a single word. When they came into sight again, the taller man was sheathing a wicked knife. They passed across her field of vision to the left, heading toward the canals. It was some time before she realized they were leaving. Their voices trailed away and were gradually lost.

Tilly remained frozen in place until her limbs were stiff and cramped, then inched toward the doorway. The view was peaceful again. Near the edge of the jungle a squirrel sat on its haunches, munching a tasty tidbit, and a trio of Muscovy ducks waddled across the clearing. The intruders were gone.

There was no sign of their victim. She didn't know if he was dead or merely unconscious. There might be nothing she could do to aid him, yet she could not turn her back on him. Moving cautiously, she crept through the plant growth toward the side of the temple and made her way to the bottom. All the way down, Tilly was aware that her position was fairly exposed, and that the attackers, if they were still in the area, might spot her. It was a profound relief to reach the ground safely without being seen.

It didn't take her long to locate him. The man lay on his left side, face down, arms and legs flung out awkwardly. His shirt had been almost ripped off. Kneeling, she put her hand upon his side and turned him over. The limp body flopped lifelessly and lay still. From the angle of his left leg she was certain it was broken.

Tilly leaned down in an attempt to see his face better and recoiled in shock. Although she didn't know him, his face seemed horribly familiar. The shape was slightly longer than it was wide and slashed by a generous mouth. The cheekbones were carved in high relief, flanking a jutting nose of patrician shape and large proportions.

Recognition dawned. It was a certain type of face, specific to a certain place. She'd seen it in Catherwood's engravings, and she'd seen it on several stelae within a hundred yards of this temple. This man, in his simple peasant clothes, was a direct descendant of the ancient Mayan people.

Her fingers tangled in a piece of string tied around his neck and a small metal cross touched her wrist. She freed it and put her hand upon his chest. Still alive, thank God! The heartbeat was there, faint and rapid. But when her hand came away it was sticky and wet. There was a gaping wound where his collarbone joined the shoulder, which was bleeding copiously, and there was another on his back. She knew nothing of medicine and was frustrated by her helplessness. There were probably several things that needed to be done immediately—all she could do for him was bind his wounds.

Then she must get away before the would-be murderers came back. Flynn would be returning and had to be warned that there were dangerous men around. In the back of her mind lurked the terrifying awareness that they might have already met, that Flynn had run afoul of the vicious attackers and his body lay hidden in the thick jungle growth. The thought was too ghastly to contemplate and she pushed it away.

There was no time to dwell on morbid fears. Tilly set to work. Deftly tearing strips from the remains of her ragged dress, she made them into a thick pad. Although she did not begrudge him the sacrifice of the material, she had lost more of it than she retained. All that was left of her skirt were jagged strips, like the petals of a giant peonie—certainly not the proper outfit for a modest female. Thank goodness her unmentionables almost reached her knees! At the moment the important thing was to keep this poor man's blood from draining away.

Quickly she wrapped the fabric inside his wide neckerchief. Next she removed the long piece of cloth he wore tied around his waist for a belt. It would serve admirably to hold the makeshift bandage in place. As she shook it a small object fell out and rolled into the darkness. Winding the cloth around his shoulder, she bound his wound tightly. To her great relief, the pressure of the bandage seemed to have stopped, or at least slowed, the bleeding.

She sat back on her heels. Not too bad for an amateur, she decided. Now for the next step. Whatever *that* might be.

She tried to lift the unconscious man. Oh, if only Flynn was here! He was too heavy for her to carry, but she could drag him farther along the base of the temple, where he would be shielded from the cruel sun.

Tilly dragged him as far as she could and made him as comfortable as possible. There was nothing more she could do until Flynn arrived, except bathe the unconscious man's face and dribble a bit of water into his dry mouth. It would be quicker to go to the canal than to climb the steps again, and the risk of being seen from a distance was also much less.

She turned to check the courtyard for movement, and her bare foot came down on something small and cold and hard. Even before she stooped to retrieve it, she knew what it was.

Another emerald.

An unpolished hexagonal crystal, some two inches long, and greener than the sea. A chill ran over her skin like an icy caress. The coincidence was uncanny. Of course, there could be no connection with this stone and the emeralds that had precipitated her on her own perilous adventures; and, if the attackers had been after this emerald, why had they not taken it with them?

Mysteries upon mysteries surrounded the stones. There seemed to be an evil spell attached to the precious green gemstones, one that brought violence in its wake. Tilly had never had a particular preference for emeralds—now she had a positive aversion to them!

Knotting the gem into a torn piece of her bodice, she tucked it between her breasts. She peered into the clearing. The sun was intense, reflecting from the exposed limestone blocks until they shone blinding white. Beyond them the dense jungle rose in deep silhouette. Tilly saw no sign of the attackers in the open area, and the sounds of the birds and monkeys held no note of disturbance. She put a foot into the sunshine then pulled it back. The stone was as hot as a stove top.

Her toes smarted painfully. The jungle loomed yards ahead, but it might have been miles away. Without shoes she couldn't cross it. Perhaps a bit of bartering was in order. She returned to the injured man's side. Just as she had thought: he wore sandals, simple woven soles tied on with twisted cords.

Guilt nagged at her. It wasn't as if he'd be needing them in the immediate future, Tilly kept reminding herself, as she removed them from his dusty feet. They were a bit long, but when she crossed the cords over her arch and tied them around her ankles, they fit snugly enough. It took only a few turns back and forth to learn how to walk in them quite noiselessly.

She darted out and down the steps to the small platform, taking cover behind the trunk of a short, twisted tree. It grew incongruously from the roof of a small, low building, the strong roots taking nourishment from the thin layer of soil that covered it. Belatedly she appreciated that if she took refuge in the jungle, she might not be able to warn Flynn away from the temple. If he returned from the same direction she could cut him off, but if he chose another route? As she unsnagged her frayed sleeve from a brambly shrub, her quick mind jumped to a solution.

Ripping another bit from what was left of her skirt, she tied a length of fabric to one of the lower branches. The pale cloth would scarcely show against the flowering shrubs and limestone wall, but Flynn would not rush in without scanning the clearing first. The fluttering would catch his wary eye and he would recognize it. Then, while he reconnoitered the area she could make her way to his side.

It seemed the only option open to her. Taking advantage of every bit of cover, Tilly eventually reached the dappled shadows of the first rank of trees. There was a great change from the brazen heat of the clearing to the twilit green world of the jungle. It was like plunging from the heart of the sun into a massive, dim cathedral.

A mottled vine, as big around as her arm, came to sinuous life. It writhed around the trunk of a fallen sapodilla, lifted its fist-sized head and stared at her with dark, unblinking eyes. Tilly stared at the boa as it stared back. A moment later it uncoiled itself and slithered away into the underbrush.

The silent confrontation was over so quickly she was not sure she had seen it. The snake had come and gone like something in a dream, heightening her growing sense of unreality. She was in a world so unlike anything her imagination could have designed that nothing existed but the present. England and Jamaica were the dreams: this landscape of vine-swathed ruins and jungle primeval was all there was. And somewhere within it there were two murderous villains.

And Flynn.

Tilly was so afraid for him she hardly had time to worry about herself. At least she was aware of the danger and had taken precautions to conceal herself from the men, but...

She had only a brief glimpse of a white sleeve as an arm came around her shoulders, immobilizing her. Simultaneously a hand clamped over her mouth. She tried to kick her attacker but was lifted right off her feet. The only thing to do was bite—and she did!

"Damn it, Tilly! Hold still!" a low voice whispered.

Flynn! Immediately her struggling ceased. He set her down and she turned, flinging herself into his arms. "Thank God you're safe!"

His arms came around her again, this time to comfort and protect. She grasped the open collar of his shirt tightly. He rested his chin against her hair and held her until she stopped trembling. He forced her chin up and smiled reassuringly.

"I'm sorry. I didn't mean to frighten you out of your wits, but I was afraid you might cry out. We're not the only ones running loose among the ruins here."

"I know. The two brigands have gone off somewhere together, but the injured man is still unconscious at the foot of the temple. At least I hope he is. He might be dead by now."

She was babbling and unable to stop herself. "Otherwise," she explained, or thought she did, "I wouldn't have taken his sandals."

For once Flynn's composure slipped. He held her away. "What do you mean?"

Tilly pointed at her feet, noting in the detachment of delayed shock that her finger trembled. "The sandals. I had to take them from him because the stones were too hot to walk on barefooted."

His hands clamped down on her shoulders. "I don't give a damn about the sandals right now. What about these men?"

"I heard men shouting," she began, "not more than an hour after you left." She sketched in the details quickly and succinctly.

When she was finished Flynn looked grim. "I should never have left you alone! Thank God you are a woman of sense and enterprise."

"Sense and enterprise?" Tilly asked tartly. "Is that the reason I am standing here in the middle of a jungle—dirty, hungry and half-naked—and surrounded by pagan ruins, assorted cutthroats and recumbent bodies?"

His eyes crinkled at the corners. "I imagine so, but you'll have to wait until we're well away from here before continuing your scold." Flynn took her hand.

"I am not scolding!"

"No?" He tried to lead her away but she dug in her heels.

"We can't just leave that poor man without knowing if he's dead or alive."

"For all we know, he may be as much a villain as the other two."

Flynn's evaluation startled her. It was something she hadn't considered. "I'm sorry to say that possibility never occurred to me."

"And," he said, clasping her hand in his, "I would be a far greater villain myself if I left you unprotected, knowing that those men are still in the area." He frowned thoughtfully.

As she was about to respond he put a warning finger to his lips. His posture changed from easy alertness to tense vigilance. The alteration was amazing. Tilly strained her eyes and ears. No threats revealed themselves. The jungle creatures went about their normal tasks and created their usual ruckus, so they were not aware of any trespassers in their territory. A lizard scuttled nonchalantly over the surface roots of the tree and disappeared among a tangle of leaves. She flinched but Flynn remained still, poised for action.

The tension grew, frazzling her nerves. Tilly wanted desperately to ask Flynn what had focused his attention, but intuition told her to be still and follow his lead. Time crept by. Suddenly a brightly colored macaw burst from the branches overhead, squawking hoarsely. Another bird picked up the alarm. They flapped away singly and in scattered groups, and the monkeys, after shrill screeches, fell mute. The wilderness held its breath and watched.

She hadn't noticed Flynn move, yet instantly a long, wicked knife appeared in his hand. The muscles and tendons stood out in relief as he motioned her to silence. Nothing happened. The birds flapped to their perches and settled down sociably. Whatever had threatened briefly was gone.

Flynn waited, his face all hard angles and planes. Slowly his tension eased. "I'll check on the fellow, then on the surrounding area. Meanwhile, you stay put. The men you saw earlier might still be lurking nearby."

Tilly started to protest. Flynn pointed sternly to a hollowed place where the roots of tree arched above the ground. "Scoot inside until I come back—and stay there!"

She slipped into the pocket of tree roots. It was like a tiny cave, three feet high but less than a foot deep, and smelled overpoweringly of moldy humus and animal droppings. Flynn watched until she was safely ensconced, then darted away. As the time passed, Tilly grew restless. It seemed all she did was twiddle her thumbs while he faced dangers. The inactivity drove her wild.

The strain was intolerable but she wouldn't have budged an inch except for the cramp. It developed in her right calf without warning, a sharp jolt of agony that drove up from the sole of her foot to the knee, knotting the muscles until she almost cried out.

There wasn't enough room inside the root cave to straighten her leg. Tilly gritted her teeth against the pain, but it became unbearable. Beads of sweat dotted her forehead. When she had no choice, she ducked out and put her weight upon the cramped leg to counteract the cramp. The pain eased, but only for as long as she pressed down upon it.

A twig snapped behind her and she whirled. The cramp threw her off balance and she staggered before clutching the tree trunk for support. When she saw a tall, white-clad figure moving through the dense growth, she let her breath out in a rush and clambered out of her hiding place.

She didn't realize her mistake until it was too late. She turned and tried to run, opening her mouth to call out to Flynn. A hand clamped over her mouth and nose. It was impossible to shout or even breathe. Strong arms bruised her ribs as she was picked up off her feet.

She would not give up without a fight. Swinging her elbows back with all her might, a dull gasp told her she'd connected. Following up her advantage, she tried to yank free. The butt of a machete crashed down at the base of her skull.

Tilly didn't realize she'd been struck. There was no pain, only a queer, numbed feeling in her head and neck and a growing sensation of paralysis. Her ears filled with a dull, pulsing roar; then an enormous black bird rushed down upon her, enfolding her in its soft, dark wings.

Chapter Twelve

Discomfort. A hard floor and a throbbing at the base of her skull. Intense burning at her wrists and ankles. Tilly fought her way up from a dense fog of unconsciousness. She came to with her head reverberating like a gong. Her hands and feet were numb yet pulsating with pain. A low moan squeezed from between her parched lips.

A boot prodded her arm. "Awakening, Sleeping Beauty?"

The voice was masculine. Cruel. And indisputably English. She opened her eyes and closed them again as the world revolved giddily. Again the boot nudged her, this time more roughly.

"There's no use pretending you're still unconscious. You'll have to open your eyes eventually, and it might as well be now."

Her lids flew open and this time she was able to focus. She was lying on her side with her arms bound behind her back and her feet tied at the ankles. It appeared that she was in some sort of round storage shed or abandoned dwelling. Tattered palm leaves thatched the conical roof and the walls were undressed saplings, tied crudely together near the top and bottom. Once mud had been plastered over them, but it had mostly crumbled away, and sunlight sifted through the gaps. It was still day, then. But where was she?

And where was Flynn? Had they captured him, too? There was no time to think. A pair of scuffed boots came into view. One came out and up, pushing her onto her back.

The cords bit into her flesh and she felt as if her arms were being torn from their sockets. The agony made her cry out. Beads of sweat stood on her forehead as Tilly gasped for breath.

The man hunkered down beside her. He was young and blond. There was dissipation in the lines of his face and a curious blankness in his ice-blue eyes that froze her blood. His features were smoothly carved over fine bones, almost inhuman in their cold perfection. Like a statue of an angel, she thought, carved from some base stone. A shudder ran through her.

He took note of her fear and smiled. "There's no need to be afraid. If you cooperate you will be much more comfortable, I assure you."

She answered him with a blunt challenge. "Are you mad? I demand to be released, at once!"

His smile twisted. "You are under a misapprehension. *I* am the one who will be asking the questions and issuing orders."

She struggled painfully into a more dignified position. "Who are you, and why have you brought me here?"

"Explanations will come from a higher source. Consider me a deputy of the person who 'brought you here,' as you phrase it. I am merely an...assistant, shall we say?"

As he spoke Tilly was thinking rapidly. Intuition told her that his smooth words and empty eyes hid a deep, malicious streak. She had seen his like in a dozen village bullies, though his viciousness was magnified a hundredfold. Pleas for pity would only inflame him. A show of strength was the only thing he would respect. She would have to bluff. Forcing herself to speak with a calmness she certainly didn't feel, Tilly adopted a haughty tone.

"An assistant?" she said coldly. "I do not deal with subordinates. I refuse to speak to anyone but the person in authority."

Her attack threw him off balance. Anger and uncertainty were plainly reflected in his features. He was a man filled with resentment of those over him, but his rancor was tempered with fear. While he wrestled with his conflicting emotions, she pressed her advantage.

"Well," she said, in a voice several degrees sharper than the one she'd used to quell unruly choirboys. "Why are you dawdling? I have nothing to say to a mere underling."

His face went white with anger, then flooded with a dull, ugly red. The fine lips curled into a grimace of hate until she wondered how she had ever imagined anything angelic in such a demonic face.

"You'll be sorry you talked to me that way. You'll see. I could have made it easier on you. But you're all alike, you rich ones! Think you're better than me because you was born with a silver spoon in your mouths..."

Tilly stared at him. The change in his speech was as surprising as the alteration in his face. A shadow haunted both, born of the dark streets that ran through the depths of London. Years of suppressed rage and frustration poured out of him in a filthy torrent that would have horrified Tilly had she been able to understand more than one word out of every four. It took every bit of courage she possessed to keep her chin up and a condescending smile on her lips. It vanished when he switched to words she understood.

"...strutting strumpet...diseased bawd! You filthy whore! You..."

A man entered, frowning. "Shut your mouth, Dawson, or I will rip your tongue from your throat!" Despite the violent words his voice was mild.

The scream of abuse slowed to a disgusting trickle. Dawson glared at the newcomer. "Don't you go telling me what to do, Minas!" he mumbled. "I'm not afeard of you."

The other man stared him down for the space of three seconds. Dawson brushed past and went out. Minas was swarthy and dark, but Tilly could not place his accent. He stood over her and regarded her for a moment from hooded eyes.

"You are beautiful, English miss." He pronounced it *meese*. "That is an added bonus." He stroked his bearded chin thoughtfully. "They said you were, but I did not be-

lieve them. Men such as we, living away from women, are
likely to think a crone as beautiful as a princess.''

He knelt beside her and offered her a swig from a metal
canister. She drank gratefully, not caring that half the water splashed down her chin and onto her bodice. When she
finished he pulled out a knife and cut the cords that held her
ankles.

''Such soft skin as you have, miss. It would be a shame to
scar it.''

''I am glad we're of the same opinion,'' she snapped.
''Now, if you will be so good as to untie my arms, we can
preserve them from damage also.''

''I regret that is not possible, miss. Come. I must show
you something.''

He pulled her to her feet. She staggered and almost fell.
Her legs were as heavy as stumps, and there was no feeling
from her knees down. He caught her and held her erect
while her feet came alive again. Her toes cramped as the
circulation was restored. It felt as if thousands of stinging
nettles were trapped inside her skin. They burned and itched
and sent splinters of pain through her limbs until her eyes
watered.

Minas's face softened. His brown eyes held a sad, kindly
light. Tilly was suddenly convinced that he knew what she
was going through, that his sympathies were with her. She
clutched at the hope. ''Please,'' she said. ''You are not a
brute like that other man. Help me! Let me go!''

He shook his head. ''I regret I cannot, miss. Like
Dawson, I take my orders from a higher source.''

''Oh, please! Help me escape! That man...'' She shivered.

''Come. Soon you will understand.'' He steered her to the
door. She moved awkwardly, limping and unable to keep a
steady course. ''Yes, there is something about Dawson that
chills the marrow, is there not? But I am sure there need be
no unpleasantness. After all, we are all civilized people.''

He flung the door wide, and his wild burst of laughter
echoed in her ear. Beyond the shed was a building of stone
and thatch, and ranged across its front were several of the

most *un*civilized men she had ever seen. They leered and grinned when they saw her and Tilly was shamefully aware of her appearance. Her legs were bared to the thigh and the torn neckline of her dress revealed the upper curves of her bosom.

The men started clustering closer. One shouted something, preening and stroking his long mustachios. Another pointed at her and made a crude gesture, calling out to her at the same time. She did not have to understand the language to understand his meaning. The dark lust stamped on his face was mirrored in a dozen others. She shrank back.

"So you see," Minas said amiably, "that not everyone in this camp is such a gentleman as I. A woman, half-undressed as you are, would have provided good sport for them. Already they are getting impatient."

He shut the door, and the sound of their jeers was muted. Without warning he let her go. Tilly staggered and fell, unable to save herself. She landed on her side with such force that her jaw snapped shut and her teeth clicked together jarringly. She bit her tongue and salty blood filled her mouth. Now she had several new aches and scrapes to add to the others.

Tilly hardly noticed them. She knew she should have been filled with fear; instead she was consumed with rage. For the first time in her life she wished she were a man, able to take on this fellow ounce for ounce and pound for pound. By God, if she was free, if she had a knife or club, she'd make him sorry!

Minas turned her on her back and squatted in the dirt beside her. He saw the helpless anger sparkling in her eyes. It amused him. "Such a fierce little one! If you were not tied up, miss, I would tremble in my boots. Ah, you would cut my gizzard out."

He tipped back his head and laughed again, then pulled out a large, sharply honed blade. "But it is I who have the knife, and not you. And the men outside, they would each like to prove their manliness to such a beautiful miss. Now, since you have seen the alternative, I think you will not be so eager to withhold the information we seek, eh?"

Tilly nodded. "I will tell you whatever I can, if it is within my power. What is it you wish to know?"

Although she wasn't sure why she'd been captured, she had her suspicions. They turned out to be wrong. He leaned down until his face loomed over hers, then grabbed her hair and pulled her up by it until her shoulders lifted off the ground. It smarted so badly it brought tears to her eyes.

"First, miss, I would like to know what urgent matters have driven you away from the safety of your little excavation party? Matters of spying, perhaps?"

"I don't know what you are talking—"

Her words broke off as he slammed her against the ground. "Do not be foolish, miss. I am not a patient man."

"Excavation party? Spying? I think you have mistaken me for someone else."

Her remark was never answered. A curt voice called outside and footsteps approached. Tilly's captor jumped to his feet and spun toward the door, knife ready for action. Someone jiggled the primitive latch and opened it cautiously and a dark head poked around the corner. He jerked his head toward the clearing, then flung the door open wide.

Tilly's heart skipped, stopped and started again. Not thirty feet away, Flynn stood in profile, the sun-lightened streaks of his hair turned to gold in the afternoon glare. After her first rush of admiration at his bearding the bandits in their den, cold fear settled over her like a pall. He was deep in conversation with one of the ruffians, and the others were closing in on him. Flynn seemed unaware. What on earth was he doing standing there obliviously—didn't he realize the danger?

Before she could call out a warning, Flynn turned and came purposefully toward the shed. The cry of alarm was never given. He was, she realized with a sinking feeling, not in any apparent danger. In fact, he appeared to be very much at ease. One of the men approached him, bowing and beaming. The bandit with the fierce mustachios was listening intently, nodding from time to time—as if, she thought, he was used to taking orders from Flynn.

For a moment Tilly thought that hope had made her see something that wasn't really there: the man merely had a passing resemblance to Lucas Flynn. But no, it was definitely Lucas Flynn coming toward the shed, waving an occasional greeting to one of the others.

Beside her Minas relaxed and sheathed his weapon, as a welcoming smile creased his leathery face. "Flynn!" he said, making the name sound like *Fleen*. "Why did you not send word? I had heard you were still in Kingston."

Flynn strolled forward. "You heard wrong, Minas. My information, however, is more current. You still have the woman? She didn't get away?"

Minas stepped back and gestured. "You make a joke, Flynn. No one escapes from Minas. She is in here, trussed like a pig."

Flynn's form filled the doorway, blocking the light. Tilly could not see his face, but she knew he could see her quite clearly.

"Well, well, well. So this is the mysterious English-woman."

He ducked under the low lintel. His face was still in shadow. Tilly cringed beneath his gaze, aware of her disheveled vulnerability. Flynn made an appreciative sound.

"Good work, Minas. Did you get any information from her yet?"

"She is a stubborn one, this little miss! But give me a bit more time alone with her, and she will be as wax in my hands."

Flynn moved into a shaft of sunlight. It highlighted his high cheekbones and struck gold and green sparks from his narrowed cat's eyes. They were the eyes of a stranger, and Tilly felt a spurt of fear rising in her chest until it threatened to smother her.

With a cool smile, Flynn shook his head at Minas. "Perhaps it will be best if I question our guest. Your methods of persuasion tend to be quite rough. It would be a shame to leave scars on such a beauty, don't you think? And we have a saying that more flies are caught with honey than with vinegar."

He came closer and glanced at Tilly. "Good evening. My friends aren't used to entertaining ladies of quality. I trust they haven't treated you too roughly?"

"I might have known they were your friends!" she said bitterly.

"Yes, I suppose you should." Flynn braced his hands on his hips and towered over her. "Get up."

"I can't, you...you *imbecile*! My hands are still tied, and my feet are numb from where the ropes dug in. But the moment I am free, I vow I'll..."

"Quiet!" Flynn's roar drowned out the rest. He knelt beside her and his face was dark and unreadable in the filtered light. "You are completely in my power. I can do with you what I will. You would do well, my dear, to remember the hazards of your present predicament, and keep your pretty mouth shut!"

"Are you threatening me?"

"I am merely warning you."

There was a pause in the hostilities, while Tilly weighed his words. She clamped her lips over the heated words she had been about to pour forth. It took considerable effort.

Flynn smiled. "I knew you were a sensible woman."

He pulled something from his pocket and flipped it into the air. A small object that winked green in the sunbeam's light. Flynn caught it in his palm as it fell.

"Now, where did you come upon this pretty little bauble? Dawson said you had it hidden in your bodice."

Tilly realized he wasn't lying. Her bodice gaped open, and the stone she'd hidden there was gone. Her skin crawled. She was sick at the thought of Dawson's evil hands searching her body, touching her breasts while she lay unconscious. Minas chuckled.

"You are fortunate, miss. For all his cold looks, Dawson is a hot-blooded man. I hate to contemplate what might have happened if I had not intervened."

Flynn concentrated on the gem in his hand, ignoring his companion. In the filtered light the emerald took on its characteristic glow, a cool green ember surrounding a heart of fire. It might have been her imagination, but for just an instant Tilly saw an identical green flash reflected in his eyes.

His fingers closed around the stone and he tucked it away somewhere inside his shirt. "Not talking yet? Perhaps a few more hours of confinement will make you change your mind."

He put his hand on the other man's shoulder. "No food or drink for our prisoner until I give the word. Meanwhile, I've acquired a damnable thirst. Minas! Let us broach the new cask of rum."

Tilly couldn't believe her ears. "Wait! Even you, *Mr.* Flynn, could not be so cruel as to leave me here like this. I demand to know what you intend to do with me."

"Do you really think so? You'll know soon enough, my dear, when I return."

She had always known that a current of danger ran just beneath his surface, but had never suspected the depth; Jonas was right. He was not only dangerous, but deadly. Her mouth felt suddenly dry.

Flynn and his companion exited, closing the door behind them. The latch was left undone: there was no way Tilly could untie herself, and even if she could, the only exit was past the ranks of the men. She was left to ponder Flynn's connection with Minas and his bandit crew.

The change in him astonished Tilly. She had given her heart to him, and all that went with it, and he had looked at her with the detachment of a complete stranger. There was no sign of the passionate lover who had taken her so tenderly among the graceful reeds of the canal. Even his voice had altered. It had been so aloof and indifferent it was as if nothing had ever passed between them—or as if, she amended, that it had meant nothing at all to him.

Lying there in the gloom, with nothing but her wits and her pride, Tilly waited for Flynn's return. It was close and stuffy, and sweat trickled down her temples. It seemed as if hours passed, but she realized it was still daylight. Gradually the sounds from without grew louder and less restrained.

A deep voice started singing, stumbling over the melody and slurring the words. They were drinking, and already halfway to being drunk. After a boisterous shout the door opened once more to let in a shaft of lurid light. Almost sunset, she thought, wondering if she would be alive to watch it rise again.

The man called Dawson wavered in the entrance, his face ruddy with alcohol and the rays of the dying sun. A hand clamped on his shoulder and pulled him roughly away. It was Minas who had stopped him: the tableau was clearly visible beyond the open door. Tilly watched fearfully as Dawson tore himself free.

"Keep your hands off me, damn you." His words were slurred. "I found the woman first. She's mine!"

"Leave her alone," Minas ordered from outside. "Flynn has laid claim to her for himself."

"The hell he has!"

The argument stopped short when Flynn arrived on the scene. Dawson swung wildly at Flynn, who caught his assailant with a swift uppercut. Dawson staggered back, then crumpled to the ground. Flynn looked down at him and then at Minas. "Your men lack discipline. That can prove fatal."

Minas went pale under Flynn's hard glare. "It was the drink talking. Dawson is a good man, but rum is his downfall. I will see there is no repetition."

"There'll be more of this if she stays here, and not just from Dawson. I will take her with me tonight."

Minas rubbed his chin. "She is only a woman, after all...."

"One," Flynn snapped, "who will prove valuable in the near future. Cut her loose."

Minas hesitated, then entered the shed and did as he was bid. Tilly felt pain as the ropes that bound her wrists tightened against the blade and broke. At first they were numb, and when feeling returned she wished they had remained so. Her arms and hands were pulsing masses of agonized nerve endings, as circulation returned with a vengeance. She stifled a cry, biting her lip in the process.

"She cannot stand," Minas said.

Without answering, Flynn bent and scooped her up in his arms. "I'll carry her until she's able to walk. We'll be there before the dark is absolute."

Minas shrugged. Everyone knew the English were mad. "Whatever you say. It is you, and not I, who must keep a lookout for *el tigre*." He barked out a laugh. "But then you are *El Tigre*, also. Perhaps your namesake will protect you, eh?"

Flynn tossed Tilly over his shoulder like a sack of meal and ducked beneath the low lintel. Shadows had fallen across the clearing, but she could see groups of men sprawled drunkenly beneath the trees. They paid no heed as Flynn moved away with his burden. At the edge of the camp a small beast of burden was cropping plants with dogged persistence. It brayed and breathed through its nostrils loudly as they neared.

"Easy, you ugly imp!" Minas untethered the bony mule. "He is not handsome, this one, but he is tireless. Treat him like you would a woman. Feed him, beat him and show him you are master—he will become your devoted slave."

Flynn dumped Tilly unceremoniously upon the creature's bony rump and she slumped forward against the rolled blankets strapped in front of her. If she had been much taller her feet would have dragged on the ground. Her position was acutely uncomfortable, but she was too limp to sit up. Flynn passed strips of leather beneath the animal's body and knotted them over Tilly's back.

"This will keep her from slipping off."

While she lay sprawled across the mule's back in her undignified position the two men exchanged farewells and Flynn gave some last-minute instructions; then Minas went back to the others, eager for his generous ration of rum. The mule, led by Flynn, covered the uneven ground easily. It was Tilly who found the movement difficult.

"You," she announced baldly, "are the greatest beast in nature."

"You are reaping as you have sown," Flynn told her angrily. "I do not want you to speak again until I say you may. Do you understand me? Not a single word."

In his present mood he was perfectly capable of throttling her, and they both knew it. Gritting her teeth, Tilly put up with the swaying, jostling ride. She wiggled her toes but couldn't feel whether they responded. Her fingers felt cold and clammy and as big as plums, but at least she could move them now. Her head ached abominably. Suddenly she realized she had not eaten anything since the previous day.

They went north and west, she noted, into the twilight encroaching from the east. The mule's gait was hypnotic, and the rhythm lulled her. Tilly was not aware of dozing, yet the rasping bark of an animal jolted her awake. If not for the restraining leather she would have surely fallen. The sound was repeated, followed by a rumbling snarl.

"What is it?" she whispered.

"*El tigre*. King of the forest."

"But there are no tigers in the Americas!"

"*El tigre* is the name the inhabitants have for the jaguar. I'd appreciate it if you'd not call his attention to us."

They were deep in the jungle now, surrounded by the emerald blackness. There was just enough light sifting through the screening leaves to make out shapes. Flynn stopped the mule and Tilly squinted, trying to pierce the gathering shadows. Man-made forms distinguished themselves from the background. The remains of two conical-roofed houses squatted in the moonlight, already half-reclaimed by the hungry vegetation.

"Where are we?" she whispered.

"Quiet!" Flynn surveyed their surroundings, then whistled a light, falling phrase. If Tilly had not been beside him she would never have doubted the notes came from a night bird. Flynn repeated the whistle. In response a figure came out of one of the huts. He signaled to Flynn, then turned and vanished into the jungle. Flynn followed, leading the mule.

They stirred up the grass and a cloud of bloodthirsty mosquitoes swarmed over them. The insects descended in droves, and although she tried to brush them away, Tilly was soon covered in welts from head to toe. The intense itching, on top of everything else she had endured, was too much to bear. One had bitten her just below the right eyebrow, and the resultant swelling forced her eye half-closed.

"Untie me!" she demanded wrathfully, trying to scratch her itchy cheek against the mule's rough coat. "If I can't scratch these damnable...these insect bites, I shall go mad."

"All right. I think we've kept up the charade long enough." Flynn undid the leather strips that had held her on the mule, and she slipped off awkwardly. Her limbs were still weak and she almost fell. He caught her shoulders and supported her until she was able to navigate on her own.

Tilly scratched her arms and neck until they felt raw. The mosquitoes had dined well. Even the palms of her hands itched unbearably. Her entire body seemed to be one gigantic, burning welt. Her eyes focused in the dimness on the one person most responsible for her misery.

"Tired?" Flynn asked.

"Exhausted—not to mention bruised—from the manhandling you gave me. The insects have eaten me alive, but do you care? No! I thought you were going to haul me across the Yucatan on that horrible beast."

"I would have, had it been necessary. But remember, if you'd stayed hidden, as I'd told you to do, you would never have put yourself in such danger."

"*I* put myself in danger? Was it I who stole the emeralds in the first place? If not for you and your unpleasant acquaintances..."

He put his hand over her mouth tightly. "Lower your voice at once. Didn't I warn you back at Minas's camp to guard your wretched tongue? You might have gotten us both killed."

She drew away. "Until you did, I was certain you were hand in glove with them. And from what I saw, you very well may still be. If you expect thanks from me, you will be sadly disappointed."

His fingers clamped over her shoulders. "What is that supposed to mean?"

She struggled to get free, in vain. "I think I made my meaning sufficiently clear. My life was in danger, not yours. Not for a single minute. You could not have walked in and out of their camp so boldly unless you are part and parcel of their villainy."

"I see. You are accusing me of being in league with Minas and his desperate band."

Tilly ignored his implacable tone. "I am merely stating the facts. Minas had authority over Dawson but said he was in turn responsible to his superior. And if you thought I didn't notice that Minas took his orders from *you*, you are in error."

"Most shrewd of you," he said with dangerous calm. "May I know what reason I had for saving your life and, er, virtue?"

She was rigid with fury. Her hand swung toward his cheek, but he caught both her wrists and held her tightly. Even in her anger she felt the irresistible magnetism of his touch. It reminded her forcibly of what a fool she'd been.

"You may insult me as you please," she hissed. "You gave yourself away earlier, when you told Minas I would prove valuable in the future. Otherwise I would still be in that horrid shed. Or—" her voice faltered "—or worse."

"Keep that in mind if you are inclined to wander away during the night, Miss Templeton."

Last night she had been darling and my love; this evening she was once again Miss Templeton. She could not look at him after all that had happened. He had used her for his own convenience, and she, blinded by what she had mistaken for love, had fallen into his trap. How could she have been so foolishly wrong! Her face crumpled for a moment as she fought back tears.

Flynn took her roughly by the arm. "Start walking. We have a lot of ground to cover."

They snaked along past the giant trunks and under myriad vines that garlanded their way. It was more moist and humid as they worked deeper into the jungle and the scents of mold and decaying vegetable matter were stifling. There were sweeping ferns and colorful lichens. Orchids as graceful as butterflies, and butterflies as lovely as exotic blooms.

The alien beauty of the rain forest distracted her. Hopping over a root, she avoided collision with a green lizard and stepped instead on the bushy tail of a mouselike creature. She gasped and the animal squealed before dodging into its burrow. Tilly had barely recovered when she felt something light drop onto her hair. Visions of giant spiders flashed before her eyes and she jumped, flailing her hands ineffectually at her head.

"Oh! Oh! Get it off me!"

Flynn chuckled and brushed several dried twigs out of her hair. "Just one of the monkeys, having a bit of fun."

Tilly looked up. A howler monkey sat on a limb twenty feet above her head. It seemed to be grinning at her. Without warning the monkey jumped away and sent out shrill warnings. The stillness of the canopy burst into movement. Dark figures bounded through the treetops, joining the outcry. They fled in the same direction and the leaves quivered with their passage.

Flynn had come to a dead halt. His gaze raked the great branches overhead, searching for something. Suddenly the air was rent by a terribly gusty growl, half roar and half sigh. Tilly felt her hackles rise. The sound was repeated, this time farther away. Tilly moved closer to Flynn's side. She recognized it now: *el tigre*, patrolling his kingdom.

Flynn led her rapidly away from the direction of the jaguar's snarl. Tilly looked over her shoulder. "It isn't following us."

He whisked her along. "You wouldn't see it if it were. They move like shadows through the trees, leaping from branch to branch like creatures of the air. Beautiful, but at times deadly."

She shivered and hurried her pace. After a while her sense of direction was totally skewed. She would never be able to find the ruined city again alone. Exertion and heat were affecting her but Tilly stumbled on in Flynn's wake. Her stomach rumbled its hunger so loudly she was sure every creature in the forest could hear it. An answering rumble came from the treetops some distance away. Tilly picked up her speed again. She would be exceedingly thankful when they left the jaguar's domain.

As if in answer to an unspoken prayer, the trees thinned. The hardwoods gave way to assorted palms, which dwindled to seven-foot plants in definite, if straggling rows. Tilly could scarcely believe her eyes. They were in the middle of a cultivated field. A speckled hen clucked her way down the row, stopping to peck every foot or so.

Somewhere a lamb bleated. *Hallucinations from heat and hunger,* she decided. Flynn strode purposefully along and she kept up, although her sandals slipped in the ridged furrows. Ahead was a tiny clearing backed by an extensive grove of enormous palms. Beyond loomed the ever-present jungle. As they drew closer she noticed the small house for the first time. It was similar to the structure where she'd been held captive by Minas and his crew, but larger. This one had smooth mud plaster covering the upright sticks that formed the walls, and a brown and cream blanket hung over the entrance. It seemed as if it had sprouted right out of the stuff of the clearing—and she would not have been at all surprised if at any moment it returned to its origins.

Flynn stopped and whistled a falling trill so high and sharp it made her ears ring. She clapped her hands over them and glared at him. The foliage parted and she saw a long, brown face peeking through the stalks. Beneath a mustache a Spanish grandee would not have scorned, the man's full mouth widened in a gleeful smile. He was of indeterminate age with leathery skin and black hair, and he wore white cotton trousers and a shirt like the one Flynn had on.

"Tomaso, you old devil!"

"Aye-aye, Flynn! Imy told me you were coming. Welcome, welcome."

They shook hands and Tomaso clapped his thin hands on Flynn's shoulder. A spate of greetings followed in a hodgepodge of Spanish, English and what Tilly deduced was a dialect native to the Yucatan. Since she could make out less than one word in twenty, she was unable to follow the rapid exchange.

Tomaso plucked at his mustache and examined her curiously from the corner of his eye as he spoke. Flynn switched to English for her sake. "I would trust Tomaso with anything I have. He is one of my oldest friends."

"That," she snapped, "is not much of a recommendation."

Flynn turned from Tilly to his friend, but not before winking at her brazenly. "Miss Templeton," he said suavely, "is accompanying me on my travels."

"Ah, *si*. Eet is my pleasure, Mees Templeton, to make your acquaintance. Welcome to my humble home."

Tilly admired his poise. If he thought it peculiar for a young Englishwoman to be traipsing through the jungle clad in remnants of clothing, he certainly hid it well. Well, three could play at this little face-saving game of manners. Ignoring her disheveled appearance and Flynn's delighted grin, she held her hand out to him as if such introductions were everyday affairs.

A gracious smile accompanied her reply. "You are most kind, *Señor* Tomaso. I hope our unexpected visit does not cause you any inconvenience."

The formalities concluded, the trio proceeded toward the dwelling, quite pleased with themselves. Tomaso cupped his hands to his mouth. "Uluma!"

Flynn was still grinning, and Tilly took the opportunity to needle him. "Your friend is not at all disconcerted by our appearance," she said in an undertone. "One would think you are in the habit of appearing suddenly out of the wilds, with strange women at your side."

"You are only half right," he told her. "I shall leave you to guess which."

A young woman came from behind the house. She wore a plain white garment trimmed with multicolored embroidery, and her hair was coiled neatly at her neck. When she saw Tilly she blinked. Then she recognized Flynn and hurried to greet them. After that first glance she kept her eyes lowered and did not look directly at the guests again.

The girl was quite beautiful, and in her long oval face and high-arched nose, Tilly saw echoes of ancient Mayan royalty. Her voice was low and soft, and she spoke in the native dialect, nodding and motioning with graceful, work-worn hands. Tomaso spoke to his wife and Tilly heard him repeat her name.

Flynn put his hand upon Tilly's arm. "This is Uluma, Tomaso's wife. They will shelter us for the night."

Tilly held out her hand, not realizing her gaffe until the girl shrunk away. Quickly she changed the offered handshake into a brief curtsy. Uluma blushed and smiled and bowed her head. The introductions over, Tomaso beamed with pride and waved to some stone blocks that lay near the house.

"Sit down, my honored guests, and the wife of my house, she will bring you food and drink."

"We thank you for your hospitality," Flynn replied formally. Uluma hurried up with a water bottle and drinking gourd, which she presented first to Flynn. He accepted, took a sip and passed them on to Tilly.

When Uluma left them, Tilly shot Flynn a sideways glance. "I don't mind waiting my turn for water and taking what is left, if custom demands it, but if she brings food and presents it to you, I warn you I shall snatch it out of your hands and gobble it up myself."

"You are so fond of quotes, my dear, have you forgotten the one beginning, 'When in Rome...'?"

"Not at all. But this is not Rome, but the jungle. I shall bare my claws and fight you tooth and nail for my fair share!"

His eyes flashed with appreciation. "Excellent. The only thing I like more than a spirited woman is a good fight."

"Fortunately, Uluma seems to have read my mind. She is bringing us each a bowl."

"I'm relieved. Although I sounded bold, I was quaking in my boots."

Tilly took the bowl Uluma held out to her. There was no spoon to eat with. She glanced at the others. They were scooping the gruel up on bits of flat bread. She imitated them, eagerly and awkwardly. After dumping the first bite on her bodice she acquired the knack. The food was simple but delicious. The hollow space in her middle filled up, bringing a resurgence of energy. Before she realized it, the gruel was gone.

Tomaso and his wife shared a bowl, carefully wiping out the last speck of food. Tilly followed suit. When they had finished, Tomaso spoke to his wife, who rose and collected the bowls. From the careful way she handled them, Tilly suspected they were prized possessions, used only for special occasions. Flynn and his friend exchanged a few phrases. When the woman returned Flynn nodded toward her.

"Go with Uluma. She will provide you with a change of clothing. We'll be back before sundown."

As she followed Uluma into the house, Tilly ducked her head to accommodate the low opening.

The house was cool and dim, and it took a while to make out the layout and the simple furnishings. The house was divided into two rooms by a wall of dried leaves, woven into tight patterns. Near the entrance were a low table formed by three slabs of dressed stone, a small stool and a wooden chair of lovely, simple lines. A wall niche held a wooden saint's effigy. They passed into the second room, which held only a plain wooden chest and a large hammock of loosely woven cloth.

Uluma removed a plain white garment from the chest and handed it to her guest. "Please," she said, and, "Thank you," proud of her three words of English. Which, Tilly knew, were three more words than she could speak in Uluma's tongue.

"Please. Thank you," she responded, and saw the girl's face light up with pleasure.

Both relaxed. Their communication had at least established their kindly intentions toward one another. Tilly slipped out of her rags and into the dress. The cotton had a noticeable weave, yet felt soft as Irish linen. The neckline was collarless, and like Uluma's, richly embroidered with flowers of startling hue. Something squawked in the corner. Tilly turned, expecting to see one of the omnipresent parrots; instead she saw that the bundle in the hammock was a waking baby.

Uluma followed her glance and smiled shyly. The baby, not at all bashful, squawked again and stared at the stranger. Tilly went to the hammock and looked down. An infant of three or four months, with a thatch of shiny black hair and eyes to match. "Oh, how beautiful he is!"

Uluma needed no translation. Her face took on a gentle madonna glow as she picked the infant up and handed him to Tilly. "Juan," she said. "Juanito."

Tilly took the warm little bundle in the crook of her arm. It was amazing how well he fitted. One tiny hand reached out and closed around a lock of her hair and Juanito gurgled in delight. Tilly was amazed at the surge of tenderness she felt for this wiggling bit of humanity.

Uluma and Tilly smiled at each other. The baby had worked his magic on them, as babies usually do. The differences of culture and experience faded away, leaving behind two women and the strained beginnings of something that might grow into friendship.

Later the men joined them. The sun was setting, and within minutes twilight fell. Tilly expected Uluma to light her little oil lamp; instead she put two blankets on the ground and disappeared into the other room with her husband. Flynn spread one blanket on the floor. "Lie down. It's not fancy, but it's bound to be more comfortable than a stone floor."

"Where do you intend to sleep?"

"Right beside you. If you develop any foolish intentions of wandering away in the night, I want to be nearby to put a stop to it."

"I refuse to sleep in here with you. I would rather sleep outside."

"You will do as you are told, Miss Templeton, or answer to me."

There was no use fighting him. She was too tired, mentally and physically, to even think of it. "You may have one blanket, I'll take the other."

Flynn gave her a steady look. "Do you want me to tie you up again?"

Even in the failing light those strange tiger's eyes pierced through her. Tilly shivered. Turning her back to him, she curled up on the blanket. He lay down beside her and pulled the other blanket over them. It was cooling rapidly, and would be chill by morning.

Tilly was alert to every sound. She could hear Uluma's gentle breathing and the baby's soft snore. Comfortable, homey sounds. Then Tomaso's voice, soft and low. Other sounds followed. Until the previous night she could only have guessed at what they meant; now the sighs and moans and whispery movements told her things she would rather not have known. They awakened echoes of the hours she'd spent in Flynn's arms.

Her mind rebelled, but her body betrayed her. It went soft and fluid until her breasts tingled with sensations of his mouth upon them, and a deep ache stirred in her loins. Beside her, Flynn sighed in discomfort. She was afraid of the way she might respond to him if he touched her again. Between the moments of white-hot passion they had shared and the coldness that stretched between them now, there had been no time for her to adjust. Her defenses were few, and pitifully vulnerable.

Long after Uluma and her husband fell asleep, Tilly was awake, plotting and planning and trying to make sense out of everything. Outside an animal growled once, low in its throat, then grumbled to silence. *El tigre,* in his moonlit domain.

Beyond the blanket that hung over the entrance lay a world as old as creation, all ebony and silver, mysterious and untamed. Inside were a man and a woman, sleepy and contented in the aftermath of love, and a few feet away, another couple, kept awake by the longings that neither could acknowledge or forget.

Tilly was too miserable to sleep, but at least she had the satisfaction of knowing that Flynn lay awake, too. She hoped, with scant satisfaction, that he was at least as miserable as she.

They spent a second night with Uluma and Tomaso, and it proved as lonely and wretched as the first. Once, sometime after midnight, Flynn reached out to her without speaking. His touch seared her like a flame and the desire to turn to him was nearly overpowering. In the pulsing darkness of the night her breasts ached for the roughness of his palm against them, the encircling warmth of his lips, the insistent pull of his mouth. Her nipples tingled erect, straining for his kisses.

His fingertips grazed her breasts, kneading lightly at their tips, then slid past her abdomen to caress her inner thighs. Heat pooled in her loins, weakening her will as the need grew. He stroked lightly and she gasped in a breath. There was nothing she wanted more in that moment than to feel the iron strength of his arms tightening around her and to have him take her again in the wild, sweet consummation of passion.

Instead Tilly pulled sharply away and moved to the farthest edge of the blanket, biting her lip to keep from surrendering to the moment. To Flynn. To her own surging desire. He had lied to her, betrayed her, used her. She wouldn't let it happen again, no matter how her traitorous body burned to join with his.

Flynn rolled over and made no second attempt, but both of them lay rigid and awake the rest of the night. They were up well before first light. Uluma appeared from the other room with Juanito slung over her breast. Her eyes were cast down, but she sent little curious glances in their direction from time to time. Flynn's woman did not want him.

She handed them thick leaves wrapped around cold corn cakes stuffed with bean paste. The men washed them down with beer from a wide-mouthed jug but Tilly declined. "Water is all I want. One drop of that beer and I wouldn't be able to walk."

"Go ahead. We'll have the mule a bit longer, and after that I'll carry you if need be."

She gave him an icy look. "I would rather crawl."

Flynn stifled an oath. "I'll remember that, should the occasion arise." Downing his beer, he stalked away. It seemed they could not be in the same place without striking angry sparks.

Uluma gave Tilly a striped cloth to tie over her hair and a wide hat of woven palmetto leaves to go over it. While Tilly adjusted the hat, Uluma placed a shawl around Tilly's shoulder and tied it into a sling, into which she placed her baby. Juanito opened his eyes, yawned contentedly and went back to sleep.

When they went outside the men were ready and waiting. The pack animal was loaded down with hampers and baskets of Uluma's weaving and various produce. Flynn had a strip of cloth thrown over his shoulder and wore a wide-brimmed hat. Except for his greater height, he might have been Tomaso's brother.

He stood back and examined her. "This is not an afternoon promenade, Miss Templeton. Uluma, adjust that hat forward to hide her face more."

The girl did as she was asked. Tilly was sure her hat was now at exactly the same angle as the one worn by the patient burro. All that was lacking were two ear holes.

"Does this meet your approval?" she asked frigidly.

"You'll do. From a distance no one would suspect you're an Englishwoman—"

"Or," she interjected, pointedly surveying his crumpled garments, "that you are a gentleman."

He continued, ignoring the interruption. "Unless, of course, you open your mouth for one of your blistering set downs."

The look she gave him would have peeled barnacles off a hull. "I see no need for us to trot through the jungle in disguise. You assured me that the bandits were no longer a threat."

"Let us just say that it is wiser if no one suspects our identities until we reach our destination."

"Anyone might have followed our trail here directly."

"Do you take me for a fool, Miss Templeton? Imy obscured our trail, and I took a very roundabout way here."

She fumed, remembering that uncomfortable journey, most of it made with her tied on the mule; but she was not about to gratify him by losing her temper. Tilly made no more protests until Flynn tried to make her put on an odd, basketlike contraption. She balked, forgetting her good resolutions. "And just what is *that*?"

"That goes on your back. Slide your arms through the straps and I'll load it up."

"I am not a pack animal," she said indignantly. "Put it on the mule."

Flynn bit back the first retort that came to mind and contented himself with smiling wickedly. Once again the unspoken communication worked between them. Tilly's eyes blazed and her soft mouth thinned to a hard line. Without a word she slipped into the basket harness and stomped away. Tomaso exchanged glances with his wife.

It was going to be a long journey.

Chapter Thirteen

Tomaso's prediction proved correct. Flynn had insisted they avoid contact with other people as much as possible. This meant they were unable to take the most direct course. Instead of the trails and paths worn by dozens of bare or sandaled feet, they were forced to dodge and hack their way through heavy virgin growth.

Tilly plunged over roots, around boulders and through boggy ground that squelched and sucked unpleasantly beneath her feet. Lizards and snakes were no longer cause for her to stop and stare. They clambered past fallen trees, leading the stalwart mule, and over ground so hard it felt like cast iron. Her feet were sore, but the blisters did not pain as much as they had initially.

She stepped into a hole and swore beneath her breath, but kept up with Uluma, who had known these jungles all her life. It would have shamed her not to. Flynn turned. "Are you all right, Miss Templeton?"

"As right as I will ever be in this benighted place, *Mr.* Flynn." She had reverted to his surname, using it as a shield against their earlier intimacy.

She stopped to untangle a thorn-tipped liana from her hair. "At the moment Jamaica seems a million miles away, and England a half-remembered dream."

He considered her for a moment. "When you return to England I imagine you'll be content to travel no farther than to your own garden."

"Ha! I am not such poor stuff as that. Carry on, Mr. Flynn!"

She marched briskly past him, trying not to limp. Flynn whistled something beneath his breath. Tilly thought it might be "Rule Britannia" but she could not be sure. Let him laugh at her, if it gave him satisfaction. Meanwhile, she would keep up the pace if it killed her—which it was quite likely to do.

The going was slow and the hungry mosquitoes that rose with every step made each mile seem like a hundred. Juanito was protected in his sling and the others seemed fairly immune. Tilly slapped them off when she was able, but her arms grew tired with the futile attempts.

A mosquito got inside her tunic and made severe depredations. After slapping herself three times she managed to squash it. From his place in line, Flynn heard her mutter something that sounded suspiciously like a curse. "Once again, Miss Templeton, you prove your irresistibility."

She didn't look back.

On the third day an unexpected logging operation, run by a shipbuilding concern, complicated matters. To go around it would add another day to their journey, but they might be able to pass by without attracting undue attention. Flynn decided on the latter course and led them toward it.

From their vantage point they were able to see only part of the loggers' camp. The mingled scents wafting from the cook tent were, in Tilly's estimation, an exquisite torture. For the past three days they had been living primarily on water, corn cakes and leathery strips of dried meat Flynn called "jerky." She was heartily sick of it all, especially the gritty corn cakes, seasoned only with minute bits of rock from Uluma's grinding of the kernels.

"Hot tea and coffee," she sighed. "Deviled kidneys. Chicken with dumplings and sirloin of beef! Soda biscuits!" Her mouth watered at the mere thought. She longed to taste light-textured bread made with white flour, bread so delicate it would melt away on her tongue. "I was beginning to imagine such things existed only in my memory. I think I smell heaven."

Flynn narrowed his eyes. "I smell danger," he said cryptically. "Wait here. And if anyone approaches, let Tomaso do the talking. In fact, pretend you're mute."

She shot him a look that he ignored completely. He pulled his hat down, bloused out his shirt and assumed a shuffling, stoop-shouldered posture. Tilly blinked. It seemed impossible. One moment a tall, commanding man in his prime stood before her, the next she saw a much older man with an unsteady gait and arthritic joints. While she was still staring, openmouthed, Flynn moved into the forest and vanished from view.

"How," she asked wonderingly, "did he do that?"

An appreciative grin creased Tomaso's face. "Fleen, he has many treecks up hees sleeve."

It was the longest sentence Tilly had heard him utter in English. Until now she hadn't realized his grasp of the language. Quickly she cast her mind back, wondering what embarrassing things she might have said in front of him. Her face flamed so red even the tips of her ears burned, and she focused her attention on the camp.

Within a short time something amazing happened. Down in the clearing near the cook tent, a bent man in a large woven hat sidled up to one of the men. Tilly could scarcely quell her admiration. No matter what she thought of Flynn, there was no denying his courage: he had said the loggers might be a danger to them, yet had braved the lion's den for a closer look at them.

As she watched, the disguised Flynn and the cook's assistant exchanged a few words. The assistant shrugged and grudgingly held out a plate of food and a mug of coffee. Quicker than a wink, Flynn scooped up the kidneys and eggs and gulped down the coffee. He shuffled away, his stomach filled with a good, hot English breakfast.

Tilly felt the smoke coming out her ears. "That beast!" She had admired his courage, but it was hunger that had driven him into the camp. By the time Flynn reached them her anger was blazing brightly.

"You are a selfish pig! Saying you smelled danger!"

He cocked an eye her way and didn't even try to suppress a smile. "I did. My nose told me I was in danger of passing all that wonderful food by without tasting any of it."

Tilly flounced away, sulking, and he called after her. "Miss Templeton. Catch!"

As Tilly turned a round, pale missile came at her. She caught it. A hot soda biscuit, hard and crispy on the outside, as fluffy and insubstantial as a cloud inside. Its fragrance was more alluring than any perfume. She would have liked to savor it, but was too hungry. With a few delicious bites it was gone.

Flynn, with all the flair of a conjurer, produced two more from beneath his shirt, and handed one each to Uluma and Tomaso. Another swift movement and he pulled out a gourd, filled with chunks of cooked meat he'd stolen from the stew pot.

"This will have to do until we reach the Catholic mission this afternoon. They'll give us food and beds for the night."

"I thought we were trying to avoid anyone who might recognize us or our nationality."

His eyes twinkled with green lights. "They know me there, and will give us shelter with no questions asked. I'll explain later."

"What, back to that old refrain again? I believe in your 'laters,' Mr. Flynn, as much as I do in little green men."

After making that thrust, Tilly put up no major objections to the plan. She was not enthusiastic about spending another night on the jungle floor. There were too many creeping and crawling things to interfere with sound slumber. At this point in their journey they would all be grateful for a good night's sleep. More important, Uluma, who was used to hard travel, was not used to doing so while carrying and nursing a baby. In the beginning she had seemed tireless, but for the past hours her strength had been flagging. Tilly had been keeping a close eye on her two smaller companions.

The journey to the Catholic mission was interrupted by only one incident. Flynn had been scouting a distance ahead when he doubled back suddenly. "Some of the loggers are up ahead. It might be all right, but there's no sense in taking chances. We will have to split up and cut around them. It will delay our arrival until this evening."

Tilly shook her head. "Uluma is tired. She has been faltering the past half hour and more. We must find a safe place to rest."

Flynn glanced at Uluma, who was rocking Juanito in her arms. It chagrined him that Tilly had seen the girl's fatigue and he had not. As head of this little expedition he was supposed to look out for the welfare of all. Eagerness had made him careless.

"I agree. We cannot push her so hard and so fast. Tomaso, do you know of any place suitable nearby?"

Tomaso rubbed his chin and spoke to his wife. After some conversation, Flynn interpreted for Tilly. "We will split up now. That will confuse our trail even more. Uluma has kin nearby, and can rest with them. Tomaso will join us later."

With Uluma and her baby on the mule, Tomaso guided his family into the jungle. Tilly watched them go with feelings of sadness. Just before Uluma vanished from sight, she turned and gave Tilly a dazzling smile. The leaves closed behind her and she was gone.

Flynn took Tilly by the elbow. "We'll go up that bank."

She shrugged off his hand. "I am perfectly capable of doing so under my own power."

The going was heavy since they followed no trail and the land sloped upward at a steep, broken angle. It was so hot and increasingly humid. Time and again Flynn extended his hand to help her up the steep grade or reached to lift her over some major obstacle. Although her breathing was labored and her side ached, she ignored his offers of aid.

The ground ahead was rough and pitted, and Tilly suspected there were Mayan ruins beneath the tangled covering of jungle. Her fascination with the remnants of that proud, ancient culture had deepened since arriving in the Yucatan and seeing them at firsthand. If time had not been a factor she would have liked to explore.

Ahead there were two likely routes she thought Flynn might take. Instead he chose a third one. She was sure he'd done it on purpose. Determined not to give him any reason for scorn, she came on in his wake. She was so busy guarding her pride she didn't hesitate when he jumped up, grabbed a low-hanging limb and swung himself up a massive, scarred bank. Jumping with all her strength, she sprang upward, grasped the branch—and lost her grip, tumbling backward into the ditch. With the cumbersome basket on her back and her limbs flailing in the air, she was as helpless as an overturned ladybug.

There was no sign of Flynn.

With a great deal of effort she managed to roll partially onto her side, and got hung up on the bulge of the basket. Unable to rock herself free, she lay there gasping and searching her body gingerly for broken bones. Doubts thronged her mind. Would he realize she was no longer following? Should she call out to him?

The decision was taken out of her hands. Minutes passed while she struggled futilely. At last she saw a shock of hair appear over the rim of the bank, then a pair of laughing green eyes. She realized how she must look in her undignified position. "How dare you laugh at me!" she sputtered.

"I am not laughing at you."

Tilly clamped her jaw tightly. True, his face was perfectly expressionless, but she *knew* his eyes were laughing. She closed her eyes and grimaced in frustration. With her features skewed and her teeth bared so widely, Flynn thought she was in pain.

He jumped down beside her. "You're injured. Why didn't you tell me at once?"

How like him, she thought, *to blame me!* Outraged, she squeezed her eyes shut more tightly and clamped her lips together in an effort to maintain control. Not one sound escaped her lips.

Flynn was appalled. He'd expected one of her lively scolds, or at least a brisk rebuke; but she hadn't uttered one word of reproach. The pain must be frightful. He ran his hands swiftly over her arms and legs, along her ribs and behind her head. No lumps, no bumps, no frank breaks. There must be internal bleeding. Nothing else could have caused her agonized grimace. Panic gripped him in its terrible teeth and shook him like the cur that he felt he was. He'd led her on a merry chase, and this was the outcome. He despised himself.

"Where does it hurt? Can you tell me?"

The urge to punish him was too strong. Tilly twisted her features in anguished lines and moaned softly. Flynn cursed himself beneath his breath, but she heard him quite distinctly. After all he had put her through, it was truly music to her ears.

Flynn leaned down and whispered in her ear. "Try to be brave, my dear. I know it will be painful, but I must carry you to the mission."

The image of Flynn carrying her upslope to the mission over rugged ground was another tempting morsel. What a wonderful joke on Flynn! Her lips trembled as she held back a bubble of laughter, and the only sound that came out was a pitiful mewing.

"Oh, God!" Flynn whispered. "This is all my fault. I have no one but myself to blame!"

He lifted her tenderly into his arms and staggered up the bank where the gradient was less steep. With the incline, the exertion and the fear his breathing quickened. She lay passive in his arms, her head bobbing against his shoulder. Flynn thought she'd fainted, but no, her chest was still heaving with those terrible, silent sobs.

He staggered over fallen limbs and chunks of broken limestone blocks, avoiding tree branches and the lancet thorns of the lianas. After some three hundred yards he felt her entire body quiver and began a mumbling litany of encouragement. "Only a little longer and I'll have you there safely. Hold on, Tilly! Don't give up!"

The mission outbuildings were visible just ahead through the trees. He hurried as much as possible, afraid he might stumble in the rough terrain and drop her. "Just a few more yards," he said.

She quivered again and he came to a dead halt. Her head was buried in the angle of his shoulder and her hands hung limply around his neck, but something had changed. The seed of suspicion grew into a certainty.

"By God, I have been taken in!" He set her on her feet, and she collapsed against his chest, grasping his shirt to keep erect. "Tilly, you little wretch, if you are laughing, I swear I shall strangle you here and now!"

The tide of laughter could no longer be stemmed. She burst into howls of mirth. "'This is all my fault. I have no one but myself to blame,'" she quoted in between whoops. "I have finally gotten you to admit it!"

Flynn's teeth bared in a wide grin and his strong hands closed around her throat. Weak with laughter, she threw her head back and gasped in a shaky breath. Something was dragged through the brush, and a shadow fell over them.

"My son," a mournful voice said, "think carefully of what you are doing...."

They spun around together. A man, tall and cadaverously thin in his dark Franciscan robe, stood in front of them. His eyes were shadowed with sadness at the eternal folly of mankind, yet filled with the wonderful light of faith and hope.

"Nothing," he said in soft persuasive tones, "can be solved by resorting to violence."

Flynn raised one eyebrow. "Just one little squeeze? Not too hard, mind you. Only enough to make my point."

Tilly pulled free of his grasp and dug him sharply in the ribs with her elbow. The cleric favored her with a melancholy smile.

"I see there is provocation on both sides. However it is only by overcoming our animal natures that we can find true peace and harmony in this world. Come into the church, my children, and we will talk."

Slipping in between them, he put a gentle hand on their shoulders and guided them toward the mission with an odd shuffle. He promised them food and shelter and spiritual comfort. As they strolled beneath graceful palms the undergrowth gave way to a discernable track, and eventually to a well-trodden path. A great deal of effort had gone into beating back the jungle, and the ground was swept clear of rocks, leaves and debris.

Tilly's spirits rose. A hot meal, a warm bath, a soft bed were all she wanted, sprinkled perhaps with some good conversation—just the barest bones of civilization. Those hopes withered and died when she saw the buildings.

She had expected the mission to be a substantial structure, something like the engravings she had seen of Spanish missions in the Americas; instead it was a first cousin to the little house of Uluma and Tomaso, only a bit larger. It seemed to have sprung from the mould of the jungle, and several of its posts had sprouted leaves as proof of their origins.

Tilly's feet dragged in disappointment. Her dreams of hot baths and real beds evaporated into the steamy air. Even Flynn seemed taken aback. Their guide beamed proudly.

"Yes, it is splendid, is it not? Although pride is one of the seven deadly sins, I must admit in all humility that this cathedral is as close to perfection as may be possible in this imperfect world."

He shuffled ahead of them to show the way, his face glowing. "Note particularly the stained glass of the windows and the Gothic carving of the central spire. The stonework of the buttresses, as airy and delicate as lace! As for the gilded saints above the main front, there is not their equal in the world."

Goggle-eyed, Tilly followed his pointing finger. Where the man envisioned a glorious spire, she saw the trunk of a towering tree rising toward the sky, its smooth bark almost hidden by the vines that covered it. The only window was a lopsided hole covered with a faded piece of printed muslin. While she stared at one of the gilded saints, it spotted a tasty-looking beetle flying by. It opened its beak and squawked, then left its perch in a flurry of bright orange and yellow feathers. Swooping upon the hapless insect, the parrot flew upward triumphantly.

Goose bumps rose along the back of Tilly's arms. Whether their guide was a cleric or not, one thing was sure: he was mad as the proverbial hatter. As she glanced sideways at Flynn, his bronzed hand came down on her shoulder, the fingers pressing a warning. "A marvel of artistry," he said, "worked by a master hand."

"Brother Clement has devoted all his time and energies to it," another voice added.

A burly redheaded man was coming through the jungle on the other side of the clearing. "It is a marvelous example of faith made manifest," he continued, approaching them through the trees.

His long black cassock swung with the length of his strides and a silver cross bobbed from the chain around his neck. Suddenly he stopped dead in his tracks, shook his big, bearlike head, then broke into a run, laughing and shouting. Tilly took one look and pressed closer to Flynn's side. They were surrounded by madmen!

She was ready to flee and expected Flynn to take action, as he always did in times of crisis. His muscles had tensed when he'd heard the second man's voice, but now they relaxed. His face split in a smile that could only be described as radiant. Holding out his hand, he caught the latest arrival's broad paw in it and pumped vigorously.

"Gerald, by All that's Holy!" The shake turned into a hug. The red-haired priest thumped Flynn on the back and controlled his grin long enough to address his colleague. "Carry on with your noble work, Brother Clement, and I will take our guests to the hospital."

The other man bowed, benevolence shining from his emaciated face. "That is kind of you, Father Gerald, and most perspicacious. I did not realize they were stricken with the plague."

Humming softly, he turned away and began directing imaginary workmen on the installation of an imaginary window.

With a smile, Father Gerald urged Tilly and Flynn across the clearing. "Do not be alarmed. Brother Clement—he is not really a religious, by the way—is a gentle soul, and quite harmless. Years of alcohol and . . . uh, a most tragic disease acquired in his youth have affected his mind. He believes that he is constructing a cathedral to rival Chartres in beauty and elegance.''

His ready explanation did not impress Tilly. She frowned. ''It seems cruel to reinforce his delusions. Why do you encourage them?''

Father Gerald sighed. ''His days on earth are severely numbered. If it gives him ease to spend his last days in an illusory world, it would be more cruel of me to deny him. He thinks the cathedral will be dedicated next summer on the feast of Corpus Christi. Of course, he will be dead by then.''

''How very sad,'' Tilly murmured.

Flynn shook his head. ''Not really. How many of us are fated to spend our last days in complete happiness and satisfaction?''

The priest clapped him on the back. ''It is your penchant for philosophy, Lucas, that endears you to me.''

Tilly was increasingly bewildered. ''You seem to know each other well.''

''Of course,'' both men answered simultaneously. Flynn laughed at her confusion. ''Forgive my lapse of manners. May I present my brother Gerald?''

Her mouth fell open. ''Brother!''

The two men nodded in unison. The priest was burly in contrast to Flynn's lean muscularity, and his eyes were a burning blue instead of green; but as they stood side by side, sharing matched grins at her astonishment, the resemblance was uncanny. It was not a matter of features, but of expressions: they were identical.

If surprise was her first reaction, embarrassment was the second. She wasn't sure if the worst was that the priest was Flynn's brother or that his brother was a priest. Gerald must think her a scarlet woman to be traveling alone with a man who was not related to her by ties of marriage or ancestry. The horrible truth, she realized, was that in any eyes but her own, she certainly fit all the criteria.

She prayed that Father Gerald was not as adept at reading her aspect as his brother was, and she knew her face was redder than a prize beet. They began walking toward the mission. Honesty was supposedly the best policy, and Tilly plunged into it.

"I suppose," she began hurriedly, "that you are wondering how we came to be traveling together in such an unorthodox manner."

Flynn interrupted. "Don't trouble yourself with explanations, Tilly. While my brother likes my philosophic turn of mind, the thing that most endears Gerald to me is that he never asks awkward questions."

"I think you should know," Tilly began again, "that your brother has used me shamefully."

The look Father Gerald turned upon her made Tilly blush to the roots of her hair, and Flynn choked on an explosion of laughter. "I mean," she corrected hastily, hoping the lie wasn't written on her face, "that he has abused my trust and taken advantage . . ." Tilly stammered to a halt, her face on fire with chagrin.

Flynn's eyes crinkled at the corners. In the end he said simply: "This is Miss Matilda Templeton. She is a guest of Lara and Jonas Whitby. Miss Templeton, this is my brother, known hereabouts as Father Gerald."

The priest bowed, a slight smile curving his generous mouth. "How do you do, Miss Templeton."

If he wondered how a guest of the respectable Whitbys came to be traveling without chaperon in the Yucatan, Father Gerald hid it completely. He bowed to her with such civility that Tilly could almost forget her straggled hair and sunburned face. She stammered out a reply and tried to explain, but Flynn took over.

"What she means to say, Gerald, is that I have endangered her life and reputation by planting stolen goods upon her person, caused her to be abandoned on a sandbar in the path of a hurricane, then brought her to the Yucatan so she might be kidnapped by brigands."

He sent her a challenging look. "Furthermore, for my own evil ends, I'm delivering her up to that sinister person, Dr. Julian Challfont, the eminent archaeologist and professor of history at Edinburgh University. And finally I am—as you no doubt already know—the leader of a band of murderous brigands!''

Tilly could have slapped Flynn! He made her sound like a hysterical fool.

Father Gerald's eyes widened. "Quite a catalogue of iniquity. Tell me, Lucas. Is any of it true?''

Flynn didn't miss a beat. "All of it, according to Miss Templeton. Look at her, and judge for yourself. Is this innocent face that of a lady who would make up such scurrilous accusations?''

The priest's answer was a jolt to his listeners. "Indeed no. But, my dear Lucas, if you've come to complete these nefarious deeds with Dr. Challfont, you are out of luck.''

He positioned himself casually, where he had an unobstructed view of both their faces. "You see," Father Gerald explained slowly, "the eminent Dr. Challfont is also, I regret to say, the late Dr. Challfont.''

Flynn stopped so abruptly Tilly stumbled into him. "Dead? When?'' he demanded. "How?''

His brother looked grave. "The news reached me yesterday. He'd been missing for three days. Sunday morning his body was found beneath a block of fallen stone over a mile from where he'd last been seen.''

Flynn had appeared stunned at the news but he recovered quickly. "Unfortunate! Challfont was a good man, a dedicated scientist and an able excavator. He will be sorely missed by his friends and colleagues.

"But what are you doing here, Gerald?'' he added quickly. "I certainly didn't expect to find you at the mission. The last time you wrote you were in Mexico City.''

"I was, but having had a surfeit of politics and red tape, I've come back to where I belong. And the last I'd heard, you were in Bombay.''

"I was. But Dame Fortune led me back to Jamaica.''

Gerald boomed out his hearty laugh. "Or *mis*fortune, by the looks of you.''

Tilly was filled with misgivings. Flynn had changed the subject abruptly, and now the two were chattering on like magpies, as if Dr. Challfont's sudden death was on a par with a mild change in the weather.

She dug in her heels. "I would like to know what is going on and I won't take another step forward until I do!"

Two pairs of eyes gazed at her innocently, one green, the other blue. "Don't look at me like that," she said acerbically. "I have been around members of the Flynn family long enough to know that something is in the wind."

The way their faces closed in, like houses with the shutters pulled over the windows, told her she was on the right track. Tilly's quick mind jumped to a conclusion and landed solidly. "It is something to do with the death of Dr. Challfont. I think it was not an accident, but foul play."

The two men exchanged glances. Father Gerald nodded. "You're remarkably astute, Miss Templeton. I've no proof and neither has his assistant, Mr. Scarborough, but we're of the same mind. There's been trouble at the site for several weeks—vandalism, thievery. Recently several of his most reliable workers have deserted. Challfont knew and trusted his men. They'd worked with him for the past two seasons. Something is up."

They began to walk slowly down the path and Flynn was lost in reverie for the few yards. "I'd hoped to keep you well out of this, Gerald, but there's no other way. It's imperative that I reach the excavation site as soon as possible. Every hour's delay adds to the risk, and I'll require any help you can give me to that end."

"Up to your old tricks?"

"Not at all. But I can't go into details."

"He will explain *later*," Tilly said caustically. "It is a habit with him to postpone answering any questions until some future—and no doubt mythological—date."

The two brothers locked eyes, and Tilly could have sworn some silent conversation went on between them. Unspoken undercurrents swirled around her, and she felt she was treading on quicksand again. Still the two men stared at each other. The priest seemed reluctant but Flynn was steadfast and determined.

After several seconds Gerald shrugged and gave in. "Very well. You know what you are doing and nothing I do or say will stop you. My resources are not much, but they are yours to command."

"I knew you wouldn't let me down."

"Miss Templeton will, of course, remain at the mission."

"Contrary to what Miss Templeton thinks, I've brought her to you as proof of my good intentions toward her. But now I think she'll be safer with me. We'll talk later. I'd rather not discuss it out in the open."

It irked Tilly to be discussed as if she were absent. "I am not a piece of wood to be talked over and moved around at your will."

Flynn slipped a hand beneath her elbow. "No. You are a brave and gallant woman and I should be locked up and the key thrown away for getting you entangled in this. Don't worry, my dear, I won't rest until I get you safely back to Kingston."

There was a weary bitterness in his voice she'd never heard before. Tilly didn't answer. If she had an opinion she wouldn't have voiced it at the moment. She was far too tired to argue. And the lump that had suddenly formed in her throat had nothing at all to do with it. Serious as her predicament was, returning to Kingston would only provide her with a new set of problems.

Flynn regaled his brother with an abridged version of their adventures. "As usual, the good Lord was looking after you," Gerald said.

"Ah, is that who it was?" Flynn mused. "I had suspected far otherwise. You know the old saying, that the devil looks after his own."

A few minutes later they arrived at the mission, which consisted of a thatched church and a two-room building, much like Uluma's house, that served as school, infirmary and general living quarters. Flynn's pride in his brother was apparent. Gerald, he explained, had studied medicine before finding his religious vocation. Now he dedicated his life to working among the people of the Americas.

Endemic disease and infected injuries were his worst medical problems among men, he explained, while poor nutrition and fevers caused the greatest mortality among the women and children.

"You seem happy here, Gerald, teaching the people."

"Yes. And they're teaching me even more. There are plants and herbs growing here that have miraculous properties. By combining the knowledge of the old world with that of the new world, we are making some inroads."

"If only Bishop de Landa hadn't tried to destroy all the written records of the Maya," Flynn added, "the world would have been richer for it. Their history, genealogy, religion and medicine—all gone up in Spanish smoke. By the time he changed his mind there were only three surviving books."

Tilly stared at Flynn, seeing the earnestness in every line of his face, hearing the anger and regret in his voice. "You sound like an historian or an archaeologist."

He only shrugged. "Gerald is the scholar in the family. I am, as you've already deduced, the black sheep."

His brother laughed and changed the subject, asking after some acquaintance unknown to Tilly. As they talked she watched them wonderingly. Both shared the same intensity and love of life, and the same teasing humor. As they joked and talked and exchanged news she saw a side of Flynn she had not seen before. She realized, sadly, how different their relationship was than that of hers with her own brother, Durward. Two men, so seemingly dissimilar, yet linked by unmistakable bonds of blood and affection. They were not only brothers, they were friends.

As they strolled around Tilly was surprised that Lucas Flynn was as well known to the local population as was his brother. Everyone, from the lay dispenser to the man who hoed the vegetables, came by to greet him with a smile or a few words.

"Oh, yes," Father Gerald told her. "Lucas spent a year with us. Indeed, he helped to build the infirmary."

"Please." Flynn held up his hands in protest. "You are ruining my image with Miss Templeton. Up to now she has been sure I am devoid of any virtues at all."

Gerald said nothing, but his eyes moved from his brother to Tilly and back. She lowered her lids to mask her emotions, but had the feeling the priest knew more about her than she wanted him to know. Her sharp words might fool Flynn, but they had not fooled his brother one wit. The proof of this came that evening, when it was time to retire.

Flynn tried to fight a yawn. "If you will show us where we can bunk, we will turn in for the night."

"Joseph, my deacon, has prepared a bed for you in the dormitory, Lucas."

"I cannot abandon Miss Templeton," Flynn interjected quickly. "You mentioned that the infirmary is currently unoccupied. We could spend the night there."

"I cannot abandon Miss Templeton, either, my dear brother." A walnut-skinned woman came into the common room and smiled gravely at Tilly. "This is Aneta, who aids us at the infirmary when needed. She sleeps in the office, which is the more dignified name of that tiny cubbyhole adjacent to it. She will play duenna tonight."

Flynn looked chagrined, but Tilly thanked the priest for his consideration. Gerald's blue eyes twinkled. "I am sure you will sleep more soundly there than in the infirmary."

"I am sure you are right. Good night." Tilly crossed the room to Aneta without a backward glance, and the two women went out together.

Later, when Aneta was deep in slumber, Tilly was wakeful. The night was hot and sticky and she longed for a refreshing breeze. Since the shipwreck she had spent her nights upon earth or hard stone. Now that she had the luxury of a grass-stuffed mattress and a pillow of real feathers it might as well have been high noon in Trafalgar Square, for all the sleep she was likely to get. It was an hour or two before dawn when she finally gave up.

Through the net-draped window she heard leaves rustling in the breeze, inviting her to share its benefits. She rose quietly and went to the door, which was really only half of a Dutch door. The opening was filled with more voluminous folds of mosquito netting. She was not foolish enough to wander from the building, but at least she could stand at the opening and feel the air currents against her heated skin. The netting hazed her view. The reflected moonlight covered the small mission buildings and the jungle beyond with hoarfrost.

Tilly scarcely noticed. Her mind was too busy, too crammed with thoughts and speculations. Her travels with Flynn were nearing an end, and her questions would soon be answered. She had grown accustomed to Flynn's presence beside her in the night, to the warmth of his body and the sound of his breathing. He might be many things she disapproved of, but there was no doubt she felt safe from outside dangers when he was near.

In the morning they would begin the last leg of their journey toward the archaeological expedition site to await the supply ship. From Flynn's urgency she had deduced earlier that he expected a confrontation there, one that would lay bare all the ugly secrets.

As she was about to return to her mattress, she saw a red glow outside only a few feet away. It was brief, but bright as a firefly. The smell of cigar smoke wafted on the breeze. Two figures appeared in the darkness and she retreated a step, recognizing Flynn and his brother.

"Now, Lucas," Gerald said, "before the others are up, I want you to tell me the truth of why you're dragging that unfortunate young woman along with you through the Yucatan."

There was a pause of several seconds. Tilly flinched when she heard Flynn's answer. "If I had my way, Gerald, Miss Templeton would be far away from here. She's been a confounded encumbrance."

"I thought perhaps..."

"You thought wrong."

Tilly clenched her jaw and listened in shock. "Just what are you up to?" the priest was asking.

"It's not what I'm up to, but what I'm after. Imagine this—an emperor's ransom in gold and emeralds, lost from sight these five hundred years."

"Montezuma's treasure!" the priest exclaimed.

"Don't play the fool," Flynn said sharply into the darkness. "Montezuma was an Aztec, not a Maya, as well you know."

Gerald sighed. "You can't blame me for thinking you were pulling my leg. You've done it often enough in the past to your poor little brother. But if this isn't Montezuma's treasure, whose is it?"

"Mine."

Tilly strained her ears to hear but the breeze blowing through the trees made it difficult. ". . . interested by a local legend Tomaso related to me and I set myself to figuring out the puzzle. It's truly a sight to behold! The wealth of an ancient ruler stacked from floor to ceiling like so much fire wood."

"You were always good at solving mysteries, Lucas. Almost as good as you are creating them. Why have you kept it secret?"

"It's very simple. Some unfortunate business transactions put my neck on the line. Certainly the Mayan noble whose tomb I stumbled upon had less need for them than I did. I've been smuggling them into Jamaica ever since. There's a very good traffic for emeralds between this corner of the world and Europe."

"I see." The priest cleared his throat. "I suppose that explains your generous donations to the mission hospital."

Tilly's fingers curved into fists. It explained many things, including Flynn's expensive yachts, his tiptoeing around Coeur d'Émeraude by night and his strange disappearances. Somehow she had hoped against hope that when he finally fulfilled his promises to explain things, there would be good, sound reasons for his actions. To find his romantic-hero airs were nothing but a disguise, that his entire object was financial gain diminished him in her eyes. Her disillusionment was great.

She almost wished she'd minded her own business and stayed in bed. Stubbornness kept her at her post, blinking back the tears: she'd already learned the worst, she might as well hear the rest.

"Where," his brother asked, "is this fabulous tomb?"

Flynn voice was so soft it was barely audible. "Would you like to see the tomb and the treasure for yourself, Gerald?"

There was a brief pause. "I'm a man of the cloth. I can't be part and parcel of your schemes."

"You needn't be. I've all I need or could use in a hundred years. I'd planned on revealing the location. Perhaps we could strike a deal between the authorities and Dr. Challfont's assistant. Money for your mission and treasures for rich collectors and museums."

A low chuckle floated on the air. "Render unto Caesar the things that are Caesar's, eh? Yes, I think it might be possible."

Tilly knew she should be just as horrified, or perhaps even more so, that the priest should dismiss the tomb robbing and the smuggling so lightly. Priceless artifacts were being ruined and knowledge lost forever. *Two of a kind,* she thought, *as alike as two blighted peas in a withered pod!*

She couldn't believe she been taken in by either of them. But it was only Lucas Flynn who broke her heart. She wiped away a tear. How stupid she had been ever to think...to hope...that he'd cared for her.

Their voices were suddenly closer. "Yes," Father Gerald was saying, "I'd like to see this treasure of yours."

"Good. Travel with us to Challfont's excavations on the coast tomorrow and I'll take you there. It's nearby, but so well-concealed a man could be three feet away and miss the hidden entrance."

"Very well. But I warn you, Lucas, if this is one of your elaborate jests, I'll..."

The rest of his laughing threat was inaudible as they moved past the corner of the building. For a few seconds Tilly was tempted to throw on her clothes and confront them. She changed her mind at once. There was really nothing she wanted to say. Certainly nothing more she wanted to hear!

As she was turning away, a movement attracted her eye. A form slipped through the shadows near the base of the trees, heading the same way Flynn and his brother had gone. Tilly stepped into the shadows of the room, keeping the figure in view. As it darted from tree to tree, moonlight gleamed icily along the barrel of a pistol. *Just someone keeping watch,* she thought and returned to her bed.

Tilly sank into deep and dreamless sleep, unaware that the final round of the deadly game was about to begin.

Chapter Fourteen

The sun was merciless in the afternoon sky as the small party wound its way through the lowland tangle. Scrub and thorn ruled the flat expanse, so thick it was impossible to see more than a few yards ahead. In a silence broken only by the wind, the birds and the sounds of their footsteps, three men, two women and one baby came along the almost invisible trail. Flynn dropped back until he was even with Tilly. "You're strangely silent today."

She kept her eyes straight ahead. "I have nothing to say."

"You surprise me! Perhaps you're coming down with a fever."

He touched her wrist lightly with his fingertips. A jolt of mingled pain and pleasure shot up her arm. Though part of the pleasure came from memories of the past, the pain came from the humiliation and the bleak and lonely future Tilly saw stretching out before her.

She pulled away sharply. "Keep your hands to yourself, Mr. Flynn."

Unfortunately she overbalanced on the uneven ground and lost her footing. His strong brown arm caught her around the waist and steadied her. "Easy now."

Her hair and skin were scented with the soap she'd used for her bath the previous evening and beneath that was the fragrance that was Tilly's own, sunlight and moonlight and rose-petaled flowers. The urge to take her into his arms and kiss her breathless was one Flynn couldn't follow. Anyone watching from a distance would realize they were not just another peasant couple—and Flynn was very sure that someone *was* watching them from a distance. They'd been followed from the moment they'd left the mission.

He couldn't tell Tilly. The less she knew, the better it would be for everyone. But someday, when this was all over, he might be able to pick up the pieces. The Maya had believed that everything in the world had a cyclic nature. That what once was would someday be again. Flynn hoped he'd be able to accelerate the process, at least concerning one important matter. He stepped away.

"Be patient. Just a few more days and we'll be..."

Whatever he'd been about to say was lost when he saw the sheen of angry tears in her eyes. "Whatever your plans are, Mr. Flynn, they don't include me. Once we reach the archaeological camp you can safely wash your hands of your confounded encumbrance!"

His body tensed with that tigerlike tension she knew so well. "What else did you hear?"

The dangerous edge in his voice frightened her. "Nothing! That was quite enough!"

The others had continued on. Father Gerald stopped and looked back. "Tiger?"

Tilly straightened her shoulders and marched forward, leaving Flynn to follow.

They traveled northeast until they reached their destination an hour before twilight. "Here we are."

Tilly followed Flynn through a break in the jungle and stepped back in time eight hundred years. It was an amazing sight. Instead of ruins masked by centuries of rioting growth, twin pyramids of Mayan construction stood at either end of an open plaza twice the size of Trafalgar Square. The genius of the builders was evident, even to her inexpert eyes.

Each piece of paving stone fit perfectly against its neighbors. The upper structures shone dazzling white in the light, shadows exposing their reliefs in intricate detail. The sides of the buildings had once been buried beneath twenty feet of vegetation, and the limestone blocks were stained dark with dirt and crusted with patches of moss. Tilly couldn't

believe the site had been built with primitive tools. She tried
to picture how it had once looked with coats of fine stucco
plastered over the huge stones and gaily painted. For once
her intrepid imagination failed her.

Flynn, however, was interested in more contemporary
matters. "Something's wrong. There's no activity." He held
up a cautionary hand. "Wait here."

Tilly was shocked when he pulled a pistol from beneath
his tunic and stunned when his brother removed its mate
from his garments. Father Gerald blushed. "Dueling pistols," he said by way of explanation, which only confused
her even more—emerald thieves and dueling priests! She
wondered what the rest of the Flynn family was like. Certi-
fied madmen, no doubt!

Flynn scrambled down the deep angle to the plaza below
and made his way to one of the small tents on the far side.
There was an abandoned air to them and Tilly wasn't surprised when Flynn returned with his news.

"We're half a day too late. The government canceled their
concession in the wake of Dr. Challfont's death. According
to the watchman left behind, Dr. Scarborough and his crew
left for the coast to meet the supply ship, which arrived yesterday."

Gerald tucked his pistol away beneath his garment.
"Where is it anchored?"

"A few miles as the crow flies. It's to lay over for a day.
If we're up by first light we can reach them in time for a nice,
civilized luncheon aboard ship."

The supply ship. Tilly swallowed. Tomorrow it would all
be over. Tomorrow they would be safe. And tomorrow she
would be a fallen woman, shunned by all respectable society. She played with Juanito awhile but refused to join in the
talk, even when Flynn baited her with several choice remarks. Later she helped Uluma prepare dinner over an open
fire and retired alone to one of the tents to spend a very
miserable night.

Tilly dozed intermittently and was completely awakened
before dawn by the sound of low voices. Peeking out the tent
slit, she was just in time to see Flynn and his brother dis-

appear into the growth beyond the ancient plaza. She knew where they were going, of course. All around her were towering remains of the Maya, enough to keep her busy exploring for weeks; yet perverse curiosity nibbled at her. Tilly didn't want to examine them, she wanted to view Flynn's secret find, the undespoiled tomb with its ancient remains.

She really had no choice.

Tilly pulled her hair back with a bandanna, grabbed her straw hat and sandals and followed. The going was rough and she stumbled more than once. Soon her hands were scratched by thorns and a wayward twig stung her cheek. No wonder Flynn's secret had remained undiscovered: only an idiot would wander through the brambles without a sound purpose. Sweat trickled down her temples and the nape of her neck.

They reached a treed area. Flynn quickened his pace and his brother kept up easily. Tilly wasn't so fortunate. Her skirts caught on branches and had to be tugged free. When she looked up they were out of sight. Hesitantly she went on in the direction she thought they'd taken. Suddenly a deep cough sounded from somewhere above her, followed by a frightening snarl. Shivers chased up and down Tilly's spine. *El tigre* was on the prowl.

The panther's challenge came again, closer this time. She gathered her skirts and forced her way through the scrub, eyes on the overhanging tree limbs. She couldn't see the panther and she hoped it couldn't see her. Head up, she ran her foot into the tip of a carved stone block imbedded in the ground. Sparks dazzled her eyes as she grasped her injured foot and hopped on the other.

She sat on the edge of the block and rocked in pain until the throbbing eased. Nothing broken, she realized, gingerly probing her toes. As she looked up there was a clear line of vision through the growth of tree trunks and vegetation, and framed in that opening for an instant was a flash of white cloth. Flynn was up ahead a few hundred feet. Tilly rose and hobbled after him, saying a silent prayer of thankfulness.

Limping and dodging, she hurried toward him and broke into a jumbled, open place. She skidded to a stop as the man turned toward her, gleaming knife in hand. Not Flynn, but the man she'd known as Dawson.

"Minas," he whispered hoarsely. "Look! The woman!"

Tilly whirled away as he lunged in her direction. His sudden dash caught her by surprise.

"Flynn!" she cried out once. There was no time for more. She skirted around the trunk of a fallen tree and plunged on, held back by her injured foot. Ahead she could spy the tops of the twin pyramids, gleaming gold in the sunrise. She didn't dare lead the brigands toward the camp. Tomaso couldn't defend her and his family from these desperadoes.

She could hear her pursuer gaining on her. Tilly desperately searched for a place to hide. She limped north, into a thicket of gnarled trees and murderous thorns. The ground rose and fell in irregular undulations. Suddenly she spotted a small root cave ahead, like the one she'd hidden in before. It was a dark, yawning mouth, but so near the ground in the half-light that she hoped Dawson would run right past it.

With a quick, scrabbling movement she rolled into it, heedless of any prior occupants. Tattered webs caught at her hair and clung to the side of her face. She backed in farther. There was plenty of room. Tilly wiggled backward another two feet—and went sliding down a long, black tunnel into the bowels of the earth in a shower of dirt.

Clods of soil and bits of stone slithered past her ears with the noise of an avalanche. She landed on something soft and crackly, every bare surface of arms and legs scratched and abraded. She hurt in a hundred places. Carefully she stood up. The darkness was so absolute it was like wearing a black velvet blindfold. She couldn't tell if Dawson had heard the commotion or not.

Gingerly she went a few steps in every direction. She seemed to be in a cavern. The floor was solid, but strewn with obstacles. A falling pebble sent hollow echoes through a large space. The cavern must be quite high and wide. She thought the left-hand wall was closer, and moved slowly

oward it, feeling her way. Tilly estimated she had gone some
ifteen feet before her hand made contact. It was not the
ough wall of a cave, she realized, but a surface of dressed
tone. She slid her hands along the wall, and found the impossibly tiny crevices that were the joined surfaces of
mooth, unmortared blocks.

Farther along her fingertips traced the curved lines of
inely preserved carving. The edges were as sharp as the day
hey had been made.

Tilly wrapped her arms about her to keep out the grow-
ng chill. She understood about the thicket now. The irregular ground rising from the plane was not a product of
nature. She was alone, underground, in the ruins of a bur-
ed Maya center. Possibly inside a tomb. She tried not to
hink of her dream.

Another chunk of earth fell down, widening the acciden-
al entrance. Some burrowing animal had made its home in
he shelter of the tree roots, and over the years the seasonal
ains had eroded the ground further. Finally a huge root had
pierced its way through a weakness in the structure, pene-
rating through to the chamber.

Her teeth chattering with cold and reaction, Tilly sat on
he stone floor and prayed for light. Eventually the sun rose
igh enough for faint lights to sift into the hole in the
chamber's roof. First the walls took on a dim, luminous
glow, growing more solid minute by minute. Now she could
see faintly. Tilly rose and her heart caught in her throat. On
he plastered surface of the walls bizarre figures leaped to
sudden, menacing life: Chac-mool, god of rain, and An
Puc, the skeleton-jawed representation of Death.

From one side her keen eye caught the telltale gleam of
gold. Her heart pounding with excitement, she crossed the
littered floor and stepped over the scattered bones. The
jungle rodents had discovered this place only recently when
the opening was breached, but had left their traces.

She hobbled toward the far corner like a woman in a daze.
Yes, it was gold that she'd seen. The massive gem-studded
collar and pectoral gleamed on the suit of jade mosaic that
covered the remains of a once-proud Mayan aristocrat.

Holding her breath Tilly moved in for a closer look. The engraved glyphs were identical to those in her dreams and confirmed what she already knew: she had quite literally stumbled upon Queptil, the lost city of the Mayas.

There was a scraping sound above and behind her. Wheeling, Tilly prepared to face danger, warily seeking the face of her adversary, the secret enemy who had followed her into the tomb. Instead she heard a low whisper. "Tilly?"

The hair on her arms and at her neck stood up. She backed up until she bumped into the wall. Bits of plaster flaked away and fell to the ground with a dry, crumbling sound. Something blocked the light from the entrance. "Tilly?"

Her mouth was dry. She knew if she answered that call she wouldn't live to see another sunset. Clumps of earth and several stones fell into the tomb and Tilly looked around for a hiding place. A short alcove was built into one corner, and framed a kind of shield. It was her only hope. The noises from the entrance concealed the sounds of her movement. Peering through a small opening, she watched a figure slide into the chamber. She saw his face in profile and blinked. Not Dawson's cold, handsome face that hid the cruelty inside, but one she hadn't expected.

George Keating. He stood in the center and surveyed the room. "I know you're in here somewhere. You can come out. I won't hurt you."

For a moment Tilly thought she was dreaming again, that this time the nightmare had taken her deeper. But no, the pain in her foot and the sick feeling in the pit of her stomach told her she was horribly, irrevocably awake. Keating spotted her hiding place and came forward. "Come out, my dear. It's all right. There's no need to hide. You know how I feel about you."

Yes, she knew. The pieces clicked into place. He cared enough to have her lured out and abandoned on a sandbar with a hurricane coming. The Lord only knew what else he was capable of! Then she remembered that Dr. Challfont was dead and had no trouble putting the blame in the proper quarter. Tilly looked around for something to use as a weapon, wishing she'd thought of it earlier. Her palm brushed something smooth and heavy. She ran her fingers over its surface. A ceremonial ax, heavy—and potentially deadly. Her hand closed over it.

Keating turned his head as another shower of debris cascaded into the tomb. He waited. Tilly waited. Nothing happened. As he started toward the shield again a shaft of sunlight pierced the gloom. The beam lit the golden pectoral on the yellowed skeleton and caught Keating's attention. Crossing toward the grave goods, he stepped on fragile bits of fabric and pottery, grinding them into dust.

The treasures seemed to hypnotize him and Tilly wondered if he'd forgotten her. He lifted the jade-mosaic breastplate and the wires broke apart, sending thin squares of the precious substance all over the floor. Another spurt of stones and soil fell from the entrance above. He didn't seem to care. His eyes were on a second golden pectoral that had lain beneath the armor. It was studded with glowing emeralds.

Even from her vantage point, Tilly could see that the workmanship was exquisite, the massive pieces covered with delicate gold beading and scrollwork. It was magnificent—but it certainly wasn't Mayan. She had seen similar designs in York during an exhibition of pre-Roman Celtic art. The implication was interesting—but this was no time to consider the possibility of contact between the New World and the Old.

She watched as Keating turned it over and over in his hands. "I'll be damned." He whistled.

"You can count on that!" Flynn stood at the foot of the tunnel, feet braced and menace in his eyes. His long knife shone in his hand. "It's over, Keating. You're finished. Come quietly."

"What're you talking about?"

"The masquerade is over. You see, I know everything. How you've been smuggling emeralds and gold artifacts from the Americas into Jamaica. How you've been ransacking tombs for your own gain, forcing the natives to slave for you under threat of torture and death. How you murdered Julian Challfont when he began to get suspicious."

Flynn circled toward Keating, keeping his knife at the ready. The golden pectoral slid from Keating's fingers as he rose to a crouch. "You think you're so damned clever, Flynn. Well, Dawson and Minas are up above. Only one of us will get out of here alive and it won't be you."

"Don't be too sure of that." Flynn's face was sinister in the wavering torch light, like the visage of an ancient warrior god. The icy light in his green eyes made Tilly's blood chill.

Keating saw it, too, and changed his tactics. "Perhaps I've been hasty. There's no need for us to be enemies. Look around. There's plenty here for both of us. You shouldn't take it so personally."

"You were the one who made it personal, Keating. It was bad enough that you used Christopher Burlinghome's weakness to enslave him with drugs to get his help. Yes, I know how you arranged to hide the smuggled goods in pieces that Jonas would want for his collection, and how you forced Christopher to remove them at Coeur d'Émeraude in return for drugs. And how, when Jonas tried to cure him, you helped Christopher slip away when Leander's back was turned."

Flynn strolled casually to the center of the chamber, the knife still in his hand. "And what about Miss Templeton?"

Keating shrugged. "It wasn't an easy decision but it was the only way I knew to lure you out."

"Why did you have me captured? Why didn't you just have me killed?"

"I may have bent the rules a bit, but I'm not a murderer."

"No," Flynn lashed out, moving in on him. "You let Metcalf and Dawson do your dirty work for you! There may be no actual blood drying on your hands, Keating, but your soul is wallowing in it—may it rot in hell!"

He lunged forward. Tilly's startled movement knocked he shield down. Both men stared at her for a crucial second, as if she'd risen from the grave.

"Tilly! What in God's name...!"

Flynn moved toward her, and Keating saw his chance. He an to the entrance tunnel and grasped the dangling rope. Flynn threw himself across the room and tackled Keating around the knees, dropping his knife in the process. The two fell to the floor, punching and battering at each other. The sounds of fists on bone and flesh were more than Tilly could bear. Keating's hand moved to his boot, and when it came up it held a stiletto. She was horrified. Flynn thought he was fighting an unarmed man.

She couldn't stand by helplessly. She grabbed her weapon and flailed out. It struck Keating's hand, and his knife went spinning away. Tilly looked at her club. Not a ceremonial ax, but a human leg bone.

She dropped the grisly weapon without thinking, and the two men fell on it, wrestling for their lives. Tilly picked up the nearest pot and brought it down with all her might. At the same time the writhing figures rolled over, and it glanced off Flynn's head, shattering.

He pinned Keating down and shot her a look. "Damn it, Tilly, watch what you're doing! That pot was irreplaceable."

He tightened his grasp on his opponent's wrist and Keating's knife clattered to the floor. Flynn pinned him down and pulled back his arm for a punishing blow.

"Don't!" Tilly shouted. "There's no need. You've got him now!"

"There's every need!" Flynn drove his fist into Keating's face with all the force he could command. Keating's eyes rolled up in his head and he went limp.

For a moment Flynn bent over his enemy, and his hands clenched and unclenched. Tilly understood the battle raging within him. He wanted to kill Keating here and now. She went to Flynn and knelt, taking one of his hands in hers.

"It's all right, Flynn. It's over."

At first he didn't seem to hear her. Then the tension drained from his body and he took in a deep breath. He stood up. "Yes. It's over."

The *Laura Halford* sailed toward Kingston on a fine morning several days later with Flynn and his brother topside. "I'm glad you could come with us, Gerald, to lend veracity—and respectability—to our adventures."

"Well, now!" the priest said, "I have to find out how your adventure ends, don't I?"

He smiled as Tilly joined them, and moved a bit apart. Except for the sunburn and scratches, she looked like a totally different woman. Her shining chestnut hair was piled atop her head in a sophisticated chignon, and the blue dress the captain's wife had supplied her with was certainly more flattering than Uluma's baggy tunic. Tilly mourned the freedom of the loose, corsetless garments but was otherwise pleased with her ensemble.

At the moment, however, she was quite agitated. "Did you hear? Mr. Keating and his accomplices escaped somehow during the night when we stopped at Port Helen. It is terrible that he's escaped justice after all his crimes!"

Flynn smiled his lazy cat smile. "Don't worry. They didn't get far."

"Do you mean they've been recaptured?"

"In a manner of speaking. You see, the crew of this ship sailed with Skelly many times and they took things into their own hands. At the moment George Keating and his cronies are bound around the Horn in the hold of a rat-infested ship. If they survive the voyage they'll slave ten years in foreign mines before they earn their release."

Tilly was startled. "That's terrible!"

Flynn's smile grew more enigmatic. "Is it?"

"No. No, I suppose it's poetic justice." She turned to Father Gerald who stood only a few feet away. "You seem deep in thought this morning."

"Yes. I like tidy endings with things all wrapped up. Therefore, Lucas, I was wondering what you plan on doing about it?"

"That," Flynn replied, "is up to the lady. What do you think, Tilly, now that you know I'm not really a rogue and a scoundrel?"

Tilly frowned in puzzlement. "About what?"

"Why, the marriage vows," Flynn's brother interjected. "It would be better to exchange them before the two of you go traipsing back to Kingston together."

Flynn looked uncomfortable. "What about it, Tilly? Gerald is right, you know."

"Don't be ridiculous!"

"I see. You won't have me because of my rakish past and roguish ways." His eyes took on the mingled tones of green and gold she knew so well. "I'm disappointed in you. I thought you had more spunk."

"Spunk!"

"I admit I have a few faults," he went on. "My sense of humor is a bit off kilter, and many of my friends are disreputable, but I don't drink till I'm drunk or chase scandalous women or curse. At least, not unnecessarily."

Tilly tilted her head. "You cursed me when I hit you with that pot."

"Can you blame me?" Flynn rubbed the lump atop his head. "It was an excellent example of Mayan polychrome work, and probably unique."

"A fine lot you know about Mayan pottery," she retorted.

"Actually," his brother interjected, "he does. Lucas's paper comparing classical and preclassical ware is considered the definitive work on the subject."

Tilly looked from one to the other. Green eyes and blue, both were twinkling with laughter. "Is that true, Flynn?"

"Yes," he admitted sheepishly, "it is. I'm a bit of an antiquarian and support accurate record keeping and systematic study of ancient relics. Rather a hobbyhorse of mine."

She looked at him from beneath her lashes. "Is this another fictional invention, like your hidden emeralds?"

"That was to lure Keating's men out into the open. Of course, we had no idea the supply ship had arrived a day early, and with Keating aboard her."

Tilly pouted. "I really did have my heart set on those emeralds, Flynn. I'm afraid they're the one thing that would have made a hardened rogue like you palatable to me as a husband."

He flashed her a grin. "I'm afraid I don't have a fortune in emeralds for you, but I do have a wealth of knowledge of the ancient cultures—Mayan polychrome pottery ware, for example—for what it's worth."

"And a flourishing plantation, in addition to a silent partnership in Jonas Whitby's shipping interests," Gerald added smoothly. "So you see, you wouldn't be marrying a pauper, after all. I know my brother is a scapegrace, Miss Templeton, but I am counting on you to reform him through marriage. Think of it as your duty to mankind."

"You are both impossible," Tilly announced, and flounced away.

Flynn waited a few seconds, then went after her.

Five days later, as Flynn turned the carriage into the long drive of Coeur d'Émeraude, Tilly could not help contrasting this visit with her first arrival. The inexperienced young lady, eager to taste all the luxuries life had to offer, was now a seasoned woman, grateful for even the most modest blessings of food and clothing and a roof over her head. Then she had been unprepared for the intrigues and tensions she'd uncovered at the Whitby plantation, and as the vehicle pulled up before the portico, she wondered what she would find within this time.

As they alighted Jonas opened the door. "Flynn! Miss Templeton! Thank God you're both safe and sound."

He looked much younger, with a spring in his step and a glow of happiness lighting his eyes, as he guided them through the foyer. "The others are in here."

He ushered them into the drawing room. Tilly saw at once that the air of serenity was not due solely to the pastel decor. The peace in the house was real. Lara jumped up from the settee and ran to her.

"Tilly! It is really you? And Flynn! I was afraid to believe it until I saw you with my own eyes." She embraced them both.

Christopher and Leander stood a little away from the others, but now came forward. Lara's brother was still terribly thin, but had more color in his face, and his eyes were clear and unclouded. He took Tilly's hand. "I can't tell you how relieved I was to hear of your miraculous survival."

Tilly tipped her head to look at him. "It was no miracle that saved us—it was Flynn. But don't let him know I said so. It would only add to his arrogance." Her smile took the sting from her words. "I am sorry to learn you have been ill."

"You're kind to keep up the pretense, Miss Templeton, but I am sure you know by now that it was an addiction to opium that almost finished me, not malaria."

Christopher's smile was a faint echo of hers, but equally sincere. "My friend Leander, who was the foreman of our expedition, volunteered to stay with me and see me through because he thinks I saved his life once. Well, he has saved mine a dozen times over, and I have put him through hell for it."

"And I would do it all again." Leander spoke as softly as a mother to a child. "There are not so many good men in the world that we can afford to lose even one. And soon, my friend, you will be well again and we can return to the Yucatan and take over Dr. Challfont's work."

Christopher smiled again, pale but triumphant. "Yes. By the next season I will."

He turned to Tilly and took her hand. "Forgive me. I didn't know what I was doing at the time when I struck you down. I thought you were stealing in to take the emeralds and artifacts before I could get them to Keating in exchange for the opium."

Tilly blushed. "If apologies are in order I have one of my own to make. I'm afraid I blamed Jonas. I thought he had done it."

She didn't add that she'd thought Lara had been in love with Flynn: some things were better left unsaid. Now she knew their relationship was one of deep and abiding friendship, and that Flynn had been helping her to conceal Christopher's lapses and brief escapes. Lara, in the age-old way of women, had been trying to keep her husband and brother from further estrangement and instead had fostered it.

Jonas's face took on a strangely carefree expression. It set comfortably on the features that Tilly had once thought so stern. He looked years younger. "And I owe you profound apologies, Miss Templeton, for putting you in George Keating's way. I never suspected this affair could turn violent, and of course, I was well aware that he was quite attracted to you."

Flynn made a low sound, very like a growl. "The only characteristic of Keating's that I admired was his good taste." Tilly's gaze flew to his face. The dark look in his eyes was a revelation. Why, Flynn was actually jealous. How lovely!

Jealousy, of course, was not an emotion that bothered Tilly. Not at all. "And what of Mrs. Thorne," she asked sweetly and wished she'd bitten her tongue instead.

Lara had the answer to that question. "She packed her bags and took the first ship out the day you disappeared, leaving a mountain of debts behind her. She's halfway to Bombay by now."

Jonas nodded. "She was only one of Keating's pawns and had no idea what was afoot until it was too late. She had known him as Fritz Keating years ago. He'd blackmailed her into helping, but once things got serious she cut her losses and ran." He rubbed his hand along his jaw. "We didn't notify the authorities, but if you wish we can set things in train."

Tilly thought of the widow, running in fear with no money and no friends and only her fading beauty to comfort her. "No... I think she's learned her lesson. She only meant to be spiteful, not to harm me."

Christopher bowed over her hand. "You've been exceedingly kind after what I put you through, Miss Templeton. I hope you'll come out to the new excavation site next season. We're going to sink several test trenches and mark the boundaries. I am very sure, from the accurate description you sent me, that it is indeed the lost city of Queptil. Your name will go down in the history books.''

As her face turned pink with pleasure he smiled and Tilly saw his old charm return. "And now, if you'll excuse me," Christopher said, "I'm a bit tired. Jonas can fill you in on the rest." He bowed with wistful dignity and left the room.

Jonas left his place by the mantelpiece. "When you know the circumstances you will absolve Christopher for the greater part of his addiction. He was severely injured near Chichen Itza when they were raising a fallen stele. The ropes broke and the stone grazed and badly bruised him as it fell. Dr. Challfont had laudanum with him, but it provided little relief. When George Keating offered to supply a stronger native remedy they were grateful. Of course it was really opium he gave Christopher."

"Keating!" Tilly exclaimed.

Flynn rubbed his jaw. "And then, I suppose, by increasing the dosage he made Christopher an addict, planning to use him to smuggle out the emeralds."

"Yes," Jonas responded. "When Challfont notified me of Christopher's bizarre behavior, I went out to investigate. Recognizing the symptoms of the problem I brought him to Kingston. Later I enlisted the aid of Challfont and a few discreet men, trained in such matters, to trap Keating and his henchmen."

"And then," Flynn said sardonically, "I entered the picture and set everything on end."

"I tried to warn you off, in an effort to protect Lara and Christopher, but I must admit we made little headway until you became involved."

The masks, Jonas explained, had been used to smuggle in the emeralds, and Christopher would then exchange the gems for drugs. Tilly put her hand on Flynn's arm. "Then that is why you took the emeralds and hid them in my reticule—to throw them into disorder and stop the smuggling."

Flynn's gaze flickered to her and then away. "Yes."

"No!" Lara stepped forward, her face crimson with mortification. "I will not let you take the blame for me, Lucas. You see, Tilly, it was I who took them. I found them accidentally in the warehouse. I...I knew what he had been doing, but not how. Christopher was missing and I didn't want to take the chance of him finding the stones and getting more opium. I meant to take them from you before we reached the plantation, but there was no opportunity. When we returned from the picnic and I saw the outrage in your room, I didn't know if Christopher had done it—or if it had been someone else. I went to tell Leander."

"What a dilemma you were in, unable to tell me anything. I knew you were troubled," Tilly said hastily, "but I put it down to other things."

Now that the skeleton was out of the closet, Lara felt compelled to number all its bones. "It would have been much worse if Jonas was not so good. Although he was very angry and upset, he arranged for physicians and attendants and the guards, to keep my brother from fleeing in one of his wilder moods. When you arrived in Kingston, he had been missing for two days. Jonas had threatened to have him put in an asylum if necessary, so I turned to Lucas. He found him and brought him back safely, but I'd had no word until he arrived before dinner."

Lara twisted her ring nervously and cast a rueful glance at Flynn. "And later that evening, a woman came to tell Flynn that Christopher had overpowered Leander and escaped again."

"Then," Tilly said slowly, "it was Christopher that you were searching for in my room that night."

Jonas nodded and she turned on Flynn accusingly. "Then you made it all up about us being in danger!"

"Not one bit of it. Keating was also on the grounds, ostensibly to find Christopher, but he spotted me spying upon them and followed me to the house. The danger, at that moment, was acute. He would have shot me on sight under some pretext, and disposed of you later."

"Oh!" Tilly was abashed. Rampant female curiosity overcame her innate politeness. "I have often wondered—

who was the woman who came looking for you? The one with the baby?''

Flynn laughed and pinched her chin. ''Jealous, are you? You needn't be. She is Leander's wife of many years.''

''That was my fault,'' Lara said softly. ''Everyone misunderstood, and it created a terrible scandal. It has been a nightmare, but by far the worst was the knowledge that I was deceiving my husband by not telling him that my brother had escaped.''

She tried to continue but seemed unable to find the right words. Jonas crossed the room to her side and took her hands in his. No one could doubt the love in his eyes.

''It will be all right, my dear. You have been brave and borne up under a terrible strain. I only wish you could have been shielded from all this, that you could have had enough faith in me to let me handle it in my own way.''

''Jonas, my dearest, dearest husband, my faith in you is—and has always been—complete.'' Lara took Jonas's hands and brought them to her cheek. ''I was so ashamed of all the troubles marriage to me had brought upon you, through Christopher! I avoided your company, dear as it is to me, in fear I would betray myself. Then I saw how other women—beautiful women—looked at you, and was afraid you would turn from me in disgust. Please forgive me.''

''Foolish little thing! The fault is mine. I am a man of few words, but I should have let you know that you are the most precious thing to me in all the world.''

''Oh, Jonas!'' Tears sparkled in Lara's dark eyes, but for once they were for happiness. Jonas took her gently into his arms and Lara threw herself into his embrace. It was soon apparent that they had forgotten there was anyone else in the room.

Flynn slipped his arm around Tilly's waist and whispered in her ear. ''All's well that ends well. This seems like a good time to take a long stroll in the garden. Or better yet, a long carriage ride. We'll tell them our news later.''

Tilly nodded, dabbed at her eyes with a corner of her handkerchief and left the drawing room with him. He assisted her into the carriage and climbed up beside her. Tilly pinned her bonnet on more securely. "Where are we going?"

Flynn gave her one of his dazzling smiles. "Home. Home to the lair of the tiger. You'll like it. Blackbeard's Roost is one of the oldest estates on the island."

"Blackbeard's Roost. How intriguing! Does the old pirate haunt it?"

"Of course."

Tilly settled her hands in her lap. "Then I shall like it immensely!"

Epilogue

Tilly, in a fetching new negligee of ivory satin and point lace, was sitting up in bed with the breakfast tray when her husband came in. The marmalade kitten, which had been dreaming contented mouse dreams, opened one eye and winked. Flynn eyed the creature.

"I think, Esmerelda, that you might like a stroll in the morning sunshine."

The kitten agreed. Like its father, she always paid attention to Flynn's wishes: he was, after all, a friend. It stood, stretched, jumped down lightly and sauntered out. Flynn shut the door firmly behind the animal and grinned.

Tilly smiled back at him, feeling the love well up inside her. What a splendid figure he cut in his tight-fitting coat and breeches and his high, polished boots! She could not help flushing with pleasure and pride. "How very handsome you are in your new riding clothes, Flynn!"

He came forward and shot her a look of mock reproach. "Hoping to turn me sweet with your compliments, my beautiful sleepyhead, when you promised faithfully to be up and ready for our morning ride?"

"Well, you see I am not merely idling away in bed. I am weighing a proposition from my brother Durward and his wife-to-be."

Flynn noticed the envelope and several sheets of paper scattered over the embroidered sheets. He cocked an eyebrow in surprise. "I hope your brother isn't ill. For a man who is a moth-pocketed miser, he must have been prodigal with the paper and posting."

She smothered a chuckle. "Don't be alarmed, darling. Durward is well and practiced his usual economy. He was very careful to see that his letter cost nothing for me to receive—or for him to send. When he went to London he hand-carried it to the docks and presented it to the captain of one of the Whitby merchant ships, with instructions to deliver it to Lara, who had it sent over earlier."

Flynn had been toying with the ribbons that tied her negligee together and gave a little tug. The bow came undone, revealing a gown of gauzy silk beneath it, and the rounded tops of her breasts above the lacy ruffle. The low-cut bodice of the gown was laced with a row of tiny ribbons. Before she could remonstrate, he had them undone halfway to her waist. He cupped one soft breast in his bronzed palm and leaned forward purposefully.

"Flynn!" she warned him laughingly, and wriggled away. "We have an important matter to discuss."

"What could be more important than this?"

He dropped a kiss in the perfumed cleft between her breasts, sending ripples of pleasure across her skin. The heat of his mouth burned through her, creating a longing for further and bolder intimacies. She no longer tried to escape his amorous play but held up the crumpled sheets of notepaper. Flynn's lips hovered over one breast, and his fingers closed over her wrist to push it away.

"Why waste time reading dull letters from dull people when there are more delightful ways to pass the time?"

He kissed the upper swell of her breast, the soft side, the tender curve beneath, all the time circling inward toward its peak. She arched her back sensuously as his breath stirred across her skin, sending eddies of sensation over it. As she shifted against the pillows to accommodate his seeking mouth, the letter from England crackled beneath her elbow. "But our morning ride...and the letter..."

"Durward and his letters may go straight to the devil, and the morning ride as well!"

Taking his face between her hands, Tilly brought it to hers nd kissed him soundly. His hair was tousled and she ran her ingers through it a moment. Then she sat up determinedly. You are right. There are several delightful things I can hink of that we might indulge ourselves in. But first, you ust hear Durward's proposition."

"Curse all interfering brother-in-laws and their interfer- ng proposals! Read the damned thing," Flynn replied, re- igning himself.

He sat up and pulled off his cravat and coat, then Tilly ested her head against his broad shoulder. He eyed the losely written sheets with misgiving.

"I hope he does not propose to spend his honeymoon in amaica trespassing on my good nature—for I promise you, have none where he is concerned. Not after the way he isled and mistreated you. And for that," he said grimly, he will answer to me as your husband."

"Oh, but he had no notion, when he wrote this, that he s a brother-in-law, as our letters must have crossed one an- ther. And he is not only ready but willing to make up to ne, as he puts it, for any errors of judgment he *may* have nade in the past in his dealings with me."

"Generous!" Flynn commented sarcastically. He glanced own, realizing he had missed the last ribbon lacings. "I now, the damned letter!" he said before she could pro- est, and watched in fascination as the bodice of her gown ell away to either side.

"Do listen!" Tilly clutched ineffectively at her gown and retended to ignore him. She scanned the lines and para- hrased their contents.

"Durward and his bride plan to make an extended tour of he continent, and it occurred to him—more likely to He- ena!—that I have never been abroad except for this Jamai- an excursion. They propose that I join them on their six- nonth tour, entirely at Durward's expense."

She gave her husband a wide-eyed, innocent look. "Now, lynn, tell me what you think of the plan."

"That I will!" This time his scowl was genuine. He leaped up, took the letter and tore it into little pieces. They floated to the polished wood of the floor as he sat again, facing her

"I think, my dearest Tilly, that your miserly brother and his abhorrent fiancée are planning to save the expense of a combination maid and companion by offering you that position disguised as a treat! For your room and board, and of course the pleasure of their company, you would be expected to fetch and carry and serve as general drudge, all the while exuding gratitude for their extreme generosity!"

Tilly laughed. "How fierce you look! And how very clever you are, my love. Of course he doesn't know of our marriage yet, but that is *exactly* what Durward proposed— although he couches it in less frank language."

She leaned back on the ruffled pillows, a beguiling picture with her hair hanging loose and her bare breasts white and tempting. Flynn was unable to resist. As he reached for her, he saw the impish look in the depths of her eyes.

"Yes," Tilly said thoughtfully. "I will answer his letter today."

"And what do you mean to tell him?"

She held out her arms and pulled Flynn into her embrace. "I mean," Tilly said huskily against his mouth, "to take your advice, Flynn, and tell Durward to go straight to the devil!"

He leaned down and kissed her lips, then sat on the side of the bed. "And now that we have been married a week, don't you think you might begin using my given name?"

She made a saucy face at him. "You know it is fashionable for a wife to address her husband by his surname—very sophisticated."

"What you really mean is that you are so used to calling me Mr. Flynn in your strict little voice that you keep forgetting I have another name."

Her arms wound around his neck and pulled him down for another, more lingering kiss. "If it matters to you," she said, when the kiss ended, "then I shall make the effort— Lucas darling."

Tilly sat up a bit straighter. "And now that we are on the subject of names, I have been meaning to ask you how you got the nickname of Tiger."

His eyes gleamed with mischief. "Have you been listening to common gossip, my love? I never suspected you of having such low tastes."

She tipped her head sideways. "You are trying to change the subject. I insist you tell me the truth."

Flynn sighed. "Who would have thought that I would end up under the cat's paw, overruled by a strict and dominating wife!"

"Flynn!" The stern tone was belied by the laughter in her warm gray eyes. "I mean, Lucas, my dear!"

He toyed with a lock of her hair, winding it around his fingers, and his eyes danced. "Very well. There are several versions, as you might know—that I tamed a ferocious Indian tiger using nothing but my voice and certain mystical powers, that I strangled a man-eating Chinese tiger with my bare hands, and even that I was lost in the jungle and raised by a tigress. There is also a fourth story, not widely known. That account is less heroic. It concerns a small boy and a very battered toy tiger, which he carried with him everywhere."

She waited. Apparently he was finished. "Well? Don't keep me in suspense. Which story is the true one?"

Flynn's white grin creased his bronzed face. "That, my dear, you will have to decide for yourself. I will tell you this much, however. Two of the accounts are complete fabrications—and two of them are true."

Tilly picked up a lace-edged pillow and proceeded to hit him with it, laughing so hard she was almost incoherent. "You...you are the most incorrigible...the very worst...!"

He stopped her protests by lowering his mouth to hers and kissing her until she was breathless. "Such impertinence, my dear *Mrs.* Flynn, is exactly what I would expect from a woman with the effrontery to bash me over the head with a priceless ceramic pot."

He frowned and tried to look severe, but failed completely. The green tiger's eyes were warm and filled with glints of gold dust. They always were these days, especially when they were focused on his wife.

"I did apologize," she reminded him laughingly. "And if you are going to tease me so before I've risen from my bed, I will send you packing to the stables alone."

"Do you really think so?"

He stripped away his shirt and did the same with her silk gown. All thoughts of Durward and morning rides and Kingston gossip were banished. Nothing existed but the two of them, lost in passion, secure in their love.

Outside the marmalade kitten smiled a knowing cat smile at the world in general, and a grinning groom led the horses back to their stalls. Inside the chambermaids smiled and lowered their voices as they passed the closed bedroom door.

The Tiger and Tigress were safe in their lair. And if this kept up, soon there'd be a few little cubs rollicking over the lawns and terraces of Blackbeard's Roost.

All was right with the world.

*   *   *   *   *

Author's Note

Invoking artistic license, I have taken a few liberties; the June hurricane, the Isle of Shells and the lost Mayan city of Queptil exist because of them.

H A R L E Q U I N
American Romance®

November brings you...

SENTIMENTAL JOURNEY

B A R B A R A
B R E T T O N

Jitterbugging at the Stage Door Canteen, singing along with the Andrews Sisters, planting your Victory Garden—this was life on the home front during World War II.

Barbara Bretton captures all the glorious memories of America in the 1940's in SENTIMENTAL JOURNEY—a nostalgic Century of American Romance book and a Harlequin Award of Excellence title.

Available wherever Harlequin® books are sold.

HARLEQUIN
American Romance®

RELIVE THE MEMORIES....

From New York's Lower East Side immigrant experience to San Francisco's great quake of 1906 to the muddy trenches of World War I's western front to the speakeasies of the Roaring Twenties...A CENTURY OF AMERICAN ROMANCE takes you on a nostalgic journey through the twentieth century.

Glimpse the lives and loves of American men and women from the turn of the century to the dawn of the year 2000. Revel in the romance of a time gone by. And sneak a peek at romance in an exciting future.

Watch for all the A CENTURY OF AMERICAN ROMANCE titles coming to you one per month in Harlequin American Romance.

Don't miss a day of A CENTURY OF AMERICAN ROMANCE.

The women...the men...the passions...the memories....

If you missed #345 AMERICAN PIE, #349 SATURDAY'S CHILD, or #353 THE GOLDEN RAINTREE and would like to order them, send your name, address, and zip or postal code, along with a check or money order for $2.95 plus 75¢ postage and handling ($1.00 in Canada) *for each book ordered*, payable to Harlequin Reader Service, to:

In the U.S.
3010 Walden Ave.,
P.O. Box 1325
Buffalo, NY 14269-1325

In Canada
P.O. Box 609
Fort Erie, Ontario
L2A 5X3

Please specify book title(s) with your order.

ARC-1R